Dear Reader,

Thirty years ago I began my career by writing
romances under several pseudonyms. These were
stories of women and men who meet, fall in love
despite the odds against them and endure the
heartache and joy that is unique to that experience.

These stories reflect those classic themes, which have
engaged and entertained audiences since storytelling
first became a popular pastime. They have been
reissued at your request and for your enjoyment.
I hope you have as much fun reading them as I did
writing them.

As in all romance novels, expect a happy ending…

Sandra Brown

# SANDRA BROWN

*Led Astray*
*&*
*The Devil's Own*

MIRA

ISBN-13: 978-0-7783-1856-9

Recycling programs for this product may not exist in your area.

Led Astray & The Devil's Own

Copyright © 2015 by Harlequin Books S.A.

The publisher acknowledges the copyright holder of the individual works as follows:

Led Astray
Copyright © 1985 by Sandra Brown

The Devil's Own
Copyright © 1987 by Sandra Brown

For questions and comments about the quality of this book, please contact us at CustomerService@Harlequin.com.

www.MIRABooks.com

**Printed in U.S.A.**

# CONTENTS

# LED ASTRAY

# *One*

If they didn't stop talking about it, she was going to scream.

But they weren't going to stop talking about it. It was the one subject on everyone's mind and the chance of them switching to another was remote. The topic under discussion had carried them through the pot roast dinner. It was the type of meal usually reserved for Sundays, as though this were an occasion to be celebrated rather than lamented.

Sarah had outdone herself in preparing the food. There had even been hot, fluffy yeast rolls fresh from the oven to dip in the thick, savory beef gravy and a homemade pudding that was so rich, the calories fairly shouted.

But Jenny's taste buds might as well have been dead for all she had enjoyed the meal. Her tongue seemed to cleave to the roof of her mouth with every bite, and her throat rebelled against swallowing.

Now, over coffee, which Sarah was pouring into the china cups with the yellow primrose pattern, they were still talking about Hal's imminent trip to Central America. The trip would encompass an unspecified period of time, virtually make him an outlaw, and probably imperil his life.

Yet everyone was excited about it, especially Hal, whose cheeks were flushed with enthusiasm. His brown eyes shone with expectation. "It's a tremendous undertaking. But if it weren't for the courage of those poor souls in Monterico, everything we've done and will do would be in vain. The honor belongs to them."

Sarah touched her younger son's cheek affectionately as she resumed her chair after refilling everyone's cup. "But you've instigated this underground railroad to help them escape. I think it's wonderful. Simply wonderful. But—" her lower lip began to tremble "—you will be careful, won't you? You won't really be in danger?"

Hal patted the soft hand that clung to his arm. "Mother, I've told you a thousand times that the political refugees will be waiting for us at the border of Monterico. We're only picking them up, escorting them through Mexico, and—"

"Illegally smuggling them into the United States," Cage supplied dryly.

Sarah glanced at Hal's older brother sourly.

Accustomed to such disdain, Cage remained unaffected by his mother's disapproving glance. He stretched his jean-clad legs far out in front of him as he slouched in his chair in a way that had always irritated Sarah. During his youth she had harped on his table posture until she was blue. Her lectures had never done any good.

He crossed one booted ankle over the other and eyed his brother from beneath a shelf of dust-colored eyebrows. "I wonder if you'll be so fired up with fanatic zeal when the Border Patrol slams your ass in jail."

"If you can't use better language than that, kindly leave the table," Reverend Bob Hendren snapped.

"Sorry, Dad." Unrepentantly Cage sipped his coffee.

"If Hal goes to jail," the pastor went on, "it will be for a good cause, something he believes in."

"That's not what you said the night you had to come bail me out," Cage reminded his father.

"You were arrested for drunkenness."

Cage grinned. "I believe in getting drunk occasionally."

"Cage, please," Sarah said with a long-suffering sigh. "For once try and behave."

Jenny stared down at her hands. She hated these family scenes. Cage could be provoking, but she felt in this instance he was right to bluntly point out the risks of Hal's involvement in this venture. Besides, even she could see that Cage's derision was a response to his parents' obvious preference for Hal, who shifted uneasily in his chair. Though he basked in Bob's and Sarah's approval, their blatant favoritism made him uncomfortable as well.

Cage relented by erasing the smirk from his handsome face, but he continued arguing. "It's just that this labor of love, this mission of Hal's, seems like a good way to get killed. Why is he risking his neck in some banana republic where they shoot first and ask questions later?"

"You couldn't possibly understand Hal's motives," Bob said with a dismissive wave of his hand toward his elder son.

Cage sat up straighter and propped his arms on the

table, leaning forward for emphasis. "I can understand his wanting to liberate people marked for death, yes. But I don't think this is the way to do it." Impatiently he ran a hand through his dark blond hair. "An underground railroad, escorting political refugees through Mexico, illegal entry into the United States," he said scoffingly as he enumerated the stages of Hal's mission by ticking them off his fingertips.

"And how are they going to survive once you get them here to Texas? Where will they live? What will they do? Have you thought of jobs, shelter, food, medicine, clothing? Don't be naive enough to think that everyone will welcome them with open arms just because they're from a strife-torn country. They'll be thought of as wetbacks just as all illegal aliens are. And treated as such."

"We're trusting all that to God's will," Hal said a little uncertainly. His steadfastness always faltered under Cage's pragmatism. Just when Hal thought one of his convictions was unshakable, Cage shook it—to the core. Just like an earthquake, Cage's arguments opened up fissures in beliefs Hal had previously thought of as sound and indestructible. Hal prayed about it often and always came to the conclusion that God used Cage to test him. Or was Cage's astuteness a gift of the devil used to tempt him? His parents would no doubt opt for the second theory.

"Yeah, well, I hope God has more common sense than you have."

"That's enough!" Bob said sharply.

Cage hunched his shoulders and propping his elbows on the tabletop, carried his coffee cup to his mouth. He didn't use the tiny handle. Jenny doubted his long finger would fit in that narrow china crook. He held the cup by folding both his hands around it.

He was out of place in the parsonage kitchen. It had crispy ruffled curtains at the windows, a pastel plaid yellow vinyl floor, and a glass-fronted china cabinet that held delicate serving pieces that were treasured and used only on holidays.

Cage shrank the kitchen until its coziness became clutter. And it wasn't that he was inordinately muscular or tall. Physically Cage and Hal were much the same. From a distance and from the back, the brothers were almost indistinguishable, except that Cage was slightly more robust than his younger brother. That added brawniness was due more to the differences in their occupations than to a whim of heredity.

But there the similarity between the two ended. The main difference between them was one of attitude. Cage had a presence that made any room seem smaller when he entered it. An indefinable something surrounded him like an aura and was as much a part of him as his darkly tanned skin.

Indoors he was like an oversized body straining at the seams of clothing that was too small. He seemed to be squeezed into most rooms, as though what he needed around him was wide-open spaces, earth, and sky. An essence of the outdoors clung to him, as if he carried the wind inside on his clothes and in his hair.

Jenny had never gotten close enough to him to find out, but she thought his skin must smell like sunshine. The ravages of long hours in the sun were evident on his face, particularly around his tawny eyes. Those web-fine lines made him appear older than he was. But then he had crammed a lot of living into his thirty-two years.

And tonight, as always wherever Cage went, there was likely to be discord if not downright warfare. Mischief and malcontent followed him like a shadow. He was a predator, stalking through the jungle, upsetting the peaceable inhabitants, raising shackles and ruffling feathers and rustling the stillness even when he wasn't looking for trouble.

"You're certain you've worked out all the rendezvous points?" Sarah asked. She was distressed that Cage had spoiled her perfect farewell dinner for Hal, but was valiantly trying to ignore her recalcitrant son and set things back on an even keel.

As Hal rehashed his travel plans for at least the hundredth time, Jenny unobtrusively began to clear the table. As she leaned over Hal's shoulder to pick up his plate, he took her hand, squeezed it, raised it to his lips, and kissed the back of it, but all without a pause in his zealous dialogue.

She longed to bend down and kiss the crown of his blond head, to clasp it to her breasts and plead with him not to go. But of course she didn't. Such an action would be outrageous and everyone at the table would think she had gone stark, staring mad.

She suppressed her emotions and finished carrying the dishes to the sink. No one offered to help. No one even took notice of her. It had been Jenny's chore to do the dinner dishes since she had come to live in the parsonage.

They were still talking fifteen minutes later when she dried her hands on the cup towel and neatly draped it over the peg beside the sink. She slipped out the back door and went down the porch steps. She crossed the yard to the white rail fence and leaned her arms over the top.

It was a lovely night, almost windless, which was a rare blessing in West Texas. There was only a trace of dust in the air. A huge round moon looked like a shiny gummed sticker someone had pressed against a black felt sky. What stars the city lights didn't diminish were large and near.

It was a night for lovers to be clinging, snuggling close, whispering outlandishly silly and romantic things to each other. It wasn't a night to be saying goodbye. Or if goodbyes must be said, they should be overflowing with passion and regret, seasoned with endearments rather than the details of an itinerary.

Jenny was restless, as though she had an itch she couldn't quite locate.

The screened back door squeaked open and then closed with the soft slapping sound of old wood against old wood. Jenny turned to see Cage sauntering down the steps. She brought her head back around as he moved to stand beside her at the fence.

Without speaking, he fished in his breast pocket for a pack of cigarettes, shook it, and, closing his lips around one, drew it from the foil top. He lit it with a lighter whose flame flared briefly in front of his face. He clicked the lighter off and returned it and the cigarettes to his pocket as he drew the tobacco smoke deep into his lungs.

"Those things are killers," Jenny said, still staring straight ahead.

Cage turned his head and stared at her silently for a moment, then his body came around until he was leaning with his back against the fence. "I'm not dead yet and I started smoking when I was about eleven."

She glanced up at him, smiling, but shaking her head. "What a shame. Think what that's done to your lungs. You should quit."

"Yeah?" he said with that one-sided lazy grin that never failed to trip the hearts of women—young, old, single, or married. There wasn't a female in La Bota who could remain indifferent to Cage Hendren's smile. Some paused to consider exactly what it implied. Most knew. *I'm male, you're female, and that's all that needs to be said.*

"Yes, you should quit. But you're not going to. I've heard Sarah ask you to stop smoking for years."

"Only because she didn't like nasty ashtrays and the lingering smell of tobacco smoke. She never asked me to quit because she was worried about my health." There was the merest glimmer of bitternness in his amber eyes. Someone with less sensitivity than Jenny wouldn't have noticed it.

"I worry about your health," she said.

"Do you, now?"

"Yes."

"Are you asking me to quit smoking on that basis?"

She knew he was only teasing her, but she played along. Her chin lifted a notch and she said decisively, "Yes."

He tossed the cigarette into the dirt and ground it out with the toe of his boot. "Done. There. I've quit."

She laughed. Little did she know how remarkably pretty she was when she threw her head back like that and laughed. Her throat arched gracefully, showing off her honey-toned complexion. Her soft brown hair swung free and silky against her shoulders. Her green eyes sparkled. Her pert nose wrinkled delightfully. She had a whiskey-husky laugh that was flagrantly seductive, though Jenny never realized it.

But Cage did. His body responded to the sultry sound and there wasn't a damn thing he could do about it. He lowered his eyes to her petal-soft lips and glistening teeth.

"That's the first time I've seen you smile tonight," he said.

Jenny sobered instantly. "I don't feel much like smiling."

"Because Hal's leaving?"

"Of course."

"Because you've had to postpone the wedding again?"

She ducked her head and scraped the fence rail with her thumb nail. "Certainly, though that's not important."

"Why the hell not?" Cage demanded roughly. "I thought a woman's wedding was the most important day in her life. At least to a woman like you, it is."

"It is, but when measured against this mission Hal's going on—"

Cage muttered a scandalously obscene word beneath his breath which effectively silenced her speech. "What about the other times?" he asked brusquely.

"You mean the other postponements?"

"Yeah."

"Hal had to get his doctorate. It was important that he finish his dissertation before we got married and... and started a family."

As always, Cage had made her stammer like an idiot. She wanted to ask him not to stand too close, but he wasn't that close. He only seemed to be. He had always had this effect on her. He caused her to go breathless, to suffer a slight vertigo. She felt a need to clasp her hands tightly together, to hold herself intact as though she might fly apart if she didn't. He unsettled her. She had never found a reason why that should be so, but it was. Tonight especially, when her nerves were already ragged and her carefully maintained control was frayed, she found it difficult to meet Cage's intent stare. He saw too much.

"When did you and Hal actually start dating?" he asked abruptly.

"Dating?" Her tone implied that the word wasn't part of her vocabulary.

"Yeah, you know, going out. Holding hands. Necking at the drive-in. Dating. It must have been while I was up at Tech, because I don't remember it."

"Well, we never actually started dating. It just…just evolved, I guess you'd say. We were constantly together. We were considered a couple."

"Jenny Fletcher," Cage said, crossing his arms over his wide chest and staring at her incredulously, "do you mean to tell me that you've never had a date with anyone else?"

"Not because I wasn't asked!" she retorted defensively.

Cage put up his hands in surrender. "Whoa, girl. I wasn't hinting that. You could have had all the young bucks in town panting after you."

"I didn't want them panting after me. It sounds very undignified."

She blushed becomingly and Cage couldn't resist rubbing the back of his hand against her cheek. She averted her head and his hand fell to his side. "I figure a man could lose his dignity over you, Jenny," he said reflectively, then picked up in a lighter vein, "but you didn't go out with any other guys because that would have been unfaithful to Hal."

"That's right."

"Even while the two of you were at Texas Christian?"

"Yes."

"Hm." Cage automatically reached for his pack of cigarettes, remembered, and stuffed them back in his pocket. Never did his eyes leave Jenny. "When did Hal propose?"

"A few years ago. I think we were in our senior year at TCU."

"You think? You don't remember? How could you forget an earth-moving moment like that?"

"Don't tease me, Cage."

"The earth didn't move?"

"It isn't like it is in the movies."

"You've been seeing the wrong kind of movies." His eyebrows bobbed up and down lecherously.

"I know what kind you see," she said, slanting him an accusing glance. "The kind Sammy Mac Higgins shows in the back room of his pool hall after hours."

Cage tried to keep a straight face at her lofty tone, gave up the attempt, and let that dazzling smile break across his features. "Ladies are invited. Wanna come with me sometime?"

"No!"

"Why not?"

"Why not? I wouldn't be caught dead seeing that kind of movie. They're disgusting."

He leaned forward and taunted, "How do you know

if you've never seen one?" She punched him on the shoulder and he moved back, but not without first filling his head with her fresh, flowery scent. Gradually his smile faded to a somber expression as he searched her eyes. "Jenny, when did Hal ask you to marry him?"

"I told you, it—"

"Where were you? Describe the surroundings. What happened? Did he go down on bended knee? Was it in the backseat of his car? In the daytime? At night? In bed? When?"

"Stop it! I told you I don't remember."

"Did he ever?" His voice was so quiet that she snapped to attention.

"What do you mean?"

"Did he ever voice the words aloud? 'Jenny, will you marry me?'"

Her eyes fell away from his. "We've always known we were going to get married."

"Who's always known? You? Hal? Mother and Dad?"

"Yes. Everybody." She turned her back on him and started back toward the house. "I've got to go in and—"

His warm, hard hand closed around her wrist and brought her up short. "Tell Hal not to go on this fool's trip."

She spun around. "What?"

"You heard me. Tell him to stay at home, where he belongs."

"I can't."

"You're the only one he might listen to. You don't want him to go, do you? Do you?" he repeated with more emphasis when she failed to answer.

"No!" she cried, wrenching her hand free of his. "But

I can't stand between Hal and a mission he feels that God has called him to do."

"Does he love you?"

"Yes."

"And you love him."

"Yes."

"You want to marry him and have a house and babies and all the trimmings, right?"

"That's my business. Hal's and mine."

"Dammit, I'm not trying to interfere into your personal life. I'm trying to keep my kid brother from getting blown away. Now, whether anybody likes it or not, I'm still a member of this family and you're going to answer me."

She quelled beneath his anger, but felt ashamed, too, for shutting him out of family matters as his parents so often did. When it boiled down to it, she was the outsider, not Cage. She met his eyes levelly. "Of course that's what I want, Cage. I've waited years to get married."

"All right, then," he said more calmly, "put your foot down. Issue an ultimatum. Tell him you won't be here when he gets back. Let him know how you feel about this."

She was shaking her head. "This is something he feels led to do."

"Then lead him astray, Jenny. I'm thinking of him as much as you. Hell, if presidents and diplomats and mercenaries and God knows who else can't straighten out that mess down there in Central America, how the hell does Hal think he's going to? He's going into something he knows absolutely nothing about."

"God will protect him."

"You're only repeating what you've heard him say. I know my Bible, too, Jenny. It was drilled into me. At one time I actually studied the Hebrew war generals. Yes, they pulled off a few miraculous battles, but Hal hasn't got an army behind him. He doesn't even have the endorsement of the U.S. Government. God gave each of us a brain to reason with and what Hal's doing is unreasonable."

Jenny agreed with him wholeheartedly. But Cage was an expert at twisting words and truths to make them fit his own ends. Aligning herself with Cage's way of thinking was flirting with heresy. Besides, her loyalty had to be with Hal and the cause he had dedicated himself to.

"Good night, Cage."

"How long have you lived with us, Jenny?"

She paused again. "Since I was fourteen. Almost twelve years."

The Hendrens had taken her in when both her parents were killed. One day while she was at school, a gas heater had exploded in their house and it had burned to the ground. Later she remembered hearing the fire truck and ambulance sirens during algebra class. She hadn't known then that it was already too late for her parents and a younger sister, who had stayed home that day with a sore throat. Her daddy had come home on his lunch hour to check on her. By nightfall, Jenny was left alone in the world, without a thing to her name except the clothes she had worn to school that day.

The Fletchers had been friendly with their pastor, Bob Hendren and his wife, Sarah. Since Jenny had no living relatives, there had been little discussion about her future.

"I remember coming home from college for Thanksgiving break and finding you here," Cage said. "Mother had converted her sewing room into a bedroom fit for a princess. She finally had the daughter she had always wanted. I was told to treat you like one of the family."

"Your parents have been very good to me," Jenny conceded in a small voice.

"Is that why you never stand up to them?"

She was offended and it showed. "I don't know what you're talking about!"

"Oh, yes, you do. It's been twelve years since you made a decision of your own. Are you afraid they'll kick you out if you disagree with them?"

"That's ridiculous," she exclaimed, flabbergasted.

"No, it isn't. It's sad," Cage said, jutting his hard, square chin into the air. "They decided who your friends could and could not be, the kind of clothes you wore, the college you went to, even who you were going to marry. And now it looks like they'll decide when the wedding will take place. Are you going to let them plan your kids, too?"

"Stop it, Cage. None of that is true and I won't listen to any more of it. Have you been drinking?"

"Unfortunately, no. But I wish to hell I had been." He moved toward her and gripped her arm. "Jenny, wake up. They're smothering you. You're a woman, a damn good-looking woman. So what if you do something they disapprove of? You're not fourteen now. They can't punish you. If they did kick you out, which they never would, so what? You could go someplace else."

"Be an independent woman, is that it?"

"I guess that capsulizes it, yeah."

"You think I should cruise the honky-tonks the way you do?"

"No. But I don't think it's healthy for you to spend ninety percent of your time cooped up in Bible study groups either."

"I like doing church work."

"At the exclusion of everything else?" Agitated, he raked his fingers through his hair. "All the work you do in the church is admirable. I'm not taking anything away from that. I just hate to see you shrivel up like an old lady long before your time. You're throwing your life away."

"I'm not. I'm going to have a life with Hal."

"Not if he goes off to Central America and gets himself killed!" He saw her face drain of color and softened his stance and his tone of voice. "Look, I'm sorry. I didn't mean to get into all that."

She accepted his apology graciously. "Hal's the real issue."

"That's right." He clasped her hands. "Talk to him, Jenny."

"I can't change his mind."

"He has to listen to you. You're the woman he's going to marry."

"Don't place so much confidence in me."

"I won't hold you responsible for his decision, if that's what you mean. Just promise you'll try to convince him not to go."

She glanced toward the kitchen. Through the windows she could see Hal and his parents still grouped around the table, deep in discussion. "I'll try."

"Good." He squeezed her hands before releasing them. "Sarah said you're spending the night." For some reason she didn't want Cage to know it had been she who had prepared his room for the overnight stay, airing it out that afternoon and putting fresh linens on the bed. She wanted him to think his mother had gone to the trouble.

"Yeah, I promised to be here for Hal's big send-off in the morning. I hope it never materializes."

"Well, anyway, Sarah likes having you sleep at home now and then."

He smiled ruefully and touched her cheek. "Ah, Jenny. You're such a diplomat. Mother issued the invitation and then told me to clear out all the football and basketball trophies from my bedroom while I was here. She said she was tired of dusting all that junk."

Jenny swallowed a knot of emotion and her heart went out to Cage. Only a few weeks ago she and Sarah had carefully folded clean cloths around Hal's sports trophies and stored them in boxes in the attic. For twelve years it had been clear to Jenny which was the favored son. But Cage had no one to blame but himself. He had chosen a way of life his parents couldn't possibly approve of.

"Good night, Cage." Jenny suddenly wished she could hold him. He often looked like he needed to be held, which was a ridiculous notion considering his reputation as the town stud. But was that kind of loving enough, even for someone as wild as Cage?

"G'night."

Reluctantly she left him alone and entered the house by the back door. Hal raised his eyes to her and indicated with his head that she should move behind his chair. He was listening attentively to what his father was saying about collecting a statewide offering for the support of the refugees once they arrived in Texas.

Jenny, standing behind Hal's chair, wrapped her arms around his shoulders and leaned down to tuck his head beneath her chin. "Tired?" Hal asked her when Bob stopped speaking. The Hendrens beamed at them proudly.

"A little."

"Go on up to bed. You'll have to get up early in the morning to wave me off."

She sighed and laid her forehead on top of his head, not wanting his parents to see the despair on her face. "I won't sleep."

"Take one of those sleeping pills the doctor prescribed for me," Sarah suggested. "They're so mild, one can't hurt you, and they do help me get my brain to slow down long enough to fall asleep."

"Come on," Hal said, scraping his chair back, "I'll go up with you."

"Good night, Bob, Sarah," Jenny said listlessly.

"Son, you didn't give us the name of the Mexican contact," Bob reminded Hal.

"I'm not turning in yet. I'm coming right back. I won't be a minute."

Together Jenny and Hal climbed the stairs. At the top, he paused outside his parents' bedroom. "Do you want that sleeping pill?"

"I suppose so. I know I'll toss and turn all night."

He left her and came back a few moments later with two small pink tablets lying in the palm of his hand. "The instructions on the bottle said one or two. I think you should take two."

They went into her bedroom and she turned on

the bedside lamp. Cage was right. As soon as she had moved into the parsonage, this room had been outfitted to suit a princess. Unfortunately, Jenny had had little choice in the decorating.

Even a few years ago, when Sarah had suggested it was time for a change, the hated powder blue dotted swiss had been replaced with white eyelet. The room was too juvenile and frilly for Jenny's taste. But she wouldn't have hurt Sarah's feelings for the world. She only hoped that as soon as she and Hal were married, she would be allowed to decorate their bedroom suite. There had never been any mention of their moving to their own house because it was also understood that when Bob retired, Hal would assume his ministry.

"Take your pills and put on your jammies. I'll wait to tuck you in." Jenny left Hal standing in the middle of the room and slipped into the bathroom, where she did as she was told, swallowing both capsules. But she didn't put on "jammies." She put on a nightgown she had surreptitiously bought in the hope that she would have an occasion like tonight to put it to use.

She faced herself in the mirror and made up her mind to take action as Cage had dared her to. She didn't want Hal to go. It was a dangerous, fool's mission. Even if it weren't, it was stalling their marriage plans again. Should any woman have to stand for that?

Jenny had a premonition that her future hinged on tonight. She had to stop Hal from leaving or her life would be forever altered. She had to take the gamble; and the stakes were all or nothing. And she would use the oldest device known to woman to assure a victory.

God had sanctioned Ruth's night with Boaz. Maybe this was another one of those times.

But Ruth hadn't had a nightgown that slithered down her naked body, feeling sinfully slinky and sensuous against her skin. Straps as fine as violin strings held up a bodice that plunged down far between her breasts, showing the ample inner curves. The pearl-colored nightgown had a trim, body-hugging fit that didn't miss a single detail of her figure until it flared out slightly at her hips. Its fluted hem brushed her insteps.

She misted herself with a flowery, light perfume and ran a brush through her hair. For a moment after she was ready, she closed her eyes and tried with all her might to gather the courage to open the door. She groped for the light switch first, snapping it off before she eased the door open.

"Jenny, don't forget to..."

Whatever Hal had been about to say left his mind the instant he saw her. She was a vision, both ethereal and sensual, as she glided toward the door on bare feet and softly closed and locked it. The lamplight bathed her skin with a golden glow and cast the shadows of her legs against the sheer nightgown as she moved.

"What are you... Where'd you get that, uh, gown?" Hal stammered.

"I was saving it for a special occasion," she answered softly as she reached him. She laid her hands on his chest. "I guess this is it."

He laughed uneasily. His arms went around her waist, but lightly. "Maybe you should have saved it until after we're married."

"And when will that be?" She pressed her cheek to the open V of his cotton shirt. He was dressed casually in jeans.

"As soon as I get back. You know that. I've promised you."

"You've promised before."

"And you've always been so understanding," he said fervently. His lips moved in her hair and his hands smoothed her back. "This time I won't break the promise. When I come back—"

"But that could take months."

"Possibly," he said grimly, tilting her head back so he could see her face. "I'm sorry."

"I don't want to wait that long, Hal."

"What do you mean?"

She took a step closer, matching her body to his in a way that made the pupils of his eyes contract as if too much light had been let in. "Love me."

"I do, Jenny."

"I mean…" She wet her lips and took the dive. "Hold me. Lie with me. Make love to me tonight."

"Jenny," he groaned. "Why are you doing this?"

"Because I'm desperate."

"Not as desperate as you're making me."

"I don't want you to go."

"I have to."

"Please stay."

"I'm committed."

"Marry me," she whispered against his throat.

"I will, when this is over."

"I need a pledge of your love."

"You've got it."

"Then show me. Love me tonight."

"I can't. It wouldn't be right."

"For me it would."

"For neither of us."

"We love each other."

"So we have to make sacrifices for each other."

"Don't you want me?"

In spite of himself, Hal pulled her closer and pressed his mouth against her neck. "Yes, yes. Sometimes I daydream about what it will be like to share a bed with you and I... Yes, I want you, Jenny."

He kissed her. His lips parted over hers as one hand slid down the curve of her hip. She responded, pressing closer, rubbing her thigh against his. His tongue barely breached the soft damp interior of her mouth before her tongue came out questing. He moaned again.

"Please love me, Hal," she said, clutching at his shirt. "I need you tonight. I need to be held and petted, reassured that what we have is real, that you're coming back."

"I am."

"But you don't know for sure. I want to love you before you go." She covered his lips and face and neck with quick, fiery kisses. He edged away from her, but she wouldn't be stopped. Finally, he gripped her upper arms and pushed her away sternly.

"Jenny, think!" She gaped at him wide-eyed as though she had been slapped. Gulping in air, she swallowed hard. "We can't. It would go against one of the principles we stand for. I'm going on a God-called mission tomorrow and I can't let you, beautiful and desirable as you are, distract me from that. Besides, my parents are right downstairs." He bent down and kissed her chastely on the cheek. "Now get into bed like a good girl."

He led her to the bed and peeled back the covers. She obediently climbed in and he pulled the sheet over her, determinedly keeping his eyes off her breasts. "I'll see you early in the morning." His mouth touched hers softly. "I do love you, Jenny. That's why I won't do as you ask." He switched out the lamp, crossed to the door, and closed it behind him, plunging the room into total darkness.

Jenny rolled to her side and began to cry. Tears, scalding and salty, rivered down her cheeks and into the pillowcase. Never had she felt so forsaken, not even when she had lost her family. She was alone, more dismally alone than she had ever been in her life.

Even her bedroom seemed alien and unfamiliar. But maybe that was the effect of the sleeping pills. Through the darkness she tried to distinguish the shape of the furniture and the outline of the windows, but everything was blurred around the edges. Her perception was dulled by the drug she had taken.

She had the sensation of floating and drifted toward sleep, but a fresh batch of tears kept it at bay. How humiliating. She had gone against her own staunch moral code. She had offered herself to the man she loved. Hal vowed he loved her. But he had flatly and outrightly rejected her!

Even if their love hadn't been consummated, he could have lain with her, held her, provided her with some evidence of the passion he claimed he felt, given her a shred of a memory to cling to while he was gone.

But his rejection had been total. How low she must be in the order of priorities of his life. He had more important things to do than love and comfort her.

Then the bedroom door opened.

Jenny turned toward the sound and tried to focus tear-laden eyes on the wedge of light that was cut into the consuming blackness. A man was silhouetted against the sudden brightness for only a second before he stepped into the room and shut the door behind him.

Jenny sat up and stretched her hands out toward him, her heart leaping and racing with joy. "Hal!" she cried gladly.

# Two

He made his way toward the bed and sank down on the edge of it. His shadow was barely discernible against the others in the room.

"You came back, you came back," Jenny repeated as she clasped his hands and raised them to her lips. She rained kisses across the ridges of his knuckles. "My heart was breaking. I need you tonight. Hold me." Her words broke into sobs and his arms encircled her with warmth. "Oh, yes, hold me tight."

"Shh, shh."

The sudden movement of sitting up, the few words she had spoken, taxed her dwindling, drug-affected coordination. Spent, she let her cheek fall into the cradle of his palm. His thumb stroked her cheekbones, sweeping off the tears. "Shh." When the tears were dried, she buried her face in the hollow between his shoulder and throat.

He bent his head down over hers. His beard was rough against her temple. With mindless curiosity her hand inched up his chest to touch his face. She gently scratched her nails over the rasping stubble on his chin, accidentally glancing his lips with her fingertips.

She heard him gasp. It seemed to come from far away, though she felt the quickening of his body. Uttering a low, rumbling sound deep in his chest, he tilted her head back and his mouth moved down to greet hers. His arms drew her possessively against his chest. Head falling back in wanton offering, Jenny surrendered her last conscious thoughts and entrusted herself only to sensual instinct.

His lips parted. This time his hesitation was short-lived. A heartbeat ticked by, possibly two, before his tongue came swirling down into the sweetest depths of her mouth, touching secret places, stroking madly.

Jenny whimpered and clung to him dizzily. Her head buzzed and she didn't know if it was the power of his kiss or the sleeping pills that made all her senses hum so deliciously. The kiss continued, gaining in fervor with each second, with each pounding heartbeat, until she thought her heart would break through her rib cage.

Had the sheet and blanket fallen away? They must have because her skin was suddenly cooled. Then warmed. As his hand… His hand? Yes. Moving over her. Touching her breasts. Caressing, kneading, finessing.

She felt her head sinking into the softness of the pillow and realized he had lowered her back onto the bed. The straps of her nightgown were lifted off her shoulders. Her moan could have been one of protest or permission. She wasn't certain. She was certain of nothing save the hands ghosting over her nakedness, acquainting themselves with her shape by touch. Fingertips grazed her nipples, again and again, plucking softly.

Then she fell victim to hot, encompassing sensations, surrounding, tugging. His mouth? Yes, yes, yes. The wet wash of his tongue flaying her gently. It caressed. Around and around. Long and slow. Quick and light.

She wanted to clasp his head and hold him against her, but couldn't. Her arms were heavy, useless, lying on the bed at her sides as though restrained by invisible bands. Her blood was pumping like molten lava through her veins, but she had neither the energy nor the will to move.

She welcomed his weight as he eased himself onto the bed and partially covered her, his tongue prowling the interior of her mouth, but softly, like a stealthy intruder. It was delicious. He was delicious. As was the whisper of cloth against her bare breasts.

Directed by his hands, she raised her hips and aided him in slipping her nightgown off. Beneath him she lay naked and vulnerable. But the hands that moved over her were kind, gentle, pleasure-giving. They touched every part of her, pausing frequently, making a gift of every caress.

The very tips of her toes were brushed by his thumb. Or was it his tongue? Her calves were gently squeezed. Her knees. Thighs. The hands lifted her, positioned her, until she felt the cool bed linens against the soles of her feet.

Mindlessly she obeyed every silent direction. To have refused, to have balked, would have been unthinkable. She was a servant of this seductive master, a priestess of sensuality, a disciple of desire.

His hair pleasantly tickled her belly as his head moved from side to side. He lightly pinched the soft flesh between his lips, laved it with his tongue, sucked at it gently.

And when he opened his hand over her mound, she bowed her head against his chest and savored the cherishing caress that revolved slowly, ground gently.

Oh, yes! her mind cried joyfully. He loved her! He wanted her! She proved her willingness by moving her body in a tempestuous ballet.

Tantalizing, investigative fingers left her flesh slippery against his. His thumb applied a massaging friction that accelerated her breathing, made a drumbeat of her pulse.

Faster. Surer. Ever whirling with a pagan beat. Until— Her soul seemed to open up and release a flock of colorful songbirds that scattered on a flurry of wings.

It wasn't enough! *I'm still hungry,* her soul cried in protest.

His denim jeans were rough, but not unpleasantly so, against her open thighs. Buttons. Cloth. Then—

Hair. Skin. Man. Hard warmth and smooth strength. A velvety spearhead. All rubbing against her. Probing. Seeking its mate. Until they meshed the way they were intended.

The penetration was swift and sure.

She heard the sharp cry an instant after feeling the brand-hot pain shoot through her, but it didn't occur to her that she had made that surprised sound. She was too enthralled by the steely manhood imbedded tightly inside the giving folds of her body. But no sooner had she come to realize the splendor of his possession than he began to ease away.

"No, no." The words echoed through the darkened chambers of her mind, and she wondered if she had actually spoken them aloud. She was consumed with the determination that it not end yet, not quite yet.

Of their own volition, her hands slid beneath his jeans and pressed the hard muscles of his buttocks with her palms. She felt the spasm that shuddered through his body, heard his animal groan, felt the rush of his warm breath in her ear, felt, miraculously, still more of his hardness delving into her.

Pliant, malleable, she let him gather her beneath him, positioning her for comfort and maximum sensation. Random kisses fell on her throat, her face, her breasts, leaving stinging impressions on her skin.

Her whole body responded to the myriad sensations rioting through it. She seemed trapped in the rhythm that rocked their bodies together in perfect harmony. Then the coil that had been winding tighter and tighter in her middle suddenly sprang free again. Thighs, hands, belly, breasts, replied in an ageless physical manner that milked life from him.

The body above hers tensed. Against the walls of her womb she felt each precious eruption of his love. Until there was nothing but the full pressure of him still filling her.

Replete, but selfish, her body closed around him like a silken fist. She was almost asleep when he finally left her, rolled to his side, and tucked her against him. She cuddled up to his solid frame, her fist clutching a handful of his damp shirt. She was embraced by a peace and sense of belonging she had never known before.

Still woozy, still entranced, still dazed by the experience, she was smiling when she drifted into a dreamless sleep.

\* \* \*

She awoke early. She awoke alone. Sometime during the night Hal had left her. That was understandable and she forgave him, though it would have been wonderful to wake up in his arms. But the Hendrens would never have approved what had happened last night. Jenny, as much as Hal, wanted to protect them from finding out.

There were footsteps on the landing and whispered conversations that carried through the hallways of the old house. She could smell coffee brewing. Preparations were underway for Hal's departure. Apparently he hadn't spoken to his parents yet.

Last night had changed everything. He would be as anxious for marriage now as she. She clung to the precious memory of their lovemaking and could find no shame in it, even if she had used it to make him stay.

He belonged there with her. He would continue as associate pastor until his father retired and then take over the full ministry. She was well trained in being a pastor's wife. Surely Hal could now see that that was what God willed for them.

But how would the Hendrens react to his change in plans?

Not wanting him to have to face the music alone, she flung the covers off, almost surprised to find herself naked. Oh, yes, he had removed her nightgown, hadn't he? And quite frantically, she thought with an impish smile.

She was blushing furiously as she entered the bathroom and turned on the taps in the shower. She looked no different, though upon close inspection she saw there were rosy whisker burns on her breasts.

All the same, he had left an indelible print on her.

When she thought about it, she could still feel the welcome weight of his body atop hers, still feel the supple movements of his muscles beneath her hands, still hear his moans of gratification. She was both ashamed and thrilled when her body responded to the recollections.

She dressed hurriedly and sailed downstairs, eager to see Hal. By the time she reached the kitchen, her heart was pounding with expectation. Breathless, she hovered on the threshold, taking in the scene.

The Hendrens, sitting at the breakfast table, were in an attitude of prayer. Cage was there, too, reclining on his spine in the ladder-back chair. His head was bowed, but he was staring broodingly into his coffee cup, which he had balanced on his belt buckle.

Where was Hal? Surely not still asleep.

Bob pronounced the amen and raised his head. He spotted Jenny. "Where's Hal?" she asked.

Silently the three of them stared back at her. She could feel a blackness closing in, like storm clouds rushing closer from a threatening horizon.

"He's already gone, Jenny," Bob said gently. He stood, scraped his chair back, and took a step toward her.

She retreated a half step as though he posed a threat to her. The encroaching blackness smothered her. She couldn't breathe. All color drained from her face. "That's impossible." The words were barely audible. "He didn't say goodbye to me."

"He didn't want to put you through another heartbreaking farewell scene," Bob said. "He thought it would be easier this way."

This wasn't happening. She had played the scene in her mind. Hal would be mesmerized by the first sight of her. She had imagined them gazing into each other's eyes, lovers sharing a marvelous knowledge that was secret from the rest of the world.

But he was gone and all that she saw were three faces gazing back at her, two with pity, Cage's with a remarkable lack of emotion.

"I don't believe you!" she cried. She dashed through the kitchen nearly falling over a chair before she pushed it aside and barreled through the back door. The yard was deserted. There were no cars on the street.

Hal was gone.

The truth hit her hard. She felt like throwing up. She felt like collapsing onto the ground and pounding her fists against the hard earth. She felt like screaming. She was swamped with disappointment.

But what had she expected? Hal was never demonstrative where his affection for her was concerned. Now, in the light of day, she realized how fanciful she had been. He hadn't made any promises not to leave. He had sealed their covenant of love with a physical expression of it. That was what she had asked of him. To have expected more was unrealistic. And it was characteristic of him to spare her the humiliation of begging him not to go. He would have wanted to avoid that for both their sakes.

Then why did she feel deserted? Bereft. Forsaken. Dejected and rejected.

And mad.

Damn good and mad. How could he leave her like this? How? How, when she had regretted that they couldn't even finish the night lying in each other's arms?

Jenny stood on the cracked sidewalk staring at the

empty street. How could he have left her so blithely, without so much as a goodbye? Was she no more important to him than that? If he loved her—

The thought brought her mind to an abrupt standstill. Did he love her? Truly love her? Did she love him the way she should? Or was it as Cage had suggested last night? Had she and Hal merely drifted into the relationship everyone had expected of them, one that was convenient to her because it was safe, and convenient to him because it didn't cost him time away from his ministerial duties?

What a dismal thought.

She strove to push it aside. Why couldn't she dwell on the happiness she had basked in last night in the aftermath of their love?

But the ambiguities wouldn't be swept under the rug. They stayed there in the forefront of her mind and she realized that before Hal came home, she had to reach some conclusions. It would be foolhardy to enter into a marriage harboring the kind of doubts she had. The union of their bodies had been glorious, but she knew that wasn't the soundest foundation on which to base a marriage. And she had been dopey with the sedative. Maybe she was remembering the lovemaking as more earthshaking than it had actually been. Maybe it had all been an erotic, drug-induced dream.

Turning on her heel to return to the house, she almost collided with Cage, who had come up behind her so silently she hadn't realized he was there.

She almost jumped under the impact of his stare.

He was studying her from beneath a hood of dusty blond brows. The golden brown eyes were as unflinching and unblinking as a great cat's. He was motionless, completely motionless, until one corner of his mouth lifted involuntarily.

Jenny attributed that telltale gesture to regret and remorse. Was he feeling sorry for her because she had failed to persuade Hal to stay at home? Was that how everyone in town would see her, a pitifully forsaken lover, pining away for the man whose life's work was more important than she?

Irked by the thought, she tore her eyes from Cage's stare, straightened her shoulders, and tried to go around him. He sidestepped and blocked her path.

"Are you all right, Jenny?" His brows were pulled down into a low V over his eyes. His squint lines were pronounced. His jaw looked as hard as granite.

"Of course," she said brightly, faking a huge smile. "Why shouldn't I be?"

He shrugged. "Hal left you without saying goodbye. He's gone."

"But he'll be back. And he was right to go like that, make a clean break. I couldn't have stood to tell him a final goodbye." She wondered if her statements sounded as false to him as they did to her.

"Did you talk to him last night?"

"Yes."

"And?" he probed.

Her smile faltered and her eyes skittered away from the penetrating power of his. "And he made me feel much better about things. He wants to get married as soon as he gets back."

It wasn't quite a lie. It wasn't quite the truth either, and Cage's searching eyes told her he wasn't convinced. She brushed past him hurriedly. "Did you eat any breakfast? I'll fix you something. Two eggs over easy?"

He smiled, pleased. "You remember how I like them?"

"Sure." She held the screen door for him, standing straight and shrinking against the jamb as he wedged himself past her. When his body made brief contact with hers, every cell ignited. Her breasts flared to rigid points. Her thighs tingled with heat. Her heart did handstands.

Jenny was flabbergasted. She rushed to cover her agitation by hastily preparing Cage's breakfast. Her hands shook so she could barely control them, and as soon as she set the plate of food on the table in front of him, she fled to her room.

Now that her sleeping body had been awakened to sexual awareness, it seemed not to want to lie dormant again.

But, Lord, didn't it have any discernment? Any discrimination? Would it now react to every man she came in contact with?

The thought sent a surge of embarrassment through her. Nevertheless, she stripped, crawled between the covers of her bed, and pulled her knees to her chest. She let the events of last night parade through her mind again and relished the naughty sensations that still rippled through her like aftershocks.

The dark amber contents of the highball glass didn't offer any absolution for Cage's guilt, but it held his attention as though it could.

Three longneck beer bottles were neatly lined up on the highly glossed tabletop. They were empty. He had switched to Jack Daniel's about an hour ago, but the

guilt poisoning his system refused to be diluted even
by near-lethal amounts of alcohol.

He had violated Jenny.

There was no sense in using euphemisms to try to
blunt the edges of his guilt. He could say he had made
love to her, initiated her into the rites of sexual loving, deflowered her. But no matter how his conscience
juggled with semantics, he had violated her. It hadn't
been a brutal rape, but she had been unwittingly in no
condition to give her consent. It had been a violation
of the vilest sort.

He took another swig of the stinging whiskey. It
burned all the way down. He wished he could get drunk
enough to vomit. Maybe that would purge him.

Who the hell was he kidding? Nothing was going to
purge him of this. He hadn't felt guilty about anything
in years. Now he was swamped with guilt. And what
the hell could he do about it?

Tell her? Confess?

"Oh, by the way, Jenny, about the other night, you
know the one, the night Hal left and you made love with
him? Yeah, well, that wasn't him. It was me."

He cursed savagely and polished off the drink in
one gulp. He could just imagine her face, her dear, dear
face, shattering before his eyes. She would be horrified.
Knowing she had been with him would probably put
her in a catatonic state from which she would never recover. The most notorious skirt chaser in West Texas
had taken sweet Jenny Fletcher.

No, he couldn't tell her.

He'd done bad things before, but this time he had
sunk to an all-time low. He liked his reputation as a
hell-raiser. He lived up to it, worked at keeping it alive,

kept reminding folks of it should they think Cage Hendren was mellowing with the passing years. He'd even take credit for some things he hadn't done. He would let that slow, lazy smile answer allegations for him, and his cronies could draw their own conclusions as to whether the latest rumor was true or not.

But this…

Signaling to the bartender, Cage became aware of his surroundings. They were dismally familiar. Tobacco smoke fogged the close, stuffy, beery atmosphere of the tavern. Red-and-blue neon lights advertising various brands of beer winked from the walls like phosphorescent sprites hiding in the paneling. A sad strand of gold tinsel, left over from last Christmas, dangled from a wagon-wheel-shaped chandelier. A spider had made a home between the spokes. Waylon Jennings mourned a love gone wrong from the jukebox in the corner.

It was tawdry. It was tacky. It was home.

"Thanks, Bert," Cage said laconically as the bartender set another glass of whiskey in front of him.

"Hard day?"

Hard week, Cage thought. He'd lived with his sin for a week now, but the gnawing guilt hadn't abated. Its fangs were as sharp as ever as they ate their way into his soul. Soul? Did he even possess a soul?

Bert bent over the table and transferred the empty beer bottles to a tray. "Heard something that might interest you."

"Yeah? What about?" There was a droplet of water on the outside of the highball glass. It reminded him of Jenny's tears. He wiped it away with his thumb.

"'Bout that parcel of land west of the mesa."

In spite of his black mood, Cage's interest was instantly piqued. "The old Parsons' ranch?"

"Yep. Heard the kinfolks is ready to talk money to anyone interested."

Cage slipped Bert a smile worthy of a toothpaste ad, and a ten-dollar tip. "Thanks, buddy." Bert smiled back and ambled off. Cage was a favorite of his and he was glad to oblige.

Cage Hendren was indisputably one of the best wildcatters around. He could smell oil, seemed to know instinctively where it was. Oh, he'd gone to Tech and earned a degree in geology to make it all official and to inspire confidence. But he had a knack for sensing where the stuff was, a knack that couldn't be book learned. He had drilled a few dry holes, but very few. Few enough to win him the respect of men who had been in the business more years than Cage was old.

He'd been trying to lease the mineral rights on the Parsons' land for years. The elderly couple had died within months of each other, but the children had held out, saying they didn't want their family's land to be desecrated by drilling rigs. That was a crock, of course, and Cage knew it. They had been holding out while the price went up. He'd pay a call on the executor of the estate tomorrow.

"Hiya, Cage."

He had been so lost in thought that he hadn't seen the woman until she sidled up to his table, managing to nudge his shoulder with her hip as she did so. He glanced up with a notable lack of interest. "Hi, Didi. How're things?"

Without a word, she laid a single key on the polished surface of the small, round table, covered it with the pad of her index finger, and slid it toward Cage. "Sonny and I have finally called it quits."

"'S that a fact?"

Didi's marriage to Sonny had been on the rocks for months. Neither upheld their vows, especially the one promising faithfulness. She had made inviting moves toward Cage before, but he'd stayed away from her. He didn't have many scruples, but he was loyal to one; never with a married woman. Something inside him still believed in the sanctity of marriage, despite everything, and he never wanted to be responsible for helping break one up.

"Uh-huh. That's a fact all right. I'm a single woman now, Cage." Didi smiled down at him. If she had licked her lips, she would have been the perfect imitation of a well-satisfied she-cat that had just lapped up a bowl of cream. Her generous figure had been poured into a pair of jeans with a Neiman-Marcus label, and a low-cut sweater. Leaning down, she gave him an unrestricted view of her deep cleavage.

Rather than inciting desire, she made him feel like he needed a bath.

Jenny. Jenny. Jenny. So clean. Her body so neatly feminine. Not overblown, not lush, not voluptuous, just womanly.

Damn!

Mentally he jerked himself erect, though he still slouched in his chair, nonchalantly twirling the bottom of his glass on the table.

Didi dragged a long fingernail down his arm. "See ya, Cage," she said with a seductive certainty as she undulated away.

One corner of his mouth twisted sardonically. Had

he ever thought such a bold invitation was attractive? Didi's blatancy was almost laughable.

Jenny didn't even know she was sexy. She wore such a subtle fragrance. In comparison, Didi's heavy perfume lingered after her distastefully.

Jenny's voice was nervously breathless, a voice Cage found far sexier than Didi's affected purr. And Jenny's amateurish caresses had stirred him more than the calculated foreplay any of his former lovers had practiced.

Closing out the seamy setting before him, he let his mind wander back to that innocent bedroom that should have belonged to a child, not to a woman who wore silk nightgowns. And it had been silk. His touch was educated to the matchless feel of silk against a woman's body. But Jenny's skin had been almost as soft. And her hair. And—

Her virginity had been a shock. Surely, surely his brother wasn't that saintly. How could Hal, how could any man, have lived in the same house with Jenny all these years and not made love to her?

Were he and his brother that different? Weren't they similarly equipped? Of course they were. There was nothing wrong with Hal physically. Cage had to admire Hal's unflagging morality, though he couldn't imagine anyone imposing such a rigid code of morality on himself.

Jenny hadn't, had she?

She had been willing to give herself to Hal on the night of his departure. What a sap Hal had been not to accept that precious gift. Cage hated to think of his brother in such derisive terms, but that was how he felt about it. Hadn't Hal realized what a sacrifice Jenny had been making for him? At the moment he had encountered the frail barrier of her virginity, Cage had.

God above, had he ever known such rapture as when he was sheathed inside her? Had he ever heard any sweeter sound than the little catches in her throat when passion claimed her?

Never. It had never been so good.

But then, no other woman was Jenny. She was the unattainable one. The one forbidden and off-limits. Even beyond his far-reaching boundaries.

He had known it for years. Just as he had known that she belonged to Hal. It was understood. Years ago, Cage had had to reconcile himself to that. He could have any woman he wanted. Except the one he really wanted. Jenny.

He was rotten to the core. No good. Didn't give a damn about anyone or anything. That was what folks said about him and it was mainly true. But he had cared enough about Jenny and Hal not to ruin their lives with his interference.

He had kept his secret well. No one knew. No one would even guess. Least of all her. She had no idea that every time he was near her, he ached to touch her. Not sexually. Just touch her.

Her affection for him was purely fraternal. Yet he had always sensed that she was afraid of him, too. He made her uncomfortable and that had often broken his heart. Her fear was justified, of course. He had a scandalous reputation and any woman who valued her good name stayed away from him as though his sexuality was as contagious and dreaded as leprosy.

But he had often wondered what would have happened if Jenny had come to live with them sooner. If he hadn't been off at college, if he hadn't already been known as a hell-raiser without equal, if they had had time to develop a relationship, would Jenny have turned to him instead of Hal?

It was his favorite fantasy to think so. Because he sensed that beneath Jenny's reserve, there was a free spirit longing to be released, a sensual, sexual woman trapped in an invisible cage of circumspection. If she were given her freedom, what would happen?

Maybe she wanted to be rescued. Maybe she made silent appeals to be freed that no other man had responded to. Maybe—

*You're fooling yourself, man. She wouldn't want to get her life tangled up with yours under any circumstances.*

He shoved his chair back and stood, angrily tossing a pile of bills onto the table. But in the process, his hand paused as a thought struck him.

*Unless your life changed.*

He hadn't gone into her bedroom that night with the intention of doing what he'd done. He had heard her crying and knew that her appeal to Hal had failed. She had been heartbroken and it had been his intention only to comfort her.

But then she had mistaken him for Hal and, like the tide washing into shore, he had been compulsively drawn to her. He had crossed the dark room to her bed, telling himself that at any moment he was going to identify himself.

He had touched her. He had heard the desperation in her voice. He had understood the despair of craving love and not receiving it. He had answered her plea and held her. And once he had kissed her, felt the responding warmth of her body beneath his hands, there had been no turning back.

What he had done had been unforgivable. But what he was going to do was almost as bad. He was going to try to steal her from his brother.

Now that he had had her, he couldn't let her go. Not if hell opened up and swallowed him. He wouldn't let her spirit be stifled by his family any longer. Hal had been given a golden opportunity to claim her love forever, but he had rejected her. Cage wouldn't stand by and see the yearning in her face eventually become defeat, her vitality become resignation, and all her animation be smothered in a cocoon of righteousness.

He had months to win her before Hal returned, and, by God, that was what he was going to do.

"Didi." She was cuddled in a dark booth with a roughneck who had a hand under her sweater and his tongue in her ear. Annoyed by the interruption, she disengaged herself. "You forgot something," Cage said, flipping the key toward the booth.

She missed it and it clattered noisily onto the table. Didi snatched it up and looked at Cage blankly. "What's this for?"

"I won't be using it."

"Bastard," she hissed venomously.

"Never said otherwise," Cage said breezily as he pushed open the door of the tavern.

"Hey, guy," the roughneck called after him, "you can't talk to the lady—"

"Oh, let it go, honey," Didi cooed, smoothing a hand down his shirtfront. They picked up where they had left off.

Cage stepped into the cool evening air and drew it in

deeply to clear his head of alcohol fumes and the odor of the tavern. Sliding beneath the wheel of his '63 split window Corvette Stingray, he gunned the engine to a low growl and sped off into the night.

The restored classic car was the envy of every man within a hundred-mile radius of La Bota and was readily identified with Cage. It was a mean midnight black with a matching leather interior that was equally as devilish.

Sleekly it rocketed down the barren highway, then slowed to silently take the corners of the town's streets. Half a block away from the parsonage, Cage pulled it to the curb and cut the engine.

The window in Jenny's room was already dark. But he sat and stared at it for a full hour, just as he had done for the past six nights.

# *Three*

Jenny glanced up from the altar at the front of the church when a tall silhouette loomed in the sanctuary door, dark against the bright sunlight outside. The last person she expected to see here was Cage. Yet it was he who took off a pair of aviator sunglasses and strolled inside and down the carpeted aisle of the church.

"Hi."

"Hi."

"Maybe I should increase my tithe. Can't the church afford to hire a janitor?" he said, nudging his chin toward the basket of cleaning supplies at her feet.

Self-consciously she stuck the handle of her orange feather duster into the rear pocket of her jeans, which left the plume sticking up like a tail feather. "I like doing it."

He grinned. "You seem surprised to see me."

"I am," she replied honestly. "How long has it been since you came to church?"

She had been dusting the altar in preparation for the bouquet of flowers the florist had delivered. Sunlight poured through the tall stained glass windows and made the fuzzy dancing motes look like a sprinkling of fairy dust. The light cast rainbows on Jenny's skin and her hair, which had been pinned into a haphazard knot on the top of her head. Her jeans fit snugly. The tennis shoes on her feet were appealingly well-worn. Cage thought she looked as cute as a button and sexy as all get-out.

"Last Easter." He dropped down onto the front pew and laid his arms along the back of it, stretching them out on either side of him. He surveyed the sanctuary and realized it had remained virtually unchanged for as far back as he could remember.

"Oh, yes," Jenny said. "We had a picnic in the park that afternoon."

"And I pushed you in the swing."

She laughed. "How could I have forgotten that? I screamed for you not to push me so high, but you kept right on."

"You loved it."

There was a trace of mischief in her eyes as she smiled down at him, the corners of her mouth turning up adorably. "How did you know?"

"Instinct."

When he sent a lazy smile in her direction, Jenny guessed that Cage had many instincts about women, none of them holy.

Cage was thinking back to the previous spring, to the Sunday they had mentioned. It had been a late Easter and the skies had been purely blue, the air warm. Jenny had worn a yellow dress, something soft and frothy that had alternately billowed around and clung to her body with each puff of south wind.

He had loved drawing her close against his chest as

she sat in the swing, the old one with ropes as thick as his wrists suspending it from the giant tree. He had held her against him for an unnecessarily long time, teasing her by almost letting her go before jerking her back. It had given him the opportunity to breathe in the summery scent of her hair and enjoy the feel of her slender back against his chest.

When he did release her, she laughed with childlike glee. The sound of her laughter still rang in his ears. Each time the pendulum of the swing carried her back to him, he pushed the seat of it, almost touching her hips. Not quite, but almost.

It was true what the romantic poets penned about the fancies of young men in spring. Virile juices had pumped through his body that day, making him feel full and heady, heavy with the need to mate.

He had wanted to lie in the grass with Jenny, letting the warming rays of the sun fall on her face as gently as his lips kissed her. He had wanted to rest his head in her lap, gazing up into her face. He had wanted to make soft, unhurried, gentle love to her.

But she had been Hal's girl that day, just as always. And when Cage had taken all he could of seeing them together, he had stalked to his car to drink a cold beer from the cooler he kept there. His parents had demonstrated their extreme disapproval.

Finally, to keep from ruining everyone's good time, especially Jenny's, because Cage knew that dissonance within the family distressed her tremendously, he had bade everyone a snarling farewell and roared away from the park in his black Corvette.

Now he felt the same compulsion to touch her. Even in her mussed state, she looked so touchable and soft. He wondered if the wall of the church would cave in if he took her in his arms and kissed her the way he longed to.

"Who donated the flowers this week?" he asked before his body could betray his lusty thoughts.

Each year a calendar was circulated through the membership of the church. Families filled in a Sunday when they would provide flowers for the altar, usually in honor of a special occasion.

Jenny read the card attached to the bouquet of crimson gladiolas. "The Randalls. 'In loving memory of our son, Joe Wiley,'" she read aloud.

"Joe Wiley Randall." Cage squinted his eyes, a smile on his face.

"Did you know him?"

"Sure did. He was several classes ahead of me, but we ran around together some." He leaned his head far back and looked over his shoulder at a pew several rows behind him.

"See that fourth row there? Joe Wiley and I were sitting there one Sunday morning. When the offering plate came by, Joe Wiley stuck his chewing gum to the bottom of it. I thought that was hilarious. So did Joe Wiley. We followed the progress of that offering plate through the sanctuary, up one aisle, down another. You can imagine the expressions on people's faces when their hands got stuck in the gum."

Jenny, her eyes sparkling, sat down beside him. "What happened?"

"I got a spanking. Reckon he got one, too."

"No, I mean, the card says 'in memory of.'"

"Oh. He went to Nam." He stared at the flowers for a long moment. "I don't recall seeing him after he graduated from high school." Jenny sat motionless, saying nothing, listening to the silence. "He was a helluva basketball player," Cage said reflectively. Then he hunched his shoulders and ducked his head as though God's wrath might strike him like lightning for his curse. "Ooops. Can't say that in church, can you?"

Jenny laughed. "What difference does it make? God hears you say it all the time." Suddenly she took on a serious mien and gazed at him, her eyes probing deeply into his. "You do believe in God, don't you, Cage?"

"Yes." There was no doubt he was telling the truth. His face was rarely that somber. "And in my own way I worship Him. I know what people say about me. My own parents think I'm a heathen."

"I'm certain they don't think that."

He looked doubtful. "What do you think of me?"

"That you're a stereotypical preacher's kid."

He threw back his head and laughed. "That's an oversimplification, isn't it?"

"Not at all. When you were growing up, you acted ornery to keep from being thought of as a goody-goody."

"I'm grown up, but I still don't want to be a goody-goody."

"No one would accuse you of that," she teased, poking his thigh with her index finger. She drew her hand back quickly. His thigh was hard, just like Hal's, and it reminded her too well of hard, jean-clad muscles rubbing against her naked legs.

To cover her consternation she asked, "Do you remember trying to make me laugh when I was singing in the choir?"

"Me?" he asked indignantly. "I never did any such thing."

"Oh, yes, you did. Making faces and looking cross-eyed. From way back there in the back row where you sat with one of your girls, you would—"

"With 'one of my girls'? You make it sound like I had a harem."

"Didn't you? Don't you?"

His eyes lowered significantly and took a leisurely tour of her body. "There's always room for one more. Wanna fill out an application?"

"Oh!" she cried, jumping from her seat and facing him with mock fury, fists digging into her hips. "Will you get out of here. I've got work to do."

"Yeah, so do I," he said, sighing and pulling himself to his feet. "I just signed a contract leasing a hundred acres of the old Parsons' place."

"Is that good?" She knew little about his work, only that it had something to do with oil and that he was considered successful.

"Very. We're ready to start drilling."

"Congratulations."

"Save those for when the first well comes in." Playfully he yanked on an errant strand of caramel-colored hair that had escaped the knot on top of her head. Turning, he sauntered up the aisle of the church toward the door.

"Cage?" Jenny asked suddenly.

"Yeah?" He turned back around, looking rugged and handsome, windblown and sunbaked, disreputable and dangerous. His thumbs were hooked in his belt loops. The collar of his denim vest was flipped up to bracket his jaw.

"I forgot to ask you why you came by."

His shoulders bobbed in a brief shrug. "No special reason. 'Bye, Jenny."

"'Bye."

He stared at her for a moment before he put on his sunglasses and stepped through the door.

Jenny struggled to anchor the damp bedsheet to the clothesline before the strong wind ripped it from her grasp. The linens she had already hung up popped like sails and flapped around her like giant wings.

As she shoved the clothespin over the last corner and dropped her arms in exhaustion, her ears were met with a monster's roar. A threatening form reared up behind the sheet and grabbed her. It enfolded her in its massive arms as it made rapacious devouring noises.

She screamed softly, but her exclamation of fright was muffled by the smothering embrace she had been wrapped in.

"Scared you, didn't I?" the as-yet-unseen attacker growled in her ear as he pulled her close.

"Let me go."

"Say please."

"Please!"

Cage released her and peered around the sheet, laughing at her efforts to extricate herself from its folds. Miraculously it had stayed on the clothesline in spite of their tussle.

"Cage Hendren, you scared the daylights out of me!"

"Aw, come on, you knew it was me."

"Only because you've done that to me before." She made exasperated attempts to push her windblown hair out of her eyes. They were as futile as the efforts she made not to smile. Finally a grin broke through and she laughed with him. "Someday…" She let the threat dwindle, but she shook her finger at him. His hand whipped out and snatched it, entrapping it in his fist.

"What? Someday what, Jenny Fletcher?"

"Someday you're gonna get yours."

He lifted her finger to his mouth and closed his teeth around it in a playful bite, growling cannibalistically. "Don't bet on it."

Just the sight of her flesh imprisoned between his strong white teeth flustered her and she wished she could think of a way to pull her finger away from his mouth without creating an awkward moment. At last he released her hand and she stepped back as though she had moved too close to a fire and hadn't realized it until the flames singed her.

She wondered why he had come to the parsonage today, though his visits weren't nearly as rare as they had been before Hal left. Since then Cage had been dropping by frequently on unimportant errands.

Ostensibly these visits were to ask if they had received news from Hal, but his excuses were so lame that Jenny wondered if he was coming around for the benefit of his parents. If so, she was touched by the gesture.

He had made several trips to the parsonage in order to empty his former bedroom of all the "junk" Sarah had asked him to remove, though it all could have been handled in one load.

Then he had come by bearing a cake he had bought at the FHA fund-raising bake sale and offered it to them, since he knew he couldn't possibly eat it all.

One evening he had stopped by to borrow an electric sander from Bob so he could polish his car with the buffer attachment. All these devices were valid enough, but Jenny still thought there was an ulterior motive behind them.

It wasn't like Cage to show such interest in the goings-on at the parsonage. His evenings were usually spent in local watering holes where he caroused with roughnecks and cowboys and businessmen—when he wasn't in the company of a woman.

And the more time she spent with him, the less Jenny liked to think about Cage and his women. The pangs of jealousy she felt were uncalled-for and she couldn't imagine why they should have suddenly sprung up from nowhere.

"Is the clothes dryer broken?" Cage asked now, swinging her empty laundry basket over his shoulder and following her toward the back door.

"No, but I like the way the sheets and pillowcases smell after they've dried outside."

He smiled down at her as he held the door open. "You're a hard case, Jenny."

"I know, hopelessly old-fashioned."

"That's what I like about you."

Again she felt the need to put distance between them. When he was standing this close, looking at her in that peculiar, penetrating way of his, she couldn't breathe properly. "Would you...would you like a Coke?"

"That'd be great." He returned the basket to the laundry room, off the kitchen, while she went to the refrigerator. She plunked ice cubes into the glasses she took down from the cabinet and poured the fizzing soft drink over them.

"Where are Mother and Dad?"

"There were several people in the hospital they needed to visit."

Realizing that she and Cage were alone in the rambling old house made her unaccountably nervous. Her hand was shaking slightly when she set his drink down in front of him on the table. She didn't want to risk touching him. She had always avoided touching him if possible, but lately…

Nervously she dropped into the chair across the table from him and thirstily sipped at her cold drink. He was watching her. Though she wasn't looking directly at him, she could feel his eyes touching her. Why wasn't she wearing something beneath the old T-shirt she had on?

Then, to her mortification, as though thinking about them had coaxed forth a response, her breasts began to bead against the soft cloth.

"Jenny?"

"What?" She jumped as though she had been caught doing something dirty. She felt feverish and light-headed, much as she had the night she had made love to Hal. He had been dressed as Cage was now, in jeans and a cotton Western-cut shirt.

She could almost feel the different textures of fabric against her naked skin, the cool bite of his metal buckle before he had unfastened it, the warm proof of manhood when he did. She squirmed in her chair and pressed her knees tightly together beneath the table, trying to keep her face impassive.

"Have you heard from Hal?"

She shook her head fiercely, both in answer to his question and to deny the sensations rioting inside her. "Not since that last postcard dated a month ago. Do you think we should read anything into that?"

"Yes." Her head snapped up, but Cage was smiling. "That everything is okay."

"No news is good news."

"Something like that."

"Bob and Sarah keep up a good front, but they're worried. We didn't think he'd have to go into the interior of the country, only to the border. We thought he would have been well on his way home by now."

"He might be, but just hasn't had the opportunity to notify us yet."

"Maybe." Selfishly she was hurt because the few times Hal had written, the notes had been addressed to them all. They had stressed that conditions in Monterico were bad, but that he was well and safe. He hadn't included one private word for her. His own fiancée. Was that characteristic of a man in love, especially after what had happened the night before he left?

"Do you miss him?" Cage asked her softly.

"Terribly." She raised her eyes to his, but they fell away almost immediately. One couldn't lie while staring into those tawny eyes. One couldn't even fudge on the truth. She missed Hal, but not "terribly," not like she had thought she would, not like she should. In a way, she was relieved that he wasn't constantly underfoot. And wasn't that odd?

Now that she had been to bed with him, didn't she want him anymore? What kind of depravity had she sunk into?

Oh, she longed to experience that kind of total joy again, that indescribable physical high, but she wasn't particularly anxious to see Hal. Probably because she was still angry with him for leaving without even saying goodbye to her. At least that was the answer she gave herself. It wasn't satisfying, but it was the only one she had.

"He'll be fine. Hal always comes out of scrapes smelling like a rose." Cage leaned back in his chair, balancing it on the two rear legs. "There was a family who lived through the alley there…long before you ever came to live with us. I was about twelve; Hal was eight or nine. Their poor daughter was extremely overweight. Obese. All the kids at school called her Tank, Fatso, Porky, unkind things like that. A group of bullies used to wait for her on the corner and laugh and catcall when she walked past them on her way home."

Jenny was lulled by the tone of his voice. It was deep, a shade raspy, as though some West Texas sand had collected on his vocal cords. As he talked his fingers idly slid up and down the glass where condensation had made it slippery. The hairs on his knuckles looked very fair against his bronzed hand. Funny, she had never noticed that before. The way his fingers stroked the glass was mesmerizing and she could imagine…

"One day Hal was walking home with her and flew into the bullies when they started the name-calling. He got a bloody nose, a black eye, and a busted lip for his efforts to defend her. But that night Mother and Dad hailed him a hero for taking on a foe larger than himself. Mother gave him a double helping of dessert. Dad analogized Hal's good deed by comparing him to young David taking on Goliath.

"I thought, hell, if that's all it takes to make them happy, I can do that. I knew how to fight, and a lot better than Hal did. So the next day, I waited for those bullies behind the garage. I had two scores to settle with them.

One, for beating up my kid brother. The other was for making fun of that poor girl."

"What did you do?"

"They were real proud of themselves and came chasing down the alley, laughing. I stepped from behind the garage and slammed the lid of a garbage can into one's face. Broke his nose. I buried my fist in the other's gut and knocked the wind out of him. I kicked the other one in the…where it hurts little boys."

Jenny smiled in spite of herself and ducked her head blushing. Then she lifted her eyes back to him. "What happened?"

"I was expecting the same kind of praise Hal had gotten the night before." A wry grin twisted his sensual mouth and he shook his head. "I got sent to my room with no dinner, a blistering lecture, a spanking, and a suspension in my allowance and the use of my bike for two weeks."

The front legs of the chair hit the floor with a finality compared to the way he had concluded the story. "So you see, Jenny, if I'd taken on this Central American mission, I'd have been labeled as a troublemaker and a rabble-rouser looking for a good fight. But Hal, Hal is considered a saint."

Without even thinking about it, her hand shot across the table to cover his. "I'm so sorry, Cage. I know it hurts."

His hand automatically covered the one clutching his and his eyes speared into hers. There were tears of empathy standing in the emerald depths.

"Jenny? We're home. Where are you?"

The Hendrens were coming in the front door. Cage and Jenny remained captives of each other, releasing their hands and eyes only heartbeats before his parents blustered into the kitchen.

"Oh, here you are. Hello, Cage."

Jenny jumped up, offering to get the older couple a cold drink or coffee. Cage rose to his feet, too. "I've got to be going. I just stopped by to see if you'd heard from Hal. I'll check back later. 'Bye."

There was no reason to prolong the visit. He had wanted to ask about Hal, but his main reason for coming to the parsonage had been to see Jenny.

He had seen her.

She had touched him.

Actually reached out and touched him.

He felt good.

Jenny bent over to place a sack of groceries in the backseat of her car. The Hendrens had given her the economical compact when she graduated from TCU. A long wolf whistle brought her around quickly, so quickly she almost bumped her head.

Cage was sitting astride a vicious-looking motorcycle wearing an expression that matched his whistle. A shiny black helmet was dangling from his hand. He had on a blue chambray shirt from which the sleeves had been ripped. Either the wind had tugged all the buttons from their holes, or he had left them carelessly undone. In either event, the only thing that saved him from indecency—and then just barely—was that the shirt was tucked into the waistband of his jeans.

There was nothing decent about them.

A faded red bandanna was knotted around his neck. He looked like a bandit. Hell's Angels would have welcomed him with open arms and probably elected him their president.

Jenny was intrigued by the network of light brown hair that matted his chest. It fanned out over the upper muscles and grew inward toward that satiny ribbon of hair that bisected his stomach. She had a difficult time tearing her eyes away from the beguiling sight of all that tanned skin and the crisp carpet of masculine body hair.

"You're not very nice," Jenny chided insincerely.

"Thank you, ma'am."

She laughed.

"You're not very nice either," Cage countered.

"What did I do that wasn't nice?"

"You wore a tight pair of jeans that could inflame a man's imagination."

Glancing down at herself, she retorted, "Only some men. The ones with their minds in the gutter."

"Hm. I suppose that means me."

"If the shoe fits… No other man has whistled at me today."

"Then no other man caught you bending over."

She shot him an acid look. "Sexist."

"And proud to be one."

Placing her hands on her hips, she demanded, "What if I came up behind you and whistled like that?"

"I'd drag you into the bushes."

"You are incorrigible."

"That's what they tell me." When he smiled, his teeth shone brightly in the sunlight. Bracing his hands on the handlebars of the bike, he leaned forward slightly. The muscles in his arms bulged and Jenny could detect the strong veins beneath the taut skin. "Go for a ride with me?"

Drawing her eyes away from him, she closed the backseat door with emphasis and opened the driver's. "A ride? You're insane." She looked askance at the cycle.

"Nope. Only incorrigible." She made a face at him and his grin broadened. "Come on, Jenny. It'll be a blast."

"No way. I'm not getting on that thing."

"Why?"

"I don't trust your driving."

He barked a short laugh. "I'm stone sober."

"For once."

It was his turn to make a face.

Jenny said, "I've ridden with you in a car before and risked life and limb every mile. Even the highway patrolmen salute you when you whiz by. They know they couldn't possibly catch you."

He shrugged, sending all sorts of muscles into play. "So I like driving fast. I'm safe."

"I'm safer. No, thank you," she said politely and slid beneath the steering wheel of her car. "Besides, the ice cream's melting," she said through the window as she started the engine.

He followed her home, weaving the cycle in and out and around her, making her stop and start lurchingly a dozen times in an effort to keep from crashing with him. Beneath the shaded visor of his helmet his grin was wide. Through her windshield she tried to look stern and disapproving, but she was laughing by the time they reached the parsonage.

"See?" He parked the motorcycle beside her car and pulled off his helmet. "Perfectly harmless. Come for a ride with me."

The sun struck his hair just right, turning it the color

of ripe wheat. Through his dense, sun-tipped lashes, his eyes were compelling. Jenny hesitated, the sack of groceries growing heavier in her arms.

"When's the last time you did something spontaneous?" he asked her temptingly.

*The night I seduced Hal.*

But she didn't even want to think about Hal. He had been gone for ten weeks. Cage visited the parsonage often. He always popped up unexpectedly, as he had today in the grocery store parking lot. If she didn't know better, she would think he was following her.

"I can't, really," she hedged.

"Sure you can. Hurry. I'll help you put away the ice cream."

There was no arguing with him. The groceries were stashed in the pantry and refrigerator with dispatch, and since Bob and Sarah weren't at home, Jenny was fair game. Cage knew exactly how to sniff out weakened prey and bring it down.

"Pretty please," he begged, bending his knees to bring his face down on a level with hers. The lines on either side of his mouth deeped into dimples that should have been outlawed as a public menace. "With sugar on it."

"Oh, all right," Jenny surrendered with an irritated sigh. Actually her heart was pounding with anticipation.

He gripped her arm firmly and dragged her outside before she could change her mind. "I even have a helmet for you." He eased it over her head and reached beneath her chin to snap the strap closed. For an instant, only an instant, their eyes locked. He touched her cheek. But before she could determine exactly what the gleam in his eyes meant, the moment was over and he was instructing her on how to mount the motorcycle.

When she was situated on the padded seat, he swung his leg over and said, "Now put your arms around me."

She hesitated, then gingerly closed her arms around his middle. When her hands came in contact with his bare front, the fuzzy hair tickled her wrists, and she yanked her hands away. "I'm sorry," she muttered, as though she had bumped into a stranger on an elevator. Her heart was knocking painfully against her ribs.

"It's all right." He took her hands in his and folded them together just above his waist, pressing them against him. "You have to hold on tight."

Jenny's head was buzzing. Her throat had gone dry. If she hadn't been afraid of becoming dizzy and possibly falling off, she would have shut her eyes as he started the motorcycle and guided it down the street. She kept her hands perfectly still, though she had the mad urge to comb her fingers up through his chest hair and to knead the hard muscles of his chest with her fingers.

"How do you like it so far?" he shouted back at her.

Having gotten over her initial shyness, she could honestly answer, "I love it!"

The hot wind beat at them mercilessly as they left the city limits and Cage opened the cycle's motor to full throttle. They sped down the highway with the straight flying precision of a hornet. There was something wildly exciting about having only the two wheels of the cycle between her and the macadam that sped past beneath her. The motor thrummed up through her thighs, her middle, her breasts. That steady vibration was thrilling.

He turned off the highway onto a narrow blacktopped

road and eventually drove through a gate. The house at the top of a gradual rise in the otherwise flat barrenness was authentically Victorian. Grass and shrubbery had been planted in the fenced yard and there was a variety of trees lending their shade. The front porch, which wrapped around three sides of the house, was shielded from the sun by the balconies of the second story. An onion-shaped cupola domed one front corner. The picture-book structure was painted the color of sand with an accent trim of rust and slate.

To one side there was a garage. Jenny noticed the Corvette parked there, along with a selection of other vehicles. Beyond the garage was a stable. Several horses grazed in the pasture behind it.

"This is my house," Cage said simply. He drew the bike to a halt and cut the engine. He let Jenny alight before he did. She stared at the house as she lifted the helmet from her head.

"This is where you live?"

"Yep. For two years now."

"I never really knew where your house was. You've never invited us out here." She turned to him. "Why, Cage?"

"I didn't want to be turned down. My folks consider this a den of iniquity, they wouldn't set foot in it. Hal probably wouldn't have come because he knew they would disapprove. It seemed simpler not to ask and just make it easier for everybody."

"What about me?"

"Would you have come?"

"I think so." But neither of them believed she would have.

"You're here now. Would you like to see it?"

He asked humbly. For all his machismo he looked

extremely vulnerable. Jenny didn't hesitate this time. She very much wanted to see his house. "Please. Can we go inside?"

His mouth broke into a wide grin and he led her up the front steps. "The house was built just after the turn of the century. It went through a series of owners, each one letting it deteriorate a little more. It was truly derelict when I bought it. What I really wanted was the land that went with it, and I thought about tearing the house down and starting over with something low and sprawling and contemporary. But the house began to grow on me. It seemed to belong here, so I decided to let it stay. I've fixed it up."

That was an understatement.

"It's lovely," Jenny observed as they wandered through the tall-ceilinged, airy, sunlit rooms.

Cage had decorated simply, painting everything off-white, the walls, the shutters, the woodwork, the portiere, which separated the central hall from the parlor on one side and the rounded dining room on the other. The oaken floors had been rubbed to a soft patina. The furniture, with an emphasis on comfort, was a pleasing mixture of old and new, all tasteful and well arranged.

The kitchen was a space-age wonder, but all the modern appliances were aptly hidden behind a facade of century-old charm. The upstairs boasted three bedrooms. Only one had been fully restored.

From the doorway Jenny gazed at the room Cage slept in. Decorated in desert colors of sand and sienna, it matched his dusty-blond coloring. The massive bed was covered with an irregularly shaped, unhemmed suede spread that looked as soft as butter. Through a connecting door Jenny caught a glimpse of a lavish bathroom with a picture window immodestly placed over the enormous tub.

Cage noted the direction of her eyes. "I like to lie in the water and look over the landscape. From there the sunset is spectacular." He spoke close to her ear, close enough for his warm breath to stir her hair. "Or at night when the moon is full and the stars are out, it's a breathtaking sight."

Jenny felt herself being hynotically drawn closer to him and jerked herself erect. "The house suits you, Cage. At first, I didn't think it would, but strangely it does."

He seemed to like that. "Come see the pool."

He led her back down the stairs, through a screened "sleeping porch," and onto the limestone patio. It was a riot of color. Terra-cotta pots held clusters of blooming red geraniums. In one corner a cactus garden boasted bright yellow and pink blooms. Silvery sage bushes with their purple flowers lined the fence. The pool was as deep and blue as a sapphire. "Wow," she whispered.

"Wanna swim?"

"I don't have a suit."

"Wanna swim?"

The raspy inquiry was laden with implication, subtle and seductive, but indubitably clear.

Everything inside Jenny stilled. Her blood stopped flowing through her body because her heart ceased pumping. Her lungs shut down operation. She couldn't even blink, so captivated was she by his intent amber stare and the intoxicating huskiness of his invitation.

It was unthinkable, of course.

But she thought about it anyway.

And the thoughts, making a kaleidoscope of her

mind, sent her temperature rising. She could see them naked, the sun beating down on their bare skin, the dry wind swirling around them. Cage naked, his toasty skin garnished with that soft golden brown body hair. And herself, shyly baring herself to the elements, to the man.

The fantasy made her mouth water.

She saw herself touching him, saw her hands gliding over those sleek bare arms, saw her fingertips tracing the veins that showed beneath the surface, saw her fingers winding through that soft pelt on his chest.

She saw him touching her, saw his strong hands reaching out gently to caress her breasts and their aching crests, to slide down her belly to her thighs, to touch—

"I need to get back." She turned and virtually ran across the patio and through the house as though the devil were after her. Cage didn't have a forked tail and horns, but the simile wasn't all that inaccurate.

He caught up with her on the porch and she waited stiffly beside him while he relocked the door of the house. When he took her arm to guide her down the steps, she flinched away from him. "Is something wrong, Jenny?"

"No, no, of course not," she said, wetting her dry lips with a nervously flicking tongue. "I like your house."

Why was she acting like this? Cage wasn't going to hurt her. She had known him for years, lived in the same house with him when he came home for summer vacations from college.

Why now did he suddenly seem like a stranger to her, yet one she knew better than any other human being on earth? She hadn't shared her heart with Cage the way she had with Hal during their quiet discussions. But she felt a kinship with this man that was beyond reason or explanation. Why?

Feelings for him churned inside her. They were all so foreign, all so sexual. But, miraculously and unnervingly, all so right.

"Okay, you've been initiated," he said, jumping onto the cycle once she had resumed her place. He revved the engine. "Hang on tight, girl."

"Cage!"

That was the last full breath she drew. He sped down the highway until the landscape was no more than a blur. Hanging on for dear life, she clung to him, no longer timorous about splaying her hands wide over his stomach and gluing her front to his back. Her thighs cradled his hips and she propped her chin on his shoulder.

When they reached the street of the parsonage, he slowed down considerably but jumped the curb and weaved in and out of the mulberry trees that some civic-minded individual had planted there decades ago. There were no pedestrians, so it was safe, but Jenny squealed, "You're crazy, Cage Hendren!"

They were gasping with laughter when he pulled into the driveway of the parsonage and killed the motor. "Want to go again tomorrow?" he asked over his shoulder.

She climbed off and her knees nearly buckled beneath her. Excitement had robbed her of equilibrium and it took her a moment to regain it while she clutched his shoulder. "No. Definitely not. That last ride was death defying."

Her cheeks were rosy and her eyes shone green. Cage had never seen her smile quite like this. Gone was the conservative mask she hid behind. Jenny had an adventurous streak to her nature and he was seeing it emerge for the first time.

He got off the bike and pulled the helmet from his head. "Pretty soon you'll get the hang of it." He helped her with her own helmet and it seemed the most natural thing in the world to comb his fingers through her matted hair. "Next time we'll break the sound barrier."

He draped his arm around her shoulders. Still weak-kneed, she slumped against his support and looped her arm around his waist. Together they staggered toward the back door.

It opened. Bob stepped out onto the steps. He looked at Cage accusingly, then at Jenny. His hard expression brought them to an abrupt halt.

"Dad?" "Bob?" they asked in unison.

But they already knew.

"My son is dead."

# *Four*

"Jenny?" Cage's urgent whisper elicited no response. "Jenny, please don't cry. Can I have the flight attendant bring you something?"

She shook her head and lowered the damp tissue from her eyes. "No, thank you, Cage. I'm fine."

But she wasn't fine. She hadn't been since yesterday afternoon when Bob Hendren had told them that Hal had been shot by a firing squad in Monterico.

"Why the hell I let you talk me into letting you come along, I'll never know," Cage said with bitter self-reproach.

"This is something I had to do," she insisted, still blotting her puffy red eyes and dabbing at her nose.

"I'm afraid it's going to be an ordeal that will only make things more difficult for you."

"No, it won't. I couldn't just sit at home and wait. I had to come with you or go mad."

He could understand that. This was a gruesome errand, traveling to Monterico to identify Hal's body and arrange for its transport back to the United States. There would be mounds of paperwork from the U.S.

State Department that must be dealt with, not to mention the tenuous negotiations with the petulant military junta in Monterico. But grappling with all that was better than staying at home and witnessing the Hendrens' abject grief.

"Jenny, where have you been?" Sarah had cried. She had stretched both arms in Jenny's direction when the younger woman rushed into the living room of the parsonage after Bob had told her and Cage the news. "Your car was here...we looked everywhere... Oh, Jenny!"

Sarah had collapsed against Jenny and sobbed heart wrenchingly. Cage sat down on the sofa, spread his knees wide, bowed his head low, and stared at the floor between his booted feet. No one comforted him on the loss of his brother. He might not have been there, save for the condemning looks Bob directed toward the motorcycle helmets Cage had dropped on the hall floor as they rushed inside the house.

Jenny smoothed back Sarah's light brown hair. "I'm sorry I wasn't here. I... Cage and I went riding on his motorcycle."

"You were with Cage?" Sarah's head popped up and her eyes swung toward him. She looked as though his existence was a great surprise to her, as though she had never seen him before.

"How did you find out about Hal, Mother?" he asked quietly.

Sarah seemed to have fallen into a stupor. Her expression was blank, her skin pasty.

It was Bob who had told them what little they knew. "A representative of the State Department called about half an hour ago." The pastor seemed terribly old suddenly. His shoulders sagged, reducing his posture to that of an old man. The skin beneath his chin looked flabby and wobbly for the first time. His eyes weren't as clear and lively as usual. His voice, which sounded impressive and full of conviction from his pulpit, wavered pitifully.

"Apparently those fascist hoodlums in control of the government down there didn't like Hal's interference. He and members of his group were arrested, along with some of the rebels they were going to rescue. They were all—" he cast a sympathetic glance at Sarah and amended what the government official had told him "—killed. Our government is making a formal protest."

"Our son is dead!" Sarah wailed. "What good will protests do? Nothing will bring Hal back."

Jenny had silently agreed. The two women had clung to each other for the remainder of the evening, weeping, grieving. Word had spread through the congregation of the church. Members began arriving, filling the large rooms of the parsonage with sympathy, and the kitchen with food.

The phone had rung incessantly. Once Jenny glanced up to see Cage speaking into it. At some point he had gone home and changed clothes. He was wearing a pair of tailored slacks, a sport shirt, and a jacket. As he listened to the party on the other end, he rubbed his eye sockets with his thumb and index finger. Slumped against the wall as he was, he looked tired. And bereaved.

She hadn't even taken time to go upstairs long enough to brush her hair after that madcap ride with Cage. But no one seemed to notice her dishevelment. Everyone moved about like robots, going through the motions of living with disinterest. They couldn't believe that Hal's presence in their lives had actually been snatched away in such a cruel, violent, and irreversible way.

"You look exhausted." Jenny had turned from pouring herself a cup of coffee to find Cage standing behind her. "Have you eaten anything?"

The dishes of food brought over by members of the church were lined along the countertops of the kitchen. They didn't entice Jenny, indeed, the thought of eating anything was repugnant. "No. I don't want anything. How about you?"

"I guess I'm not hungry either."

"We really should eat something," Bob had remarked as he joined them. Sarah was clinging to his arm as he eased her into a chair.

"A man named Whithers from the State Department called, Dad," Cage had informed them. "I'll go down there tomorrow and accompany Hal's body back." Sarah whimpered and crammed her fingers against her compressed lips. Cage looked down at her sadly. "This Whithers is meeting me in Mexico City. He'll go with me, and hopefully cut through some of the red tape I'm bound to run into. I'll call you as soon as I know something, so you can make funeral arrangements."

Sarah folded her arms on the table, laid her head on them, and began crying again.

"I'm going with you, Cage."

Jenny had spoken her intentions calmly. The Hendrens' reaction to her announcement hadn't been so calm. But her mind was made up and they were too distraught to argue with her about it.

She and Cage had left early that morning, driving to

El Paso to catch a plane to Mexico City, the same flight Hal had taken almost three months before.

Now Cage was sitting close to her. Though there was an empty seat in their row, he sat in the middle beside her, as though shielding her from the rest of the world. When her tissue began to shred, he passed her a handkerchief from the breast pocket of his sport coat.

"Thank you."

"Don't thank me, Jenny. I can't bear to see you crying."

"I feel so guilty."

"Guilty? For godsake, why?"

She waved her hands in frustration and returned her gaze to the void outside the window of the airplane. "I don't know. A million reasons. For being mad at him when he left. For feeling hurt and angry when he didn't send me a special postcard. Silly, stupid things like that."

"Everybody feels guilty for slights like that when someone dies. It's natural."

"Yes, but…I feel guilty for…being alive." She turned her head and looked at him with tear-shiny eyes. "For having such a good time with you yesterday when Hal was already dead."

"Jenny." Something hard and painful ground into Cage's chest. That same guilt had visited him, but he wouldn't tell her that.

He put his nearest arm around her and drew her against his chest. His other hand sifted comfortingly through her hair as her head rested on his shoulder. "You mustn't feel guilty for being alive. Hal wouldn't want that. He chose to do this. He knew the risks involved. He took them."

Cage didn't want to be consciously aware of how good it felt to hold her. But he was. He had wanted to hold her plenty of times. He hated the reason for being granted the opportunity now. On the other hand, he was human. He couldn't ignore the sheer pleasure of feeling her small, dainty body pressed against his.

Why did Hal have to die? Dammit, why? Cage had wanted to win Jenny in a fair fight. There was no victory in her suddenly becoming available by Hal's death. Would her own guilt be the next obstacle he must overcome?

"Why were you mad at Hal when he left?" Had she had a change of heart and later regretted what had happened in her bed that night? Oh, please, no. He might get an answer he didn't want to hear, but he had to ask.

Jenny hesitated so long, Cage was beginning to think she wasn't going to answer. Then she said haltingly, "Something happened the night before he left that brought us very close. I thought it had changed things. But the next morning he left without even saying goodbye as though it had never happened."

Because it hadn't happened to Hal.

"I halfway expected him to call off his trip." She sighed and Cage felt her breasts expand with the deep breath. "I felt rejected when he didn't. Deep down I really didn't believe that my feelings were more important to him than his mission, but…"

Cage had been desperate to know what she was thinking and feeling that morning. As he stared at her across the breakfast table, a thousand questions had tumbled through his mind, but he hadn't been able to ask any of them. He had been forced into silence by his own treachery.

He had wanted to say, "Are you all right?" "Did I hurt you?" "Jenny, did I imagine how wonderful it was, or was it really that good?" "Did it actually happen or was it all a fantastic dream?"

And he still didn't know the answers to those questions. But whatever her answers to them were, they belonged to Hal, not to him. She had been hurt by Hal's apparent casualness about having made love to her for the first time. She couldn't understand how he could have left the way he did if it meant something to him. Hal didn't deserve her anger. But she was innocent, too. There was only one culprit, and as usual, it was he.

Should he tell her now, explain that Hal hadn't been indifferent to their lovemaking because he hadn't experienced it? That would absolve her of the guilt she was feeling now. Should he tell her?

No. God, no. She had Hal's death to deal with. How would she cope with the knowledge that she had made love to the wrong man? How could any woman ever forgive herself for that? How could she ever forgive the man who had tricked her?

Jenny must have felt the tension in his arms, because she sat up suddenly and put space between them. "I shouldn't be bothering you with this. I'm sure my personal life is of little interest to you."

Oh, yes, it was. They had once been as personal with each other as two human beings could be. Only she didn't know it. She didn't know that he had caressed her skin until the texture of it was engraved on his palms and fingertips. He knew the shape of her breasts and how they felt against his lips and tongue. The sounds she made in the throes of passion were as familiar to him as his own voice because his mind had played them like a tape recorder over and over again when he was alone at night in his bed, thinking of her.

And he was certain no man, not even his brother, had kissed her with the same degree of intimacy he had. No one knew her taste like he did.

Abruptly his mind snapped to attention. What the hell was he doing? What kind of a sorry son of a bitch was he? His brother was dead and here he was thinking about what sex with Jenny was like.

"We'll be landing soon," he said gruffly to cover his own guilt and confusion.

"Then I'd better repair my face."

"Your face is lovely."

Her head whipped around. In spite of his disgust with himself for his previous train of thought, Cage couldn't keep himself from looking at her.

She gazed back into his eyes, realizing that no one had thanked him for all the necessary details he had attended to. He had taken on the unwelcome tasks without having even been asked to. "You've been a tremendous help through all this, Cage. With your parents. With me." She laid her hand on his arm. "I'm glad we have you."

"I'm glad you have me, too," he said with a soft smile.

He'd been right not to tell her he had been her lover that night. The old selfish Cage wouldn't have let his brother take the credit for the joy he had given Jenny that night. But this new changed Cage would continue letting her think she had been with Hal to spare her from having to heap shame onto tragedy.

The captial city of Monterico was noisy, nasty, and hot. Concrete-and-steel skeletons were grim reminders that buildings had once stood where now there was only ruin. Piles of rubble made some streets impassable. Political slogans, painted on in bloodred, screamed the grisly story of civil war from every available billboard.

Soldiers, wearing fatigue pants and combat boots and tank tops, patrolled the streets. Their expressions were surly, their attitude arrogant and rude. The civilian population was cowed, their eyes watchful and afraid, their movements furtive, as they went about their workday activities.

Jenny had never seen such a depressing place. She began to feel an empathy with Hal's cause and to experience some of his determination to correct this wrong and put an end to this suppression of the human spirit.

Whithers, the State Department official who had met them in Mexico City, was a disappointment. Jenny had expected a Gregory Peck type whose very carriage proclaimed authority and commanded obedience. Mr. Whithers looked like he couldn't withstand a strong wind, much less adversity from a government hostile to the United States. He looked far from authoritarian and commanding in his wrinkled seersucker suit. She could visualize him being the butt of cruel jests, rather than posing any threat to a military junta.

But he had been kind and sensitive to their grief as he walked Cage and her through the crowded airport to the plane that would carry them to Monterico. He had treated her with deference.

Jenny let Cage do most of the talking. But while he took official matters into his own hands, he never let his attention slip from her. She was never far from him; he was constantly at her side, usually with a protective arm around her shoulders or a tender hand beneath her elbow.

She drew on his strength, relied on it without apology. Lord, what would she do without it? She wondered why people didn't credit Cage with having any sensitivity.

"Cage Hendren doesn't give a damn about anybody or anything."

That was how people saw him.

But they were wrong. He cared a great deal. About his brother. And he couldn't have been kinder to her.

Upon their arrival in Monterico, Jenny, Cage, and Mr. Whithers had been packed into the backseat of an aging Ford. In the front seat were a driver and a soldier with a Soviet AK-47 tucked beneath his arm. Every time Jenny looked at the automatic weapon, shivers went down her spine.

The driver and his partner represented the government currently in control of the country. They made no effort to disguise their contempt for their passengers.

After a circuitous journey through the city, they were finally deposited in front of a building that had formerly housed a bank. Now it served as government headquarters. A goat was tethered to one of the columns of the building's facade. He seemed as ill-tempered and hostile as the other residents of Monterico.

Inside, overhead fans vainly tried to circulate the thick, stifling air. But at least the former bank lobby provided a repose from the scorching sun. Jenny's blouse was sticking to her back. Cage had long since taken off his jacket and tie and rolled up his shirtsleeves.

They were ungraciously shown a seat by a soldier who poked his rifle toward a dilapidated couch and grunted what they assumed was an order for them to sit down. Mr. Whithers was ushered in to confer with the military commander. He was agitatedly mopping his brow with a handkerchief when he left the office a few minutes later. "Washington will hear about this," he said indignantly.

"About what?" Cage demanded.

Standing with his feet spaced widely apart, his jacket slung over his shoulder by a crooked finger, his shirt open to reveal that breath-snatching chest, and virtually growling through clenched teeth, he looked more fearsome than any of the soldiers.

Mr. Whithers explained to them that Hal's body hadn't yet reached the city. "The village where the… uh…"

"Execution," Cage provided bluntly.

"Yes, well, the village where it took place is sealed off by guerrilla fighting. But they expect the body to be delivered by nightfall," he rushed to add reassuringly.

"Nightfall!" Jenny exclaimed. Spending one afternoon in this war-torn place was a dismal prospect.

"I'm afraid so, Miss Fletcher." Mr. Whithers cast a nervous glance toward Cage. "It might be sooner. No one seems to know for certain."

"What are we supposed to do in the meantime?" she asked.

He cleared his throat and swallowed. "Wait."

And they did. For endless hours that ticked by with monotonous sluggishness. They weren't allowed to leave the building. When Mr. Whithers used all his diplomatic powers to get them food and drink, they were brought stale ham sandwiches and glasses of rusty tepid water.

"No doubt these are leftovers from the prison camps," Cage said and with scathing disgust tossed the offensive sandwich into the nearest overflowing trash can. Jenny couldn't eat hers either. The ham had a slightly greenish cast. But they drank the water out of fear of dehydration. They sweltered in the afternoon heat while the soldiers propped themselves and their rifles against the walls and took their siestas.

Cage paced, incessantly cursing and mouthing epithets about Monterico in general and their guards in particular. Jenny's light hair and green eyes were a novelty in this country, where most of the populace was of Latin descent. Cage was aware of that even if she wasn't. Every time one of the cocky soldiers cast a speculative glance in her direction, Cage's eyes narrowed dangerously.

The guards weren't aware that he was fluent in Spanish and when one guffawed a crude remark about Jenny to his buddy, Cage went storming toward the soldier, his hands balled into fists. Mr. Whithers grabbed him by the sleeve.

"For godsake, man, don't do anything stupid. Otherwise we might have three bodies to ship home to your parents."

Whithers was right, of course, and Cage belligerently returned to his seat on the couch. He clasped Jenny's hand hard. "Don't leave my sight for an instant, for any reason."

Just as the sun was sinking over the top of the dense

jungle in the distance, a large military truck rumbled up the street and wheezed to a halt outside the government building. The driver and his cohorts came out of it leisurely, lighting up cigarettes, joking among themselves, stretching after what must have been a long, dusty ride. The one with the biggest belly and highest rank waddled into the commander's office.

"This must be it," Mr. Whithers said hopefully.

He was right. The commander came out of his office, waving a sheaf of papers, beckoning them to follow him outside. The canvas flaps at the back of the truck were flung aside and the commander heaved himself up. Whithers followed. Then Cage.

"No," he said to Jenny, when she placed her foot on the tailgate.

"But, Cage—"

"No," he repeated firmly.

Inside the truck there were four caskets. Hal was in the third one they opened. Jenny knew by the expression on Cage's face when the top was pried off. As though someone had stamped a new expression on his face, it changed drastically. He squeezed his eyes shut and grimaced, baring his teeth. Whithers asked him a brief question and he nodded.

When his eyes opened, they roved the interior of the truck as though he couldn't bring himself to look down at his brother again. But eventually he did. And his face softened and tears sprang into his eyes. He extended his hand and lovingly touched his brother's face.

Then the commander issued a curt order in rapid Spanish and the casket was resealed. Cage and Whithers were prodded out of the truck and four soldiers were ordered up into it to lift the coffin out.

The moment Cage jumped out of the truck, he put his arms around Jenny. Until then, she hadn't realized she was crying. "Get us out of here," he said to Withers, who hovered nearby. "Have them take the coffin to the airport and let's leave immediately."

Withers rushed off to do Cage's bidding. Placing a finger beneath her chin, Cage lifted Jenny's head. "Are you all right?"

"Was he… Is his face…"

"No," he said, smiling gently and brushing back her hair. "He looks untouched, like he's sleeping. Incredibly young. Very peaceful."

She heaved a sob and buried her face in the collar of his shirt. He bent his head down low over hers and held her close. His hands smoothed her back. Despite her confused feelings for Hal, he was like a brother. She had lived with them long enough to feel that kind of kinship with him. Cage knew what she was suffering. He felt like a part of himself was in that casket.

Whithers cleared his throat loudly and uncomfortably. "Uh, Mr. Hendren." When Cage lifted his head and looked at him, he said hurriedly, "They're taking your brother's body to the airport now." He indicated a rickety pickup truck that was jostling its cargo as it lumbered up a hill, its gears grinding.

"Good. I want to get Jenny the hell out of here. We can be in Mexico City by—"

"There's, uh, a problem."

Cage was already in motion. He stopped and wheeled around, bringing Jenny, who he had by the arm, with him. "What kind of problem?" he asked with a glower.

Whithers shifted his weight from one foot to the

other, then back again. "They won't let a plane take off after dark."

"What?!" Cage exploded. The sun had set by now. The dusk was impenetrable, the way only a tropical dusk can be.

"Security precautions," Whithers explained. "They won't turn on the landing strip lights after nightfall. If you'll recall, the runways were camouflaged when we landed today."

"Yeah, yeah, I remember," Cage said irritably, raking a hand through his hair. "When can we leave?"

"First thing in the morning."

"If we don't, I'm going to raise hell. I can fight dirty, too, by God. They've yet to meet a guerrilla fighter meaner than me." His warning carried with it jabbing thrusts of his index finger. "And if they think I'm going to subject Jenny to a night in that bank building, they're wrong!"

"No, no, that won't be necessary. They've made arrangements with a local hotel for us to spend the night."

"I'll bet they have," Cage spat. "We'll find our own hotel."

But the selection was limited and as it ended up they stayed where the government officials had assigned them in the first place. If the rooms were as sad as the lobby, Jenny thought, they were in for an uncomfortable night. The furniture was dusty and stained. The fans overhead turned desultorily. The drapes were shabby and their hems straggled to the scarred floor. A rack of magazines had been there so long the covers were faded and dust obscured the titles.

"Not exactly the Fairmont," Cage said from the side

of his mouth. The lobby was patrolled not by brisk bell-men, but by sardonic soldiers carrying automatic rifles.

After a conference with the unkempt concierge, Whithers handed them each a key. "We're all on the same floor," he said happily.

"Terrific. I'll have room service bring up champagne and caviar and we'll have a party."

Whithers actually looked hurt by Cage's snideness. "Miss Fletcher, you're in three nineteen."

Cage intercepted the key before it could be passed to Jenny and checked the number on his own. "Miss Fletcher is in three twenty-five with me. Come on, Jenny." Cage took her arm and led her across the lobby toward the stairs, opting to walk up rather than take the elevator. If it was in the same derelict condition as everything else in this godforsaken country, he wouldn't risk their lives by using it.

"But they were specific about the rooms," Whithers protested, trotting after them like a pesky puppy. "We were assigned rooms."

"To hell with that and them. Do you think I'm going to leave Jenny alone and at their mercy? Think again, man."

"But this is a breach of our agreement."

"I don't give a damn if this breach in your agreement brings on World War III!"

"I seriously doubt if they'd do anything to harm Miss Fletcher. After all, they're not savages."

Cage spun around and glared at the other man so hard, the state official shrank back. "She stays with me."

There was no arguing with the finality with which Cage spoke those four words.

Room three twenty-five was as hot and stuffy and

dusty as all of Monterico seemed to be. Cage turned the lamp down low. He crossed to the window and checked outside. Just as he suspected, three stories below, they were being watched by two soldiers, distinguishable only by the glow of their cigarettes in the dark. He left the window open but adjusted the louvered shutters to give them a measure of privacy. Some of the cooler night air filtered in, making the hotel room at least livable.

"Whithers said they're sending up dinner."

"If it's anything like lunch, I can hardly wait," Jenny said, listlessly dropping her handbag onto the bed and flopping down on its edge. There was a definite droop to her shoulders, but Cage was glad to see she was still capable of humor.

"Take your shoes off and lie down."

"Maybe I'll just rest a minute," she said weakly and lay down. The bedspread had a red florid print that seemed to gobble her small form alive.

A half hour later a soldier knocked once on the door, then swung it open to carry in a tray. Jenny, who had been dozing, jackknifed into a sitting position on the bed. Her skirt slid back to the top of her thighs. The soldier leered at her.

Cage, disregarding Whither's warning, grabbed the tray and shoved the soldier outside. He snapped closed the flimsy lock and braced a chair beneath the doorknob. Such measures wouldn't stop a round of AK-47 bullets, but it made him feel better to show even that much defiance.

"Dinner" was a dish comprised of rice, chicken, beans, and enough hot peppers to bring tears to Jenny's eyes. She didn't feel like eating anyway and after only two bites set her fork down.

"Eat," Cage commanded, pointing at her plate.

"I'm not hungry."

"Eat it anyway. Anything that doesn't move, that is."

He was unrelenting and she forced down half the portion, picking out the stringy pieces of chicken. Murky red wine accompanied the meal. Cage poured some from the foggy carafe, tested it, and made a face. "I think they clean commodes with this."

"Is this the lush of La Bota County speaking?"

"Is that what they call me?" he asked, arching one brow.

"Sometimes."

He poured her a glass of the wine. She took it but looked at him as if to say, "What am I supposed to do with this?"

"Drink it," he said, answering her unspoken question. "I don't trust the water, and believe me, no germ could live long in that brew," he said of the wine.

She sipped, made a face that he laughed at, and sipped again. She managed only five swallows. "That's all I can take," she said, shuddering at the bitter aftertaste.

Cage placed the tray with their dirty dishes on the floor near the door. He listened there for a long moment, but he didn't think anyone was monitoring them. At least not just outside the door. But he knew that sentinels must have been posted near the elevator and stairs.

"Do you suppose the shower works?" Jenny asked, venturing into the bathroom.

"Try it out."

"Do you think I'll catch an infection?"

He laughed. "At this point, we'll have to chance it." He lifted his soiled shirt away from his chest. "I have no choice."

"I guess I don't either," she said, glancing at her reflection in the wavy mirror.

Closing the door between them, she peeled off her clothes and stepped into the shower stall. Ordinarily she wouldn't have considered setting her bare foot in such a mildew-ridden cubicle, but as Cage had said, she didn't have much choice. It was either use the shower or live with herself grimy and dusty.

Surprisingly the water that rained down on her was hot, and the soap was a United States export. She even used it to wash her hair in lieu of shampoo.

After she had dried herself off, she was in a dilemna as to what to put on. She had to rinse out her underclothes and blouse or she wouldn't be able to force herself to put them on again in the morning. She settled on wearing her full slip to sleep in and put her suit jacket over it for modesty's sake. It was a ridiculous-looking outfit, but it would have to do.

She hand-laundered her lingerie in the sink and hung the panties, stockings, brassiere and blouse on the only towel rack available. Switching off the light, she opened the door.

Her hesitant eyes met Cage's curious ones across the room. Self-consciously she fingered the buttons on her jacket as she kept it pulled over her breasts. Her bare toes bashfully curled downward. Had Cage ever seen her with wet hair? "I, uh…there was only one towel. I'm sorry."

"I'll air dry." He smiled and made his voice sound

flippant and light, but his eyes were on the deep lace border of her slip just above her knees.

She moved toward the bed and he brushed past her on his way into the bathroom. Once the door was closed behind him, she remembered her intimate apparel hanging up to dry. Scalding color rushed to her cheeks. Which was foolish. They had lived in the same house. When he was home from college, their clothes had been washed together. One couldn't go into the laundry room without seeing a garment belonging to somebody else. Cage had seen her in nighties and robes and in various stages of dishabille on numerous occasions.

But this was different. There was no use pretending that it wasn't. And the thought of Cage's eyes on her underwear made her go hot all over.

By the time he came out of the bathroom, she had taken off her jacket and was lying beneath the top sheet.

He smelled of damp male flesh and soap. He had pulled on his trousers, but that was all. His feet were bare. The hair on his chest was curly and damp. He must have rubbed his head with the towel. The dark blond strands weren't dripping, but they were still wet and tousled.

He flipped out the light and crossed to the bed, sitting down on the edge of it. "Comfy?"

"All things considered, yes."

He reached for one of the hands clutching the sheet to her chin and laced his fingers through hers. "You're something, Jenny Fletcher," he said softly. "Did you know that?"

"What do you mean?"

"You've been put through hell today, but you haven't murmured one word of complaint." With his free hand he wound a strand of her hair around his finger. "I think you're terrific."

"I think you are, too." There was a tremulous catch in her voice. "You cried for Hal."

"He was my brother. Despite our differences, I loved him."

"I keep thinking about—" She broke off and clamped her lower lip with her teeth when a tear slipped over the brim of her eyelid and rolled down her cheek.

"Don't think about it, Jenny." He smoothed her cheek with the backs of his fingers.

"I've got to!"

"No, you don't. You'll go mad if you think about that."

"You've thought about it, too, Cage. I know you have. What was it like right before he died? Was he tortured? Was he frightened? Was he—"

He laid his finger along her lips, stilling them. "Sure I've thought about it. And I think Hal must have faced it bravely. He had unshakable faith. He was doing what he felt led to do. I don't think that faith would have deserted him, no matter what."

"You admired him," she whispered with sudden insight.

He looked chagrined. "Yes, I did. Our reactions to circumstances were always different. I was violent, Hal was peaceable. Maybe it takes more courage to be meek and docile than it does to be a hell-raiser."

Without thinking, she reached up and laid her hand along his cheek. "He admired you, too."

"Me?" he asked incredulously.

"For your defiance, grit, whatever you want to call it."

"Maybe," Cage said pensively. "I'd like to think so."

He replaced the sheet over her shoulders and patted it into place. "Get some sleep." He turned off the lamp and hesitated only a moment before bending down and pecking a brotherly kiss on her forehead.

He moved the only moderately comfortable chair in the room to the window and settled into it. The day had taken its toll. In minutes both of them were asleep.

"What was that?" Jenny bolted upright in the bed. The room was dark, but bright light flashed periodically at the unfamiliar window.

Cage whirled around at her fearful exclamation and crossed to the bed quickly. "It's all right, Jenny." He sat down and tried to ease her back onto the pillows, but she was rigid. "It's several miles away. It's been going on for about half an hour. I'm sorry it woke you."

"It's not thunder," she said hoarsely.

He paused before saying, "No."

"It's fighting."

"Yes."

"Oh, Lord." She covered her face with her hands and fell back against the pillows. "I hate this place. It's dirty and hot and they kill people here. Good people, beautiful people like Hal. I want to go home," she cried. "I'm scared and I hate myself for being scared. But I can't help it."

"Ah, Jenny."

Cage lay down beside her and rolled her against him, holding her close. "The fighting is far away. Tomorrow morning we'll leave and you won't ever have to think about Monterico again. In the meantime, I'm here with you."

His fingers combed through her hair to massage her

scalp, as though to press the reassuring words into her brain. He rubbed his chin on the top of her head and planted a fervent kiss there. "I won't let anything hurt you. God, as long as I'm alive, nothing will hurt you."

She took comfort from his words and the husky, soothing voice that kept repeating them. His physical strength was like a lifeline that she clung to. When he propped his back against the headboard and pulled her across his chest, she didn't resist but curled up against him, instinctively craving contact with another being who was larger and stronger.

Her fingers wove through the thick mat of hair on his chest and she pressed her cheek against the muscled wall. Her other arm hugged his waist tight as she burrowed beneath the shelter of his securing arms.

He held her in a close embrace, whispering the promises she was desperate to hear. Cage's mind wasn't on what he said, but on the precious feel of her lying against him.

Her slip showed up smooth and pale in the dark room. The lace-trimmed silk dipped at her waist and molded over the tantalizing curve of her hip. Her breasts felt soft and feminine against his chest.

Frequently a tremor rippled through her and he would kiss her hair while his hands caressed her bare shoulders. He marveled over the smoothness of her skin and tried to keep his touch impersonal.

Then she slept. He could tell by the even, warm breathing that sifted through his chest hair. And, when in sleep, she moved one leg to cover his shin, he ground his head against the headboard. Her thigh rested atop his, her knee almost nudging the fly of his trousers. He clenched his teeth against the desire that knifed through him. He stared at her hand where it lay in repose on his lap. His need for her to touch him was so profound, it almost killed him. Yet if she had, he probably would have died in a spasm of agony and ecstasy anyway.

He listened to the rumbling echoes of the distant battle until all was still again. He watched the dawn creep over the eastern horizon. And still he held her, Hal's fiancée.

But his love.

# *Five*

HHal Hendren's funeral drew public attention. It was thought by all those in attendance that he had been martyred. Those who had scoffed at his fanaticism before he left, now had their heads bowed reverently at the grave site. Television news teams from major Texas cities and several national networks crawled over the cemetery like ants, setting up their camera angles.

Jenny, sitting with Bob and Sarah beneath the temporary tent, still couldn't believe that Hal's mission had resulted in this. It still seemed impossible that he was dead. She expected any moment to wake up from a bad dream.

Since she and Cage had returned from Monterico, the parsonage had been in chaos. The telephone never stopped ringing. There was a steady stream of visitors. Government agencies sent representatives to interview Cage and her about their impressions of the Central American country. With the interference of well-meaning church members, the whole event had taken on a carnival atmosphere.

Jenny had slept very little since she had awakened

in Cage's arms in the hotel room in Monterico. She had come awake slowly, and when she realized that she was sprawled across his naked torso, wearing only her slip, she shoved herself up to find his eyes open and watchful.

"Ex…excuse me," she stammered as she scrambled off the bed and retreated to the bathroom.

Tension between them crackled like a bonfire as they dressed to leave. They seemed prone to bumping into each other accidentally, which required awkward mumbled apologies.

Every time she hazarded a glance in Cage's direction, his eyes had been as sharp as razors, studying and analyzing her. So she had avoided looking at him, and that had seemed to irritate him.

They had been driven to the airport in another rattle-trap car and put on the aircraft bearing Hal's coffin. In Mexico City Mr. Whithers had scuttled around like a beetle, making arrangements for their flight to El Paso, where a funeral home limousine from La Bota would meet them to carry the body home.

Cage had stood at the window of the airport staring at nothing, his shoulders hunched, his face tense, chain-smoking. When he caught her eyes on him and saw the surprise on her face—she hadn't seen him smoke since that night before Hal left—he cursed under his breath and ground the cigarette into the nearest ashtray.

They had said little to each other on the flight to El Paso. The drive from there to La Bota, which had seemed interminable as they followed the white limousine with its grim cargo, had been virtually silent.

They had said little to each other ever since.

The comradeship that had developed between them

in Monterico no longer existed. For reasons she couldn't even name, Jenny was even more uneasy around him than she had been. He entered a room; she left it. He looked at her; she averted her head. She couldn't say why she took such pains to avoid him, but she knew it had something to do with that night in the Monterico hotel room.

So he had held her. So?

So he had held her against him on a bed while they slept. So?

So he had held her against him on a bed while they slept, while she had been wearing nothing but a slip and he only a pair of slacks. So?

They had been surrounded by danger. They were friendless aliens in a foreign land. People did things in situations like that they wouldn't ordinarily do. One couldn't be held accountable for uncharacteristic behavior.

And it was probably insignificant that when she was first roused from sleep, one of his hands had been splayed wide on her derriere, the other closed loosely, but possessively, around her neck, and that her fingers had been entwined in his chest hair, her lips alarmingly near the flat disk of his nipple.

Now Jenny stared straight ahead at the flower-bedecked coffin and willed away the memories of that morning. She didn't want to recall that infinitesimal span of time just after waking when she had felt warm and safe and serene, before she came to the jolting realization of just how wrong that serenity was.

She wouldn't risk getting close to Cage again. His strength and endurance were like a magnet that relentlessly pulled at her. She might even be tempted to look to him for support now if he weren't sitting on Bob's far side, his parents between them.

The bishop concluded the grave-site service with a long prayer. In the limousine that took them home, Sarah wept softly against her husband's shoulder. Cage stared moodily out the window. He had loosened his tie and unbuttoned his collar button. Jenny twisted her handkerchief and said nothing.

Several ladies from the church were already at the parsonage, brewing coffee, ladling punch, slicing cakes and pies for those who would come by to pay their respects after the funeral. And there were many. Jenny thought the parade would never stop. Weary of being consoled, she left the living room and went into the kitchen, where she insisted on washing dishes.

"Please," she said to the woman she replaced at the sink. "I need to keep busy."

"You poor dear."

"Your sweet Hal is gone."

"But you're young yet, Jenny."

"Your life must go on. It might take a while…"

"You're holding up well."

"Everybody says so."

"That trip you took to that horrid country must have been a nightmare."

"And with Cage."

The last speaker made a tsking sound with her lips and shook her head mournfully as if to say that, for a woman, traveling in Cage's company was tantamount to a fate worse than death.

Jenny wanted to lash out at them all, to tell them if it hadn't been for Cage, she probably would have fallen apart altogether. But she knew their comments were guileless and stemmed from ignorance. As they left one by one, she thanked them, forgiving them their stupidity, because their concern was sincere.

She finished the dishes that were stacked on the counter and went searching for others scattered throughout the house. When she entered the living room, she was relieved to find only the Hendrens there. Finally everyone had gone home. Gratefully Jenny sank into an easy chair and let her head flop back on the headrest.

Her eyes popped open when she heard the click of Cage's cigarette lighter. The flame burst from it to ignite the end of the cigarette he held between his lips. He returned the lighter to his pocket and drew on the cigarette.

"I've told you not to smoke in this house," Sarah snapped from her place on the sofa. Her eyes were dry but ringed with muddy shadows. She looked wrinkled and shrunken, almost skeletal. Her expression was so bitter, it bordered on meanness.

"I'm sorry," Cage said with genuine apology. He went to the front door and flicked the cigarette into the night, which had fallen without anyone noticing. "Habit."

"Must you bring your nasty habits into this house? Don't you have any respect for your mother?" Bob asked.

Cage halted on his way back to his chair, stunned by Bob's harsh and condemning tone. "I respect both of you," he replied softly, though his body strained with tension.

"You don't respect anything," Sarah said tersely. "You haven't told me once that you're sorry about your brother's death. I've gotten no sympathy from you."

"Mother, I—"

She went on as though he hadn't spoken. "But then I don't know why I expected it from you. You've done nothing but give me trouble from the day you were born. You were never considerate of me the way Hal was."

Jenny sat up straight, wanting to remind Sarah that for days Cage had been taking care of the media and relieving them of the legal details surrounding Hal's death. She didn't get a chance to say anything before Sarah continued.

"Hal would have been at my side constantly through something like this."

"I'm not Hal, Mother."

"You think you have to tell me that? You couldn't hold a candle to your brother."

"Sarah, please don't," Jenny cautioned, sliding to the edge of her chair.

"Hal was so good, so good and sweet. My baby." Sarah's shoulders began to shake and her face crumpled with another burst of tears. "If God had to take one of my sons, why did He take Hal and leave me with you?"

Jenny's hand flew to her mouth. "Oh, my God."

Bob dropped to his knees in front of his wife's chair and began to comfort her. For a long moment Cage stared down at his parents in total disbelief, then his face hardened. He spun on his heel and strode toward the door. The screen was brutally punched by the heel of his hand and went crashing against the outside wall. He bounded across the front porch and down the steps.

Without pausing to think about it, Jenny went tearing after him. She raced across the yard and caught up with him at the curb where his Corvette was parked.

He was shrugging out of his dark suit coat as though it were on fire and ripping at the buttons of his vest.

"Go back where you belong," he shouted at her.

He squeezed himself into the low seat of the sports car and twisted the key in the ignition. It surprised Jenny that the key didn't break off. Stamping on the clutch, he shoved the car into first gear. She yanked open the passenger door and scrambled in just as he stamped on the accelerator.

The car shot forward like a missile. It fishtailed into the middle of the street and careened around the next corner without the benefit of brakes to slow its turn. Jenny reached for the door handle and miraculously managed to slam it closed without falling out onto the pavement or wrenching her arm from its socket.

Cage had shifted up to fourth gear by the time they reached the city limits sign. As he worked the gear stick, he ground his jaws together as though that would command better performance from the car. Jenny didn't risk looking at the speedometer. The landscape was no longer distinguishable. The headlights sliced through the endless darkness in front of them.

He reached for the knobs on the radio, controlling the car with one hand until he found the acid-rock station he wanted. He turned the volume up full blast, filling the interior of the car with the deafening clamor of metallic music.

"You made a big mistake," Cage shouted over the cacophony. "You should have stayed home tonight."

Reaching across the car and fumbling around her knees, he opened the glove compartment and took out a silver flask. Wedging it between his thighs, he unscrewed the cap, then raised it to his lips. He drank

long. The face he made when he swallowed let Jenny
know the liquor was potent. He drank again, and again,
speeding down the center stripe of the highway with
only one hand on the wheel.

The windows of the car were open and the wind
tore at her hair, tugging it free of the pins that had contained it in a neat, demure bun for the funeral. The wind
sucked the breath from her nostrils. She didn't know
how Cage had managed to light his cigarette, but the
tip of it glowed against his dark face, illuminated only
by the lights on the dashboard.

"Having fun?" He leered at her mockingly.

Seemingly unaffected by his sarcasm, she turned
her head and stared out the windshield. She refused to
honor him with an answer. The speeding car terrified
her. She disapproved of it all, but she would remain
mute if it killed her. And she thought it very well might,
as he turned the car off the main highway onto a road
that had no markings. How he had known it was there,
Jenny was never able to figure out.

He abused the vintage Corvette by driving it over
the dirt road, which was as corrugated as a washboard.
Jenny's teeth slammed together and she clenched down
on them to hold them intact. She gripped the cushioned
seat beneath her in an effort to keep her head from
bumping the ceiling as they bounced jarringly over the
pockmarked road.

They were climbing. She could sense the change in
altitude, though there was nothing to be seen, no relief
from the darkness that surrounded them. The headlights bobbed crazily with each erratic movement of
the car. Even the moon had slipped behind a cloud and
lent no light, as though to say that Cage Hendren was

pulling one of his wild stunts and no one should have to be witness to it.

He brought the car to an abrupt halt that almost sent Jenny through the windshield and made the tires skid fifty feet before coming to a complete standstill.

Cage cut the motor, creating a sudden silence as the blaring radio died with the engine. He propped his arm on the open windowsill, took the cigarette from his mouth, and replaced it with the spout of the flask. He drank deeply again and smacked his lips with satisfaction after he had swallowed.

He turned to Jenny, who was watching him in silent reproof. "I'm sorry. Where are my manners? Drink?" He tilted the flask toward her. She didn't move and her bland expression didn't change. "No?" he said, shrugging. "Too bad." He drank again, then offered her the pack of cigarettes. "Smoke? No, no, of course not."

He swigged more liquor. "You're the lady without blemish, aren't you? The viceless Miss Jenny Fletcher. Untainted. Untouchable. Fit only for saints like our dearly departed Hal Hendren." He dragged a goodly portion of nicotine into his lungs and released the smoke in a long gust aimed directly at her face.

Still she showed no reaction.

Then, as though her composure angered him, he threw the cigarette out the window. "Let's see, what would rattle your cage? What would get you to shriek in terror? What would provoke you into getting the hell out of my car, out of my sight, and out of my goddamned life?"

He was shouting. His breathing was labored and harsh. Jenny watched him visibly rein in his temper and control himself. When he spoke again, his voice still shook with hurt and fury, but he was calmer.

"What would disgust you enough to flee in fear for your virtue? A barrage of dirty words? Yeah, maybe. I doubt if you even know any, but we'll give that a try. Should I put them in alphabetical order or just say them as they come to my mind?"

"You can't disgust me, Cage."

"Wanna bet?"

"And nothing you say or do will make me leave you now."

"Is that right? You've set out to save me. Is that it?" He laughed mirthlessly. "Don't waste your time."

"I won't leave you," she repeated softly.

"Oh, yeah?" A sardonic curl lifted one corner of his lip. "We'll see."

He lunged across the console. One hand cupped the back of her head and hauled her against him. His lips crushed down on hers, hard and bruising. His teeth brutally ground against her tender mouth. She didn't fight him. Even when his tongue plunged between her lips to violate her mouth in the most demeaning way, she withstood its violent pillage without resistance.

The dress she had worn to Hal's funeral was a two-piece black knit. Cage fumbled at her waist, lifted her top, and plowed his hand beneath it.

"You've no doubt heard of my reputation with women," he rasped hotly against her neck. "I'm ruthless, without scruples. A despoiler of virgins, a wife-stealer, a sex machine run amok. It's said I'm so horny, it's tough for me to keep my pants zipped." He parted her knees with one of his. "Know what that means to you, Jenny? Bad news. You're in a heap of trouble, girl."

He brutalized her mouth again with another insulting kiss as his hand found her breast beneath her top. He pressed his hand over it, then dug into the fragile cup of her brassiere to lift her out. He massaged her breast roughly and rolled his thumb over its tender crest.

Despite her determination not to react, Jenny's back bowed off the seat. She drew herself up taut and tense against him. But she didn't fight or struggle. She resisted with passivity.

Her soft gasp was as effective as a siren's blast in Cage's head. He came to himself, realized what he was doing, and sagged against her like an inflatable toy someone had just punctured with a hat pin. He drew in several restorative breaths against her mouth, where his lips no longer exacted their revenge.

The oxygen served to clear the fog of alcohol and rage from his head. Contritely he withdrew his hand from her brassiere and in a pathetic attempt to make amends, tried to adjust the lace cup back over her breast. When he pulled his hand from beneath her top, he moved back to the driver's side of the car and got out.

Jenny buried her face in her hands and gulped in shuddering breaths. When she was somewhat composed, she straightened her clothing, opened her door and stepped out.

Cage was sitting on the hood of the car, staring out at nothing. She recognized their surroundings now. They were on the mesa, a table of land that rose above the surrounding countryside. It extended for miles. Beneath them the prairie was dark and still. The hot, dry wind plastered her clothes to her body and whipped through her hair. It whistled mournfully, nature's keening.

She moved to stand directly in front of him, blocking

his view, such as it was. Their knees almost touched. He raised his head, looked at her briefly, then let his chin drop to his chest.

"I'm sorry."

"I know." She touched his hair, smoothing it back from his forehead, but the wind immediately whisked it from her fingers.

"How could I have—"

"It doesn't matter, Cage."

"It does," he insisted through gritted teeth. "It matters."

He raised his head again and reached out to gently lay his hand on the breast he had assaulted only moments before. There was nothing sexual in his touch. He could have been touching the shoulder of an injured child. "Did I hurt you?"

His hand was warm, healing, and Jenny brought her hand up and covered his where it lay. "No."

"I did."

"Not as much as they hurt you."

They stared deeply into each other's eyes. An unlabeled emotion arced between them like an electric current. Jenny dropped her hand. He lowered his just as quickly.

Jenny sat down beside him on the hood of the car. The waxed surface was hot even through their clothes, but neither of them noticed.

"Sarah didn't mean what she said, Cage."

He snorted a laugh. "Oh, yes, she did."

"She's distraught. That was grief talking, not her."

"No, Jenny." He shook his head sadly. "I know how they feel about me. They wish I'd never been born. I'm a living reminder that somehow they failed, a perpetual embarrassment to them and a constant insult to what they believe. Even if it is never spoken aloud, I know what they are thinking. It's probably what everyone is thinking. Cage Hendren deserves to die. His brother didn't."

"That's not true!"

He got up and walked to the brink of the mesa, sliding his hands into his pockets. His white shirt showed up starkly against the blackness. Jenny followed him.

"When did it start?"

"When Hal was born. Maybe before that. I can't remember. I just know it's always been like that. Hal was the fair-haired child, literally. I should have had black hair. Then I really would have been the black sheep."

"Don't say that about yourself."

"Well, it's true, isn't it?" he asked brusquely, turning to face her belligerently. "Look what I almost did to you. I came close to raping the woman I—" He broke off in mid-sentence and Jenny wondered what he had been about to say. He made a taut, thin line of his lips to seal the unsaid words inside and turned away again.

"I know why you did that to me, why you were drinking and driving fast. You were trying to make your point that they're right about you. But they're not, Cage." She moved closer to him. "You're not some bad seed that turned up as a genetic accident in an otherwise flawless family. I don't know which came first, your naughtiness, which your parents didn't handle well, or their scorn, which made you act naughty."

She caught his sleeve and forced him around to face her. "Isn't it apparent? You've been reacting to them all your life. You work at being bad because that's what you know people expect of you. You've made a career of being the black sheep of the minister's family. Don't you see, Cage? Even as a child you did outlandish things to get their attention because they doted on Hal. That was wrong of them. Their failure, not yours.

"They had two sons and each of you had a different personality. But Hal's suited them best, so he became the model child. You tried to win their approval and when that failed, you turned around and did just the opposite."

His grin was patronizing. "You've got it all figured out, I see."

"Yes, I do. Otherwise I would have been terrified by what happened tonight. Even a few months ago I would have been. But tonight I knew you wouldn't hurt me. I know you better now. I've watched you lately. I saw you cry over your brother's body. You're not nearly as 'bad' as you want people to think you are. You couldn't compete with Hal's goodness, so you made it your goal to be a champion in another arena."

She had his attention. He was listening. And as much as he wanted to dispute her, what she said made sense. He stared at his feet as the toe of his shoe stirred up clouds of dust that swirled in the wind.

"I just worry about how far you'll carry it."

His head came up. "Carry what? What do you mean?"

"You've been made to feel you have no self-worth. How far will you go to prove them right? How far will you go to prove just how unworthy you are?"

He hitched his thumbs in the waistband of his pants and tilted his head arrogantly to one side. "You've gone this far. Why don't you just come right out and say what you're skirting around? You think I'm living a death wish."

"People who have no self-esteem do stupid things."

"Like drive fast and drink irresponsibly and live recklessly?"

"Exactly."

"Aw, hell. Ask anyone. They'll tell you about my self-esteem. They'll tell you how conceited I am."

"I'm not talking about how you act, but how you feel on the inside. I've seen the other side of you, Cage, the sensitive side you don't show anyone else."

"You think I'm committing a slow form of suicide?"

"I didn't say that."

"But that's what you meant," he said, shoving his hair off his forehead with aggravated fingers. "You've taken your armchair psychology a step too far, Jenny."

He was defensive enough to convince her that maybe she had. "All right, I'm sorry," she said. "But I'm only worried because I care about you, Cage."

He relaxed his stance immediately and his eyes softened. "I appreciate your concern, but you don't have to worry about me disposing of myself. I like driving fast and drinking irresponsibly and... What was the other thing?" he asked teasingly.

But Jenny wasn't finished with being serious yet. "I think your parents care about you, too."

His humor was fleeting. With bleak amber eyes he gazed over and beyond Jenny's head, out onto the barren landscape. "Doesn't Mother realize that I wanted to hover around her, around them both? Since we heard about Hal, I've wanted to go to them and hold them." His voice dropped a decibel. "I've wanted them to hold me."

"Cage." Jenny reached out to touch his arm. He yanked it away. He didn't want anyone's pity.

"I didn't go near them because I knew they didn't want me near them. So I tried to show my love and sympathy in other ways." He sighed. "Only, they didn't notice."

"I noticed. I was grateful."

"But you didn't let me come near you either, Jenny," he said abruptly, lowering his eyes to meet hers.

She looked away quickly. "I don't know what you mean."

"Like hell you don't. When we were in Monterico, you depended on me, leaned on me emotionally and physically. Since we've gotten back, I'm a leper again. It's 'hands off.' No touching. No talking. Hell, you wouldn't even look at me."

He was right, but she wouldn't admit it.

"Does your avoidance of me have anything to do with that night we shared in Monterico?"

Her head snapped up and she wet her lips, though her tongue had gone dry. "Of course not."

"Sure?"

"Yes. What difference could that have made?"

"We slept together."

"Not like that!" she exclaimed defensively.

"Exactly," he said, taking steps forward until he loomed over her. "But by the way you're acting, it could have been 'like that.' What are you feeling so guilty about?"

"I'm not feeling guilty."

"Aren't you?" he pressed. "Aren't you thinking that you had no business sleeping in my arms, wearing nothing but your slip? Don't you feel that we were somehow being disloyal to Hal while he lay dead in his coffin? Isn't that what you're thinking?"

She turned her back on him and crossed her arms over her stomach as though it pained her. Tightly she clasped her elbows with the opposite hands. "I shouldn't have been with you like that."

"Why?"

"You know better than to ask."

"Because you know what everyone thinks of a woman who spends a night on a bed with me."

She said nothing.

"What are you afraid of, Jenny?"

"Nothing."

"Are you afraid that someone will find out about that night?"

"No."

"Afraid that your name will be added to the list of Cage Hendren's has-beens?"

"No."

"Are you afraid of me?"

Even the relentless wind couldn't disguise the hesitation and heartbreak in his voice. She whirled around and saw the misery on his face. "No, Cage, no." To prove it, she stepped forward and put her arms around his waist, laying her cheek on his chest.

Instantly his arms went around her and held her close. "I wouldn't blame you if you were, especially after what happened tonight. But, God, I'd hate that. I'd hate that worse than anything else. I couldn't bear for you to be afraid that I'd hurt you."

She could have told him that she wasn't as afraid of him as she was of her own reactions to him. When he was near her, she stepped out of the shell she lived behind in the parsonage and became another woman.

He made her heartbeat escalate, her breathing accelerate, her palms grow moist. She was never herself when she was with Cage, whether it was riding a motorcycle and loving it, or sharing a bed with him. With him she forgot who she was and where she came from, living only for the moment.

It was almost as if she had been in love with Cage all these years instead of Hal. She had made love with Hal, but the night she had slept in Cage's arms had been almost as wonderful. She couldn't quite reconcile herself to that. How was it that only a week after Hal's death, she could be wondering what making love with Cage would be like?

Startled by the thought, she backed away from him. "We'd better go home. They'll be worried."

He looked disappointed but escorted her to the car without argument. Ruefully he recapped the flask and returned it to the glove compartment. He tossed the pack of cigarettes out the window.

"Litterbug," Jenny said from her side of the car.

"Women," Cage muttered in exasperation as he put the car into low gear. "They're never satisfied."

They grinned at each other. Everything was all right.

When they arrived at the parsonage after a sedate trip back into town, he came around and opened the door of the car for her. He placed his arm around her waist as he walked her toward the door, and companionably, she did the same.

"Thank you, Jenny."

"For what?"

"For being my friend."

"Lately you've been mine often enough."

"Thanks anyway." At the door they stood facing each other. He seemed reluctant to leave. "Well, good night."

"Good night."

"It may be a while before I come visiting."

"I understand."

"But I'll be calling you."

"It breaks my heart for this chasm to be between you and your parents at a time when you need each other the most."

His sigh was laden with sadness. "Yeah, well, that's the way it goes. If you need anything, anything, holler."

"I will."

"Promise?"

"Promise."

He squeezed her hand and bent down to press a soft kiss on her cheek. His lips lingered before he finally withdrew them. Or perhaps that was only her imagination. She hadn't quite decided as she let herself in and climbed the stairs to her room. The house was dark. The Hendrens were already in bed.

She opened the door to her room and stepped inside. She gazed around the childishly decorated bedroom. Now what? she thought.

What was Jenny Fletcher going to do with the rest of her life?

She pondered the question as she undressed, and for long hours after she got into bed the problem kept her awake.

By morning she had an answer. But how was she going to tell the Hendrens? As it turned out, they made it easy for her to broach the subject.

# Six

Bob was making toast when Jenny entered the kitchen the following morning. She smiled at his apron as she kissed him on the cheek. After pouring herself a cup of coffee, she sat down at the table with Sarah, who was idly shifting a portion of scrambled eggs from one side of her plate to the other.

"Where did you go last night?"

No "Good morning," no "How did you sleep?" Nothing. Just that bald question.

As she asked it, Sarah's lips were pinched. There was a strained expression on her face.

"We," Jenny stressed the word, "just went for a drive."

"You came in awfully late." Bob tried to make the comment sound offhanded, but Jenny knew this conversation wasn't offhanded or spontaneous by any stretch of the imagination. There was an air of hostile suspicion among them, as though there were an enemy in the camp that had to be sniffed out.

"How do you know when I came in? You were already sleeping."

"Mrs. Hicks came by this morning. She saw…she saw you and Cage together last night."

Jenny looked from one of them to the other. She was both bewildered and angry. Mrs. Hicks was the nosiest neighbor on the block. She loved to spread rumors, especially if they were bad. "What did she say?"

"Nothing," Bob said uneasily.

"No, I want to know. What did she say? Whatever it was, it obviously upset you."

"We're not upset, Jenny," Bob said diplomatically. "It's just that we don't want people to start linking your name to Cage's."

"My name is already linked to Cage's. He's a Hendren, your son," she reminded them angrily. "I've spent the last twelve years of my life in the Hendren household. How could my name not be linked with his?"

"You know what we mean, dear," Sarah said. Tears were glistening in her eyes. "You're all we have left. We—"

"That's not so!" Jenny cried angrily, getting out of her chair. "You have Cage. I never thought I'd say this, but I'm ashamed of you both. Sarah, do you realize how you hurt Cage last night? You might not be pleased with everything he does, but he's still your son. You wished him dead!"

Sarah bowed her head and burst into tears. Jenny, ashamed of her outburst, sat back down. Bob patted Sarah's shoulders in a feeble attempt to comfort her.

"She was distressed last night when the two of you raced out of here," Bob explained to Jenny. "She realized what she had said and was sorry about it."

Jenny sipped her coffee until Sarah's tears subsided.

Finally she set her cup in her saucer. "I've decided to leave."

As Jenny had anticipated, they were stunned. For several moments neither of them moved. They stared at her with blank, disbelieving eyes. "Leave?" Sarah wheezed at last.

"I'm going to move out of the parsonage and begin a life of my own. For years I've been living here, biding my time until Hal and I got married. Perhaps if we had married and had children…" She let that thought dwindle away. "But since we didn't, and since we never will now, there's no reason for me to stay. I have to make a future for myself."

"But you have a future with us," Bob argued.

"I'm a grown woman. I need to—"

"We need you, Jenny!" Sarah cried, clamping a damp, cold hand on Jenny's arm. "You remind us of Hal. You're like our own daughter. You can't do this to us. Please. Not now. Give us time to adjust to Hal's death first. You can't go. You just can't." She broke down again, burying her face in a sodden tissue.

Jenny felt a cloak of guilt closing around her. She had a responsibility to them, didn't she? They had taken her in and given her a home when she had had nothing. Didn't she owe them something? Time? A few weeks? A few months?

The thought of it depressed her, but then duty often did feel shackling.

"All right," she conceded dispiritedly. "But I won't live under Mrs. Hicks's censorship or anyone else's. I was engaged to Hal and I loved him, but he's dead. I've got my own life to lead."

"You've always been free to come and go as you

like," Bob said, happy now that talk of her leaving was over. "That's why we bought you the car."

That wasn't the kind of freedom Jenny referred to, but she didn't think they would understand if she tried to explain it to them. "My other condition is that you both apologize to Cage for what you said last night."

When they would have protested, she stared them down. Their eyes fell away from her steady gaze. "Very well, Jenny," Bob said at last. "For your sake we will."

"No, not for my sake. For his and for yours." She stood up and headed for the door. "I think Cage will forgive you because he loves you. I only hope God will."

The grocery baskets crashed together. Jenny's rattled upon impact. A box of detergent toppled over. Canned goods rolled about noisily. A roll of paper towels bounced onto the carton of eggs.

"Hi."

"You bully. You did that on purpose."

His grin was slow, lazy, and totally unrepentant. "It's a great device to meet a pretty woman on a slow afternoon. Crash into her grocery cart. Then she's flustered, sometimes angry, but always at your mercy. Ideally I try to lock up the wheels of the carts." He glanced down and frowned. "You were too quick for me."

"You're without conscience, Cage Hendren."

"Absolutely."

"Then what happens?" Jenny asked him. "I'm fascinated."

"You mean after—"

"After you've crashed into her grocery basket and gotten the wheels locked together and she's flustered, etc. What do you do then?"

"Ask her to go to bed with me."

Jenny took that piece of information like a soft cuff on the chin. "Oh." She maneuvered her basket around his, which was empty, and continued down the aisle of pet food. Since the Hendrens didn't have a pet, the attention she gave the shelves was rather ludicrous.

"Well, you said you were fascinated," Cage said defensively, pushing his cart up beside hers.

"I am, I was, but I thought you'd lead up to the seduction a little more subtly."

"Why?"

"Why?" She spun around to look up at him, letting her perusal of tender morsels and chewy bits lapse for the moment. "You mean it's that simple? Just like that?" She snapped her fingers.

He wrinkled his brow in feigned concentration. "Not always. A few times it has required more time and effort." His golden brown eyes swept over her, taking in her neat slacks and cotton knit pullover. "Now, take you for instance. I'm betting you'd be a difficult case."

"Why do you say that?"

"Will you go to bed with me?"

"No!"

"See. I'm right every time." He tapped his forehead with his index finger. "When you've been doing this sort of thing as long as I have, you learn a few things along the way. You develop a sixth sense. I could tell immediately that I would have to use the long, slow, easy approach with you. It was the way you frowned slightly when the box of Tide mashed your bag of marshmallows. A dead giveaway that you weren't going to be easy."

She gazed at him in mute wonder for several seconds, then burst out laughing. "Cage, I swear, you're amoral."

"Shameless." He winked. "But I'm sincere."

She turned out of the pet food aisle into another. He barged in front of her, blocking her path. "You look terrible."

"Is that an example of the long, slow, easy approach? If so, it needs work," she said dryly.

When she tried to go around him, he adroitly turned his basket sideways to block the aisle entirely. "You know what I mean. You look tired. Way too thin. What are they doing to you over there?"

"Nothing." She avoided his eyes.

But she knew she wasn't deceiving him any more than she had been deceiving herself. The Hendrens hadn't listened well to her declaration of independence. Or else they had listened, but were ignoring what she had said. They had every day's activities outlined for her before she came down to breakfast.

First there had been all the acknowledgments to be written after Hal's funeral. She had been almost grateful for that job because it had allowed her to call Cage and ask him to pick them up and mail them. That had created an opportunity for his parents to aplogize to him.

It had been an awkward reunion. Cage had stood at the front door, looking like he feared they wouldn't invite him in. Jenny had held her breath, unable to distinguish the words he and Bob exchanged in the hallway. Then he was standing in the living room, looking at Sarah, who was huddled on the sofa. At last she raised her head.

"Hello, Cage. Thank you for coming by."

"Hello, Mother. How are you feeling?"

"Fine, fine," she said absently. She shot a questioning glance toward Jenny, who nodded her head slightly. Sarah wet her lips. "About the other night, the night of Hal's…funeral… What I said—"

"It doesn't matter," Cage had rushed to say. He crossed the room and knelt on one knee in front of his mother's chair, covering her pale, bloodless fingers with his hand. "I know you were upset."

Jenny's heart had gone out to him. He wanted so badly to believe that. But whether Sarah's apology was sincere or not, whether he believed it or not, they were at least voicing aloud the sentiments they should feel.

Jenny's chores at the parsonage seemed endless. The Hendrens had even discussed the possibility that she continue Hal's crusade to help the political refugees in Central America. Even the thought of tackling such a campaign exhausted her, and she refused to speak at rallies and such. But she had taken on the job of sending out a newsletter that detailed the problems as she had witnessed them firsthand and asked for donations to further the relief cause.

She knew her eyes were shadowed with fatigue, knew that she had lost weight due to a notable lack of appetite, knew that she was wan and pale from not spending any time outdoors.

"I'm worried about you," Cage said softly.

"I'm tired. Everyone is. Hal's death, the funeral, it's all taken its toll."

"It's been over two weeks. You spend more time in that parsonage than ever. That's unhealthy."

"But necessary."

"The church is their calling, not yours. They're going to make an old woman out of you if you let them, Jenny."

"I know," she said wearily, rubbing her brow. "Please don't badger me about it, Cage. I told them I needed to move out, but—"

"When?"

"The day after the funeral."

"Why didn't you?"

"They got so upset, I couldn't. And, really, it would have been cruel to move out right after they had lost Hal."

"So what about now?"

She smiled and shook her head. "I don't even have a job. At least not a paying one. I know I've got to make a life for myself, but I've let them manage things for so long, I don't know how to go about it."

"I've got an idea," Cage said suddenly and grabbed her arm. "Come on."

"I can't leave the groceries."

"You don't have the ice cream as an excuse this time. I caught you before you got to the freezer."

Figuratively she dug her heels in. "I can't leave a full basket of groceries in the aisle of the store."

"Oh, for heaven's sake," Cage said irritably. He spun the basket around and, taking long striding steps, pushed it to the front of the store. "Hey, Zack!" The store manager peered over the partial wall of his office. He was counting back money to someone who had cashed a check.

"Hiya, Cage."

"Miss Fletcher's leaving her groceries here," he said, parking the basket near a display of pots and pans that could be obtained with saved coupons. "We'll be back for them later."

"Sure, Cage. See ya."

Cage picked up a Milky Way bar as they passed the candy counter and saluted the manager with it before looping his arm over Jenny's shoulders and leading her from the store.

"Did you steal that?"

"Sure," Cage said, peeling the candy open and cramming half of it into his mouth. "This half's for you."

"But—" He stopped her protest by popping the remainder of the candy bar into her surprised mouth.

"You never stole a candy bar?" Jenny shook her head, shifting the huge bite of candy from one side of her mouth to the other in an effort to chew it before it choked her. "Well, it's about time you did. Now you're my partner in crime." He opened the door of his Corvette and gently, but inexorably, pushed her into the passenger's seat.

Cage drove through the busy downtown streets with only a little more discipline than he drove on the highway. He turned into a curbside parking space in front of a row of offices. When he got out, he reached beneath the seat of the car and took out a cloth bag. It was the kind the city used to cover parking meters on holidays. He slipped it over the meter in front of the Corvette and winked at Jenny before catching her elbow and ushering her to the door.

"Can you do that?" she asked, worriedly glancing at the covered meter.

"I just did."

He unlocked the office and she stepped in ahead of him.

But she came to an abrupt halt on the other side of the threshold and stared around her in dismay. The room was in semidarkness, but it only looked worse when Cage went to the window and adjusted the dusty blinds to let in more sunlight.

Jenny had never seen a room in such disorder. A sad sofa, straight out of a fifties television situation comedy, was pushed against one wall. The rose-colored upholstery, which hadn't had much going for it in the first place, was grayed with generations of dust. The cushions were hollowed out in their centers.

Ugly metal shelves took up another wall. They were stuffed with papers and ledgers and maps, the corners of which were curled and yellowed.

Every available ashtray was full to overflowing.

The desk in the middle of the far wall should have been junked years ago. A deck of playing cards held up the corner where one caster was missing. It was piled with dated magazines, littered with empty coffee cups, and crisscrossed with scratches and scars. An egotistical vandal had carved his initials in one corner.

Jenny turned to Cage slowly. "What is this?"

"My office," he said abashedly.

Incredulity caused her jaw to drop open. "You actually run a business out of this trash heap?"

"I wouldn't go so far as to call it that."

"Cage, if Dante were alive, this is how he would describe hell."

"That bad?"

"That bad." Jenny ambled toward the desk and picked up a half inch of dust on her finger when she dragged it over the marred surface. "Have you ever had this place cleaned?"

"I think so. Oh, yeah, once I hired a janitor service. The guy they sent over was a real cutup. We got to drinking and—"

"Never mind, I get the picture." She edged around an overflowing wastepaper basket and went toward a door she assumed belonged to a closet.

"Uh, Jenny..." Cage lifted his hand and tried to forestall her, but it was too late.

As the door opened a giant wall calendar swung outward and tipped her on the shoulder. She jumped back, startled. But not nearly as startled as she was when the calendar seesawed back and forth until it came to rest on its nail and she saw the glossy photograph.

The pouting redhead was sporting a strategically placed shiny blue star that had "Deep in the Heart of Texas" inscribed on it. Pillow-sized breasts with nipples as large and red as strawberries took up a good portion of the picture.

Cage cleared his throat uncomfortably. "A crew of roughnecks gave me that last Christmas."

Jenny shut the closet door firmly and turned to face him. "Why did you bring me here?"

He pushed his hands into the back pockets of his jeans, withdrew them, then lightly slapped his thighs nervously. "Here, Jenny, sit down," he said, suddenly lunging forward to clear off a place on the sofa for her.

"I don't want to sit down. I want to get out of here so I can breathe some fresh air. Tell me why you brought me here."

"Well, you said you wanted a job and I was thinking—"

"You can't be serious," she interrupted him, gleaning his thought.

"Now, Jenny, hear me out. I need someone to—"

"You need a demolition squad, then a bulldozer.

After they're done, I suggest you start from scratch." She headed toward the door.

He blocked her escape and clasped her shoulders. "I'm not talking about someone to clean it up. I'll get it straightened up. I thought you could answer the telephone, do general office work, you know."

"You've survived without someone all these years. Who's been taking your calls?"

"An answering service."

"Why change now?"

"It's damned inconvenient to check in every hour."

"Wear a beeper."

"I tried that."

"And?"

"I had it hooked to my belt, but I, uh, lost it."

Her eyes flew up to his. He looked away guiltily. "Hm, I can see how having it hooked to your belt could get inconvenient." She tried to move around him again. He held her forcibly.

"Jenny, please, listen. You need and want a job. I'm offering you one."

"A chimpanzee could be trained to sit and answer a telephone. Besides, you said you have an answering service."

"But how do I know they get all the calls? Besides, there are other things to be done."

"Such as?"

"Correspondence. You'd be surprised how much."

"Who's doing it now? You?"

"No, a friend of mine."

She gave him another I'm-onto-you-mister look and he sighed in exasperation. "She's about eighty-seven and myopic and uses a vintage typewriter. The capital

*T* is always half a step up from the other letters. And she has a crooked *S*."

Narrowed green eyes glared up at him suspiciously. "Was that a subtle play on words?"

"No, I swear, but I'm glad you caught it anyway. It means you're not a totally hopeless case."

She ignored that and gazed around her. "You don't even have a typewriter."

"I'll buy one. Any kind you like."

The thought of being more productive was intriguing and challenging, but she knew she couldn't accept his offer. With a defeated stoop to her shoulders, she shook her head. "I can't, Cage."

"Why not?"

"Your parents need me too much."

"You hit the nail on the head. They need you too much. Do you think you're doing them any favors by waiting on them hand and foot? They're middle-aged, but if they don't have a purpose in their lives, they'll grow old very fast. They need to get their lives going again, but they won't ever do that if they become so reliant on you.

"I've never had a child, so I don't know what it's like to lose one. But I can imagine that the temptation would be to curl up and die yourself. If you keep catering to Mother and Dad, that's what they're likely to do."

He was right, of course. Every day the Hendrens seemed to shrivel up more. And as long as she was convenient for them to rely on, they would use her until all their lives had been wasted.

"How much would you pay me?"

His face broke into a strong, wide grin. "Mercenary little bitch, aren't you?"

"How much?" she demanded, not nearly as piqued by his vulgarity as she should have been.

"Let's see," he said, rubbing his jaw. "Two-fifty a week?"

She had no idea if that was fair or not, but she wanted to leap at it anyway. Still, she hedged, pretending to be considering it. "How many paid holidays do I get?"

"Take it or leave it, Miss Fletcher," he said sternly.

"I'll take it. Nine to five with an hour and a half off for lunch." That would give her time to go to the parsonage and take the meal with the Hendrens, though the thought of eating lunch out every day was much more exciting. "Two weeks paid vacation, plus all the holidays the postal service takes. And I'll work only until noon on Fridays."

"You drive a hard bargain," Cage said, frowning. Actually he was thrilled. If he'd had to double the salary and meet any conditions, he would have done so to get her free of the parsonage and out from under his parents' control.

"I won't set foot in this place until it's been cleaned up. I mean clean."

"Yes, ma'am." He clicked his heels together.

"And the calendar has to go."

He looked toward the closet door and his face drooped in comic disappointment. "Aw, shoot! I was really coming to like her." He shrugged. "Ah, well. Anything else?"

Jenny was thinking how absolutely adorable he was, but her mind snapped back to the problem at hand. "Yes. How am I going to tell your parents?"

"Don't give them a choice." He stuck out his hand. "Is that it? Do we have a deal?"

"Deal." She gave him her hand, but instead of shaking it, he drew it up and placed it on his chest.

"A handshake is no way to finalize a deal with a gorgeous woman."

Before she could react, he bent his head down and slanted his mouth over hers. The hand now pressing hers to his chest went to her waist, where it settled lightly. His thumb gently stroked her lowest rib.

The kiss was long. His lips were open over hers, but he didn't use his tongue. He only kept her held in breathless suspension, teasing her with the possibility that at any moment he might send it delving into her mouth. But he didn't. And when he raised his head, he merely smiled.

Later, after he had deposited her back at the grocery store and she had finished her shopping, she wondered why she hadn't done something, anything, to stop the kiss. Why hadn't she slapped his face, or stamped her foot, or even laughed? Why, when he finally lifted his mouth off hers, had she just gazed up at him with limpid eyes and throbbing dewy lips, a pounding pulse, and melting thighs?

The only answer she could provide was that her limbs had felt leaden, deliciously so. And weak with pleasure. She couldn't have raised a finger to protect herself from Cage's kiss if she had wanted to. And she really hadn't wanted to.

The Hendrens didn't take the news of her job too well. Sarah dropped her fork on her dinner plate when Jenny made her announcement. "I start Monday."

"You're going to work—"

"For Cage?" Bob finished for his wife.

"Yes. If you have any projects for me to do before then, let me know."

She left the kitchen before their dumbfoundedness wore off. As Cage had advised her to do, she hadn't given them a choice in the matter.

One minute before nine o'clock the following Monday morning, Jenny entered the office. The door had been left unlocked. For a moment, she thought she had gone in the wrong door. The office hadn't only been cleaned, it had been transformed.

The gunmetal-gray walls were now painted a soothing cream. The hideous sofa had been replaced by two leather armchairs in a rich shade of chocolate brown. A walnut table was tucked between them.

The linoleum tile floor had been covered with parquet wood. An area rug of ethnic origin took up the center of the floor. Where the metal shelves had been, there was now a wall of wood shelves and cabinets. All the components had been tastefully arranged to maximize space so that everything was stacked neatly.

The surface of the desk now dominating the room was as glistening as an ice rink. Behind it was a leather chair of thronelike proportions. On the desk's shiny top was a bouquet of fresh flowers, still beaded with moisture from the florist's refrigerator.

"The flowers are for you."

Jenny spun around to see Cage standing just inside the closet. The door was open. "How did you do it?" she asked, aghast.

"With my checkbook," he said wryly. "That works better than magic wands these days. Do you like it?"

"Yes, but..." Jenny was suddenly contrite. "I

shouldn't have criticized. You've gone to tremendous expense."

"Hey, don't go soft on me. You spurred me on to do something I should have done years ago. I've been entertaining clients at the drugstore's soda fountain because I was ashamed of this 'trash heap,' as someone we all know and love called it." He grinned when her cheeks flushed. "By the way, I have a selection of calendars for you to choose from."

He held up the first one and she gasped softly. "Buns of the Month," Cage said solemnly, trying hard not to smile. The muscular model, posed lying on his stomach, was wearing a jock strap, a football helmet, and a wicked grin. "This is Mr. October. Football season, you understand. Would you like to see the other months?" he asked guilelessly, thumbing through the calendar.

"That will be sufficient," Jenny said hoarsely. "What else do you have?"

Cage set that calendar aside and picked up another. "A Hunk a Day. No heads, just bodies." An oiled chest, bulging biceps, and a washboard stomach graced the picture he held up. Jenny made a squeamish face and shook her head. "Or," Cage said, spreading open the third choice, "Ansel Adams."

"Hang the Ansel Adams." Cage looked pleased and turned to do her bidding. "But leave the others in the closet," Jenny added mischievously. He gave her his most crestfallen expression, then they both burst out laughing.

"Cage, the office is beautiful, really. I love it."

"Good. I want you to be comfortable here."

"Thank you for the flowers," she said, moving behind the desk and tentatively sitting down in the leather chair.

"This is a special occasion."

Their eyes met and locked for a moment before he showed her where his business stationery was stored and how to operate the new typewriter. "You can start on these letters," he said, passing her a folder. "I've roughed them out in longhand, which I hope you can read. Gertie managed to."

"The friend with the crooked *S*?" Jenny asked innocently.

He yanked on a strand of her hair. "Right." He left shortly thereafter, saying he was going out to the Parsons' ranch.

"How does it look?"

"The samples look great. If we don't strike oil, I'm an archangel." He put on his sunglasses and reached for the doorknob. "'Bye."

"'Bye."

He paused, staring at her for a long moment. "God a'mighty, you look good sitting there."

Then he was gone.

He came back a few minutes before noon, carrying a large sack. "Lunchtime!" he yelled as he barged through the door.

Jenny waved her hand, motioning for him to be quiet. She was on the telephone, jotting down notes as the other party talked. "Yes, I have it and I'll give the information to Mr. Hendren when he comes in. Thank you." She hung up and proudly passed him the message.

He read it and thumped the paper. "Terrific. I've been waiting for permission to have a look-see at this property. You've brought me luck." He grinned and set the sack on the edge of the desk. "And I've brought you lunch."

"Can I expect this kind of treatment every day?" She stood up to peer into the sack.

"Absolutely not. But as I said earlier, today is a special occasion."

"I really should go home and check on Sarah and Bob."

"They'll be fine. Call them later if you must."

His lighthearted mood was infectious and she caught it as they unloaded the lunch he had carried out from the town's only delicatessen. "To top it all off..." He disappeared into the closet and came back carrying a bottle of champagne. "Ta-da!"

"Where'd you get that?"

"I've had it cooling in the refrigerator."

"There's a refrigerator in there?"

"A tiny one. Haven't you looked?"

"No. I've been busy." She pointed toward the stack of letters that were waiting for his signature.

"Then you deserve a glass of champagne," he said, working the cork free. The effervescent wine popped but didn't foam over. Cage poured her a paper cup full.

She took it, too overwhelmed not to. "I really shouldn't, Cage."

"How come?"

"You might find this hard to believe, but we don't usually serve champagne with lunch at the parsonage," she said sarcastically. "I'm not used to it."

"Good. Maybe you'll get drunk, strip off all your clothes, and dance naked on top of the desk."

He passed a speculative glance down her body that

clearly intimated he wondered what such a sight would be like. Embarrassed, she watched him pour himself a cup of champagne. "Do you do this sort of thing often?"

"Drink champagne in the middle of the day? No."

"Then how do you know you won't get drunk, strip off all your clothes, and dance naked on top of the desk?"

He touched the rim of her cup with his. "Because, my Jenny," he whispered roughly, "if we were both naked on top of the desk, we wouldn't be dancing."

Her stomach did a backward somersault. She managed to tear her eyes away from the hypnotizing power of his and noticed that her hand was trembling.

"Take a sip," Cage urged in that same husky voice. Grateful for something to do, she did. The champagne was cold and biting on her tongue. "Like it?"

"Yes." She took another sip.

He moved his head closer until they were almost nose to nose. His eyes fairly smoldered. "How do you feel about…"

"About what?"

"Hot pastrami?"

Hot pastrami had never tasted so delicious. In fact, it was one of the most fabulous meals Jenny had ever eaten. As they ate he told her more about his business and was pleased with her intelligent and intuitive questions.

He couldn't coax her into drinking more than half the paper cup of champagne. When they were finished, he carefully picked up the empty cartons and put them back in the sack. "I wouldn't dare litter up your office," he said with a crooked smile.

For a long time after he left she couldn't stop think-

ing about both of them being naked. What had he meant
when he'd said they wouldn't be dancing? But she knew
what he'd meant.

And she couldn't stop thinking about that either.

The days fell into some sort of pattern, though life
with Cage was always spontaneous and unplanned. It
was like traveling down a mysterious jungle river. One
never knew what unexpected surprise would be waiting around the next bend.

He left her small presents that shouldn't have been
significant, but to someone who had never been courted,
they were very much so.

A small cake with a single candle was waiting on
her desk the morning of her first week's anniversary of
employment. She found a red rose lying beside the coffeemaker another time. One morning when she opened
the door she almost screamed. A giant teddy bear was
grinning at her from her chair behind the desk.

She knew the town was buzzing with gossip about
them. The tellers at the bank were shocked when she
began to handle Cage's buisness banking. Now they
were accustomed to seeing her come in on his behalf.
But she could see them clustering together when she
left.

The postmaster, who she had known for years, was
still friendly, but now that she was handling Cage's mail
instead of the church's, he looked at her in a way that
made her skin crawl.

And Cage had begun attending church regularly,
which really had the town gossips aflutter.

She loved the challenge of the new job and by the
second week was handling every situation like a pro.

"Hendren Enterprises."

"Jenny, darlin', get your celebrating shoes on," Cage said, laughing.

Jenny could hear the racket in the background. "The well came in?" she squealed.

"The well came in!" he shouted. The roughnecks around him were already breaking out the coolers full of Coors. "Sweetheart, I'm going to buy you the biggest chicken-fried steak lunch we can find. I'll be there in an hour."

"I have an errand to run. Why don't I just meet you somewhere?"

"All right. The Wagon Wheel at twelve-thirty?"

She agreed on the time and place.

But at twelve-thirty Jenny was wandering aimlessly down the main street of town, her brain registering nothing. Entranced, she stopped in the middle of the sidewalk and sightlessly gazed at the garish display of goods in the variety store's front window.

Cage drove by, spotted her, called out her name, and honked. She didn't turn around. She didn't even hear him.

He executed an illegal U-turn and whipped his pickup, which he had driven out to the drilling sight, into the only available parking space and hopped out onto the sidewalk. He jogged toward her. His boots and the hems of his jeans were caked with mud.

"Jenny," he said breathlessly, "you're going in the wrong direction. Didn't we say the Wagon Wheel?"

His broad smile collapsed when she turned and gazed up at him with vacuous eyes. Instantly alarmed, he caught her upper arm and shook her slightly. "Jenny, what's wrong?"

"Cage?" she whispered faintly. She blinked her eyes and looked around her as though only then realizing where she was. "Oh, Cage."

"God, don't scare me like that," he said, worry wrinkling his brow. "What's happened? What's the matter? Are you sick?"

She shook her head and lowered her eyes. "No. But I don't feel like going to lunch. I'm sorry. I'm very happy about the well, but I don't feel like—"

"Will you stop with all that apology crap. To hell with lunch. Tell me what's happened to you." She reeled against him as though she were going to faint. He caught her against his chest, cursing and feeling inept and stupid. "Come on, love. Let's go into the drugstore. I'll get you a Coke."

They walked half a block to the drugstore, where there was a soda fountain in back. At least Cage walked. Jenny stumbled along with his support. She virtually fell into the green vinyl booth as he called out, "Two Cokes, please, Hazel," to the waitress behind the counter.

Cage didn't take his eyes off Jenny, but she didn't look at him. She stared down at her hands where they were locked together on the Formica tabletop. Hazel set the icy fountain drinks on the table. "How're things, Cage?"

"Fine," he muttered absently.

Hazel shrugged and ambled back to the cash register. Folks were saying that Cage Hendren had undergone a change since his brother had gotten killed. They said he'd been hanging around the Fletcher girl like a fly around a jar of honey. Well, that just went to show that some gossip was true. Hazel could always count on Cage for a good half hour of bawdy joking. Today he was so taken with Jenny Fletcher, he was staring at her like she might go up in a puff of smoke if he took his eyes off her.

"Jenny, drink your Coke," Cage said, sliding it closer to her. "You're as pale as a ghost." Obediently she sipped through the straw. "Now tell me what's wrong."

Her head remained bowed for what seemed like hours to him. He was just about ready to lose control when she finally raised it.

Her eyes were glossy with tears. Two escaped simultaneously and rolled down her cheeks. "Cage," she whispered hoarsely, pausing to draw in a shuddering breath, "I'm pregnant."

# Seven

Cage felt like he had just been punched in the gut. His tawny eyes went blank. Except for swallowing hard, he remained perfectly still, his eyes trained on Jenny's face.

"Pregnant?"

She nodded. "I just came from the doctor's office. I'm going to have a baby."

He swiped his damp palms over his thighs. "You didn't know?"

"No."

"Aren't there signs?"

"I guess so."

"Hadn't you missed periods?"

Her cheeks were stained with hot color and she ducked her head. "Yes, but I thought that was because of Hal's death and all the turmoil afterward. I just never thought… Oh, I don't know," she said, wearily resting her forehead on the heel of her hand. "Cage, what am I going to do?"

Do? She would leave with him that very minute and

get married, that's what. They were going to have a baby! Sonofagun! A baby!

Joy pumped through Cage's body. He wanted to stand up and whoop, to rush out in the streets, stop traffic, and tell everybody that he was going to be a daddy.

But he saw Jenny's dejected posture, heard her quiet weeping, and knew that he couldn't let his true reaction show. She thought the baby was Hal's. Cage couldn't acknowledge that it was his because she would despise him, just when she was coming to trust him.

Was this to be his punishment for all the sins he had tallied up beside his name? He had always taken precautions to see that none of the wild oats he sowed produced an unwanted child. He had made certain every woman he slept with knew of those precautions so she couldn't frame him later for an accident that wasn't his.

But now, when he wanted to claim his paternity, he couldn't. He couldn't be granted the privilege of acknowledging the child he had created with the woman he loved, had always loved.

God played dirty pool.

*Tell her, tell her now,* a voice deep inside him whispered.

He wanted to. Lord, how he wanted to take her in his arms and reassure her that she had no reason to cry. He wanted to proclaim that he loved her and his child—yes, his child—and promise her that for as long as he lived he would take care of both of them. Selfishly that was what he wanted to do.

But he couldn't. Learning she was pregnant had been devastating enough for her. He couldn't bring her more misery by telling her that the father of the child wasn't who she thought he was.

For now, he had to be satisfied with being her friend.

"Crying won't help, Jenny." He passed her a handkerchief. She blotted her eyes and glanced around self-consciously. They had the small coffee shop to themselves. Hazel was engrossed in a movie star magazine.

"Everyone will think I'm trash. And Hal…" She bowed her head at the thought of what people would think of the young minister now.

"No one will think Jenny Fletcher is trash." Cage twirled the straw in his Coke, already feeling guilty for the way he was about to manipulate her. He cleared his throat. "I didn't know you and Hal had that kind of relationship."

"We didn't." She spoke so softly he had to lean across the table in order to hear her. "Not until the night before he left."

She raised her head to find him studying her intently. His unwavering attention made her even more uncomfortable about the subject they were discussing, and when she began speaking again, her voice faltered. "Remember you told me I should try to stop him from going? Well, I tried," she said with a shaky little laugh. "But it didn't work."

"What happened?" Cage was finding it hard to speak past the lump in his throat. But he wanted to know what she felt about that night. It wasn't fair to goad her into talking about it like this, but he had to know.

"He went upstairs with me. I…" She lowered her gaze and drew in a tremulous little breath. "I pleaded with him not to go. He wouldn't be swayed. Then I tried to lure him into bed. But he left me."

"Then I don't understand—"

"He came back a while later and we…we made love."

Several moments ticked by while neither of them spoke, each lost in his own thoughts. Jenny was remembering that burst of joy she had felt when the door opened and she had seen Hal's silhouette against the narrow strip of light. Cage was recalling the same thing, only from his perspective. Jenny sitting up in bed, her face awash with tears.

"That was the first time you ever..."

"The first and only. I never believed that a woman could become pregnant from one time." She plucked at the paper napkin growing soggy beneath her sweating glass. "I was wrong."

"Was it good for you, Jenny?" Her eyes flew up to meet his. "I mean, if you were a virgin," he improvised quickly, "didn't it hurt?"

"A little, at first." She smiled in a secretive, Mona Lisa way that made Cage's heart constrict. Then she looked him square in the eye. "It was wonderful, Cage. The best thing that's ever happened to me. I've never felt that kind of closeness to another human being. And no matter what happens, I'll never regret what I did that night."

Now it was his turn to drop his gaze. He felt dangerously close to tears. Emotion churned in his throat. His loins were thick with it. He wanted to hold her against him, to feel her body soft and warm against his. He longed to confess that he understood exactly how she felt because it had been the same for him.

"You must be about—"

"Almost four months," she supplied.

"And you haven't had any unpleasant symptoms?"

"Now that I know I'm pregnant, I recognize them. I wasn't looking for them before. I've been tired and listless. Right after we came back from Monterico I lost some weight, but I've gained it back. My breasts—" She stopped mid-sentence, glancing up at him modestly.

"Go on, Jenny," he coached softly. "Your breasts what?"

"They, uh, they've been tender and tingling sort of, you know?"

He grinned lopsidedly. "No. I don't know."

She laughed. "How could you know?" It felt good to laugh, but she covered her mouth. "I can't believe I'm laughing about something this serious."

"What else can you do? Besides, I think it's cause for celebration, not tears. It's not every day a man brings in an oil well and learns he's going to be a…an uncle."

She reached across the table for his hand and clasped it tightly. "Thank you for feeling that way, Cage. When I left the doctor's office, I was flabbergasted. I didn't know where to turn or where to go. I felt lost and alone."

"You don't have to feel that way, Jenny. You can always come to me. For anything."

"I appreciate your attitude about it."

If only she knew his real attitude about it. He was incredibly overjoyed and incredibly sad. He was having a child, but no one would know it was his. Not even its mother.

"What do you plan to do?"

"I don't know."

"Marry me, Jenny."

That stunned her speechless. She stared at him blankly while she tried to get her heart to calm down and stop hopping around in her chest like a wild bird in a cage. She knew he was motivated by pity, possibly family loyalty, but out of sheer desperation to grasp the security his offer promised, she was tempted to say yes. That was ridiculous, of course. "I can't."

"Why?"

"There are a thousand reasons against it."

"And one very good one for it."

"Cage, I can't let you do that. Ruin your life for the sake of me and my child? Never. No, thank you."

"Let me decide what would bring me ruination, please." He squeezed her hand. "Should we elope tonight or wait until tomorrow? I'll honeymoon anywhere you say. Except Monterico," he added with a grin.

Her eyes were soft and shiny with tears. "You really are wonderful, you know that?"

"That's what they tell me."

"But I can't marry you, Cage."

"Because of Hal?" His face lost all vestiges of humor.

"No. Not solely. It has to do with you and me. We would be getting married for all the wrong reasons. Jenny Fletcher and Cage Hendren. What a joke."

"Don't you like me anymore?" he asked, pouring all the charm at his command into his smile.

She smiled with him. "You know it's not that. I like you very much."

"You'd be amazed at how many married couples I know who can't stand each other. We'd have more going for us than most."

"But a wife and child hardly fit your lifestyle."

"I'll change my lifestyle."

"I won't let you make that kind of sacrifice."

He wanted to shake her and shout that he wouldn't be making any sacrifice. But now he had to give her room. She needed time to adjust to the idea of the baby before she could consider taking on a husband with a reputation for being a philanderer. This would only be a temporary postponement. Nothing in heaven or earth would keep him from marrying her, making her his forever, rearing his child in a home filled with love rather than censure.

"So if you're going to break my heart and turn me down, what are you going to do?"

"Can I still work for you?"

He frowned at her. "You have to ask?"

"Thank you, Cage," she murmured earnestly.

She let herself relax against the back of the booth and unconsciously smoothed her hands down her abdomen, which was still flat. *She's so damn tiny,* Cage thought. Was it possible that his child was growing inside her?

She had been so small. He almost groaned with the memory of his intrusion into that smooth sheath. He had loved her tightness then, but now it worried him. What if she had difficulty delivering the baby?

His eyes wandered up to her breasts. They weren't noticeably larger, but there was a ripe fullness to them. They were round and maternally plump and he wanted nothing more than to caress them softly and cover them with adoring kisses.

"Your parents will have to know."

Reluctantly Cage pulled his eyes away from her breasts and his mind from its fantasy. "Would you like me to tell them?"

"No. That responsibility falls to me. I only wish I knew how they are going to take it."

"How else can they take it? They will be delighted." It cost him tremendously to say it, but he added, "They'll have a living legacy of Hal."

She fiddled with the wet napkin. By now it was almost shredded. "Maybe. Somehow I don't think it will be that simple. They're very moral people, Cage. I don't have to tell you that. For them the boundaries of right and wrong are clearly defined. To their way of thinking, there are no gray areas of morality."

"But my father has preached Christian charity all his adult life. God's grace and loving forgiveness have been the topics of many sermons." He covered her hand with his. "They won't condemn you, Jenny. I'm certain of that."

She wished she could be as confident, but she smiled at him as though she were.

Before they left he made her drink a chocolate malt, saying that it was more important than ever that she gain weight and keep up her strength. They toasted the oil well and the baby with their glasses.

"I might have to share my teddy bear with the baby," she said as they walked outside, hands clasped and swinging between them.

"Put up a good fight," he said, smiling down at her. "For a long time, you'll be bigger than the baby." He walked her to her car and unlocked the door for her. "Go home and take a nap."

"But I've only put in half a day," she objected.

"And it's been a bitch. Rest this afternoon. I'll call and check on you tonight."

"Sometime between now and then, I'll have to break the news to Sarah and Bob."

"They'll be as thrilled about the baby as I am."

That was impossible. No one was as thrilled about the baby as he was. God, he was bursting at the seams to declare how happy he was, how much he loved her, how much he loved the child they had made.

He was forced into silence, but he yielded to the temptation to hold Jenny. He drew her against him. She went into his arms willingly, and they held each other close in broad daylight, unaware of everything around them, prying eyes included.

His heart beat steady and strong beneath her ear. She drew warmth from his body. Cage had become important to her, almost unnervingly so. But she desperately needed a friend and he hadn't failed her. So she clung to him for strength and support. And while she was at it, she enjoyed the blended fragrances of sun and wind and spicy aftershave, scents that belonged so uniquely to Cage.

Cage cradled her against him, loving the feel of her lush breasts against his chest. He pressed his lips to the crown of her head for a prolonged kiss that really wasn't a kiss at all. It hurt like hell that he couldn't thank her for blessing him with a child. He couldn't lay his hands on her tummy and foolishly talk to the baby nestling inside. He couldn't fondle her breasts and tell her how he longed to see his baby suckling there. Worst of all, it hurt to have to let her go.

But eventually he did.

"Promise me you'll lie down as soon as you get home."

"I promise."

He tucked her into the front seat of her car and made her fasten the seat belt. "To protect you and baby from drivers like me," he said with a self-derisive smile.

"Thanks for everything, Cage."

He watched her drive away, wondering if she would thank him if she knew he was responsible for the predicament she now found herself in.

\* \* \*

Cage arrived at the parsonage shortly after seven o'clock.

After sending Jenny home, he had spent the remainder of the afternoon at the drilling site. Busy as he was, she was never off his mind. He was worried about her, her mental state, her physical condition, her anxiety over telling his parents about the baby.

From the outside, the parsonage looked as it always did. Jenny's car was there, parked next to the one belonging to his parents. There were lights on in the kitchen and living room. Nonetheless, Cage had a gut instinct that something was wrong.

He knocked on the front door and then pushed it open. "Hello," he called out. He went in without invitation and found Bob and Sarah sitting together in the living room.

"Hello, Cage," his father said unenthusiastically. Sarah said nothing. She was twisting a handkerchief round and round her index finger.

"Where's Jenny?"

Bob was apparently finding it difficult to speak because he swallowed several times. When he did manage to make a sound, he spoke economically. "She left."

Anger and fear began to coil inside Cage. "Left? What do you mean she left? Her car's here."

Bob dragged his hand down his face, distorting his features. "She chose to leave without taking anything with her except her clothes."

Cage turned on his heel and bounded up the stairs two at a time, the way he had done in his youth. It had been an infringement of house rules, but he had ignored them then and he did now.

"Jenny?" She wasn't in her room. He lunged for the closet and yanked open the door. Except for a few garments, all the hangers were empty. In the drawers he frantically pulled from the bureaus, he found the same mute testament that she was gone.

"Dammit!" he roared like a thwarted lion and went charging down the stairs again. "What happened? What did you do? What did you say to her?" he demanded of his parents. "Did she tell you about the baby?"

"Yes," Bob said. "We were appalled."

"Appalled? Appalled! You found out Jenny is carrying your first grandchild and your only reaction is that you're appalled?!"

"She claims it's Hal's baby."

Had it been any man other than his father who maligned Jenny's integrity and virtue that way, Cage would have jerked him up by the shirt collar and beat him until he lived to regret ever having uttered so much as a breath of slander against her.

As it was, Cage only made a low growling sound in his throat and took a threatening step forward. That, in fact, it wasn't Hal's child didn't matter at the moment. Jenny thought it was. She had thought she was telling them the absolute truth.

"You doubt that?"

"Certainly we doubt it," Sarah said, speaking for the first time. "Hal wouldn't have done anything so…so… so sinful. Especially not on the night before he left for Central America as she claims."

"This may come as a surprise to you, Mother, but Hal was a man first and a missionary second."

"Is that supposed to mean—"

"It means that he had the same apparatus as every

other man since Adam. The same drives. The same desires. It's only a wonder to me he waited so long to take Jenny to his bed." Hal never had taken Jenny to his bed, but Cage wasn't thinking very reasonbly at the moment.

"Cage, for heaven's sake, shut up," Bob hissed, rising to face his oldest son. "How dare you speak to your mother in such crude terms."

"All right," he said, slicing the air with his hands. "I don't give a damn what you think about me, but how could you have driven Jenny out at a time like this?"

"We didn't drive her out. She made the decision to leave."

"You must have said something to provoke her into taking such a drastic action. What was it?"

"She expected us to believe that Hal had…had done that," Bob said. "Mother and I conceded that he might have. As you pointed out, your brother was a man. But if he did, she must have tempted him to do it beyond his endurance to resist."

Frankly Cage didn't know how Hal had resisted her that night. He never could have. Not in a million years. Not if the jaws of hell had opened up to welcome him as soon as it was over. "Whatever happened, it was done out of love." That much was the truth.

"I believe that. Even so," Bob said, stubbornly shaking his head, "Hal wouldn't have distracted himself from his mission unless he was sorely tempted. And possibly, just possibly, he was still distracted, or feeling guilty about the sin he had committed, or was otherwise in conflict with himself when he was in Monterico. Maybe that's why he was careless enough to get himself captured and killed."

"My God," Cage breathed, falling back against the

wall as though he had just sustained a stunning blow. He stared at his parents, wondering how two such self-righteous, narrow-minded, judgmental people could have spawned him. "You told Jenny that? You blamed her for Hal's death?"

"She is to blame," Sarah said. "Hal's convictions were so steadfast, she must have seduced him. Can you imagine how betrayed we feel? We reared her as our own daughter. For her to turn on us like this…to have an illegitimate child… Oh, Lord, when I think of what this is going to do to Hal's memory. Everyone loved and admired him. This will destroy everything he stood for." Sarah clamped her lips into a thin white line and turned her head away.

Cage was torn by indecision. They were laying the blame for Hal's death on Jenny, thinking she had seduced him. Hal's death couldn't be blamed on anyone but Hal, because he hadn't been distracted or guilty over a night of passion with Jenny. Cage could absolve her now by telling them that she had been with him instead. But if they condemned Jenny for sleeping with Hal, they would stone her in the streets for sleeping with him.

Their attitude made him sick. He had reassured Jenny that they would be glad about the baby. Instead they had judged her and scorned her in a most unchristian way. He wanted to call them hypocrites to their faces, but he didn't have the time. And why waste the energy? As far as he was concerned, they were a lost cause. He had only one purpose in mind now. To find Jenny.

"Where did she go?"

"We don't know," Bob said in a tone that indicated he didn't care either. "She called a taxi."

"I pity the two of you," Cage said before storming out.

\* \* \*

"How long ago?"

"Well, let's see." A gnarled finger traveled down the column of departure times, then traced a line across to the listing of cities. "'Bout thirty minutes ago. It was due to pull out at six-fifty, and as well as I recollect, there weren't no delays."

"Does it make any stops?"

The clerk at the bus depot checked the schedule again with a meticulous precision that was driving Cage crazy. Didn't the man know anything without having to consult the damn schedule?

After talking with the owner of the town's only taxi service and learning that Jenny had been chauffeured from the parsonage to the bus depot, Cage had driven there at top speed. A rapid survey of the dingy passenger lounge assured him she wasn't there. Only one ticket had been sold to a young woman matching Jenny's description. A one-way ticket to Dallas.

"Nope. No stops. Not until Abilene, that is."

"Which highway do they take?"

The clerk told him and by the time he finished his painstaking directions, Cage was already running toward the door. The idling Corvette was shoved into gear, but Cage cursed when he checked the gas gauge. He couldn't go forty miles on what was in the tank. Turning into the next service station he came to he filled the tank with gasoline as fast as the pump would permit.

"You've only got a fifty-dollar bill?" the attendant whined. "Jeez, Cage, that's gonna take practically all the money out of my till."

"Sorry. That's all I have and I'm in a hurry." Damn,

he needed a cigarette. Why had he promised Jenny he'd give them up?

"Heavy date?" The attendant winked lecherously. "Blonde or brunette tonight?"

"As I said, I'm in—"

"Yeah, a hurry, I know, I know," he said, winking again. "Is she the one running hot or are you? Well, let's see what we can do here." He peered down into the cash register's tray over the top of his eyeglasses. "There's a twenty. Nope, it's a ten. And here's a five."

Had the whole damn town been drugged with a mind-stealing chemical? Everyone had been reduced to an imbecile. "Tell you what, Andy, you keep my change and I'll pick it up later."

"Got the itch that bad, have ya?" he called to Cage's retreating back. "She must be somethin' special."

"She is," Cage said as he slid into the Corvette. Seconds later darkness swallowed his taillights.


Jenny had learned not to fight the swaying motion of the bus, but to let her body rock with it. It had become almost lulling. The sheer monotony of it was soothing, and it kept her mind off her future.

What future?

She had none.

The Hendrens had made their feelings plain. She was a Jezebel who had tempted their sainted son, who had tried to lure him away from his life's calling by getting herself pregnant by him.

Stinging tears filled her eyes, but she wouldn't submit to them. She closed her eyes and laid her head on the seat cushion behind her, wishing she could sleep. But that was impossible. Her mind was in turmoil and the passengers around her were becoming increasingly restless and vocal.

"Would you look at that."

"A maniac."

"Does our driver see him?"

"What does he think this is, the Indy Five Hundred?"

Curious as to what had captured their attention, Jenny peered through the window. She saw nothing but her own reflection in the glass and a stygian blackness beyond it. Then she saw the sports car skid alongside the bus, coming dangerously close to the oversized wheels.

"A madman for sure," Jenny heard someone mutter just as her eyes went wide and her mouth went slack with recognition.

"Oh, no," she breathed.

Suddenly the bus gave a lurch as the driver applied the brakes and steered it to the shoulder of the highway. "Ladies and gentlemen," he said into the microphone mounted near the steering wheel, "I'm sorry for this delay, but I'm making an unscheduled stop. This is obviously a drunk driver who's intent on running us off the road. I'll try to reason with him before he kills us all. Stay calm. We'll be on our way again shortly."

Several passengers leaned forward in their seats to see better. Jenny scrunched down in hers, her heart pounding. The driver pushed open the automatic door of the bus and made to leave his chair. Before he could, however, the "madman" bounded inside.

"Please, mister," the driver pleaded, obviously concerned for the safety of his passengers. He patted the air in front of him with raised hands. "We're just innocent folks and—"

"Relax. I'm not a robber. I'm not going to hurt anybody. I'm just going to relieve you of one of your passengers."

Cage's eyes were busily scanning the passengers. Jenny sat quiet and still in her seat. He began making his way down the aisle. "Sorry for this inconvenience," he said in friendly fashion to the passengers, who eyed him warily. "This will only take a minute, I promise." When he spotted his quarry, he stopped in the aisle and sighed with relief. "Get your things, Jenny. You're coming back with me."

"No, I'm not, Cage. I explained it all to you in a letter. I mailed it just before I left. You shouldn't have come after me."

"Well, I did, and I didn't make the trip for nothing. Now come on."

"No."

They had everyone's attention.

Aggravated with her the way a parent is with a lost child when he's found, he put his hands on his hips. "All right. If you want to air the dirty laundry in front of all these nice people, it's fine with me, but you'd better think about it before we get down to the juicy details."

Jenny's eyes skittered around the other passengers, who were looking at her with open curiosity. "What'd she do, Mama?" a little girl piped up. "Was it bad?"

"What's it going to be, Jenny?"

"You don't have to go anywhere with him, miss," the driver said gallantly from behind Cage. It wasn't going to be said that he had let a wife-beater haul his hapless victim off his bus.

Jenny looked at Cage. His jaw was set. His eyes were glowing like yellow flame. He seemed as unmovable as the Rock of Gibraltar. He wouldn't relent, and she didn't want to be held responsible for a brawl aboard a Greyhound bus.

"Oh, all right. I'll go." She edged into the aisle after retrieving her small suitcase. "I have another bag in the luggage compartment," she told the driver softly, aware that every eye in the bus was focused on her.

The three of them stepped outside and the driver opened the luggage compartment beneath the bus. As he handed over her suitcase, he asked, "You're sure you want to go with him? He's not going to hurt you, is he?"

She smiled at him reassuringly. "No, no. It's nothing like that. He's not going to hurt me."

After shooting Cage a fulminating look and mumbling something about maniacal speedsters, he climbed back aboard his bus. A moment later it lumbered onto the highway, its passengers craning their necks in the windows to see the two people left behind.

Stiffly Jenny turned to face Cage. She dropped her suitcases with an emphatic plop. "Well, that was quite a stunt, Mr. Hendren. Just what did you expect to gain by it?"

"Just what I did. To get you off that bus and stop you from running away like a scared rabbit."

"Well, maybe that's what I am," she cried, giving vent to the tears that had been welling up since the scene in the parsonage.

"What did you have in mind, Jenny? Running to Dallas and having an abortion?"

Her hands knotted into fists. "That's a despicable thing to even suggest."

"What then? What was your intention? Were you going to have the baby and give it away?"

"No!"

"Hide it?" He stepped forward. How she answered the next question was of utmost importance to him. "Don't you want the baby, Jenny? Are you ashamed of it?"

"No, no," she groaned, covering her stomach with both hands. "Of course I want it. I love it already."

Cage's shoulders slumped with relief, but his voice still had an angry edge to it. "Then why were you running scared?"

"I didn't know what else to do. Your parents made it obvious they didn't want me around any longer."

"So?"

"So?" She jerked her arm in the direction the bus had just taken. "Not everyone is brave enough or crazy enough to come chasing after a Greyhound bus. Or drive ninety miles an hour down the highway on a motorcycle. I can't be like you, Cage. You don't give a damn what people think about you. You please yourself." She splayed her hands wide over her chest. "I'm not like that. I do care what people think. And I am scared."

"Of what?" he asked, thrusting his chin out belligerently. "Of a town full of petty minds? How can they hurt you? What's the worst they can do to you? Gossip about you? Scorn you? So what? You're better off without the people who would do that.

"Are you afraid of besmirching Hal's name? I hate it that some righteous hypocrites will think badly of him. But Hal is dead. He'll never know. And the work he instigated will continue. You've seen to that yourself by setting up that fund-raising network. For godsake, Jenny, don't be so hard on yourself. You are your own worst enemy."

"What are you suggesting I do? Go back and work in your office?"

"Yes."

"Flaunt my condition?"

"Be proud of it."

"Have my baby knowing he'll be labeled with a dirty name all his life?"

Cage pointed a steely finger toward her middle. "Anyone who labels that kid anything but wonderful is risking his life."

She could almost laugh at his ferocity. "But you won't always be around to protect him. It won't be easy for this child in a small town where everyone knows his origin."

"It won't be easy for him to grow up in a big city where his mother doesn't know anyone either. Who would you call on for help, Jenny? At least any hostile faces you encounter in La Bota will be familiar ones."

She hated to admit how the thought of moving to another city without much money, without a job or a place to live, without friends or relatives, had terrified her.

"Isn't it time you showed some backbone, Jenny?"

Her head snapped up. "What do you mean by that?" she asked tightly.

"You've been letting other people make your decisions for you since you were fourteen."

"We had this same argument a few months ago. I tried to direct my own destiny. Look what a mess I made of it."

He looked offended. "I thought you said the love-making was beautiful. You're going to have a baby as a result of it. Do you really consider that a mess?"

She hung her head and pressed her hands to her

stomach. "No. It's wonderful. I'm awed by the thought of the child. Awed and humbled by the miracle of it."

"Then hold that thought. Come back to La Bota with me. Have that beautiful baby and thumb your nose at everybody who doesn't like it."

"Even your parents?"

"Their reaction tonight was a knee-jerk reflex. When they think about it, they'll come around."

Meditatively she stared at nothing. "I suppose you're right. I can't find a future for me and the baby. I have to make one. Right?"

He grinned and gave her the thumbs-up sign. "I couldn't have put it better myself."

"Oh, Cage," she sighed, her arms dangling uselessly at her sides. She was suddenly sapped of energy. "Thank you once again."

He moved toward her, his boots crunching on the gravel. Cupping her face between his hands, he whisked his thumbs over her cheekbones. "You could make this a lot easier on yourself if you'd just marry me. The baby would have a daddy and everything would be neat and nice and legal."

"I can't, Cage."

"Sure?"

"Sure."

"That's not the last time I'll ask."

His breath was hot and sweet on her lips before they actually made contact with his. He eased her face upward to his descending mouth and kissed her with gentle possessiveness.

As before, his lips were open and moist. But unlike the other time, his tongue touched hers. Just the tip. Just enough to make her breath catch in her throat and her heart beat erratically. Just enough to make her breasts flare in instantaneous response.

He slid the end of his tongue back and forth over hers in a lazy movement. Then he withdrew and left her wanting. When he stepped away from her and took her arm to guide her to the car, she felt chilled with the absence of his body heat.

He stored her suitcases behind the seats of the Corvette as best he could. "The first thing on the agenda is finding you a place to live," he remarked when they were under way.

Somehow her hand had come to rest on his thigh. "Have any ideas?" she asked vaguely.

"You could move in with me."

Their eyes locked across the console. His were inquiring and mischievous; hers were chastising. "Next suggestion."

He chuckled good-naturedly. "I think I can fix something up with Roxy."

# Eight

"Roxy Clemmons?" Jenny asked, snatching her hand away from his thigh.

"Yeah. Do you know her?"

Only by reputation, Jenny thought snidely. Only by reputation as one of Cage's regulars. "I've heard of her." She turned her head away to gaze out the car window. Despair and disappointment tasted acrid in her mouth.

He had kissed her with such sweet intimacy. His embrace had been warming and security-lending. She was coming to like it when he touched her, liking it even more when he kissed her. But he wasn't doing to her what he hadn't done to hundreds of others. His kisses might set off fireworks in her head, but that kind of passion wasn't a new experience for him. His kissing technique could have been perfected only by hours of practice.

Was she destined to become one of Cage Hendren's "women"? Did he plan on lumping her into that sorority, actually ensconcing her under a roof where she would always be convenient to visit?

"You don't sound very enthusiastic about the idea," he commented.

"I don't have much choice, do I?"

"I offered you an alternative. You rejected it."

She sat in stony silence. She was angry and couldn't quite pinpoint why. Why should she be feeling mad and insulted? She certainly had nothing in common with that Clemmons woman. There was one major distinction between them.

Jenny Fletcher wasn't one of Cage's women...yet.

Had she been subconsciously harboring the thought that they would become lovers? Why? Because he had kissed her a few times? Because of the night in Monterico? Or because she had always felt an inexorable gravitation toward him? It had frightened her and she had resisted it. Until recently.

Well, if he thought she was going to join the ranks of his other women, he had another think coming. Roxy Clemmons and so many other women were strung like beads on a thread of sexual encounters that wound through several counties. Maybe because of her fall from grace with Hal, Cage now considered her fair game. He couldn't be more mistaken.

They didn't speak for the remainder of the trip back. The streets of town were deserted by the time they reached La Bota. Cage pulled his car into the parking lot of an apartment complex and cut the engine. "What's this?" Jenny asked.

"Your new address, I hope. Come on." He led her up to the apartment with a discreet sign reading Manager stuck in the front yard.

He rang the bell. Through the walls, they could hear Johnny Carson amusing his audience. When the door opened, Jenny came face-to-face with Roxy Clemmons. The woman looked at her with polite curiosity, then spotted Cage in the shadows. "Hiya, Cage." The smile she flashed him caused Jenny to wither inside. "What's going on?"

"May we come in?"

"Sure." Without reservation Roxy stood aside and held the door open for them. After she closed it, she went to the television set and turned the sound all the way down.

"I'm sorry to bother you so late, Roxy," Cage began.

"Hell, you know you're welcome anytime."

Jenny's heart twisted and her gaze dropped to the floor.

"Roxy, this is Jenny Fletcher."

"Yeah, I know. Hi, Jenny. It's nice to meet you."

Her open friendliness surprised Jenny and she raised her head. "Nice to meet you, too, Ms. Clemmons."

Roxy laughed. "Call me Roxy. Y'all want something to drink? I've got a cold beer, Cage."

"Sounds good."

"Jenny?"

"Uh, nothing, thank you."

"A Coke?"

She didn't want to appear impolite, so she answered with a weak smile. "Yes, all right, a Coke."

"Sit down and make yourselves at home."

Roxy turned toward the swinging barroom doors, which led to the kitchen. Her hips showed full and shapely in a pair of tight jeans. Voluptuous breasts swung free beneath her sweatshirt. She was barefoot. Her coppery hair was tousled, but attractively so. She looked either like she had just gotten out of bed or was on her way. She was the kind of woman a man could curl up and relax with, custom-made to be a mistress. Friendly, hospitable, warm, and willing. The thought brought a scalding rush of nausea to Jenny's throat.

Cage had settled down on the sofa and was leafing through an issue of *Cosmopolitan* that Roxy had left there. "Sit down, Jenny," he said, noting that she was standing awkwardly in the middle of the room.

Uneasily, as though she might dirty her skirt if she wasn't careful, she lowered herself onto a straight chair. Cage looked amused. That irritated her.

Roxy came back with their drinks, and after Cage had taken a long swallow from the can of beer, he said, "Do you have any vacancies? We need an apartment."

Roxy cast a dumbfounded glance at Jenny, then her eyes swung back to Cage. "Gee, that's great, congratulations. But what's wrong with your house?"

He laughed. "Nothing that I know of. I think you misunderstood. Jenny will be living in the apartment alone."

Jenny could have killed Cage for making it sound like they would be living together. Her cheeks were flaming scarlet. Now that he had clarified the situation, she watched Roxy for signs of relief. Surely Roxy would be glad that he wasn't going to move in another mistress right under her nose. But all Jenny saw on Roxy's face was chagrin at her mistake.

"Oh!" She looked at Jenny and smiled. "You're in luck. I have a one-bedroom apartment vacant."

Jenny opened her mouth to speak, but Cage cut in before her. "How large is the bedroom? Jenny's going to have a baby. Is there enough room for a crib?"

Roxy's reaction to that piece of news was shock. Her

mouth hung slack for several moments as she stared at Cage. When she turned back to Jenny, her eyes moved unerringly down to Jenny's still-trim middle.

"You don't have any restrictions on tenants with babies, do you?" Cage asked.

"No. Hell, no." Visibly Roxy collected herself and put things in their proper perspective. She bent down to slip her bare feet into a pair of sandals. "Let's go see the apartment and you can decide if it's what you're looking for."

"It's in a good location," she said over her shoulder a few minutes later as they followed her down the sidewalk between the buildings. She had gotten the key to the vacant apartment from the spare bedroom in her unit, which served as an office. "Private and quiet, but not so isolated that you'll be afraid to live here alone, Jenny." She prattled on about the complex's amenities, pointing out the laundry facilities and the pool area.

Jenny wasn't listening. She was casting murderous glances at Cage for blurting out her condition to this... this woman. By morning everybody in town would know she was pregnant.

"Here we are." Roxy unlocked the apartment and led them inside. She switched on the light. "Whew! It's a little close. I haven't opened it since the cleaning crews and painters were here."

The apartment did smell of disinfectant and new paint, but Jenny didn't mind that. It was spotlessly clean as a result.

"This is the living room, of course. You have a kitchen in here." Roxy led Jenny through a louvered half door like the one in her own apartment. The built-ins were all clean and shiny. Jenny opened the refrigerator. It was clean, too.

They finished touring the apartment, which didn't take long. There was only a bathroom and bedroom beyond the living room. "How much is the rent?" Jenny asked.

"Four hundred a month plus utilities."

"Four hundred?" Jenny squeaked. "I'm afraid—"

"Unfurnished?" Cage asked, butting in.

"Oh, jeez," Roxy said, swatting her forehead. "I misquoted. Unfurnished one bedrooms are two-fifty."

"That's more like it," Cage said.

Jenny calculated her income and expenditures. She might be able to afford it if she were frugal. Besides, this was one of the nicer apartment complexes in town, and her choices were limited. She was lucky there was an apartment available. Trying to forget that she would be living doors away from one of Cage's lovers, she said, "Do I need to sign a lease?"

"You'll take it, then?" Roxy asked.

"Yes, I suppose so," Jenny answered, wondering why the other woman was so obviously pleased.

"Fantastic. I'm glad you'll be a neighbor. Come on, let's go back to the office."

Within fifteen minutes Jenny had a copy of the contract and a set of keys in her hand. "You can move in tomorrow. In the morning I'll go over and air it out a bit."

"Thank you." She and Roxy shook hands. Cage escorted Jenny to the car, saw that she was settled in the front seat, and then returned to Roxy, who was still standing in her opened front door.

"Thanks for playing along about the rent."

"You threw me a curveball, but I picked up on it,"

Roxy said, smiling up at him. "Are you gonna fill me in on the details of this 'arrangement,' or am I gonna have to use my vivid imagination?"

"Nosy?"

"Damn right."

He laughed. "We'll talk later. Thanks for everything."

"Don't mention it. What are friends for?"

He kissed her quickly on the lips and patted her fanny before he sauntered down the steps and joined Jenny in the car. She was sitting as rigid as a statue staring straight ahead, spears of jealousy knifing into her chest.

She hadn't overheard the conversation at the door, but she had seen the way they smiled at each other and how Cage had bent down to kiss Roxy. The easy familiarity with which they touched each other wrenched at Jenny's composure. Despite her avowals that she didn't care, her heart was slowly tearing in two.

"First thing in the morning we'll hit the furniture stores," Cage was saying.

"You've done enough. I can't ask you—"

"You didn't ask, all right?" he said testily. "I volunteered. Make a list tonight of everything you'll need."

"I won't be able to afford much. Just the essentials. By the way, where are we going now?" Until that moment she hadn't remembered that for tonight she was still homeless. Where would she spend the night?

"I didn't think you wanted to go back to the parsonage."

"No."

"You could come home with me."

"You don't have the room."

"In that big house?"

"There's only one bed."

"So? We've shared a bed before." The reminder was quietly and huskily spoken. She didn't comment on it. After several seconds he sighed and said, "I'm checking you into a motel."

It was no sooner said than he pulled his car under the porte cochere of a chain motel. "Wait here."

Jenny watched him enter the well-lit lobby. Through the plate-glass front she saw the night clerk swing his legs down from his desk and set his spy thriller novel aside. That he recognized Cage was obvious by the wide grin and hearty handshake he gave him.

He didn't even require Cage to sign the register, but immediately reached for a room key and slid it across the counter. Leaning forward in a conspiratorial, let's-have-a-man-to-man-chat posture, he said something that caused Cage to wave his hand in negligent dismissal.

The clerk squinted through the window toward the car. Jenny saw his surprised expression when he recognized her. Grinning up at Cage, he made another comment that drew Cage's brows into a deep scowl. It was still there when he returned to the car after bidding the clerk a brusque good-night.

"What did he say?"

"Nothing," Cage ground through his teeth.

"He said something. I saw him."

Cage didn't respond, but drove straight to the room without even having to check the numbers on the doors. He brought the car to a jarring halt and angrily cut the engine.

"You've been here before," Jenny said intuitively.

"Jenny—"

"Haven't you?"

"—drop it."

"Haven't you?"

"Maybe."

"Often?"

"Yes!"

"With women?"

"Yes!"

Her chest was in danger of caving in around her heart. She could barely speak, it hurt so much to draw sufficient air. "You've brought women here to affairs and that's what the clerk thinks I'm doing with you. What did he say about me?"

"It doesn't matter what he—"

"It matters to me," she shouted. "Tell me."

"No."

He got out of the car and jerked her bags from behind the seat. Without waiting to see if she followed him, he strode toward the door of the motel room and unlocked it. He flung the luggage on the rack in the closet and flipped on the lamp.

"What did he say?" Jenny demanded from the doorway.

Cage spun around and saw her resolved expression. She looked tired and distraught, angry and vulnerable. Her hair was disheveled and her cheeks were pale. Her eyes were ringed with violet shadows of fatigue. Her mouth was trembling slightly. She looked like a lost child and an unvanquished soldier.

He had never wanted her more. But he couldn't have her and that only fueled his anger. She was his, dammit, but he couldn't claim her. He needed her just as much as she needed him, but circumstance was keeping them apart. He was paying dearly for that one night of heaven. Desire to possess her again was making his life hell on earth.

Wanting to hurt her as much as he was hurting, he lashed out. "All right, Miss Fletcher. You want to know what he said? He said that I was keeping it in the family this time."

She clamped her top teeth over her bottom lip to keep from screaming in outrage. Indignation boiled up inside her, seeking an outlet. Cage was the only one to vent it against.

"Do you see what you've done?" she cried. "You announced to Roxy Clemmons, whom everybody knows is one of your sluts, that I'm pregnant. Now you've brought me to a motel where you regularly bring other women. It'll be all over town tomorrow that I was here with you. Well, I don't want to be dragged from lair to lair like a prize. I don't want anybody to mistake me for one of your lovers, Cage."

"Why? Because I'm so rotten? You don't want to be associated with the 'bad boy,' that wild preacher's kid that no one can control, the one who's always in trouble, always in a scrape, always involved with the wrong woman?"

He had advanced toward her with a predatory gait. She tried to back away from him, but was trapped by the dresser. "I didn't mean it that way."

"The hell you didn't," he snarled. "Well, you've got every right to be cautious where I'm concerned. I am bad. I must be. Damn bad." One hand shot out and cupped the back of her head. The strong fingers knotted in her hair and pulled her head back. "Because I have brought a lot of women to this room, but I never wanted one as much as I want you."

He encircled her wrist with his other hand and dragged her hand down. "No!" she cried when she realized his intent. She pulled on her hand, but he wouldn't release it. He shoved it past his waist and forced it flat against his body, pressing, making sure she felt the steely evidence of his arousal behind the fly of his jeans.

"That's how much I want you. I've wanted you for a long time and I'm tired of hiding the fact. Now, does that make you scared? Sick? Disgusted? Does it make you want to cringe? To scream? Or skulk back to the safety of the parsonage?" He ground himself into her palm. "Well, that's just tough, Jenny, because this is the way it is."

He kissed her with barely controlled savagery. Unleashing all his emotions, he twisted his mouth against hers, tilting his head first to one side then to the other. His tongue plunged deep, withdrew, sank again more slowly and thoroughly into her mouth, evocative of coupling.

Then just as furiously as he had possessed her, he released her. He stormed out of the door and pulled it closed behind him with a resounding slam.

Jenny staggered to the bed and collapsed. She tried to deny that she was disappointed he hadn't finished what he had started. But she was. Her body was weak and fluttery with longing. Garnering what little strength was left her, she stumbled into the bathroom and peeled off her clothes. She avoided the mirror, not wanting to see the flags of color in her cheeks or the rosy readiness of her breasts.

The shower was hot and punishing, just the ticket

for the self-flagellation she deserved. The jetting spray stung her skin like driving needles. It was still tingling when she took a nightgown from her suitcase and pulled it on. She climbed into bed and squeezed her eyes shut, hoping that would close off her mind as well.

But the kiss was too recent to be banished from her memory. She could still taste him on her lips, still feel the rigid proof of his sex against her hand, still recall the cadence of his kiss as his tongue thrust against hers.

When the telephone rang near her ear, she jumped as though lightning had struck her. "Hello."

"I'm sorry."

Neither of them said anything for ponderous moments. Jenny's breasts trembled with emotion beneath her batiste nightie. She cradled the receiver between her cheek and shoulder as though inclining her head toward Cage. "It's all right."

"I lost my temper."

"I provoked you."

"We've been through an ordeal today."

"We were both touchy."

"Did I hurt you?"

"No, of course you didn't hurt me."

"I was rough." His voice dropped significantly. "And crude."

She looked down at her hand as though to see an imprint there. She swallowed. "I survived."

"Jenny?"

"What?"

A long pause. "I'm not sorry I kissed you. I'm only sorry for the way I kissed you." He let that sink in, then added, "And if you were ever in any doubt about how I feel about you, it's no secret now."

Touched by the gentle, but imperative, tone of his voice, her throat ached with the need to cry. "I'm not ready to think about that, Cage. So much has happened."

"I know, I know. Get a good night's sleep. Sleep late. The office will be closed tomorrow. I'll pick you up, feed you breakfast, and then take you shopping. Be ready at ten sharp."

"Okay."

"G'night, Jenny."

"G'night, Cage."

"Good morning, Jenny."

"Hm?"

"I said good morning."

Jenny yawned broadly into the pillow, stretched her pointed toes as far as she could reach beneath the covers, and pried her eyes open. Then she popped erect. Cage was sitting on the edge of her bed, smiling down at her. "Welcome back to the land of the living."

"What time is it?"

"Ten after ten. I arrived at ten o'clock on the dot, knocked, and got no answer. I went to the lobby to pick up an extra key and let myself in."

"I'm sorry," she said, raking the hair out of her eyes. She blushed becomingly under his ardent perusal of her sleepy disarray and inched the sheet up higher over her breasts. "I was exhausted."

"Hungry?"

"Starving."

"I'll go order breakfast in the coffee shop while you get dressed." He dropped an airy kiss on the tip of her nose before pulling himself off the bed.

"I'll be right there," she called to him as he closed the door behind him.

She looked fresh and rested when she joined him twenty minutes later in the coffee shop. She had dressed in a simple skirt and blouse, but had accessorized them with a paisley shawl tied at her waist under one arm. Her shoes had low heels and narrow ankle straps that captured Cage's attention as she crossed the casual dining room toward him.

He knew she had taken one of her first paychecks and used it to refurbish her wardrobe. She was dressing with more flair than she had when she was engaged to Hal.

"Am I late?"

"Your food just got here. I like your shoes, by the way."

"They're new," she said absently, eyeing the platters of food at her place setting. "All of this is for me?"

"Yep."

"You don't expect me to eat it all, do you?"

"I expect you to make a big dent in it. Get busy. I'm outlining our attack."

"Aren't you eating?" she asked, spreading the napkin in her lap.

"I went ahead." His head was bent over a notepad where he was jotting down an extensive list of household items she would need.

Jenny was taken by the endearing picture he made. There were a thousand shades of blond and brown and ash in his hair, but it all added up to dusty blond color that looked rugged and perpetually wind-tossed.

His cheeks and chin had been closely shaved and the brisk scent of his cologne overwhelmed even the aroma of fresh coffee as the waitress filled Jenny's cup. His tawny brow was furrowed with concentration.

He was dressed in jeans and a sport shirt, but there was a raw silk jacket draped over the back of his chair. It was an odd wardrobe combination, and one only a man who flagrantly broke all the rules could get by with.

He was gorgeous in a sexy, dangerous way. Jenny knew just how dangerous his appeal could be. It drew a woman out of her shell until she didn't recognize herself anymore. Jenny had to consciously settle her stomach down before she could take a bite of food.

By the time she had eaten enough breakfast to suit him, he had their itinerary mapped out. "Remember my budget," she said when he enumerated the stores they would shop in.

"Maybe your boss will give you a raise."

She stopped on her way to his car and turned to face him. Her chin was stubbornly set. "Get this straight, Cage. I won't accept your charity."

"Will you marry me?"

"No."

"Then shut up and get in." He held the door of the Corvette open for her and she knew further argument was futile. She'd just have to put her foot down when it came to what she could buy and what she couldn't.

He had expensive taste and everything he liked was exactly what she would have selected had money been no object. "I can't afford this sofa. The other one costs half as much."

"It's ugly as sin."

"It's functional."

"It's hard and…boxy. This one has cushions a foot thick and is so comfy."

"That's what makes it expensive. Comfy and cushions aren't that important."

His grin was Satan-inspired and his voice was slurred with innuendo. "That all depends on what you're going to do on the sofa."

The sales clerk standing near enough to overhear snickered, but drew a serious face when Jenny turned around and glared at him. "I'll take the other one," she said with prim hauteur.

They had the same argument over the bed, chairs, a dinette, linens, dishes, pots and pans, even a can opener. In every case he urged her to pay a premium price for top quality merchandise. She was adamantly stingy.

"Tired?"

She was resting her head on the back of the car seat. "Yes," she sighed. "I'll probably never move from this apartment. I couldn't go through this again."

He laughed. "I've arranged for everything we bought to be delivered this afternoon. By nightfall that apartment will be like home sweet home."

"How'd you manage to get everything delivered today?"

"Bribes, threats, blackmail, any way I could."

He was smiling mischievously, but she believed him.

"That looks like my car!" She sat up straight when he stopped in front of her apartment.

"It is your car," Cage said nonchalantly as he assisted her out of the Corvette.

"How did it get here?"

"I had it towed." He opened the door of her compact and leaned down to fish the keys from beneath the floor mat where he had instructed the tow truck driver to leave them. He tossed them to her. "Frankly I think it's a pile of no-class junk, but I know you're attached to it."

She looked distressed. "Cage, I didn't want to take anything from your parents."

Placing his hands on his hips, he said, "For godsake, Jenny, they gave you this car as a present years ago. Why do they need three cars—theirs, Hal's and yours—in their driveway when Mother rarely even drives?"

She marched toward the car and moved him aside so she could get in. "I'm taking it back."

He bent down and stuck his head in the open window after she had shut the door. "Then I'll be your only means of transportation," he reminded her in a sing-song voice.

In weary surrender, she laid her head on the steering wheel. "That's blackmail."

"That's right."

Laughing in spite of herself, she let him lead her into the apartment. Roxy had made good on her promise. The windows had been opened and the fresh air had rid the rooms of their stuffiness.

Within a half hour her purchases began to arrive. "Oh, you've made a mistake!" Jenny exclaimed as she opened the door for the first delivery.

"No mistake, miss. Excuse me." The man transferred his fat cigar from one side of his mouth to the other and casually brushed past her as he carried in a chair. "Bring the sofa on in," he yelled back to his helpers, who were climbing down from the truck.

"But wait, that's the wrong one."

"It's the one written on the ticket." He sat the chair down and handed her the green invoice.

Her eyes quickly scanned the invoice, then went back

over it more carefully. "Oh, no! Cage, there's been some terrible—"

She broke off when she saw his smile. His backside was trying out the cushiony couch he had chosen, his arms stretched out along its back. He was smiling like a gratified Santa Claus on Christmas morning.

"What have you done?" she grated.

"*Sabotage* is the word that comes to mind."

That was exactly the word that applied. As piece after piece of merchandise was delivered, she realized that he had gone behind her and ordered the things she had wanted but couldn't afford. "How am I supposed to pay for all this?" she cried.

"Credit. Whatever you paid today went as a down payment. I arranged monthly terms for you that you can afford. A single woman should establish credit. So what's the problem?"

"I can't let you do this, Cage. You're railroading me into making decisions that go against my better judgment. But it's going to stop right now. I won't stay in this apartment if it means keeping all this furniture."

"All right." Those two words of concession should have been accompanied by a sigh and a dejected slump of his broad shoulders. Instead he was grinning broadly. He went to the front door and whistled piercingly. "Hey, fellows, load it all back up and take it out to my place. She's decided to marry me instead of living here alone."

"Oh, Lord," Jenny groaned and covered her face with her hands. "Uncle, uncle!"

Laughing, Cage closed the door and moved toward her.

"Haven't you got anything better to do than babysit me?"

"Nothing I can think of."

"Since Hal went away, you've been wonderful. Why are you doing all this for me, Cage?"

The golden eyes wandered over her face. With one index finger, he brushed a strand of her hair off her forehead. "Because I like the color of your hair. Especially when the afternoon sunlight shines on it the way it is now."

He moved closer. Her head tilted back naturally so she could gaze up into his chiseled face. "And I like your eyes," he said softly.

He reached beneath her arm and untied the ends of her shawl. He drew it off slowly, as though he were peeling away a much more personal article of clothing, and dropped it negligently onto the floor.

"I love the way you laugh. And the way the sound of it makes me feel on the inside."

He settled his hands on either side of her waist and lightly seesawed them up and down. "I like the way your body is made."

He lowered his head and nuzzled her ear. "And the shape of your mouth."

A heartbeat later his lips drifted over hers. He pecked her mouth softly, repeatedly, until her lips parted, all but begging to be possessed.

He heeded her silent yearning and melded their mouths together. His tongue slid deep into her mouth and prowled at will. The violence of last night's kiss was gone, but this tender one was just as potent and awakened her body as earth-shatteringly as it had been stirred the night before. Driven by a craving to get closer, she took unconscious steps toward him. When her body was plastered against his from chest to knees, she was almost surprised to find it so.

"God, Jenny," he whispered. His breath was hot and fragrant against her flushing cheeks. His lips were dewy as he caught her earlobe between his teeth and arousingly worried it with small nibbles.

She felt herself slipping into silky surrender again, losing control, turning her common sense and her senses over to a reckless master.

"Cage, we shouldn't do—"

"Shh, shh."

Her memory quickened. She should remember something. She knew it.

But before she could grasp the elusive memory, his mouth was making love to hers again and all thought scattered.

He lifted her arms and folded them around his shoulders. Then his hands slid from her elbows down the undersides of her arms to the shallows of her armpits. He paused an instant before continuing downward to the outer curves of her breasts. He massaged them with the heels of his hands. Jenny sighed into his mouth.

"Feel good?"

She murmured an affirmation. The kiss deepened.

She angled her head so that one of her cheeks was lying on his chest. He bent his head down low over hers, seeking, always seeking, for her taste with his agile tongue. His arms went around her and drew her closer still. One of his hands slipped below her waist to her derriere. He pressed her against him, positioning her so she would feel the full urgency of his desire.

She moaned and rubbed her middle against his. The heart of her femininity felt feverish and swollen, but it was a delicious malady she suffered from. She throbbed, achingly but wonderfully.

"Jenny, I want you."

He moved his hand between their bodies, covered her breast, kneaded it lovingly. The pad of his middle finger found the sensitive crest and coaxed it into hard arousal.

"Ah, that's sweet." He complimented her as though she had done something miraculous. "So sweet. I want to see it, taste it, taste you."

He ducked his head and kissed her breast through her blouse. His tongue moistly nudged the tight peak. "I want to make love to you." He moved his mouth to her throat, where his lips could touch her warm skin. His voice was hoarse. "Do you understand? I want to be inside you. Deep, deep." His lips claimed hers again, wildly, more demanding.

"Hey, you two, open up." There was banging on the door. "I've brought the party."

Cage lifted his mouth from Jenny's and uttered a vicious obscenity. Then he drew in a shaky breath. He looked back down at Jenny and smiled crookedly. "We can't deliberately hurt her feelings."

Jenny worked herself free of his arms.

He went to the door and welcomed Roxy inside.

# *Nine*

~~~oↄ●ↄo●ↄ●cↄ~~~

Roxy bounced in, carrying a jug of wine in one hand and a grocery sack in the other. "Hey, what's all this?" Cage asked, relieving her of the sack. He peeped inside. "Chips, dips, popcorn, and cheese."

"Just as I said, a party," Roxy chirped happily. "Hi, Jenny. Is the apartment all right?"

"It's fine, thank you."

"Gee, it looks terrific." Roxy whistled as she surveyed the new furniture. Cage had had the deliverymen arrange it as they carried it in, after having consulted with Jenny on where everything was to go. The pieces fit well within the dimensions of the room.

"Got glasses?" Roxy asked. "Come on, let's toast your new place." Without invitation she made her way into the kitchen, with Cage right behind her. Jenny had no choice but to follow, though it was crowded in the small kitchen with all three of them.

Cage ripped open a package of corn chips and popped the lid off a plastic container of prepared dip. He gouged into it with his chip and offered it to Roxy. She took a bite of it, laughing because she was trying to pull the cork out of the wine bottle at the same time. What Roxy didn't eat of the chip and dip, Cage put into his own mouth. Then he licked his fingers.

Jenny remained in the background, feeling out of her element in the midst of their hilarity. She wasn't in a party mood.

"I don't provide this service to all my tenants, you understand," Roxy told Jenny as she washed the price tags off the glasses they had bought that afternoon. Apparently Roxy had no qualms about making herself right at home in a stranger's kitchen. "But since you're a friend of Cage's and he's a friend of mine... Ugh!" She grunted when he reached around her from behind and hugged her hard, his hands locked beneath her lush breasts.

"You betcha. Friends to the bitter end."

"Get away from me, you fool, and slice the cheese."

Jenny felt like a fifth wheel. She didn't belong with them. She didn't know how to participate in their kind of teasing banter. Roxy seemed to know exactly what to say to make Cage burst into laughter. His hands were unintimidated about touching her frequently.

Why their shared familiarity should bother her so much Jenny didn't know. How had she expected them to behave around each other? After all, they were lovers. She knew that. But knowing it and actually witnessing it were two different things. It hurt her to the core that Cage had been kissing her with such tender fervor only seconds before Roxy made her untimely appearance.

Could he turn his passions off and on at will? Had he already forgotten that he had been kissing her, telling her how much he wanted her? Could he transfer his affection from one woman to another so quickly? Apparently he could. The evidence of his chameleon desires was right in front of her.

When the wine was poured, they toasted her new home. Jenny took one sip of the inexpensive vintage. She set her glass down, and, with an "Excuse me" that she wasn't even sure they heard over their laughter, went into the bathroom and closed the door. She barely made it in time to be sick in the commode.

"Jenny?" Cage tapped on the bathroom door a few moments later. His voice was laced with concern. "Is something wrong?"

"I'll be right out," she called through the door. She washed her face, rinsed out her mouth, and combed her fingers through her hair.

"Are you mad at us?" Cage asked the moment she opened the door. "I know how you feel about drinking. This is your place. We didn't mean to offend you."

It was then that she knew she loved him.

Probably she always had. But it wasn't until that moment, that instant, when he was gazing down at her with such contrition, that she realized she did.

She had been deluding herself for all these years, telling herself that if she stayed away from him, her attraction to him would wane. But all this time it had been secretly nestling inside her like an oyster in its shell, gathering grains of knowledge about Cage, a glance, a touch, a sound, until her love for him was like a rare and precious pearl imbedded in her soul.

She wanted to walk into his arms, to be held close, to cling to his strength. But she wouldn't. Couldn't. It was unheard of. Jenny Fletcher and Cage Hendren? Impossible. She was pregnant with another man's child, his brother's child. Even if that weren't so, they were totally unsuited to each other. Had any two people ever been more different? Their being together in any kind of romantic relationship was a hopeless prospect.

Oh, but she loved him!

"No, it isn't that, Cage," she said, giving him a weak smile. "I don't feel too well."

He tensed. "The baby? Is it bad? Cramps? Blood? What? Should I call the doctor?"

"No, no." She put a restraining hand on his arm but immediately withdrew it. "I'm just tired. I was on my feet all day and I think it's catching up with me."

"I should be shot at sunrise," he said. "I should have tucked you into bed the minute we got home."

"I didn't have a bed then."

He scowled at her attempt at humor. "Well, as soon as it was delivered I should have tucked you in." He took her hand and led her into the living room. "Say good-night, Roxy. We're leaving the lady so she can get some rest."

Roxy sprang off the new sofa and looked at Jenny closely. "You're pale as a ghost, honey," she said, laying the back of her hand on Jenny's pallid cheek. "Is there anything I can do?"

*Yes, leave,* Jenny wanted to shout. *And keep your hands off Cage.* Her primary illness was jealousy. She acknowledged it, but she couldn't ward it off. She just wanted Cage's mistress out of her house. "No. I'll be fine after I get to bed," she said tactfully.

Over her protests, Roxy and Cage made up her new bed, spreading the crisp sheets over it. "Tomorrow you might want to wash these and soften them up a bit," Roxy suggested. "If you need any help carrying them into the laundry room, call me."

"Thank you," she said, knowing good and well she'd never be asking Roxy Clemmons for any favors.

When the bed was made to their satisfaction, they gathered up the party snacks and wine. At the front door Cage took both Jenny's hands in his. "Lock up after us."

"I will."

"If you need me, in the middle of the night, anytime, for anything, go to Roxy's and call me."

"Don't worry about me."

"I'll worry about you if I damn well feel like it," he said crossly. "You'll have a phone installed tomorrow."

"But I didn't order—"

He placed his index finger against her lips. "I did, when you went to the ladies' room after lunch. Now, good night and get some sleep." He kissed her mouth softly. His tongue whisked across her lower lip so lightly and fleetingly, she wasn't sure she hadn't imagined it. As he stepped into the night he took Roxy's arm. "Come on, Roxy sweet, I'll walk you home."

Jenny closed the door after them. Cage was going home with Roxy. They would no doubt pick up the party where they'd left off. Images of them together, their mouths sealed, their bodies entwined, flickered through her mind. Miserable, she lay in her new bed for a long time, unable to fall asleep. She was tormented by the thought of Cage with Roxy. Cage with anybody.

It was very late when she heard the Corvette start up where it was still parked outside her door and drive away.

The next day was Saturday, so there was no rush about getting up and going to work. Jenny stripped the sheets off the bed, having already decided before Roxy mentioned it that they would be more comfortable to sleep on after they'd been washed.

Still wearing her robe, she brewed herself a pot of coffee in her new coffeemaker, which had been only one of a hundred items she and Cage had purchased in the housewares department the day before.

She was lifting the first cup to her lips when someone knocked on the door. Peering out the window first to see who it was, she sagged against the wall dispiritedly. She wasn't up to facing Roxy so soon after last night.

"Hi," Roxy said gaily when Jenny opened the door no more than a discouraging crack. "I didn't wake you up, did I?"

"No."

"Good. Cage would have killed me. Listen, I just made this yummy pastry. It's too much for me to eat alone, and if I don't share it, that's exactly what I'll do." She slapped her generous hip. "Then I'll live to regret it."

It would have been ungracious not to invite her in, so Jenny stepped aside, manufactured a smile of sorts, and said, "Come on in. I just made coffee."

"Great." Roxy set her foil-wrapped package on the new butcher block table and eased herself into one of the bentwood chairs. "You have terrific taste," she commented, glancing around the apartment. "I really like your stuff."

"Thank you, but Cage helped me pick it out."

"He's got terrific taste, too." She winked, but Jenny wasn't sure what the wink was supposed to mean. She concentrated on pouring Roxy a cup of coffee. "Cream and sugar?"

"Black with Sweet'n Low...the chubby one says as she slices the gooey dessert," Roxy said, mocking herself as she peeled back the foil. "Got a knife and two plates?"

When the pastry had been sliced and Jenny's portion passed to her, she said politely, "This looks good."

"Doesn't it? I got the recipe out of a magazine." Roxy dug into hers. Jenny was more reserved but found the pastry to be delicious. "Did you need me to help you with anything today, like carrying those linens to the laundry room?" Roxy asked her between bites.

"No, thank you."

"Sure? I'm free."

"I can manage."

"Want another slice?" Roxy said, holding the knife poised over the dessert.

"No, thank you. I appreciate your bringing it, though."

Roxy dropped the knife and placed her forearms on the table. She stared at Jenny with disconcertingly candid brown eyes. "You don't like me, do you?"

Jenny was taken aback. All her life she had avoided confrontations and she couldn't believe she was being forced into this one. She opened her mouth to deny the allegation as diplomatically as she could, but Roxy forestalled her.

"Don't bother denying it. I know you don't and I know why. Because I've slept with Cage."

The color that surged to Jenny's cheeks and the way her eyes fell away from Roxy's were as good as an admission of guilt. Roxy leaned back in her chair. "Well, save your hostility and cut the cool politeness. The truth of it is, I've never been to bed with Cage. Surprised?"

she asked when she read the incredulous expression on Jenny's face.

"Most folks would be." Roxy laughed. "Well, it wasn't for lack of wanting to, or even for lack of opportunity," she said ruefully. "Cage is a very sexy guy. A woman would have to be dead not to wonder what it's like to ride that stallion."

Jenny swallowed hard.

"Did Cage tell you how we met?" Jenny shook her head. "Wanna know?" She took Jenny's silence for consent.

"It was at a dance after a rodeo. My husband...did you know I'd been married?" Again Jenny shook her head speechlessly. "Well, I was. That night my husband was in a bad mood because he couldn't stay on some damn Brahman bull and lost the prize money to another guy. Anyhow, he took it out on me as he always did. Nearly beat me to death."

"He hit you?"

Roxy chuckled at Jenny's innocence. "Yeah, lots of times. Only, that night he was really drunk and got a little carried away. Cage heard me screaming out in the parking lot where Todd—that's his name—had dragged me. Cage beat the hell out of Todd and told him if he ever did that to me again he could expect another going over."

She dipped her finger into the slice of dessert left on her plate and licked the cream cheese off. "This had gone on for years. Todd would get mad, get drunk, get jealous, and beat up on me. But I loved the guy, you know? Besides, I had no one else. Nowhere to go. No money to get there if there was."

"Your parents?"

"My mama died when I was ten. Daddy was a roughneck. He dragged me from one oil field to another. When I got married at sixteen, he felt like he'd done his last fatherly duty and hightailed it to Alaska. Haven't heard from the lousy bastard since. So I was stuck with Todd.

"One night he got so mad, I thought he was going to kill me. He had threatened to before, but this time I think he meant it. Cage had given me his telephone number. I called and he came to get me. He took me to the hospital and paid the bill for having me fixed up. I stayed at his house for over a month after that. That's when folks started saying we were shacking up." She laughed harshly. "I wouldn't have been much fun in the sack. I was busted up real good.

"Todd was furious. He accused us of carrying on behind his back for months, which wasn't true. He drove to Mexico and got a divorce. That was fine with me. Only, then I really had nothing, and I knew I couldn't go on living at Cage's place.

"Cage talked some of his buddies into going partners with him and buying this apartment complex. He installed me as the manager. I get the apartment, plus a salary."

Jenny was transfixed by the tale. She read the newspapers, she watched television. She knew this sort of melodrama went on. She had just never known anyone who had actually experienced that kind of life.

Roxy met her stare levelly. "Cage is the best friend I've ever had. He was the first person in my whole life to care anything about me. I owe him everything, even my life."

She leaned forward across the table. "If he'd asked

me to pay him back in bed, I would have. And probably would have loved every minute of it." She lowered her voice for emphasis. "But he never did, Jenny. I think he knew all along what I came to realize. If we'd become lovers, it would have messed up the friendship. And we both valued that more than getting laid." Her hand reached out to cover Jenny's. "You don't have to be jealous of me."

After long moments of looking at each other, Jenny lowered her gaze. "You misunderstand. Cage and I don't have...we aren't...it's not..."

"Maybe not yet," Roxy said intuitively.

Jenny would have had little doubt as to the future of her relationship with Cage if she could have seen him the night before in Roxy's apartment. It was downright comical. Roxy had seen men in every human condition, but she'd never seen one so lovesick.

Cage had sat on her floor, his back propped against her couch, staring into space, wearing the silliest expression on his face. He had talked about Jenny until Roxy had physically hauled him up and ordered him to go home, telling him that she was sleepy and if she heard Jenny's name one more time, she was going to throw up.

As much to divert the conversation away from her and Cage as to apologize, Jenny said, "I've been so rude to you."

"Naw," Roxy said, dismissing Jenny's apology with a wave. "Forget it. I'm used to being snubbed as a fallen woman."

"I like you," Jenny said bluntly, realizing that it was true. One knew exactly where one stood with Roxy.

There was no pretense. She didn't put on airs and wouldn't let anyone else get by with it, either.

"Good," Roxy replied as if they had reached an agreement after days of debate. "Now eat the rest of this fattening temptation before I do. Your cute little butt can stand it, but my big fat one sure as hell can't."

Laughing, Jenny sliced herself another piece. "I promised Cage I'd eat to gain weight."

"He's worried about the baby."

"He is?" She tried to appear nonchalant but failed.

Roxy grinned. "He thinks you're too dainty to carry it. I assured him you would come through the pregnancy with flying colors."

"I'm not concerned about me. I worry about people punishing the child for something I've done."

"Forget 'people.'"

"That's what Cage says."

"And he's right. Are you glad about the baby?"

"Yes. Very," Jenny confirmed, her eyes shining.

"With his mama and his uncle Cage loving him, the kid'll have no problems," Roxy assured her.

"You never had children?"

Roxy's smile faded. "No. I always wanted kids, but Todd, he, uh…hurt me one time, you know? Ruined all the plumbing and it had to come out."

"Oh, Lord, I'm so sorry!" Jenny exclaimed in a soft voice.

Roxy shrugged. "Hell, I'm getting too old to have a kid anyway and Gary says it doesn't matter to him."

"Gary?"

"He's the guy I'm seeing," Roxy said, her ebullience restored. "Cage introduced us. He works for the phone company. In fact, he should be here soon to install your phone."

From Roxy's description Jenny was expecting Gary to be a cross between a Playgirl centerfold and Prince Valiant. He was neither. He had big ears, a long nose, and a toothy grin, but his face beamed wholesomeness and a self-effacing good humor.

It was obvious to Jenny within moments of his arrival that he and Roxy were madly in love.

"I wanted to come to the party last night and welcome you to the neighborhood," Gary said, pumping Jenny's hand, "but I got called out on an emergency. Where do you want your phones?"

"Phones? Plural?"

"Three."

"Three?"

"That's what Cage ordered. I suggest the bedroom, living room, and kitchen."

"But—"

"You might just as well go along with it, Jenny, if that's what Cage ordered," Roxy said.

"Oh, all right."

While Gary went about his business Roxy helped Jenny organize her kitchen. Later they laundered all the new bed linens and towels before folding and storing them. They talked nonstop. By noon Jenny felt she had known the other woman all her life. Despite their separate backgrounds, they liked each other immensely.

"Anybody hungry?" Cage stuck his head through the front door, which Gary had left open on one of his trips to his truck.

Jenny was so relieved to learn that Cage and Roxy hadn't been lovers, she turned toward the door at the sound of his voice and flashed him a dazzling smile. She rushed forward, stopping just short of flinging herself in his arms.

"Well, don't stop there," he said softly.

She closed the remaining distance between them and hugged him, even going so far as to boldly slide her hands beneath his denim vest. "Hi," she whispered shyly when she backed away.

"Hi." He made three syllables out of one. His eyes were busily scanning her face. "Tell me what I did to deserve that welcome and I'll do it some more."

"I'm mad at you."

"Stay mad. I like it. Hug me again."

"Once is enough."

"But my hands are full and I can't hug back, so you've got to hug me twice."

It was pure madness, but in her state of mind it made perfect sense. She reached around him again and linked her hands behind his back, tilting her head back to look up at him. "Now, what are you mad about?" he asked.

"What am I going to do with three telephones?"

"Save yourself a lot of steps." He kissed her quickly. "But you were glad to see me. I could tell. Why?"

"You brought lunch," she quipped, nodding toward the sacks he held in his hands.

"You like cheeseburgers?"

"With onions?"

"Yes," he answered warily.

"Love 'em."

The four of them had a riotously gay lunch together. "I think you guys planned this," Roxy said suspiciously, biting into a fat golden French fry.

"I didn't plan this," Cage swore, crossing his heart. "Did you plan this, Gary?"

"I didn't plan this," he said, licking salt off his fingers. "Pass me one of those little catsup doodads, please."

"Roxy and I might have made other plans for lunch," Jenny said loftily.

Cage grinned at her, pleased that she could easily join in the joking now. "We assumed you didn't."

"Assumed, huh? Don't start taking us for granted," Roxy warned. "Right, Jenny?"

"Right."

She would have taken a bite of her cheeseburger then, but Cage leaned down and kissed her solidly on the mouth.

She never remembered being happier or feeling freer. Despite her pregnancy, Jenny felt like she had shed a hundred pounds. She had left the parsonage behind like an old skin. Her whole being breathed new life.

But she didn't shirk her responsibilities at the church. She attended regularly and Cage went with her. They sat near the back and rarely saw Bob except in the pulpit. If he knew they were there, he gave no sign. They didn't see Sarah where she sat in her usual place in the second row.

She and Cage could feel the furtive glances cast in their direction and hear the whispered conversations they left in their wake, but they spoke politely to everyone. With Cage by her side, it was easy for Jenny to hold her head high and walk proudly.

She became more involved with work in the office. She had graduated from answering the telephone and writing correspondence to handling filing and research that Cage had never intended her to do.

"You're going to wear yourself out," he said one day when he stopped by to leave some mail and found her still there.

"What time is it?"

"Long after five o'clock."

"This is so interesting. I lost track of time."

"Don't expect me to pay you overtime."

"I owe you the time. I went to the doctor today on my lunch hour."

"Your lunch hour and a half."

"Whatever. Anyway, they were running behind and that put me late getting back, so stop bugging me."

"You're getting pretty feisty, Miss Fletcher. If you don't watch your step, I'm going to give up the idea of marrying you and start looking for a nice docile girl who will treat me with the respect I deserve."

She folded the chart. "If you were treated with the respect you deserve, you'd get a thrashing."

"Hm, that sounds…interesting." He came up behind her where she was now standing at the file cabinet, encircled her waist with his arms, and nuzzled her neck.

"Don't tell me you're into S and M."

"S and M?" He laughed, lifting his lips from her neck but keeping her imprisoned between him and the file cabinet. "What do you know about S and M?"

"Lots. Roxy has a book that gives step-by-step instructions."

"Roxy's corrupting you. I should have known better than to entrust you to her. Don't look at any more of her books."

"You don't have to worry that I'd get involved in anything involving whips and chains. It all looks painful. Besides," she teased, "I don't think those skimpy black leather outfits would look very good on my new figure."

"I think your new figure would look delicious in anything. It's lovely."

He lowered his hands to her abdomen and massaged soothingly, before moving them down to stroke the tops of her thighs through her skirt. Jenny whimpered and struggled to turn around. He allowed her to, but facing him didn't give her any freedom. If anything, it made her situation more precarious. "I've got to go, Cage."

"Later." He moved her hair aside with his nose and dedicated himself to pleasuring her ear.

"It's getting late," she gasped when she felt the wet stroke of his tongue. "I should be getting home."

"Later."

The word was spoken against her open lips and when he closed his mouth over hers, all her resistance melted. He braced his hands on the file cabinet and leaned into her, pressing his body against hers. He eased away, then leaned forward again, as though doing push-ups against the cabinet. Every time his body brushed against hers, the contact set off electric charges in her.

Moving his hands to her neck, he closed his fingers around it loosely, deepening the kiss as he did so.

"Hm, Cage, no," she protested feebly when she managed to work her mouth free. It was a bone-melting, mind-stealing kiss and she could feel herself succumbing to it.

"Why not?"

"Because it's unhealthy."

He moved against her suggestively. "I beg to differ."

The proof of his healthy condition probed the soft

delta between her thighs. "We shouldn't…" He moved again and she groaned in spite of her best intentions to remain immune. "We shouldn't do this in here, in your place of business."

"How about my house?"

"No."

"Your apartment?"

"No."

"Then where?"

"Nowhere. We shouldn't be doing this anywhere."

Recently, every time he kissed her, she was reminded of the night with Hal. Cage's kisses evoked memories that were startlingly vivid. The brothers kissed with similar intensity, their caresses were equally stimulating. But somehow, by responding to Cage's kisses, she felt she was betraying Hal. Had she trembled in his arms the way she did every time Cage touched her?

"Jenny, please."

"No."

"I ache. I haven't been with a woman since—" He stuttered to a halt just before saying, "Since making love to you." He changed it to "For a long time."

"Whose fault is that?"

"Yours. I don't want anybody but you."

"Go to one of your old haunts. I'm sure you'll find an obliging lady." She would die if he did. Each day she figuratively held her breath, wondering when Cage would tire of spending so much time with her and resort to his carousing. She felt compelled to press her luck. "Or check out the grocery store."

"Invite me over tonight."

"No."

"You've been living in your apartment three weeks and I've been invited inside exactly twice."

"And that was two times too many. You stay too long and don't behave while you're there." Lord, she wished he'd stop kissing her neck that way. It felt so good. "People are seeing us together around town and they're starting to talk."

"What else have they got to talk about? It isn't football season."

"Don't you see? When word gets out that I'm pregnant, everybody will jump to the conclusion that—" She didn't finish.

His head came up and his eyes drilled into hers. "What conclusion will they jump to?"

"That the baby is yours," she answered, staring at the collar button on his shirt, unable to meet his eyes.

"And would that be so terrible?" His voice was as gravelly and emotion-packed as hers.

"I don't want you to be blamed for something you didn't do."

"I wouldn't consider it being blamed. I wouldn't mind in the least taking the credit for fathering your baby."

"But that wouldn't be right, Cage."

"I've been blamed for things I didn't do before. People make up their own minds. If they get the facts jumbled, there's little you can do to change public opinions."

"I don't believe that."

"Didn't you think that Roxy was my lover?"

"No!"

"You can't lie worth a damn, Jenny," he taunted. "You even called her one of my sluts. You thought we were having an affair. That's why you pouted all the way home that night after I took you off the bus."

"If I was pouting, it was because I'm not used to being chased down by a maniac who has the unmitigated gall to stop a Greyhound bus and haul somebody off it."

Her flare of temper delighted him. "God, you're cute." He kissed the end of her nose. "But you're not going to get off the hook by changing the subject. You thought Roxy and I had a thing going, didn't you?"

"Well, can you blame me?" she said defensively. "You can't keep your hands off her."

He squeezed her rib cage where his hands were currently resting. "I can't keep my hands off you either, so we know that's not conclusive evidence that two people are sleeping together."

She felt flustered from the inside out. "Which only brings me back to my original point. You shouldn't touch me all the time." Her voice lacked conviction even to her own ears.

"You don't like it when I touch you?"

Who wouldn't like it? Who wouldn't like the way his thumbs lightly grazed the undersides of her breasts while his strong fingers aligned themselves to her ribs? "I sure like touching you," he whispered as his hands slid around her back and drew her close for another kiss that she was powerless to resist.

"Ask me to supper, Jenny. What's the harm in having dinner at your house?"

"Because when Cage Hendren has dinner at a woman's house, it automatically implies more than eating a meal."

Their mouths continued to come together and drift apart in soft, damp caresses. "Gossip."

"Based on truth."

"Okay, I confess. I want to spend an evening alone

with you. Get in a little necking and heavy breathing. What's wrong with that?"

"Everything."

"All right," he sighed. "I asked you nice, but you want to play rough. I'm not letting you leave this office until you invite me to your apartment for dinner. Now, I can stand here till doomsday kissing you, only, I'm getting very aroused."

He wedged his legs between hers and fit their hips snugly together. "Soon, kissing's not going to be enough. I'll be driven to undo those buttons on your blouse. I've counted. There are exactly four. That should take three seconds, three and a half at the most. Then I'll know if your brassiere is lilac or blue. I know it's sheer, but I can't quite tell the color. And then—"

She pushed him away. His grin was undiluted devilry, but he spoke like a good little boy who had just gotten all A's. "I'm free Friday night."

"Don't play so hard to get, Cage," she said sarcastically.

"Jenny, where you're concerned I'm as easy as Ruda Beth Graham was in the tenth grade."

"Oh, you're horrible!" She shoved him aside and picked up her purse. "You're blackmailing me again, but come at seven o'clock."

"Six."

She shot him a disparaging look and reached for the doorknob. "Jenny?" She turned back. "What color is that brassiere?"

"That's for me to know," she said saucily as she swung out the door.

"And for me to find out," Cage said with a sly grin.

# *Ten*

Jenny flattened her hand over her stomach in the hope of subduing the butterflies inside. She wet her lips. She touched her hair. She drew a deep breath and opened her front door.

Cage was standing on her threshold. He was wearing a pair of tailored brown slacks, a light cream-colored shirt, and a camel sport jacket. The ensemble couldn't have been better coordinated with his own sandy coloring.

His hair was clean and shiny, but, as usual, any styling had been left to chance. As tousled as it was, he could have just gotten out of bed. Indeed, that was what his expression insinuated. His eyes looked like smoky Mexican topaz as they toured Jenny. One corner of his sensuous mouth was hiked into a sly smile.

"Hi," she said timidly.

"Are you dessert?" he drawled. "If so, I'm opting to skip dinner."

The butterflies soared and sailed despite her previous efforts to calm them.

The sensations pulsing through her were ridiculous.

She had spent the morning with Cage in his office, catching up on the week's correspondence. They had worked companionably, in carefree camaraderie.

Where had this tension between them come from? What had caused this tingling awareness? The air crackled with suppressed sexuality, and she knew Cage felt it as keenly as she did.

As long as they were working, they were able to control these undercurrents. But the moment they let down that professional barrier, the latent desire between them began to churn and bubble like the waters in a hot tub.

Jenny had left the office at noon, as she did every Friday. But this afternoon she hadn't rested. She had thrown herself wholeheartedly into preparations for the evening. She wanted the meal, the apartment, herself to be perfect.

With each passing hour her expectancy had mounted until now, when she stood face-to-face with him, she felt like fainting.

"Are those for me?"

He was holding a large bouquet of pink roses and baby's breath. The long stems were wrapped in green tissue and they filled the air with nature's sweetest perfume.

"Do you have a twin?"

"No."

"Then I guess they're for you." He passed them to her and she moved aside so he could step into the room. He halted before he had taken two steps. "What the—"

He gazed around him in awe. The room had undergone a transformation since he'd last seen it. Jenny had spent her lunch hours and afternoons browsing through thrift shops and garage sales looking for "goodies."

With Roxy's help she had made the apartment into a home, and she was proud of the results. She was twenty-six years old, yet this was the first time in her life that she'd had the privilege of choosing her own decor in her own home. Unlike her room in the parsonage, there wasn't a ruffle to be found. Her taste was simple and elegant, but warm.

"Do you like it?" she asked anxiously, wringing her hands.

"Like it? I may move in tonight."

She laughed, knowing he wasn't suggesting anything illicit, only complimenting her on a job well done.

"I paid a decorator an astronomical fee to do my house. I should have let you do it. I didn't know you had a hidden talent for this kind of thing." Cage scoured her speculatively with narrowed eyes. "What else do you have a hidden talent for?"

She felt a swell of emotion and rushed to lighten the mood. "You should have seen Roxy bargaining over the plants. We found them at a garage sale. The man was asking fifty dollars for all of them. Roxy got him down to ten, then called Gary to come over in his pickup and load them up before the man changed his mind. I rode in the back of the truck so none of them would get crushed."

"I would protect my benjaminia with my life. I couldn't stand for it to get crushed."

His face was too angelic for her not to be suspicious. There was a play on words in there somewhere, but she had better sense than to ask him to expound.

She cleared her throat. "I bought the bentwood rocker there, too, for five dollars. All it needed was a coat of paint."

"I like what you did to that wall."

"The fabric was a remnant I found at Kmart. Roxy helped me tack it to the wall so I would get the pattern straight." She had used what was left over to make small throw pillows for the sofa.

The colors she had selected to accent her new furniture were restful, yet oddly stimulating—mulberry, navy, slate and beige. "The candles smell good," Cage said, nodding toward the attractive arrangement on the end table.

"I found the brass candlesticks in an antiques store, one of those dim, ratty places out on the Pecos highway. I had to move aside cobwebs to get to them. It took two cans of Brasso and three nights of elbow grease to polish them up."

"Everything looks great."

"Thank you," she replied demurely.

"Especially you." He suddenly bent his head to kiss her. She expected a soft, fraternal, hello-type kiss. Instead, his lips were commanding and his tongue bold. After several moments, she pulled away breathlessly.

"I'd better get these flowers in water before they wilt."

*Or before I do,* she thought as she hurried into the kitchen to look for something to serve as a vase worthy of the roses. She didn't have anything, and they ended up in an orange juice carafe. She had already arranged a bunch of heather to serve as an abstract centerpiece for the dining table, so she carried the roses into the living room and, with an apologetic smile for their humble container, placed them on the coffee table.

"Is that a new outfit?"

"Yes," she answered nervously. "Roxy picked it out and made me buy it."

"I'm glad she did."

The long skirt and oversized blouse were raw silk in its natural color, and unlike anything that Jenny had worn before. A wide braided belt was knotted around her waist. She had on the flat, ankle-strap shoes Cage had admired before. Her hair had been swept up, but with a calculated messiness so that soft wisps escaped to lie on her neck and cheeks.

"It's sort of a Gypsy look," she said, self-conscious under his assessing eyes. "I only let Roxy talk me into it because the blouse has a long tail and will be full enough to wear when I start showing."

"Turn around." She made a slow three-hundred-and-sixty degree pivot until she faced him again. "I love it," he said with a slow smile. "But are you sure you're in there? All that cloth is camouflaging."

"I'm in here, all right," she said, patting her tummy. "I've gained two pounds."

"Good for you! Does the doctor say everything is okay?" His brow wrinkled with concern. "You're halfway through your pregnancy, but you barely show."

"Barely show? You should see me without my clothes on."

"I'd like that."

His expression was altogether too sexy. "What I mean is," Jenny said quickly, "I'm showing a little in my tummy. The doctor said the baby is growing nicely. He's just the right size for almost five months."

"He?"

"The doctor thinks it's a boy because of the heartbeat. Typically, boys have a slower heartbeat than girls."

"Then I'm atypical," Cage whispered. "My heart's racing."

"Why?" His amber eyes seemed to pull at her like a magnet. She inclined toward him slightly.

"I'm still thinking about seeing you without your clothes on."

The impulse to gravitate toward him was almost irresistible, but she drew on enough self-discipline not to. Pulling herself both mentally and physically away from him, she turned toward the louvered half doors that led into the kitchen. "I need to check on dinner."

"What are we having? It smells scrumptious."

He reached the swinging doors in time to see her bending down to check the simmering contents in the oven. The view was captivating and stirred up another of Cage's appetites, one more ravenous than that in his stomach.

"Stuffed pork chops, asparagus with hollandaise… Do you like asparagus?" He nodded and she looked relieved. "Potatoes with parsley and butter, hot rolls, and Milky Way ice cream."

"You're kidding! Milky Way ice cream?"

"No, I'm not kidding, and I paid for the Milky Way bars."

He ignored the jibe and pushed through the swinging doors. As soon as she had slid a cookie sheet of rolls into the oven, he clasped her arms and turned her to face him. "Trying to impress me?"

"Why do you ask that?"

"You went to a lot of trouble for me." He captured a free strand of her hair and wound it around his index finger. "Why, Jenny?"

"I like to cook." She watched, mesmerized, as he

lifted the strand of her hair to his lips and kissed it, at the same time drawing her face dangerously close to his. "And…and…uh, your parents didn't like to experiment. I like to try out new recipes, but they always wanted to eat the same—"

His mouth stopped the flow of nervous chatter with a kiss. "Do I get to choose dessert?" he asked in a soft murmur when he lifted his lips from hers.

"No."

"I choose you," he said, heedless of her denial. "You're the sweetest thing I've ever tasted."

He moved forward until he had backed her against the countertop. It caught her in the small of her back. Cage molded his body to hers in a complementing fit that left little doubt as to who was female and who was male. Seconds later she was shamelessly responding to the subtle nudges against her middle, and her hands were crawling up his back. The fiery embrace lasted until the smell of warm yeast rolls permeated the small kitchen.

"Cage," Jenny gasped, drawing enough breath to dispel the ringing in her ears, "the rolls are burning."

"Who gives a damn?" he growled against her throat.

"I do." She pushed him away. "I worked hard on them."

He sighed and stepped back so she could retrieve the rolls from the oven. "Do you mind if I take off my jacket?"

"Are you too warm?"

For answer one of his sand-colored eyebrows arched upward. "Hot, Jenny, darling, hot."

He joined her at the table a few moments later in his shirtsleeves. "This looks delicious," he said, seating her before he sat down. She served him and waited anxiously for his verdict after the first bite. "Better than my mother used to make," he said.

Pleased, she smiled and began eating. "Have you seen them, Cage?"

"Who? Oh, Mother and Dad? No. At least not to speak to. Have you?"

"No. I feel guilty about driving this wedge between them and you."

He laughed mirthlessly. "Jenny, that wedge has been there since I was old enough to toddle."

"But my moving out and the baby have made things worse. I hate that. I was hoping you'd be drawn closer together. They need you now."

His eyes wandered around the apartment. "You know, I think they'd be jealous if they could see what you've done here."

"Jealous?"

"Yes. I think they wanted you to need them as much as they needed you. And you didn't. You don't. They were afraid to let out your leash on the chance you'd discover that. So they kept you bound to them by obligation."

"That's unfair, Cage. They're not manipulative."

"Don't get me wrong," he said, covering her hand briefly. "I didn't mean to suggest that they did all this consciously. They'd be horrified to think themselves capable of such selfishness.

"But think about it, Jenny. I wasn't what they wanted their son to be, so they gave up on me completely and poured all their hopes and energies into Hal. Luckily he was a perfect candidate for what they had in mind and they groomed him meticulously. Then you came along. You were a sweet, obedient little girl who would make them a charming daughter-in-law."

"I'm sure they don't feel that way now."

"I'm sure they don't either, but it's healthier for everyone this way. You're a free agent. That doesn't mean you love them less." He shook his head in puzzlement. "That's what they never could understand. I loved them. I wanted them to love me. If they had shown me any affection, I wouldn't have been so unmanageable. It wouldn't have been necessary." His eyes came back to hers. "You've rebelled in your own way. Maybe this time they'll see the light."

"I hope so. I hate to think of them alone in that big house after having suffered Hal's death. I guess sooner or later, with or without our support, they'll adjust to the loss."

"And what about you, Jenny? Have you adjusted to it?"

Finished eating, she laid her knife and fork diagonally on her plate. "I miss him. Hal and I were very close. We used to talk for hours." A vein was ticking in Cage's temple, but she didn't notice as she went on musingly. "He was such a sweet person. I don't think he would have intentionally hurt anybody."

"Do you still love him?"

She was on the verge of saying, "I'm not sure I ever did," but she caught herself in time. For years she had thought she was in love with Hal. Had she only been trying to convince herself that it was so?

She had had a deep and abiding affection for him, but his kisses had never made her dizzy as Cage's did. Her heart hadn't begun to flutter each time Hal walked into a room. No, she had never felt this yearning, aching need for Hal the way she did for Cage. It was a persistent longing, as constant as her heartbeat.

Out of respect for Hal, she couldn't discuss her feelings for him with Cage. She evaded giving him a definitive answer. "I'll always love Hal in a special way."

Cage was unaccustomed to being put off. He never skirted an issue and wasn't going to tolerate it from Jenny. "If he were still alive, would you want to marry him?"

Her eyes flickered toward his, then away. "There would be the baby to—"

"If the baby weren't a consideration?"

She hesitated, because she had to come to terms with that hour spent in bed with Hal. Had it only been one of those magical comets of emotion that rocket through one's life before burning out? Had it been a fluke? Had each of them been so emotionally high strung that particular night that it had been easy to lose their heads?

She was beginning to believe that such was the case. As splendid as it had been for her, she now knew that her passion wasn't necessarily limited to one person. She had been just as aroused by Cage's kisses as she had been by Hal's that night.

Knowing that he was waiting for her answer, she softly replied, "No, I don't think so. After living on my own, I realize that Hal and I weren't intended to be man and wife. Friends. Good friends. Perhaps brother and sister. But I don't think I would have been the kind of wife Hal needed for the life he chose."

Cage kept his features under control so that his relief and elation wouldn't show. "Let me help you with the dishes," he said, standing.

"You haven't had your dessert yet."

"I'm letting the anticipation build."

His inflection hinted at an underlying meaning, but again Jenny thought it best not to pursue it. His eyes held a golden glint that was only partially due to candlelight.

They conversed easily while they cleared up the kitchen. The second oil well had come in on the Parsons' property and a third was already being drilled. Cage had his eyes on another tract of land he was sure topped a basin of oil.

Jenny loved the excitement that he emanated when he talked about wildcatting. He was successful, but money wasn't his incentive. The challenge, the gamble, and the flirtation with disaster were what motivated him. Most would call him reckless, but she knew better. He drove fast, but he knew what he was doing behind the wheel of a car. He used the same dashing skill in his business dealings.

He dished up the ice cream, unabashedly licking the dipper as he did so, while Jenny arranged the coffee things on a tray. Together they moved into the living room. "Don't drip any of that on my new sofa," Jenny scolded as Cage raised a spoonful of the ice cream to his mouth.

"Sinful, positively sinful." He let the ice cream melt in his mouth.

"Then it's true what they say?"

"What's that?"

"That the way to a man's heart is through his stomach."

He was holding the spoon upside down in his mouth. His tongue cleaned out its shallow bowl, then he pulled it through his lips slowly as he gazed at Jenny. "That's one way to get there, I guess, but I can think of another route that's much more fun to take. Want me to give you the guided tour?"

"Cream or sugar?" she asked in a thin, high voice.

He chuckled at her shaking hand as she poured his coffee. "Jenny, you've been pouring coffee for me for years. You know I drink it black."

"I forgot."

"Like hell. You're just all atremble over what I said."

"It was outrageous and uncouth." She still couldn't look him straight in the eye. Her cheeks were burning.

"You're a paradox," he observed, leaning back against the cushions to drink his coffee. He had finished his ice cream and had set the empty bowl on the tray.

"A paradox?"

"Yes. You're carrying a child, yet anytime the subject of sex is even hinted at, you come all undone."

Her sweet tooth suddenly went sour and she set aside her bowl of ice cream after having taken only a few bites. "You think I'm a prude, a holdover from another era, a Victorian dinosaur trying to survive in the age of sexual enlightenment?"

"Don't put words in my mouth. I didn't mean to imply any such thing. Your innocence is endearing."

"I'm hardly innocent," she mumbled, her chin tucked against her chest. She closed her eyes, recalling the sound of her own breathing at the point of climax. The moans of fulfillment echoed in her head even now when she remembered how her body had exploded into full bloom like an exotic neon flower. She could feel again her back bowing, her hips lifting, her limbs quaking, all greedily experiencing the pleasure.

"You said you were a virgin the night—"

"I was."

"Never before?"

"No."

"Close?"

"No."

Cage placed his coffee cup on the tray. He moved closer to her, resting his bent elbow on the back of the sofa. He lightly stroked her cheek with his knuckles. "You must have been deeply moved that night to give away what you had cherished for so long."

"I've never felt like that in my life."

Cage's heart leaped in his chest. What he was about to do was unforgivable, but that had never deterred him. "Tell me how you felt."

Deep in thought, Jenny unconsciously lifted her hand to his chest. Her fingers strummed the placket of his shirt. "It was like I had stepped out of myself and was watching what was happening to someone else. I shed all my inhibitions. I cast aside the restrictions I normally impose on myself. I existed only for those moments. I became purely carnal, and yet my spirit had never felt more elevated or expanded." She raised her eyes to his like a confused little girl. "Do you understand what I mean?"

"Yes. Perfectly," he answered honestly.

"Nothing that we did seemed sordid or wrong. It was all beautiful. I wanted to love and to be loved. It wasn't enough to verbalize our love; I wanted it demonstrated."

"And Hal was willing?"

"Not at first."

His hand cradled one side of her face. "But you talked him into it."

"That's a nice way of saying I seduced him."

"All right, you seduced him. What happened then?"

She smiled and ducked her head shyly. "Then he was more than willing. He'd never been that way with me before."

"What way?" If Jenny had been looking at Cage's face, she would have read the hungry expression there.

She closed her eyes briefly, as though to get a hold of herself and carefully choose her words. Cage studied the path her tongue took as it wet her lower lip before she continued. "Lusty, a trifle wild, sensual." She laughed lightly. "I don't know how to describe him."

"Rough? Too rough?"

"No, I didn't mean to imply that."

"Tender?"

"Yes. Through it all, he was extremely gentle, but… passionate."

"Were you afraid when he slipped your nightgown off?" Her eyes swung up to his inquiringly and Cage cursed himself for a careless damn fool. "You were wearing a nightgown, weren't you?"

For the last few minutes his soft, sand-raspy voice had been inducing a trance, and like someone who is hypnotized, she had responded to it. But his last question snapped her out of her stupor. "I shouldn't be talking to you about this, Cage."

"Why not?"

"It's embarrassing," she cried softly. "Besides, it's not fair to Hal. Why do you want to know about that night?"

"Because I'm curious."

"That's sick!"

"Not sick, Jenny, normal." He leaned over her, forcing her against the corner cushions of the sofa. He braced one hand on the back cushion, the other on the armrest, and trapped her in the triangle his arms formed. "I want to know what you think about making love."

"Why?" she asked on a near sob.

He lowered his head until his words fell as soft, emphatic puffs of air against her lips. "Because I want to make love to you. You've resisted me at every turn. I want to know what made you step out of yourself that night. What made you live only for the moment? What did your lover do that made you shed those inhibitions and lift the restrictions you normally impose on yourself? What made you purely carnal? In short, Jenny, what turned you on?"

In spite of herself, she was aroused by his demanding tone and the hard strength of his body as it stretched across hers. Her chest was rising and falling with accelerated breathing. Her eyes were incapable of leaving the magnetic field of his.

"Was it the setting that broke through your reserve?" he asked. "Did he set such a romantic scene you couldn't restrain yourself?"

She shook her head and heard herself answer. "It happened in my room."

"God knows that wasn't sexy."

"It was dark."

Cage reached above and behind her, almost covering her, and switched off the lamp on the end table. She hadn't noticed until now that he had turned off the lights in the kitchen and dining alcove as they left them. They were plunged into darkness, save for the incandescent glow of the candles. They cast long, wavering shadows on the walls and highlighted the rugged planes of his face. "Like that?"

"No. Totally dark. I couldn't see anything."

"Nothing?" His strong fingers delved in her hair and held her head steady, forcing her eyes to do battle with his.

"No."

"You couldn't see your lover's face?"

"No."

"Didn't you want to?"

"Yes, yes, yes," she moaned and tried to turn her head away. He wouldn't let her.

"Then this is better. Look at your lover's face this time, Jenny. For godsake look at all of me."

His mouth came down hard on hers and she was ready for it. Her lips responded to the possessive fury of his and parted to receive the thrilling thrust of his tongue. Her arms slid under his and around his back. She kneaded the rippling muscles beneath his shirt.

"What did he say to you, Jenny?" He breathed kisses across her cheeks and mouth. "Did he tell you all the things you wanted and needed to hear?"

While his lips toyed with hers, her mind went on a probing search into her memory. "He said…" She drew a blank. "He didn't say anything."

"Nothing?"

"No. I think he sighed my name…once."

"He didn't tell you how beautiful and desirable you are?"

"I'm not."

"You are, my love, you are. So beautiful." His breath was warm and moist as he whispered directly into her ear. "You can feel how hard I am, Jenny. How can you think you're not desirable? I desire you. I want you more than I've ever wanted any woman."

"Cage," she whimpered when he finally released her mouth from an inflaming kiss. He licked her lips gently, flicking at the corners teasingly.

His hand slid to her waist and untied her belt. He touched her throat and caressed her chest with his callused fingertips. "Did he tell you that your skin is as soft as silk?"

His head dipped lower to nuzzle her neck with his nose and mouth. "And that you smell heavenly?" He planted a hot kiss in the hollow of her throat, applying his tongue.

She was unmindful of the buttons on her blouse being undone until she felt him moving it aside. His harsh whisper could have been a curse but might have been a prayer. He groaned. He touched her lovingly. Jenny closed her eyes and reveled in the sensations his stroking fingers and soothing palms elicited.

"He should have told you that your breasts are beautiful." He kissed her through her brassiere. "That your nipples are delicate and sweet and perfect. He should have said all that. Because it's true." Deftly he unhooked the fastener and peeled away the veil-sheer cups. "Ah, Jenny, let me love you."

And, holding her cupped in his hands, he did.

Jenny hadn't known kisses could be so adoring and yet so hedonistic, that lips could suckle so ardently without causing pain, or that a tongue could be so nimble but still unhurried.

His caresses went on and on until she was swirling in an effervescent ocean of feeling. Geysers of sensation sprung up along her nerve endings. She knew it was wrong to relive her night of loving Hal with his brother. But she had stepped through the boundaries of common sense long ago and there was no retreating now. She had fallen victim to Cage's legendary charm. Jenny Fletcher would now be listed on the roster of his lovers, but somehow she couldn't help but believe that tonight was different for Cage, too.

"Did you like the feel of his body against yours, Jenny?"

"Yes."

"The touch of his skin?"

"He didn't undress," she confessed breathlessly as his mouth continued to play upon her breasts.

"And you?"

"Yes, I was…"

"Naked?"

"Yes."

"And how did you feel about that?"

She thought back to that moment when her night-gown had been stripped from her body and she had lain naked and vulnerable beneath her lover. "I felt no shame. I only wanted…"

"What?"

"Never mind."

"What?" he pressed.

"To feel him against me."

He levered himself up and penetrated her eyes with his. "Unbutton my shirt."

She hesitated only a moment before she lowered her eyes from his and looked at the first fastened button on his shirt. She watched her fingers move toward it mind-lessly, as though obeying an unspoken command. The button slipped through its hole. All the others followed.

She sighed a soft yearning sound deep in her throat when his chest was revealed. The sun-kissed brown hair spread over the sculpted muscles like a wide golden fan. His nipples were dark in the dim light.

Tears gathered in Jenny's eyes. His masculine perfection made her want to weep. He was beautiful. She caught the fabric of his shirt in her hands and peeled it back over his shoulders and down his arms as far as it would go. Her hands smoothed over him. His skin was tan and sleek, spattered with coppery freckles on the tops of his shoulders. Her fingertips traced the faint blue lines of veins in the bulging biceps.

Gradually he lowered himself over her until they were chest to breast, hair-roughened skin to smooth, masculine muscle to feminine softness.

"Jenny, Jenny, Jenny."

Their mouths meshed as surely as their bodies did. He settled against her carefully, rolling slightly to his side, so she wouldn't absorb all of his weight. He felt the pounding of her heart against his. The tips of her breasts felt achingly sweet against his furred skin.

He loved her. God he loved her. And he couldn't believe that she was finally going to be his.

"Aren't you glad we got the soft couch?"

"Hm. Is this what you had in mind when you persuaded me to buy it?"

"This and more."

They kissed. Eternally. Erotically.

"Jenny, let's go to bed."

"Cage—"

"I won't hurt you. I swear it."

"It's not that."

"Then what?"

"Oh, please don't touch me there," she gasped.

"Isn't it good?"

"Oh, Lord. Too good. Cage, please—"

"Like that? There?"

"Yes."

Their mouths dissolved together.

"Touch me," he pleaded.

"Where?"

"Anywhere."

She laid her hand on his breast. His nipple shrank to a tiny tight pebble against her fingertips.

"Oh, God, I'm dying. Come to bed with me, Jenny."

"I can't."

"Don't you want me?"

She answered with an arching thrust against his hardness. He took it to mean yes. Easing up, he offered her his hand. She placed hers in his palm and rose off the couch willingly. They headed toward the bedroom.

The front door vibrated with a resounding knock, which was followed by a blistering curse from Cage.

"What the hell!"

Jenny dove for the sofa, yanked up her blouse, shoved her arms in the sleeves, and fumbled with the buttons. She stuffed her discarded brassiere beneath the nearest cushion.

Apparently Cage wasn't worried about his giveaway dishevelment. He stormed to the front door with his shirttails flapping and hauled it open with a vicious jerk.

Roxy and Gary were standing on the threshold.

"Is the building on fire?" Cage snarled.

"No."

"Then good night."

He tried to slam the door in their faces, but Roxy caught it just in time. "It is, however, a matter of life and death. If Gary and I don't get married tonight, I'm going to kill myself."

# Eleven

"**M**arried!" Jenny exclaimed, stepping around Cage. Astonishment had overriden modesty. She had forgotten her mussed condition until Roxy's eyes lit up with amusement.

"Did we interrupt something important?" Roxy asked, batting her eyelashes with comic innocence. Cage's scowl deepened.

"Sorry about that, pal," Gary mumbled apologetically.

"Then make this quick and leave."

"Cage, didn't you hear what Roxy said? They're getting married."

"That's right." Roxy looped her arm through Gary's and squeezed it against her voluptuous breast. "That is if you'll go with us to El Paso and drive Gary's car back."

"You're serious, aren't you?" Cage asked, his eyes going back and forth between the two of them. He was just now recovering from his frustration. "You're really getting married?"

"Yes!" Roxy said, beaming.

"Well, hey, that's great!" Cage pumped Gary's hand, then gave Roxy a bear hug.

"Congratulations, Gary," Jenny said. Getting into the spirit of the occasion, she gave him a big hug, which made the tops of his large ears turn beet red. She clasped Roxy to her. "I'm so happy for you."

"Me, too, kid, me, too. He's the best thing that's ever happened to me. I don't deserve him."

"Yes, you do." Jenny smiled at her and they hugged again.

"Now, what's this about driving to El Paso?" Cage asked when the two women fell apart, dabbing at their moist eyes.

"We've got reservations on a noon flight from there to Acapulco tomorrow. Gary's so conventional," Roxy teased, "he thinks we should get married before the honeymoon.

"So we're driving to El Paso tonight to a justice of the peace. We want you to go along so you can bring Gary's car back, if you don't mind picking us up in a week and bringing us home. Besides, it'll be more fun having you there with us when we tie the knot."

Gary stood by, wearing a silly grin and nodding his head in agreement to Roxy's explanation.

Cage flashed his notorious grin. "I'm game. Jenny?"

It was after ten o'clock. She couldn't imagine striking out on such a trip in the middle of the night. Between here and El Paso there was nothing but sand, tumbleweeds and jackrabbits.

But the idea of such an impetuous trip was exciting and unlike anything she'd ever done before. She had come to like Roxy and Gary tremendously and wanted to be a witness to their marriage.

"It sounds great to me!"

Everyone went into a flurry of motion and decision-making that finally culminated at Roxy's front door twenty minutes later.

"I think we got everything," Roxy cried, waving a bottle of champagne high over her head. She locked her door behind her after having made sure the apartment was secure for a week. Her and Gary's luggage had been stored in the trunk of the car. "The assistant manager, Mrs. Burton, is going to keep an eye on things while I'm gone, Cage," she explained as she climbed in the front seat beside Gary.

"No problem. Jenny and I will be around, so don't worry. You just concentrate on having a fantastic honeymoon."

"I intend to," Roxy said, snuggling next to Gary. She touched him in a place intimate enough to make him jump. The car lurched when he momentarily lost control.

"This is no good," Cage said. "Gary can't drive and neck with Roxy at the same time. Let's stop at my house and get my Lincoln. Then you two can have the back-seat all the way to El Paso."

"I like that idea even better!" Roxy agreed enthusiastically. "Honey, is that all right with you?" Gary bobbed his head.

"Besides," Jenny added dryly, "if Cage is driving, we'll get there in half the time."

"You know, woman, if you don't stop smarting off like that, I'm gonna have to take drastic measures to shut you up." Cage drew her into an unyielding embrace and sealed her mouth in a hot kiss that didn't end until they pulled up to his garage.

"Time!" Roxy called out like a referee in a wrestling match.

Cage cursed softly as Jenny disentangled her limbs from his. "I had to come up for air anyway, Cage," Jenny whispered as she self-consciously straightened her clothes and smoothed down her hair.

Everybody thought that comment was hysterically funny and they were laughing as they transferred the luggage from Gary's car to Cage's. The Lincoln was as vintage as the Corvette, and had been restored to the same mint condition. It seemed half a block long and was as silver and shiny as the Lone Ranger's bullets.

"Make yourselves at home." Cage grinned over his shoulder at the passengers in the backseat.

"We intend to," Roxy answered. She fell back into the corner, dragging an unsuspecting, but certainly willing, Gary with her.

Cage laughed as he steered the car onto the highway. "That's the last we'll hear from them until we get to El Paso." Just then a contented groan rose from the shadows of the backseat. "Well, maybe not," he corrected himself, chuckling.

The Lincoln straddled the center stripe of the two-lane highway as it ate up the miles. Cage had it cranked up to ninety or better, but Jenny felt safe. They could see the headlights of other vehicles for miles before they met them. There was nothing on the landscape to block them from sight.

"Comfy?" Cage asked her after several moments of silence. He had tuned to a soft FM station on the radio. The stereo mood music was interrupted infrequently by a modulated, disembodied voice that kept the listeners apprised of the time and weather conditions.

"Hm, yes," Jenny sighed.

"Sleepy?"

"Not particularly."

"You're awfully quiet."

"Just thinking."

"You know, even though this car is monstrous by modern standards, we're not required to use the entire front seat."

"What does that mean?"

"To put it in the vernacular, haul your buns over here."

She smiled and slid over to sit hip to hip beside him. "That's better." He draped his right arm over her shoulders and immediately covered her breast with his hand.

"Cage!" She flung his hand off.

"I developed and perfected that move in junior high school. Don't tell me that after all these years it doesn't work."

"It doesn't work with me," she retorted primly.

"It never did work with the nice girls," he grumbled. "But you can't blame a guy for trying." He crooked his elbow and drew his hand back so that his fingers were free to strum her neck. "What were you thinking about?"

Quite naturally she let her head fall back onto his shoulder. Her hand landed on his thigh and she left it there. "That this is really fun. I've never done anything this wild and reckless before."

"This is wild and reckless? We're merely driving down the highway. Of course, there's a little harmless petting going on between two people who are obviously in love with each other and are soon to be married."

"I haven't said I'll marry you."

His pause was brief but significant. "I was referring to Roxy and Gary."

Mortification swept through Jenny like a tidal wave. She yanked her hand off his thigh and tried to put space between them. Cage would have none of it. He held her against him, though she strained away.

"Come back here," he whispered fiercely. "And you can stop that wiggling because I'm not going to let you go." When her struggles subsided, he said, "I'm thrilled that you thought I was talking about us. You took it to mean that we are two people obviously in love with each other. Are we two people in love, Jenny?"

"I don't know," she mumbled, her head bowed.

"I can only speak for myself, of course." His eyes left the highway. "I love you, Jenny."

She raised her head and became captivated by the eloquent expression in his eyes. They stared at each other for long moments as the car roared down the highway. Finally he returned his attention to the road.

"I know what you're thinking. You're thinking that I've said those words to dozens of women. Well, I have. I've said whatever was necessary at the time to get them into bed with me. I've made love because I was drunk, or horny, or angry, or blue, or happy. For just about every reason you can think of.

"And sometimes I did it even when I didn't want to, but because I felt sorry for the woman and knew she needed a man. I've been with beautiful women and some not so beautiful. I haven't been discreet or discriminating.

"But I swear to you, Jenny," he said earnestly, turning his head toward her again, "that I've never been in love. Until now. You're the only woman I've ever loved. It started a long time ago. Years ago.

"But I didn't see any sense in pursuing it. Everyone would have thought I was wrong for you. You would have run in terror if I'd approached you seriously. Mother and Dad would have had conniption fits. And besides all that, there was Hal, and I didn't want to hurt him."

Tears were rolling down the cheek she pressed against his shoulder. "Why are you telling me this now?"

"Don't you think it's time you knew?" His arm hugged her possessively and he pressed a kiss to her temple. "Do you love me, Jenny?"

"Yes, I think so. I mean, I do, I know I do. It's just that I'm confused."

"Confused?"

"My life was so well planned and organized, so carefully controlled, until a few months ago. Since the night Hal left for Central America nothing has been as it was before. That night changed me. I'm different. I can't explain it."

Cage squeezed his eyes shut for a moment. He wanted to tell her then. He wanted to say, "You're changed because we made love and it was beautiful and our bodies told us something we had secretly known but had ignored for years—you were involved with the wrong brother."

But he couldn't tell her that. Not now. Not ever. It was a secret he would live with for the rest of his life, even if it meant that he couldn't acknowledge his own child. Jenny had been hurt enough. He wouldn't hurt her any more.

"I'm like an animal raised in captivity who has just been thrown into the wild. I'm feeling my way into the mainstream of life. Taking things a day at a time. It has to be a gradual process."

She raised her head and spoke to his profile. "Don't ask me for a commitment, Cage. Everything is so complex. I barely had time to straighten out my feelings for Hal before I realized how I really felt about you." Again her hand was on his thigh. Her fingers curled into the hard flesh. "I only know that if you were to suddenly leave my life, I couldn't bear it."

He covered her hand with his. "You know what would have happened if Roxy and Gary hadn't interrupted us, don't you?"

"We would have made love."

"We would still be making love."

"And it would be wrong."

"How can you say that when we've just admitted we love each other?"

"There's someone else involved."

"Hal?"

"Hal's child," she answered softly.

Cage was quiet for a long time before he said thickly, "The child is yours, too, Jenny, a living part of you. I love you. I love the child. It's as simple as that."

"Hardly simple." She returned her head to his shoulder and after several moments she confessed, "I wanted to make love with you tonight. But even that confuses me."

"Why?"

"I can't honestly say. Is it you I want, or just another night of loving like the one I spent with Hal? That sounds shabby and sordid, I know, but somehow when it comes to lovemaking, I can't separate the two of you in my mind."

Cage's heart soared. "It will be incredible with us. I promise. It'll be exactly what you want it to be. But once I have you, I won't ever let you go." He had had to give her up for Hal's sake. He wasn't willing to give her up again. "Be sure you're ready to make a commitment before you make love with me."

She smiled up at him, a shy, sexy smile that made his heart accelerate. But instead of pressing down harder on the gas pedal, he applied brakes and slowed the car to a halt on the shoulder of the highway.

"What are we stopping for?" Gary asked groggily from the backseat.

"I'm hungry," Cage said.

"Who can think of food at a time like this?" Roxy complained.

"I wasn't thinking of food." Cage pulled Jenny into his arms and lowered his mouth to hers.

It was a while before the Lincoln was once again under way.


"I thought it was extremely romantic," Jenny said with a huge yawn she unsuccessfully tried to cover with her hand.

"I thought we looked like the seediest bunch since the Barrow gang," Cage said. "If I'd been that justice of the peace, I'd have barred my door."

They had routed the public official out of bed, and he had grudgingly consented to perform the wedding ceremony. The bride and groom had then been driven to a hotel where they would spend a few hours before leaving for the airport. After drinking several cups of coffee in a twenty-four-hour diner and refueling the Lincoln, Cage had turned it toward home.

"We could get a room and sleep a few hours," he had suggested to Jenny.

"No. I feel so gritty. I think I'd rather just go the distance, then crash."

Cage looked at her now and laughed. At some point during the night she had surrendered the losing battle of keeping her hair up and had removed all the pins. The caramel-colored strands hung around her shoulders in tumbled disarray. Her new skirt and blouse were hopelessly wrinkled. She looked like the starlet of a sexy French movie during the morning-after scene.

"That funny looking, am I?"

"That adorable. Stretch out and go to sleep," he said, patting his thigh to indicate she should lay her head on it.

"I'm afraid you'll fall asleep if I'm not keeping you company."

"No, I won't. The coffee will keep me awake. Besides, I'm used to doing wild and reckless things like this." She made a face at him and he laughed. "Come on," he urged.

"Are you sure?"

"Positive."

She lay down on her side, stretching out as much as possible, and settled her head on his thigh. Closing her eyes, she breathed deeply. "That feels good."

Keeping a careful eye on the road, he pulled her blouse from underneath her belt and reached beneath it to massage her back. She sighed. "You're going to spoil me."

"That would be my pleasure." Her skin was as smooth as satin. And warm. His hand stroked up and down her spine, gently kneading away the tiredness and tension. Eventually he caressed his way around her ribs to her front. Beneath her raised arm he found the soft fullness of her breast.

"Cage…"

"It's all right," he said soothingly.

It felt so right, Jenny silently fell into agreement and relaxed again.

"Where's your bra?"

"I had to hide it under the cushion of the sofa when you answered the door." He chuckled and she smiled against the fabric of his pants leg. "I didn't have a chance to retrieve it before we left."

"I'm glad," he whispered meaningfully, and the ministrations of his hand echoed his words.

"So am I."

He continued to caress her. His intention wasn't to arouse but to soothe. His heart swelled with love to know she had come so far in trusting him, enough to permit this kind of familiarity. In a few short minutes he knew from her even breathing that she was asleep.

Temptation got the best of him and he let his fingers sweep across her nipple. His touch was airy light, but it was enough to bring an instantaneous response, even in sleep. She stirred, shifting her weight and rubbing her head against his lap, until she once again settled and became still.

Cage ground his teeth in an agony of pleasure. "Jenny," he whispered for his ears alone, "there's one thing you don't have to worry about. As long as your head is lying in my lap, I won't be accidentally falling asleep."

The car sped through the gray predawn.

* * *

"Where are we?" Jenny sat up and blinked her eyes against the sunlight. She rolled her head around her shoulders once and stretched her neck.

"Home. Well, almost. I thought you might be hungry. I'm starving."

Through the bug-splattered windshield she saw that they were at the same motel on the outskirts of La Bota where Cage had brought her before. He was parked in front of the coffee shop.

"I can't go in there looking like this!" she cried.

"Nonsense. You look terrific."

He swung out of the car door and, after stopping to arch his back and stretch, came around to Jenny's side. She was making futile efforts to smooth the wrinkles out of her clothes and straighten her hair.

"I look terrible," she said as he helped her out, a hand under her elbow. She swayed against him and clutched at his arm. "Oh, my foot's gone to sleep. You may have to hold me up."

"I won't mind," he growled in her ear. "You might as well know that I took liberties while you were asleep."

"That sounds like something you'd do." She tried to look angry, but the sparkle in her eyes gave her away.

"Hey, what's this?" Something had caught his eye in the morning sunlight. He reached behind her seat and came up with the unopened bottle of champagne. "Well, what do you know? We forgot to make a toast with the champagne."

Jenny made a tsking sound and grabbed the bottle. "We'll save it for after breakfast."

"Uh-oh. I've created a monster. You're going to be

an expensive woman to keep. I should have started you out on beer."

Slaphappy and tired, they staggered up the steps toward the door of the coffee shop. Cage reached for the door just as another couple pushed through it on their way out.

Bob and Sarah Hendren.

It had been a tradition of theirs to go out to breakfast alone every Saturday morning. Since their boys had been old enough to fend for themselves, the Hendrens had indulged in that two hours of solitude every weekend. The demands of Bob's work allowed them little time to themselves, so they treated each Saturday as an occasion and spent all week deciding on where they would go next, always choosing a different restaurant.

The couple stood rooted to the spot as they took in the condition of Jenny's clothes and Cage's day-old beard. Jenny's attempt to brush her hair back only called attention to the tangles in it. Her lips were naturally rouged from the frequent and passionate kisses the night before. Her mascara had been smeared during her nap. Had the older couple looked closely, they would have seen a smudge of it on Cage's trouser leg.

But their attention was focused mainly on Jenny, who had undergone such a metamorphosis since they had last seen her and who was now unconsciously hugging a bottle of champagne to her breasts.

"Mother, Dad, hi." Cage was the first to break the tense silence. He would have removed his arm from around Jenny's waist to relieve the awkwardness of the moment, but he was afraid she couldn't stand up under her own power. She had slumped against him heavily.

"Good morning," Bob said with a discernible lack of civility.

Sarah said nothing, but continued to stare at Jenny. They hadn't come face-to-face since that awful scene in the parsonage when she had accused Jenny of seducing Hal. Her hard expression revealed that she thought she had been right in her accusation.

"Sarah, Bob," Jenny said pleadingly, "this isn't what it looks like. We…Cage and I drove…drove…"

Cage picked up for her when she faltered. "We drove two friends to El Paso last night so they could get married. We made a turnaround trip and just got back." He was trying to emphasize that they hadn't spent the night away together, though he thought now it would have been better if they had. At least Bob and Sarah wouldn't have known about it, and this scene, which he instinctively felt was about to get nasty, would have been avoided.

Jenny laughed nervously, fearfully, as though someone had just arrested her for a hideous crime and she couldn't determine if it was a joke or not. "The champagne was for the wedding. We forgot all about it. See? It isn't even opened. Just now we were acting silly and—"

"You don't have to explain anything to them," Cage lashed out irritably.

He wasn't angry with her. He knew she was embarrassed and he would have given anything to have spared her that. But he was furious with his parents for being so judgmental and automatically jumping to the wrong conclusion. He couldn't blame them for thinking the worst about him, but couldn't they have given Jenny the benefit of the doubt?

"You were like a daughter to me," Sarah said in a trembling voice. Tears were collecting in her eyes. She blinked them back while she pursed her lips tighter.

"I still am," Jenny moaned with soft earnestness. "I want to be. I love you both and I've missed you."

"Missed us?" Sarah's harsh tone dismissed that notion. "We've heard about your new apartment. You didn't bother to let us know your address, much less take the time to come see us."

"Because I didn't think you wanted to see me."

"You forgot us as quickly as you forgot Hal," Sarah accused her.

"I'll never forget Hal. How could I? I loved him. And I'm carrying his child."

That gently spoken reminder lifted the floodgate of Sarah's tears and she sobbed against Bob's arm.

"She's been upset," he said quietly. "She misses you terribly, Jenny. I know we didn't take the news of the baby too well, but we've had time to reevaluate. We want to be a part of his life. Even this morning we talked about calling you and making amends. It's our Christian duty to keep the family intact. I can't be the kind of example I should be with this thing between us."

The minister glanced at Cage, at the incriminating champagne, at the disreputable picture the two of them made. "But now, seeing you like this, I just don't know." He shook his head sadly and turned away, holding Sarah protectively under his arm as she cried.

"Oh, please," Jenny said, taking a step forward and extending her arms as though reaching out to touch them.

"Jenny, no," Cage said softly and drew her back.

"Give it time. They have to work it out in their own minds."

He escorted her back to the car without argument. She surely wasn't up to being seen in public now. Indeed, as soon as she was in the car, she began to cry.

It seemed to Jenny that for each giant step forward, she took two backward. She had humbled herself and begged Hal to make love to her, but he had left anyway.

While he was away she had come to realize she didn't love him as a wife should love her husband. He had died, leaving her with the guilt, as though she had deserted him and not the other way around.

Piecing her life back together, she had embarked upon a new job, only to discover she was pregnant. Now she was a pariah to the beloved people she had considered her family since adolescence.

She didn't want to return to the life she had lived before Hal left. It had been stifling and she couldn't bear that kind of slow suffocation again. After having tasted independence, she wanted to feast on it. She had achieved a level of freedom, but at what price? The liberation of Jenny Fletcher had been expensive. It had cost her the love and respect of those she held most dear.

Her tears were bitter as they rolled down her face into her mouth. Knowing that fatigue and pregnancy were partly responsible for this weeping binge, she let herself indulge in it. The outpouring of emotion was cleansing and she let it happen, paying no attention to where Cage was driving until the motor of the Lincoln was turned off.

She raised her head from her hands and wiped her eyes. "This is your house," she remarked unnecessarily.

"Right."

He got out and came around to assist her. "What are we doing here?"

"I'm going to see to it that you eat a good breakfast. And," he stressed when she opened her mouth to protest, "there will be no argument about it."

She was too weary to argue anyway, so she said nothing. He unlocked the front door and she trudged upstairs behind him into the master suite. "The bathroom's yours for ten minutes." He rummaged in a drawer and came up with a Texas Tech T-shirt. The red double T against the black cotton was faded from many washings. "Take a hot shower and put this on when you get out. If you're not downstairs in ten minutes, I'm coming to get you." He kissed her swiftly and she was left alone.

The water was scalding, the soap fragrant and sudsy, the shampoo luxurious, the towels plush. When she pulled the T-shirt over her head, she felt one hundred percent better and ravenously hungry.

Hesitantly she stood on the threshold of the kitchen, feeling vulnerable and exposed. Her hair was wet and all she had on under the T-shirt was a pair of panties. The hem of the shirt reached mid-thigh, but she still felt awkward and self-conscious.

Cage seemed not to notice either the brevity of her costume or her bashfulness. The moment he saw her he said, "Well, don't just stand there. Two hands are better than one."

"What can I do?"

"Butter the toast."

She did and within minutes they were sitting down to a steaming platter of bacon and eggs. Hunger made manners dispensable and she dug right in. After several hefty mouthfuls, she caught Cage's amused eyes on her. Chagrined, she blotted her mouth with a napkin and took a demure sip of cold orange juice. "You're a good cook."

"Don't let me slow you down." By the time she had cleared the plate of food, she was so exhausted she could barely lift the cup of herbal tea Cage had steeped for her.

"Come on before you drop," he said, pushing back his chair.

"Where am I going?"

"To bed." He swept her into his arms.

"Your bed?"

"Yes."

"I should dress and go home. Put me down, Cage."

"Not until we get to the bed."

She should stop him before he took another step up the stairs, but she couldn't collect the energy. The long nap in the car hadn't been sufficient. She couldn't remember ever feeling so wrung out. Her head fell against his chest and her eyes slid closed. He was so strong. Capable. Trustworthy. And she loved him.

The sleeve of his shirt felt rough against the backs of her bare thighs. She was reminded of that night in bed with Hal and the way his clothes had felt against her skin, how sensuous it had been.

Cage set her down beside the bed but kept an arm around her as he flung back the suede spread. Then he gently lowered her to the fresh-smelling sheets. "Sleep tight," he whispered as he pulled the top sheet over her. He brushed a strand of damp hair away from her cheek.

"What are you going to do?"

"Wash the dishes."

"That's not fair. You drove all night. You cooked the food." Her mind had a difficult time organizing the words in the right order. Her lips had an even harder time forming them.

"You can make it up to me another time. Now you and baby get some rest." He kissed her lips softly, but she didn't feel it. She was already asleep.

# Twelve

It took her a moment to orient herself when she woke up. She lay without moving, taking in her surroundings with sleepy eyes until she recognized Cage's bedroom.

Memory came back intact then. She remembered the sequence of events that had led to her sleeping in his bed. So much had happened since she had opened her front door to him last night and seen him standing there holding the roses.

It was almost night again. The sky seen through the shutters was violet, deepening into purple. A milky moon seemed within touching distance of the window. And one brilliant star, like a beauty mark juxtaposed to a smile, was positioned just below and to one side of the moon.

She yawned and stretched and rolled to her back. She sat up and shook her tousled hair. The T-shirt was twisted around her waist. Her legs, bare and silky, since she had availed herself of Cage's razor when she showered, slid smoothly against the covers she kicked off as she raised her knees and bowed her back to stretch forward.

She gasped softly.

Cage was lying beside her, perfectly still, an arm's length away. Not a single muscle moved as he lay on his back, his arms raised, his hands folded beneath his head, watching her. It seemed inappropriate to say anything, so Jenny returned his silent stare and said hello only with her eyes.

He had taken a shower while she was asleep. He smelled of the same soap she had used. His jaw had been shaved clean of whiskers, and she wondered with a half smile if she had dulled his razor.

His hair was arranged as haphazardly as usual. The disorder of those dusty blond strands was rakish, cavalier, and so typically Cage, she longed to run her fingers through them. But touching him seemed inappropriate, too.

For the moment the most provocative caress was eye contact. So Jenny did nothing at all but look at him with the same intensity with which he was looking at her. Longing vibrated between them like humming harp strings. Their senses were perfectly attuned to each other, but for the time being they tacitly agreed to indulge only their sense of sight.

His eyes hadn't wavered, but she knew he was looking at all of her at once—her hair, her face, her mouth, her breasts. How could he miss seeing her breasts? Jenny could feel them trembling with emotion, their crests thrusting against the soft cloth of the T-shirt as though vying for his attention.

Nor could he miss the V where the wedge of her panties showed above her bare thighs. Surely that spot hadn't escaped those smoky topaz eyes. Under their ardent stare, the erogenous parts of her body warmed considerably and began to throb with a pleasant ache. Still, Jenny couldn't tear her eyes away from him.

She noticed that the undersides of his arms weren't as darkly tanned as the rest of him. She wanted to sink her teeth into the hard muscles of his biceps, but she knew Cage would be shocked if she did. Women were supposed to be passive, weren't they? Besides, such conduct was beyond her experience.

The tufts of hair in his armpits looked soft and downy. Would they tickle? No doubt. Did she dare find out? Her eyes fell away shyly for a moment before she raised them again.

Ever since that night in Monterico she had been dazzled by his naked torso. Leisurely now, she studied it thoroughly and took in every detail, the curved muscles of his chest, the dusting of hair, the way the broad expanse tapered into a trim rib cage. His stomach was hard and flat. His navel dimpled the center of a narrow abdomen.

He was lying with his legs crossed at the ankles. His feet were bare. He was wearing a pair of jeans.

And they were unbuttoned.

They were the regulation jeans of roughnecks and cowboys, with the old-fashioned button fly. The seams were faded white and the denim was frayed in spots. They gloved his long thighs and cupped his sex. A ribbon of hair arrowed down into the shadowed opening.

Jenny realized she had been holding her breath for a long time. She closed her eyes and exhaled on a slow sigh. It was easy to figure out what had happened. As soon as Cage had finished showering, he had given way to sleepiness and fallen onto the bed without bothering to button his jeans. After all, he had driven all night.

He was covered, it was just…

Her heart hammering, Jenny opened her eyes again. Almost against her will they trained on Cage's lap. With each breath his stomach rose and fell, setting his muscles into play in a hypnotizing and erotic ballet.

Jenny was entranced. She felt compelled. Why resist?

She touched him.

Her fingertips found that sleek center stripe of hair that bisected his torso. They rode it down to his navel. Her index finger shyly tested the depth of that beguiling indentation and twirled in the hair encircling it.

He was so warm and alive. Energy emanated from him and sent electric currents chasing up her fingertips. He was raw masculinity. She felt weak and defenseless against his power.

Inexorably drawn, her hand moved down. The hair she encountered just inside the opening of his jeans was darker and denser and springy.

She hesitated and turned her head. When she looked into his face, she cried out softly.

Tears were glistening in his eyes. He hadn't moved, hadn't altered his position in the slightest, hadn't said a word, but his eyes were filled with emotion. That touched Jenny in a way that transcended the physical.

Love had never been demonstrated for him. He had never been fondled or smothered with affection. Loving touches had been absent from his young life. He had been deprived of unselfish giving.

Jenny didn't hesitate. Indeed, she didn't even think about it. Her mind had nothing to deliberate.

Her hand disappeared inside his jeans.

A heartfelt groan erupted from Cage's chest. Low-

ering his hands, he clutched at the sheet beneath him.
He bared his teeth in a grimace of ecstasy and ground
the back of his head into the pillow. The tears were
squeezed from the corners of his eyes when he clamped
them shut against the passion that flooded through him
like a rushing river.

He hooked his thumbs in the waistband of his jeans
and pushed them down over his hips, then bicycled his
legs until he could kick them away.

Jenny, her eyes glazed with wonder, looked down
at her hand. He more than filled it. He was full, thick,
hard and hot. She admired him with uneducated yet
eager eyes.

Acting purely on instinct, she turned and lay down
close to him, resting her cheek on his thigh. Her hair
spilled over him like a silky mantle. He sifted through
it with unthinking fingers guided only by touch.

She ached with love for him and wanted him to know
how marvelous she thought he was, body and soul. She
lifted her head from his thigh, bent down, and kissed
him.

What happened then was beyond her imagination
or comprehension. With a soft moan Cage turned his
head and began nuzzling her. Her panties were somehow discarded, though she could never recall quite how
that came about.

She felt his hands on her thighs, stroking and caressing and parting. He touched her in the most supremely
intimate way.

Then his mouth was there, warm and wet and gentle.

He made love to her and she caressed him with her
lips and tongue. The world became a bowl of cream
and she was submerged in it. The atmosphere was rich

and delicious and velvety. In this realm there existed no jagged edges of feeling, no difficult emotions, no harsh realities. Everything was smooth and complete and understood. There was an absence of ugliness and ambiguity. All was beauty and light.

When he turned and braced himself above her, he whispered, "Open your eyes, Jenny. See the one who loves you."

Her eyes drifted open. They were hazy with passion, but Cage knew she saw and recognized him. With one swift thrust he sheathed himself in her satiny warmth. When he was secured deep inside, he smiled down into her radiant face.

He watched the patterns of expression dance across her features in response to his rhythmic stroking. He saw the wonder dawn in her slumberous eyes when he changed tempos and brought her to ever-higher levels of arousal.

He watched the light burn inside her soul when she experienced her fulfillment…and he saw her shine with love when he experienced his.

"You're precious to me and I love you, Jenny. I always have." His lips were close to her ear. The dusty blond strands of his hair mingled with the richer brown tones of hers on the pillow. His cheek felt as fevered as hers when he pressed them together. "I love you."

He raised his head and gazed down into her eyes, which were glimmering like emeralds. "I love you, too, Cage." She reached up to touch his cheek, his eyebrows, his lips, as though to convince herself that he was truly there and that it hadn't all been a dream.

"Remember what I promised you?"

"Yes. You kept your promise. It was beautiful, just as you said it would be."

"You're beautiful." He moved.

"No, stay inside me."

"I intend to," he whispered against her lips. "But I haven't even kissed you yet." He remedied that with a thorough kiss that kept his tongue nestled inside her mouth for breathless moments.

Working the T-shirt up, he pulled it over her head and tossed it aside. He lowered his gaze to her breasts and caressed one softly.

"I meant what I said, Jenny. I've loved you for a long time, but I couldn't do anything about it. You belonged to Hal. I accepted that without argument just as everyone did, including you."

"I sensed there was something between us. I didn't know what it was."

"Lust."

She smiled and combed her fingers through his hair. "Whatever it was, I was afraid of it."

"I thought you were afraid of me."

"No. Only of the way you made me feel."

"Is that why you avoided me?"

"Was I that conspicuous?"

"Hm." He was intrigued with her breasts, their shape, their dusky crests. He examined them lovingly. "I'd come around and you'd duck for cover."

"You were dangerous to be around. I would go to any lengths not to be left alone in the same room with you. You seemed to consume all the oxygen. I couldn't breathe." She groaned softly as he dipped his head and bathed the tip of her breast with his tongue. "You still take my breath away."

"I can't keep what you do to me a secret." He stirred inside her. He was hard again.

She palmed the firm muscles of his buttocks and drew him deeper inside. He fondled her breast, finessed the nipple until it was firm and flushed, then lowered his mouth to it.

Jenny watched him caress her, watched the flexing of his cheeks as he gratified his need for her. She wished she could fill the void inside him, erase from his past all the times he had needed loving and went lacking.

"Cage, use me. Use me."

"No, Jenny," he rasped, his tongue flicking. "I've used other women. This is different."

She wanted to concentrate on ways to please and satisfy him, but she became too caught up in the pleasure he was giving her. His arousal had heightened until he filled her again. The walls of her body closed around his hardness like a miserly fist. She thrilled to each powerful thrust and arched up to meet them.

Then another sensation spiraled through her middle. At first the rippling movements were so faint she thought she had imagined them. But then the flutterings became stronger and she realized what had caused them.

When she did, she panicked. Her body went rigid beneath Cage's and instead of striving to know more of him, she shrank away. "No, no, stop." She clasped his head and lifted it from her breasts. She squirmed free of him and pressed her thighs together tightly. "Stop, stop."

"Jenny?" His breathing was harsh and loud. It took several seconds for him to bring his eyes back into focus and set the world on its rightful axis. "What's wrong, Jenny? Did I hurt you?"

His heart contracted with fear when she turned her

back on him, raised her knees to her chest and formed a ball with her slight body. "Oh, my God, something's wrong. What's wrong? Tell me."

Cage had never felt so afraid and useless in his life. Seconds ago he and Jenny had been making love. Her body had been responsive and eager. Now she was weeping and acting as though agonizing pains were ripping through her.

He laid a hand on her shoulder. She flinched at his touch. "What is it? Should I call a doctor?" His only answer was a racking sob. "For godsake, Jenny, at least tell me if you're in pain."

"No, no," she moaned. "Nothing like that."

"Then what?" He crammed his fingers through his hair, impatiently pushing it off his forehead. "What happened? Why did you stop me? Was I hurting you?"

"I felt the baby move."

The words were mumbled into the pillow in a papery voice. At first Cage couldn't decipher them, but when he broke apart the unintelligible syllables and pieced them back together, he went weak with relief. "That's the first time?"

She nodded her head. "The doctor said I should start feeling him soon. This is the first time."

Behind her, Cage smiled. His child had spoken to him. But Jenny was obviously concerned about it. He touched her shoulder again and this time didn't remove his hand even when she stiffened with aversion. In fact, he lay down beside her and tried to take her in his arms.

"It's all right, Jenny. It won't hurt the baby if we're careful."

She sat up abruptly and glared at him. "You don't get it, do you?"

Cage stared at her incredulously as she lunged off the bed, pulled on the blanket until it came free of the other rumpled covers, and wrapped it around herself. She stalked to the window and braced her shoulder against the frame with her back to the room.

He was hurt and angry and it showed as he got off the bed as well, yanked up his jeans, and shoved his legs into them, hiking them up over his hips with a definitely angry tug.

"I guess I don't get it, Jenny. Why don't you tell me?"

She hadn't heard his footfalls on the thick, lush carpet, and it alarmed her when she turned around to find him standing so close. His eyebrows were lowered into a glower. The jeans had been left unbuttoned again and his hair was mussed from her fingers plowing through it.

He was the personification of male sexuality and was so appealing, she had to struggle to resist him.

"You might not have any morals against that alley cat type of behavior, but I do."

"You thought what we were doing was alley cat behavior?" he demanded, his voice quaking with rage.

"I didn't until I felt my baby move."

"I think it's beautiful. I wish you had shared it with me."

"It's another man's baby, Cage! Do you realize what kind of woman that makes me?"

Her anger was spent and in its place were shame and misery. She hung her head as the tears began to fall. Cage watched her shoulders begin to shake with weeping. Her small, frail hands gripped the blanket around her as Eve must have clung to that first fig leaf to hide her shame.

"What kind of woman does that make you?"

She shook her head, at first unable to voice her thoughts aloud. She sniffed back tears. "What we did together...the way I acted when we were...making love..."

"Go on," he prodded when she hesitated.

"I don't know myself anymore. I love you, but I carry your brother's baby."

"Hal is dead. We're alive."

"I've denied it, even to myself, but your parents were partially correct when they said I tried to lure Hal away from his misson."

"What do you mean?" Cage's brow knit in concern.

"That night when he came to my bedroom to tuck me in, he had no intention of making love to me. I kissed him and begged him to stay with me, to give up the trip and marry me."

"You've told me this before. You said he left, then came back."

"That's right."

"So you can't condemn yourself for seducing him. Hal made up his own mind without any coercion from you."

She rested her head against the window jamb and stared sightlessly through the shutters. "But don't you see? He might have only come back to check on me, to kiss me good-night one more time. I was desperate and he must have sensed that."

Cage's insides were knotted. How much longer could he perpetrate this lie? Why wouldn't it die a natural death and leave him the hell alone? Why must it come back to haunt him every time he glimpsed happiness with Jenny? Like a malicious gatekeeper, that one sin was keeping him from knowing heaven.

"It was still Hal's decision," he said firmly.

"But if that night had never happened, he might still be alive. I didn't have sense enough to worry about pregnancy, but maybe Hal did. Maybe that was what he was thinking about when he became careless enough to get arrested.

"I had no more conscience than to seduce him away from a God-called mission when all the time I really loved you, a love I was too weak and frightened to admit to. Now I'm sleeping with you while carrying Hal's child. The baby will never know his father because of me."

Cage stood silently for a moment before going to the foot of the bed and sitting down on its edge. He spread his knees wide, propped his elbows on them, and rested his forehead against his raised fists as he stared down at the carpet between his feet.

"You have no reason to feel guilty, Jenny."

"Don't try to make me feel better. I disgust myself."

"Listen to me, hear me out," Cage said sharply, raising his head. "You're not guilty of any of that, not of seducing Hal into your bed, not of distracting him from his mission, certainly not of his death. Nor are you guilty of making love to me while carrying Hal's child."

She turned to look at him with perplexity. The moon shone only on one side of her face, keeping the other in shadow. That was just as well, Cage thought. He feared what he might see in her expression when he told her.

He drew in a heavy breath and spoke quietly, though there was no hesitation in his confession. "Hal didn't father your baby, Jenny. I did. I came to your bedroom that night, not Hal. It was me you made love with."

Her eyes remained still and wide as she stared at

him from across the room. Slowly she slid down the wall and sank to the floor. The blanket mushroomed out around her. All that was visible was her face, pale with disbelief, and her hands, the knuckles of which had gone white.

"That's impossible," she said on a filament of breath.

"It's the truth."

She shook her head furiously. "Hal came into my room. I saw him."

"You saw me. The room was dark. I was standing against the light when I opened the door. I couldn't have been anything but a silhouette."

"It was Hal!"

"I was walking past your door and heard you crying. I intended to go get Hal. But he was downstairs, engrossed in conversation with Mother and Dad. So I went in to check on you instead."

"No," she said soundlessly, still shaking her head.

"Before I could say anything, you sat up and addressed me as Hal."

"I don't believe you."

"Then how do I know how it happened? You reached for me. There were tears on your face. I could see them reflected in the light before I closed the door. I'll admit I should have identified myself the moment you called me Hal, but I didn't. I didn't want to then and I'm damn glad now that I didn't."

"I don't want to hear." She covered her ears with her hands.

Unperturbed, he went on. "I knew you were suffering, Jenny. You were hurt and needed comforting. Frankly, I didn't think Hal would give you what you needed."

"But you would," she hissed accusingly.

"I did." He came off the bed and walked toward her. "You asked me to hold you, Jenny."

"I asked Hal!"

"But Hal wasn't there, was he?" Cage shouted, his own ire rising. "He was downstairs talking about visions and callings and causes, when he should have been ministering to his own fiancée."

"I made love with Hal!" she cried in one last frantic attempt to deny what he was telling her.

"You were upset. You had been crying. Hal and I were close enough in build for you to mistake me for him. We were dressed alike in jeans and shirts. I didn't say anything so you couldn't distinguish my voice."

"But I would know the difference."

"Who could you compare me to? You'd had no other lover."

She tried to forget how anxiously she had enticed that "lover" to hold her and kiss her, just as she tried to forget the sleeping pills she had taken that night. Hadn't she been sedated, her mind foggy? Hadn't she thought afterward that it almost could have been her imagination? Hadn't it all seemed dreamlike?

"You weren't looking for me," Cage said. "You were looking for Hal. It simply never occurred to you that it could be anyone else."

"Which is as good as admitting what a deceitful creep you are."

His eyes narrowed perceptibly. "You didn't seem to think I was a creep that night. You didn't seem to mind me at all."

"Stop it. Don't—"

"You lapped me up like a bear does honey."

"Shut up."

"Admit it, Jenny, you'd never been kissed like that before. Hal never kissed you like that, did he?"

"I—"

"Admit it!"

"I'll do no such thing!"

"Well, you can deny it to yourself all you want, but you know I'm right. I touched you and we both went off like rockets."

Jenny squeezed her eyes shut. "I didn't know it was you."

"It wouldn't have mattered."

Her eyes popped open. "That's a lie!"

"No, it's not, and what's more, you know it's not."

She mashed her fingers against her lips. "How could you be so low? How could you deceive me like that? How could you…" She choked on the rest of it.

Cage dropped to his knees in front of her. His anger had diminished and his voice trembled with earnestness. "Because I loved you."

She stared back at him wordlessly.

"Because I needed to be enveloped in you as much as you needed a man's love. I had wanted you for years, Jenny. Lust, yes, but more, much more than that. That night, you were there, in bed, naked and warm and sweet and aroused. At first I thought I'd only hold you, kiss you a few times before I identified myself. But once I'd held you, tasted you, felt your tongue against mine, touched your breasts—" he shrugged helplessly "—there was just no stopping the avalanche.

"I was surprised that you were a virgin. But even discovering that wasn't enough to stop me. Everything I am went into loving you that night. All I thought about was relieving your pain with my loving. It was the first time in my life I felt like I was doing something good. It was clean and right, Jenny. You've told me that yourself."

"I thought I was talking about Hal."

"But you weren't. I was your lover. Think back on that night and compare it to tonight. You know I'm not lying."

He stood up again and began pacing the stretch of carpet between bed and window. "Once I had made love to you, I couldn't give you up. I wanted to win you over slowly. I planned on courting you so that by the time Hal got home you'd be willing to break your engagement with him as painlessly as possible and come to me."

He stopped his pacing and smiled down at her. "The day you told me you were pregnant, I could barely keep still. I wanted to jump up, take you in my arms, and waltz you around that drugstore. Tonight when you told me the baby had moved, I felt the same way."

With the reminder of what had transpired only minutes ago, Jenny glanced toward the bed. It was terrible. Horrible. But she believed him. It all made sense. Why she hadn't seen it before she didn't know. It was obvious now. So damnably obvious. But as he had said, she hadn't been looking for it.

Or had she? Had she known? In the secret-most part of herself, had she known? No. God, please, no!

"Why didn't you tell me, Cage? I made love to one man thinking it was another! Why didn't you tell me?"

"At first because I thought you still loved Hal. It would have destroyed you to think you'd been unfaithful to him."

"I was."

"You weren't, dammit. If anyone was, I was!"

Her breasts heaved with emotion as she struggled to her feet. "Months have gone by. Why haven't you told me?"

"I didn't want to hurt you."

"You don't think I'm hurting now?"

"You shouldn't be. You're free of it. It was my sin, Jenny, not yours. You were innocent and I was trying to spare you."

"Why?"

"Because you have a masochistic penchant for taking the responsibility for other people's failures. You hold yourself accountable for everyone's shortcomings. My parents, Hal, me."

He sighed deeply. "But that's not the only reason." He bored into her eyes with his. "I wanted to do the right thing. I felt as if I owed it to Hal not to tell you. While I was out raising hell, drinking and womanizing, he had devoted his life to doing good. I took something that rightfully belonged to him…although I could argue that, because I had loved you for so long."

He stepped closer to her. "I wanted you to be a part of my life, but I knew the price I would have to pay for you would be high. Hellions like me don't get rewarded without paying a premium."

"What are you talking about, Cage? It seems to me that until tonight you've gotten off scot-free. What kind of dues have you paid?"

"One of them was having you cry out my brother's name the moment you climaxed for the first time." She ducked her head. "Another was having you think all this time that it was Hal who had first introduced you to ecstasy. Another was the night in Monterico when

I could hold you while you slept, but still couldn't express my love. The highest price was having you think that my child, my child, had been fathered by anyone other than me."

She almost forgave him then. She almost succumbed to the tremor in his voice and the fierce possession in his eyes. She almost walked into his arms and claimed his love.

But she couldn't. What he had done had been dreadful, and a sin of that magnitude couldn't be lightly dismissed. "So why tell me now?"

"Because you're blaming yourself for Hal's death. I can't have that, Jenny. He left on his mission with a pure body and a pure conscience. His death had nothing to do with you. There was no way you could have prevented it. I won't let you go through the rest of your life blaming yourself for it and thinking that you're even remotely responsible for making your child an orphan."

He reached for her hand. It lay cold and lifeless in his. "I love you, Jenny."

She snatched her hand away. "Love isn't built on deception and lies, Cage. You've been lying to me for months. What do you want me to do?"

"Love me back."

"You made a fool of me!"

"I made a woman of you!" He spun away from her, making an effort to control his temper. "If you'd stop sifting everything through your filter of propriety and conscience and guilt, you'd see things clearly. That night was the best thing that had ever happened to either of us. It freed us both."

"Free?" she cried. "Free? I'll have to bear the burden of that night the rest of my life."

"Are you referring to my baby as a burden?"

"No, not the baby," she ground out. "The guilt. Of making love to one brother while being engaged to another."

"Oh…" He blistered the walls with his expletive. "Are we back to that again?"

"Yes. And I'm weary of it. Take me home."

"Not a chance. Not until we've thrashed this thing out."

"Take me home," she said adamantly. "If you don't, I'll steal the keys to one of your automobiles and drive myself."

"You're staying here or I'll—"

"Don't threaten me. I'm not afraid of you anymore. Your threats are empty anyway. What could you possibly do to me that would be worse than what you've already done?"

His jaw bunched with fury. She watched his eyes fill with hot rage, then just as quickly harden coldly. Abruptly he turned away from her. Going to the closet, he ripped a shirt from a hanger and picked up a pair of boots. "Get dressed," he said tersely through barely moving lips. "I'll come back for you in five minutes."

When he did, she was ready. She preceded him downstairs and through the front door. It was dark as they crossed the yard to the garage. He opened the door of the Lincoln and she got inside.

They were silent during the entire trip into town. His hands gripped the steering wheel as though he'd like to tear it from its mounting. He drove fast. When he braked outside her apartment, she rocked forward with the impact. Leaning across her, he opened the door and shoved it open. She stepped out.

"Jenny?" He was leaning across the seat. "I've done some terrible things. Mostly out of pure meanness. But this is one time I tried to do the right thing. I wanted to do right by my folks, you and my baby." He laughed mirthlessly. "Even when I try to do what's right, it gets shot to hell. Maybe it's true what people have always said about Cage Hendren. He's just no damn good." He reached for the door and slammed it closed.

Then with a grinding of gears and a shower of gravel, the car shot forward and out of the parking lot.

Jenny let herself into the apartment. She felt drained, listless. Had it only been last night that she and Cage had shared the candlelight dinner? Yes, there were their ice-cream bowls and coffee cups still on the coffee table, forgotten there when they had left to drive Roxy and Gary to El Paso. It could have happened in another lifetime.

She left the lamps unlit as she went through the apartment toward her bedroom. It seemed dark, cold, empty, unlike the bedroom at Cage's house.

No, she wouldn't think of that.

But she did and there was no stopping the memories that rushed to her mind. Every touch, every kiss, every word.

She remembered the bleak expression in his eyes just before he had left. Had he been trying to do the right thing by holding his silence?

He certainly hadn't acted smug the morning Hal left. She remembered the attention he had paid her. He had been tense and watchful, but not cocky or obnoxious as he could have been. If it had only been a cruel trick he'd played, he certainly hadn't gloated over it afterward.

Did he love her? He had been willing to forfeit claiming his child. Wasn't such a sacrifice the ultimate testimony of love?

And if he loved her, what was she really upset about?

Cage had been her only lover. Didn't that give her a warm, glowing feeling inside? The enchantment of that night had been hers and Cage's. She should have known! She had never felt that way in her life before or since…until last night.

When he was inside her, hadn't his body felt familiar, like an extension of hers? Both times, hadn't she felt complete? Hadn't the addition of his body to hers brought together all the pieces of the complex puzzle that was Jenny Fletcher and made it whole?

Was she accusing Cage of deceit only to alleviate her own conscience? Because for years she had been deceitful to Hal, to the Hendrens, to the town. She had gone along with their marriage plans, knowing full well that the love she bore Hal wasn't the kind to base a marriage on.

There had been no sympathetic chord struck between them as there was with her and Cage. Hal hadn't satisfied the restless hunger of her spirit. With him she would have gone on suppressing that spirit and living under constant restraints. Cage dared her to be herself.

Couldn't she forgive Cage for keeping his secret all these months? She had been prepared to keep hers for the remainder of her life. If Cage hadn't made love to her that night, if Hal hadn't died, she would have married her fiancé. And no matter how unhappy it had made her, she would have stuck it out. Before her relationship with Cage, she wouldn't have had the courage to seek her own happiness, but would have continued letting others do it for her.

Cage had taught her to make her own future. Wasn't that alone reason enough to love him?

Tomorrow she would think about it some more. Maybe she would call Cage, apologize for her intolerance tonight, and together they would sort it all out.

Wearily she stripped off her clothes, pulled on a nightgown, and slipped into bed. But she couldn't sleep. She had slept most of the day, and the world seemed to be against her getting the peaceful rest she needed. Sirens screamed through the streets of town, and just when she had rubbed Cage from her mind enough to fall asleep, her telephone jangled loudly.

# *Thirteen*

Thinking it might be Cage, she weighed the wisdom of answering. Was she ready to talk to him yet? The phone was on its sixth ring before she gave in and reached for the receiver.

"Hello?"

"Miss Fletcher?"

It wasn't Cage and she felt a momentary pang of disappointment. "Yes."

"Is this the Jenny Fletcher who used to live with Reverend Hendren?"

"Yes. Who is this, please?"

"Deputy Sheriff Rawlins," the caller identified himself. "You wouldn't happen to know where we can locate the Hendrens, would you?"

"Have you checked the church and the parsonage?"

"Sure have."

"Then I'm sorry, I don't know where they are. Can I help you?"

"We really need to find them," the deputy said, conveying urgency. "Their son's been in an accident."

Jenny went cold. Nausea churned in her stomach.

Yellow sunbursts exploded against a field of black when she closed her eyes. By an act of will she fought off fainting. "Their son?" she asked in a high, reedy voice.

"Yeah, Cage."

"But he was just…I just saw him."

"It happened a few minutes ago."

"Is he…was it…fatal?"

"I don't know yet, Miss Fletcher. The ambulance is rushing him to the hospital now. It's bad, all right. A train hit his car." Jenny stifled her outcry with a bloodless hand. A train! "That's why we need to find his next of kin."

Lord, what an awful official expression. "Next of kin," the phrase reserved in police jargon for those who have to be notified when someone they love dies in an accident away from home.

"Miss Fletcher?"

Several moments of silence had ticked by while Jenny tried to absorb the tragic enormity of this telephone call. "I don't know where Bob and Sarah are. But I'll be at the hospital in a few minutes. Goodbye. I have to hurry."

She hung up the phone before giving the deputy a chance to say anything more. Her knees buckled beneath her when she lunged off the bed. She stumbled to the closet, where she pulled out the first garment her hands fell on.

She had to get to Cage. Now. Hurry. She had to tell him she loved him before—

No, no. He wouldn't die. She wouldn't even think of his dying.

*Oh, God, Cage, why did you do it?*

Ever since the deputy had told her about the accident, Jenny had questioned whether it was an accident or not. What was the last thing Cage had said to her? "I'm just no damn good." Had her rejection of his love been the last rejection he could stand? Was this "accident" an attempt to win approval by ridding the world of Cage Hendren?

"No!"

She didn't realize she had screamed the word aloud until it echoed off the silent walls of her apartment. She ran through the darkened rooms on her way to the front door. Tears were streaming down her face and her fingers shook so badly, she could barely insert the key in the ignition of the car.

She saw the scene of the accident from several blocks away. A wrecker had pulled Cage's car off the tracks, but police still had the area cordoned off with flares to discourage curious onlookers.

The silver Lincoln looked like a piece of aluminum foil a petulant giant had balled up in his fist and thrown away. Jenny's chest compressed painfully. Nothing could have come out of that mangled mess of metal alive. Her arms were too weak to steer the car, but she forced herself to keep going. She had to reach the hospital in time.

When she arrived, she parked and dashed toward the emergency room doors. *Don't die, don't die, don't die,* her heart chanted with each footfall. This kind of emotional upheaval and physical exertion weren't good for the baby, but Cage was first in her thoughts now.

"Cage Hendren?" she gasped breathlessly, slapping her hands on top of the nurses' station desk.

The on-duty nurse looked up. "He's already gone up for surgery."

"Surgery?"

"Yes. Dr. Mabry."

If they were operating on him, he was still alive. *Thank you, God, thank you.* Jenny gulped for breath. "What floor?"

"Three."

"Thank you." She ran for the elevator.

"Miss?" Jenny turned around. "He might be in there for a long time."

The nurse was diplomatically cautioning her not to hold out much hope. "I'll wait, no matter how long it takes."

On the third floor the woman at the nurses' station confirmed that Cage was in surgery. "Are you a relative?" the R.N. inquired politely.

"I...I grew up with him. His parents adopted me when I was orphaned."

"I see. We haven't been able to contact his parents, but we're still trying."

"I'm sure they're just out for the evening and will return soon." Jenny couldn't believe she was capable of making casual conversation. She felt like screaming the walls down. She wanted to fall to the floor and keen while she tore at her hair.

"There's a policeman waiting at the house to bring them here."

Jenny bit her lower lip. "They'll be frightened. They lost their youngest son only a few months ago."

The nurse made a clucking sound of regret. "Why don't you sit down over there to wait," she said, indicating a waiting room. "I'm sure we'll hear something about Mr. Hendren's condition soon."

Like an automaton, Jenny moved to the waiting room

and sat down on the sofa. She should go to the parsonage herself, be there to break the news of Cage's accident when the Hendrens came home. But she couldn't leave him. She couldn't! She had to stay right here telegraphing her love and encouragement through the walls into the operating room where he precariously clung to life.

His life was precious to her. Didn't he know that? How could he have—

Oh, God, she had let him leave her thinking the worst of himself. Just as his parents had rejected him on the night of Hal's funeral, she had cruelly shut him out tonight after he had opened his heart to her. The Hendrens might be too ignorant of Cage's psyche to realize what they had done to him all his life, but she knew better.

How many times had he doubted the value of his life? Wasn't he flirting with death every time he challenged authority, or got behind the wheel of a car and defied the speed limit? Hadn't he pulled his outrageous pranks only to win the attention always denied him?

*Oh, Cage, forgive me. I love you. I love you. You're the most important person in the world to me.*

"Miss Fletcher?"

She jumped at the sound of her name. Her eyes had been closed in anguish as she prayed, bargaining with God to spare Cage's life. She had expected to see a doctor bending over her in commiseration. Instead the man who had addressed her was wearing a police uniform.

"Yes?"

"I thought it was you," he said. "I'm Deputy Rawlins. I spoke to you on the phone."

She rubbed the tears out of her eyes. "Of course. I remember."

"And this here's Mr. Hanks. It was his family Cage saved."

For the first time Jenny noticed the man standing slightly behind the deputy. He stepped forward, his overalls and brogans a jarring contrast to the modern sterility of the hospital corridor. His eyes were red with tears and his balding head was humbly bowed.

"Saved?" Jenny mouthed. Very little sound came out. "I don't understand."

"His wife and kids were in the car that was stalled on the tracks. Cage came up behind them and pushed them off. He barely got them out of the way in time. 'Course, the engineer had seen what was happening and had slowed the train down as much as he could, but there wasn't time to stop it." He cleared his throat uncomfortably. "It's a good thing he hit on the passenger side and damn lucky for Cage he wasn't in his 'Vette. That would have been squashed like a bug."

Cage hadn't tried to take his own life! He had roared away from her angry and hurt, but it had never been his intention to kill himself. What a fool she had been to even suspect that.

A fresh batch of tears streamed down Jenny's face. He had been trying to save other lives. If he died, it would be as a hero and not as a suicide. She looked up at Mr. Hanks. "Is your family all right?"

He nodded. "They're still shaken up, but thanks to Mr. Hendren, they're alive. I'd like to tell him myself how grateful I am. I pray to God he pulls out of this."

"I pray so, too."

"You know," Hanks said, lowering his head and shaking it sadly, "I've always thought bad things about Cage Hendren, because of the stories goin' around. His drinking and women and all. I've seen him ripping around town in his fancy cars, driving like a bat out of Hades. I thought he was a damn fool to risk his life like that." He sighed. "Reckon I've been taught the hard way not to condemn a man I don't know. He didn't have to run up on that track and knock my wife's car out of the path of that freight train. But he did." His eyes began to fill again. Embarrassed, he covered them with his hand.

"Why don't you get on home, Mr. Hanks," Deputy Rawlins said kindly, laying a hand on the man's shoulder.

"Thank you, Mr. Hanks," Jenny said.

"For what? If it hadn't been for my sorry ol' car—"

"Thank you anyway," she said softly. Hanks gave her a solemn, encouraging nod before Rawlins led him to the elevator.

The nurse's prediction that they would soon hear something about Cage's condition proved to be false. Jenny sat alone in the waiting room. No one came out of the operating room to report on Cage.

She had been there for almost two hours when the elevator doors opened and Bob and Sarah rushed out. Their eyes were frantic, their faces wild with worry and ravaged with renewed grief.

Jenny watched them stop at the nurses' station and identify themselves. They got the same polite, tepid reassurance from the nurse that she had. Leaning into each other for support, they turned toward the alcove. When they saw Jenny, their footsteps faltered.

At first Jenny's eyes indicted them. *You didn't love him, but now you come to weep over his deathbed,* her expression said.

But she couldn't incriminate them without incriminating herself, too. If she hadn't been so frightened of what it would mean to her placid life, she would have faced up to her love for Cage years ago.

And today, today, when he had needed to know that he was forgiven and that she loved him, she had rejected his apology. The irony of it was, he had been apologizing for making love to her, for giving her the most splendid night of her life. And she had refused to accept it! How could she blame the Hendrens for their shortsightedness when hers had been so much more hurtful?

She stood and extended her arms toward Sarah. With a glad cry the older woman staggered forward. Jenny hugged her hard. "Shh, Sarah, he'll be all right. I know it."

Hiccupping on every other word, Sarah explained where they'd been. "We drove out of town to visit a sick friend. When we got back, the sheriff's car was parked outside our house. We knew something terrible had happened." Together they sat down on the sofa. "First Hal, now Cage, I can't bear it."

"Would it matter to you so much if Cage died?"

Jenny couldn't believe she had so boldly asked them the question uppermost in her mind. They looked back at her through stricken eyes. Knowing she should go easy on them in the face of tragedy, she nonetheless could find no mercy in her heart. If cruelty would wake them up to the shabby way they had treated their son, then cruel she would be. She was fighting this battle for Cage.

"I don't think Cage believes that you would care."

"But he's our son. We love him," Sarah cried.

"Have you ever told him you love him? Have you ever told him how much you value him?" Bob lowered his eyes guiltily. Sarah swallowed hard. "Never mind answering. As long as I lived with you, you never did."

"We…we had a difficult time with Cage," Bob said.

"Because he didn't fit into the mold you thought he should. He never felt accepted. You didn't appreciate his individuality. He knew he could never measure up to your expectations, so he gave up trying. He acts hard and cold and cynical, but that's a defense mechanism. He wants desperately to be loved. He wants you, his parents, to love him."

"I tried to love him," Sarah said. "He never stood still long enough. He didn't cuddle like Hal did. He wasn't well behaved like Hal. It was difficult to love Cage. His rambunctiousness, that wild streak, frightened me."

"I know what you mean," Jenny said, smiling privately and patting Sarah's hand in understanding. "I learned to see through that into the man. I love him deeply."

Bob was the first to speak. "Do you, Jenny?"

"Yes. Very much."

"How can you, so soon after Hal's death?"

"I loved Hal. But he was more like a brother to me. I only realized when Cage and I began spending time together that I had loved him for a long time. I, like you, was afraid of him."

Bob said, "It may take us some time to get used to the idea of you and Cage together."

"It's taken me some time."

"We know we haven't been fair to you," Sarah said. "We wanted to keep you with us to fill the vacancy in our lives that Hal's death made."

"I have my own life."

"We realize that now. The only way we can keep you is to let you go."

"I won't be going far," she assured them with a smile. "I love you both. It broke my heart for there to be this rift between us."

"The baby was a shock to us, Jenny." Bob's eyes flickered down to her stomach. "Surely you can understand that. But, well, it's Hal's child, too. We'll accept it and love it for that reason."

Jenny opened her mouth to speak, but another voice interrupted. "Reverend Hendren?" They turned and recognized Dr. Mabry in his operating room greens. They were sweat stained. He looked haggard. Jenny clutched her middle, as though to protect her child from hearing bad news about his father.

"He's alive," the doctor said, relieving them of their primary fear. "Barely. He's still in critical condition. He was in shock when they brought him in. His insides were a mess. He was bleeding internally. We had to give him several pints of blood. It was a real patch-up job, but I think we got everything sewed back together. His right tibia has a clean break and there's a hairline fracture in his right femur. Bruises and lacerations all over him. They're the least of his problems."

"Will he live, Dr. Mabry?" Sarah asked the question as if her own life hinged on the answer.

"He has a good chance because he's as strong as a bull and tough as a boot. He came through the crash and the surgery. If he can survive those two traumas, I'm laying good money on his making it. Now, if you'll excuse me, I'd better get back."

"Can we see him?" Jenny asked, catching the doctor's sleeve.

The doctor pondered the question, but the anxiety on their faces convinced him. "As soon as he's moved to an ICU, one of you can go in for three minutes. I'll be in touch." He turned and headed back down the hall at a brisk pace.

"I have to see him," Sarah said. "I need to tell him how much we do care about him."

"Of course, darling," Bob agreed. "You go."

"No," Jenny said firmly. "I'm going in to see him. You had all his life to tell him you love him, but you didn't. I hope you have the rest of your lives to make that up to him. But I'm going to see him tonight. He needs me. Oh, and about the baby…" She felt the last string of oppression being clipped from her heart. "Hal didn't father him. Cage did. I'm carrying Cage's child."

Their mouths fell open in mute surprise, but Jenny was beyond caring whether they approved or not. This time she wouldn't let convention or the habits of a lifetime intimidate her.

"I hope you'll love us all—Cage, me and the baby." Jenny laid a hand on each of their shoulders and spoke from her heart. "We love you and would like to be a family." She drew a ragged breath and let her hands fall to her sides. The tears she felt flooding her eyes were sniffed away quickly, lest Cage's parents mistake their source as weakness rather than relief. "But if you can't accept us for what we are, if you can't accept the love we have for each other, then that's all right, too. It will be your loss."

Courage and hope bubbled up inside her, and she took heart, smiling through her tears. "I love Cage and he loves me, and I refuse to feel guilty about that. We're going to marry and raise our child, and he'll know every day of his life that he's loved for what he is, not for what we want or expect him to be."

And half an hour later when the doctor returned to lead one of them down the hall to Cage's ICU, it was Jenny who left the waiting room and went with him.

# Epilogue

❧❧❧

"What is going on in here?"

"We're taking a bath."

"You're making a mess."

"It's Trent's fault. He's a splasher."

"And who taught him how to splash?"

From the door of the bathroom Jenny smiled at her husband and son, who were both in the bathtub. Seven-month-old Trent was sitting in the crook of his father's lap, his back against Cage's thighs, his chubby feet on Cage's stomach.

"Is he getting clean?"

"Who, Trent? Sure. He's positively squeaky."

Jenny moved into the room and knelt down at the side of the bathtub. Trent, recognizing his mother, smiled droolingly, proudly showing off his two front teeth. He pointed at her and cooed.

"My sentiments exactly, son," Cage said. "She's a knockout, isn't she?"

"She's going to be knocking heads together if you don't get out and mop up this water." Jenny tried to sound stern, but she was laughing as she bent down and lifted Trent from the tub. When she raised him up, she saw the pinkish scar on Cage's abdomen. It never failed to sober her, at least long enough to wing a prayer of thanksgiving heavenward.

"Watch him, he's as slippery as an eel," Cage said, emerging from the bath. Water streamed down his hard, lean body. Jenny had come to learn that he was completely immodest, a trait she relished.

"How well I know." Jenny was trying to hold on to her squirming son while she wrapped a towel around him. She had given up on keeping herself dry. Trent's sturdy little body had already dampened the front of her robe.

She carried the baby into his nursery, which was across the wide hall from the master suite. She had converted one of the bedrooms of the old house into a picture-book nursery for him. Following her instructions, Cage had done most of the actual labor on weekends. They were well pleased with the results.

She was so adroit at handling her wriggling son that by the time Cage joined them, dried and wrapped in a terry robe, Trent was diaper and pajama clad.

"Tell Daddy good-night." Jenny held Trent up to receive Cage's kiss. Cage took him from her, hugged him close, and kissed him soundly on the cheek.

"Good night, son. I love you." He hugged the baby to him while Jenny gazed on lovingly. Trent was tired. His head, with its cluster of dusty blond ringlets, dropped onto Cage's shoulder and he yawned broadly.

"He was ready for bed," Jenny said later as they crossed the hall into their own bedroom after seeing that Trent was safely tucked in. "And so am I." She spread her arms out to her sides and fell backward onto the bed. "The two of you wear me out."

"Oh, yeah?" Cage's eyes roamed over her reclining form, from the top of her head to the tips of her toes, which dangled just above the floor. Her robe had fallen open, revealing a beguiling length of smooth, tan thigh. Her breasts looked both wanton and vulnerable with her arms widespread. Without compunction he unknotted the belt of his robe, shrugged it off, let it slide soundlessly to the carpeted floor, and lay down on top of her. His knees wedged hers apart.

"You've got to overcome your shyness, Cage."

"Smart-ass." He chuckled as his lips toyed with her ear. She had bathed just before him and Trent, and her skin was warm and fragrant. Beneath the robe she was wearing nothing but a rosy glow. "Why fool around with preliminaries? I believe in going after what I want."

"And you want me?"

"Hm." He pecked innocent kisses on her neck. "I always have. The longest three months of my life were those after Trent was born."

"Don't forget the weeks before he was born."

"I haven't forgotten," he snarled. "I still say that doctor put the restriction on us earlier than necessary. He was getting back at me for something."

"What?"

"Nothing."

She threaded her fingers through his hair and pulled on it until he raised his head. "What?"

"Ouch!"

"Tell me."

"All right, all right. It's no big deal. Several years

ago I dated one of his nurses. When I broke it off, she got upset and left town. He's still holding a grudge."

"How many women did you…romance?"

He became very still. His teasing manner ceased. His eyes probed into hers. "Does it matter, Jenny?"

Her eyes coasted down from his to stare at his throat. "Do you miss it? That carousing?"

"What do you think?" His body nudged apart her robe and she felt him virile and warm against her belly.

"I guess not."

"You guess right."

He kissed her with a passionate hunger that dispelled any lingering doubts. By the time he raised his lips from hers, her blood was pumping hotly through her veins. "I love you, Cage."

"I love you."

"Do you know what today is?"

He thought a moment. "The accident?"

"A year ago today."

"How did you remember that?"

She touched his lips. "Because that's the day I thought I'd lost you. I spent hours sitting in that hospital waiting room, wondering if you would live just long enough for me to tell you how much I love you and how important your life is to me. At first that was all I prayed for. Then, after you survived the surgery, I got greedy and prayed that you'd live to a ripe old age."

One corner of his mouth slanted up into a smile. "I hope God answers your second prayer."

"So do I. But I don't take a single day for granted. I thank Him for every one we have together." They kissed again. This kiss was a reconfirmation of their love.

When they pulled apart, he sank his fingers into

her hair and spread it out on the bedspread behind her. "When I regained consciousness in that ICU, the first thing I saw was your face. I wasn't about to die and leave you."

"How much of those first few days do you remember?"

She thought it was strange that they'd never talked much about this. She had scolded and cajoled him through months of convalescence. He wasn't accustomed to being confined and having his activities limited. His psychological adjustment had been as difficult as the physical recovery.

But Jenny's patient diligence had paid off. Much to the doctors' surprise, within months of the accident Cage was back to normal. Better, in fact, the doctors teased him, because he was no longer smoking and wasn't drinking as much.

Then Trent had been born and they had settled into the routine of family life. Cage's business had continued to flourish, as he had been able to conduct it by telephone during his confinement. He now had two people on the payroll, a secretary who had taken over Jenny's position when Trent was born, and a geologist who took the core samples and analyzed them. But it was still Cage who speculated, who talked investors out of their money, who put the deals together, who found the oil.

The past year had been so busy that Jenny had put the harrowing hours and bleak days following the accident out of her mind. She had never really asked Cage about his impressions while he was in the hospital.

"I don't remember much, just that you were always there. One incident stands out. The first time I saw Mother and Dad. I remember trying to smile so they would know how glad I was to see them. Mother took my hand, leaned down, and kissed my cheek. Dad did the same. That might not sound like much, but it meant the world to me."

Jenny sniffed back her tears. "You would have been proud to see me standing up to them, telling them the baby I carried was yours."

The kiss that followed was considerably more heated than the one before. "Mother and Dad have come around," Cage said when they pulled apart. "They're crazy about Trent and think he's the most wonderful baby in the world."

"Wonder where they got the idea?" Teasingly she tweaked a clump of his chest hair. "Between them and Roxy and Gary, he'll be spoiled rotten if we don't keep a lid on their indulgence." She laughed. "You know when I first knew that your folks would accept us?"

"When Dad married us in the hospital room?"

"No," she said, automatically smiling at the memory. "Before that, when Gary called from El Paso, wondering why we weren't at the airport to pick them up when they got home from their honeymoon. I was upset and embarrassed. I had forgotten all about them while you were in intensive care. Bob volunteered to drive to El Paso and bring them home. I knew that if he could accept Roxy, he could accept us."

"You won a few points with them when you set up the Hal Hendren Fund to Aid Political Refugees."

"And you won even more when you made that hefty donation."

"Only because you insisted I match what I spent on your wedding ring."

"You would have anyway."

"I don't know," he hedged, glancing down at the diamond and emerald ring. "That was a damned expensive ring."

She pinched him on his bare bottom. They both laughed and when the laughter subsided, Cage stared down at her, his eyes alight with desire. "You're my darling, Jenny. I adore you. There was no light in my life until you loved me."

"Then that light will shine forever, because that's how long I'll love you."

"Cross your heart?"

"Cross my heart." She reached for his mouth with hers and when they met, their unquenchable desire was ignited. "But you're still a troublemaker," she whispered against his lips.

"I am?"

"Hm. Look what havoc you've wreaked on me." She opened her robe and carried his hand to her breast. He touched the warm fullness, the taut center.

"I did that?"

"Yes. And I used to be such a nice girl. I was led astray."

Lightly he pinched the aroused nipple between his fingers. "I'm a naughty boy, all right."

He lowered his head and rubbed his mouth against the hard, rosy peak. His tongue swept it. Again. "You still taste milky." He suckled her as his son had done until a month before.

Cage seemed to draw nurture from her, too. He got lost in her taste and texture. When he stroked his hand up her thigh, he found her dewy with anticipation. His caressing fingers and revolving thumb brought her to the edge of oblivion. Then his manhood claimed her.

"My God, Jenny, I love you so much."

Time was suspended until the universe split open and showered them with light. It took a long while for them to regain their breath. When they did, Cage eased up and smiled down into her shining face.

Her responding grin was slow and sexy and she all but purred when she said, "You're hell on wheels, Cage Hendren."

And it was good because they could laugh about it.

\* \* \* \* \*

# THE DEVIL'S OWN

# *One*

He was drunk and, consequently, just what she needed.

She studied him through the smoky, dusty haze of the cantina, where he sat on a bar stool, nursing his drink. The glass was chipped, its dark amber contents cloudy. He didn't seem to notice as he frequently raised it to his lips. He sat with his knees widespread, his head bent low between hunched shoulders, his elbows propped on the greasy surface of the bar.

The tavern was crowded with soldiers and the women who entertained them in rooms upstairs. Squeaky fans, rotating desultorily overhead, barely stirred the thick pall of tobacco smoke. The cloying essence of cheap perfume mixed with the stench of the unwashed bodies of men who had spent days in the jungle.

Laughter was everywhere, but the mood wasn't particularly jovial. The soldiers' eyes didn't smile. There was an aura of desperation to their merrymaking. They took their fun as they took everything else, violently.

They were young for the most part—tough, surly men who lived on a razor's edge between life and death every day. Most wore the uniform of the army of the current military regime. But whether they were locals or international mercenaries, all had that same hard look about their eyes. They were full of suspicion. Wariness shadowed every grin.

The man Kerry Bishop had her sights on was no exception. He wasn't Latin—he was American by the looks of him. Hard, well-defined biceps bulged beneath his sleeves, which had been rolled up so tightly they encircled his arms like rope. His dark hair hung long and shaggy over his shirt collar.

The portion of his jaw Kerry could see was covered with several days' growth of beard. That could be either a benefit or a handicap to her plan. A benefit because the partial beard would help disguise his face, and a handicap because few officers in the regular army would go that many days without a shave. El Presidente was a stickler for good grooming among his officers.

Well, she'd just have to chance it. Of the lot, this man was still her best bet. He not only looked the most inebriated, but the most disreputable—lean and hungry and totally without principle. Once he was sober, he would no doubt be easy to buy.

She was getting ahead of herself. She had to get him out of there first. When would the driver of that military truck, the careless one who had negligently left his keys in the ignition, return to find that the keys were gone? At any moment, he could come looking for them.

The keys now rattled in the pocket of Kerry's skirt each time she moved her legs on her journey across the room toward the man drinking alone at the bar. She dodged couples dancing to the blaring music, warded off a few clumsy passes and averted her eyes from the couples who were too carried away by passion to bother seeking privacy.

After spending almost a year in Monterico, nothing should surprise her. The nation was in the throes of a bloody civil war, and war often reduced human beings to animals. But what she saw some of the couples doing right out in the open brought hot color to her cheeks.

Setting her jaw firmly and concentrating only on her purpose for being there, she moved closer to the man at the bar. The closer she got, the surer she became that he was exactly what she needed.

He was even more fearsome up close than he had been at a distance. He wasn't actually drinking, but angrily tossing the liquor down his throat. He wasn't tasting it. He wasn't drinking for pleasure. He wasn't there to have a good time, but to vent his anger over something. Perhaps to blot some major upset from his mind? Had someone welshed on a deal? Double-crossed him? Shortchanged him?

Kerry hoped so. If he were strapped for cash he'd be much more receptive to the deal she had to offer him.

A pistol had been shoved into the waistband of his fatigue pants. There was a long, wicked machete holstered against his thigh. At his feet, surrounding the bar stool, were three canvas bags. They were so packed with the tools of his trade, that the seams of the bags were strained. Kerry shuddered to think of the destruction his private stash of weaponry was capable of. That was probably one reason why he drank alone and went unmolested. In a place like this, fights frequently broke out among the hot-blooded, trigger-happy men. But no one sought either conversation or trouble with this one who sat on the last bar stool in the row.

Unfortunately for Kerry, it was also the seat farthest from the building's only exit. There would be no slipping out a back door. She would have to transport him from the rear corner to the door. To succeed in getting him to leave with her, she would have to be her most convincing.

With that in mind, she took a deep breath, closed the remaining distance between them, and sat down on the bar stool next to his, which fortuitously was vacant. His profile was as rugged and stony as a mountain range. Not a soft, compassionate line in evidence. She tried not to think of that as she spoke to him.

"A drink, señor?" Her heart was pounding. Her mouth was as dry as cotton. But she conjured up an alluring smile and tentatively laid her right hand on his left one.

She was beginning to think he hadn't heard her. He just sat there, staring down into his empty glass. But, just when she was about to repeat her suggestion, he turned his head slightly and looked down at her hand where it rested on top of his.

His, Kerry noticed, was much larger than hers. It was wider by half an inch on either side, and her fingertips extended only as far as his first knuckles. He was wearing a watch. It was black, with a huge, round face and lots of dials and gadgetry. He wore no rings.

He stared at their hands for what seemed like an eternity to Kerry, before his eyes followed her arm up, slowly, to her shoulder, then up and right, to her face. A cigarette was dangling between his sullen lips. He stared at her through the curling, bluish-gray smoke.

She had practiced her smile in a mirror to make sure she was doing a fair imitation of the women who solicited in the cantinas. Eyes at half-mast. Lips moist and slightly parted. She knew she had to get that come-hither smile right. Everything hinged on her being convincing.

But she never got to execute that rehearsed, sultry smile. It, like most everything in her brain, vaporized when she gazed into his face for the first time. Her heavily rouged lips parted all right, but of their own accord and with no direction from her. She drew in a quick little gasp. The fluttering of her eyelashes was involuntary, not affected.

His face was a total surprise. She had expected ugliness. He was quite good-looking. She had expected unsightly traces of numerous military campaigns. He had but one scar, a tiny one above his left eyebrow. It was more interesting than unsightly. His face didn't have the harsh stamp of brutality she had anticipated, only broodiness. And his lips weren't thin and hard with insensitivity, but full and sensual.

His eyes weren't blank, as were those of most of the men who killed for hire. His eyes, even though they were fogged with alcohol, burned with internal fires that Kerry found even more unsettling than the heatless glint of indifference. Nor did he smell of sweat. His bronzed skin was glistening with a fine sheen of perspiration, but it gave off the scent of soap. He had recently washed.

Quelling her shock and trepidation—because for some strange reason, his lack of standard looks frightened her more than reassured her—she met his suspicious stare steadily. She forced herself to audition that seductive smile she'd spent hours perfecting and repeated her request as she pressed his hand.

"Beat it."

His abrupt words took her so by surprise that she actually flinched, almost falling off the slick, vinyl pad of the bar stool. He turned his head forward again and jerked his hand from beneath hers to remove the cigarette from his mouth. He ground it out in the overflowing ashtray.

Kerry was dumbfounded. Was she that unappealing? Weren't mercenaries supposed to have the appetites of animals? And wasn't that voraciousness particularly true of their sexual appetites? Fathers hid their daughters from them in dread of the unthinkable. Men protected their wives at all costs.

Now, when Kerry offered herself to one, he had ungraciously said, "Beat it," and dismissed her with a turn of his head. She must look worse than she thought. Her year in the jungle had apparently taken its toll in ways she hadn't been aware of.

True, her hair had forgotten the luxury of a hot-oil treatment. Mascara and moisturizing face cream existed for her only in another lifetime. But how attractive did a woman have to be to tempt a man with a bestial sex drive?

She weighed her options. Her plan was foolhardy at best. Success was improbable. It would be risky under the best of circumstances. It would work only if her "recruit" was cooperative. If he wasn't, it would be almost impossible to do what she had set out to do that night.

She glanced over her shoulder, wondering if she should desert this man in favor of another prospect. No. Her time was limited and rapidly running out. Whoever had left that truck parked outside could return at any moment. He might demand a shakedown of everybody in the cantina until the missing keys were found. Or he might have a spare set of keys. In either event, she wanted to be long gone before he returned. The truck was just as important as the man. She had to steal it, and now was the time.

Besides, she told herself, this candidate was her first and best choice. He fit all the criteria she had outlined in her mind. He was drunk, unscrupulous and obviously down on his luck.

"Please, señor, one drink." Pushing all caution aside, she laid her hand on his thigh near the lethal machete. He mumbled something. *"¿Qué?"* She used her whispered question as an opportunity to move closer to him.

"No time."

*"Por favor."*

He looked at her again. She made a motion that sent the scarf sliding off her head and from around her shoulders. She had previously decided to take off the scarf only as a last resort. When she had told Joe to find her a dress like the women in the taverns wore, she hadn't counted on him being so knowledgeable about such things.

From a clothesline, he had stolen the dress she now had on. It was faded. The cloth was thin from years of wear and stone washing. The red floral print was lurid and tacky. The woman who had owned the dress had been a size larger than Kerry. The ruffled shoulder straps wouldn't stay put and the bodice gaped open where it should have been filled.

She wanted to pull the dress against her chest and cover herself, but she forced herself to remain still. Rigid with shame, she let his gaze travel all the way from her exposed shoulder to her sandaled feet. He took his time. While Kerry burned with humiliation, his eyes drifted across her partially exposed breasts and down to her lap, which he studied for an indecently long time, then down her shapely, bare legs and feet to the tips of her toes.

"One drink," he said thickly.

Kerry barely kept herself from slumping with relief. She smiled flirtatiously as he called out for the querulous bartender to pour them two drinks. They watched each other while he carried over two glasses and a bottle of the potent, local liquor. The bartender poured the drinks. Kerry's mercenary, without taking his eyes off her face, fished in his pants pocket and slapped two bills onto the bar. Money in hand, the bartender shuffled off, leaving them alone.

The mercenary picked up his glass, tipped it toward Kerry in a mocking salute, and drank it all in one swallow.

She picked up her own glass. If it had been rinsed out since last being used, she would consider herself lucky. Trying not to think about that, she raised it to her lips and took a sip. The liquor tasted like industrial strength disinfectant. It took a tremendous amount of willpower not to spray it into the roughly hewn, handsome face of her mercenary. She swallowed the ghastly stuff. Her throat rebelled instantly. If she had gargled thumbtacks, it couldn't have hurt more. Tears flooded her eyes.

His eyes narrowed suspiciously, emphasizing the squint lines radiating from their outer corners. "You're not a drinker. Why'd you come over here?"

She pretended not to understand his English. Smiling, she covered his hand with her own again, and tilted her head so that her dark hair spilled across the shoulder left bare by the slipping strap. "I love you."

He merely grunted indifferently. His eyes slid closed. Panicked, Kerry thought he was about to pass out.

"We go?" she said quickly.

"Go? With you? Hell no. I told you I haven't got time even if I wanted to."

She wet her lips frantically. What was she going to do? *"Por favor."*

He focused his bleary eyes on her face, particularly on her mouth when she used her tongue to moisten her lips. His gaze moved down and remained fixedly on her breasts. Because she was so agitated and afraid that her mission would be thwarted, her breasts rose and fell rapidly beneath the tasteless dress.

Kerry didn't know whether to be glad or frightened when she saw his eyes glaze with passion. He rubbed one hand up and down his own thigh and she knew he was thinking about touching her. All his unconscious movements were indicative of his mounting arousal. That's what she had wanted, but it terrified her, too. She was playing with fire. If she didn't watch it, it could burn out of her control.

Almost before she had completed the thought, his hand shot out and grabbed her around the neck. She wasn't prepared for the sudden movement and had no time to counter it before he hauled her off the bar stool and against him.

His knees were opened. She landed against him solidly. Her breasts came only to the middle of his chest, which was as firm as it had appeared. Something hard gouged her stomach. She fervently hoped it was the butt of the pistol tucked into his waistband.

Before Kerry could get her bearings, or even gasp in astonishment, his mouth covered hers. It moved hotly and hungrily. His whiskers scraped the delicate skin around her lips, but it wasn't an entirely unpleasant sensation.

Every instinct urged her to resist him. But then her common sense asserted itself. She was supposed to be a prostitute soliciting customers. It wouldn't be in character to stave off the advances of a prospective source of income.

So she let herself become pliant.

The shock of having his tongue spear through her lips almost sent her over the edge of reason. It thrust deeply into her mouth as though searching for something. Its assault was wildly erotic. Kerry's reaction was to clutch handfuls of his shirt. His arms wrapped around her waist. He continued to kiss her, pulling her ever closer, until her back was painfully arched and she could scarcely breathe.

At last, he lifted his mouth from hers and pressed it, open, against her throat. Kerry's head fell back and her eyes rolled toward the ceiling. The lazily circling ceiling fan made her dizzier than she already was. She felt as though she were spinning in slow, diminishing circles, and that when she reached the center of this maddening vortex, she was going to explode. Yet she was powerless to extricate herself from it.

The mercenary slid his hands below her waist. One boldly fondled her bottom. The other came around and stroked the side of her breast. Kerry endured the caresses, but her breathing was quick and shallow. He muttered something so blatantly sexual, so disturbingly accurate, she wished she hadn't heard or understood him.

Nuzzling her neck in the sensitive spot just below her ear, he mumbled, "Okay, señorita, you've got a customer. Where to? Upstairs? Let's go."

He stood up and swayed on his feet. Kerry's equilibrium, being what it was at the moment, forced them to cling to each other until she regained her balance.

*"Mi casa."*

"Your house?" he grumbled.

*"Sí, sí,"* she said bobbing her head enthusiastically. Not giving him an opportunity to argue, she bent down and picked up one of the canvas bags at their feet. It was so heavy, it almost tore her arm from its socket. She could barely lift the bag, but managed to work the leather strap up her arm and over her shoulder.

"Jus' leave that crap and I'll—"

"No!" She bent down to pick up another of the three bags. In rapid Spanish, she began warning him about thieves and the danger of weapons getting into the hands of enemies.

"Stop that damned gibberish. I can't unnerschtand… Oh, hell. I changed my mind. No time."

"No. Back soon."

As she bent down to assist him in picking up the last of the heavy bags, she caught his eyes on the gaping front of her dress. Though she blushed beet red, she smiled at him seductively and looped her free arm through his, pressing her breasts against his upper arm the way she'd seen prostitutes do to their customers. Mutely, he fell into place beside her.

They staggered their way through the bar, which, if anything, had become even more crowded since she had come in. The mercenary drunkenly stumbled at Kerry's side. She nearly buckled beneath his weight combined with the heavy bag she was carrying over her shoulder. The other two were hooked over his shoulders, but he seemed impervious to them.

When they were almost to the door, a soldier who looked like he'd been weaned on nitroglycerin, stumbled against her and grabbed her arm. He made an obscene proposition to her in Spanish. She shook her head vehemently and splayed her hand on the mercenary's chest. The soldier looked ready to argue, but he happened to catch the fierce, possessive gleam in the mercenary's eyes and wisely changed his mind.

Kerry congratulated herself for making such a good choice. Her mercenary inspired fear in even the most fearsome. No one else accosted them on their way out of the cantina.

Her lungs were starved for air, and she greedily sucked it in. The tropical air was heavy and humid, but it was brisk and bracing compared to that inside the cantina.

Kerry was grateful for it. It cleared her head. She wished she could rest, wished she could say, "Thank God that's over." But there was still an awesome task facing her. The pickup had been easy compared to what lay ahead.

She practically dragged her staggering escort toward the military truck, which, she was grateful to see, was still parked beneath the impenetrable shadows of an almond tree. She propped the professional soldier against the side of the Japanese-made pickup while she opened the door. The truck, having once belonged to a fruit vendor, now had the government insignia stenciled over the farmer's logo.

She pushed the incoherent mercenary inside the passenger-side door and closed it before he could fall out. Then, furtively glancing over her shoulder, she lifted the bags of weapons and ammunition into the bed of the pickup. At any moment she expected to hear the rat-a-tat of a machine gun and feel bullets ripping through her body. In Monterico, they shot first and asked questions later.

She threw a tarp over the bags and climbed into the cab. Either her mercenary hadn't noticed that the truck belonged to the regular army, or he didn't care. As soon as she closed the door behind herself, he pounced on her.

He kissed her again. His desire hadn't abated. Instead, it had increased. The cooler outdoor air, which had cleared her head, seemed to have done the same for him. This wasn't the haphazard kiss of a drunk. This was the kiss of a man who knew exactly what he was doing, and knew how to do it well.

His tongue pressed insistently against her lips until they opened, then it rubbed sleekly against hers. His hands were busy. His caresses kept her gasping with shock and outrage.

*"Por favor,"* she whispered urgently, slapping his hands away and dodging his mouth.

"Whatsamatter?"

*"Mi casa.* We go."

She reached into the pocket of her skirt and produced a key. She crammed it into the ignition and started the truck, trying to ignore the nibbling he was doing on her neck and around her ear. She felt his teeth against her skin. Despite the muggy heat, her arms broke out in goose bumps.

Kerry put the truck in reverse and backed away from the tavern. The ramshackle building seemed to vibrate with raucous laughter and throbbing music. She braced herself for shouting and gunfire, but the truck moved into the street unnoticed.

Kerry was tempted to leave the headlights turned off, but decided against it. It would arouse suspicion for a military truck to drive through the city streets without its headlights on. And, it would be hazardous to drive without lights on the rutted lanes that were likely to be littered with battle debris. So she turned on the headlights. They threw light onto the war-scarred commercial buildings and shuttered housing. Even in the darkness, which was flattering, the capital city was a depressing sight.

Getting out of the city was a problem that Kerry had spent hours mulling over. No one entered or left it without having to drive through a military checkpoint. After running several reconnaissance missions, Kerry had selected the gate she would drive through now. It was one of the busiest checkpoints. Had she picked one of the less-traveled roads, the guards might be more thorough. They would more than likely stop and search a military truck driven by a woman. At the busy gate she had chosen, she would probably get no more than a cursory inspection. At least, that's what she was hoping for.

She mentally went over her plan and what she intended to say one more time.

However, it was difficult to concentrate on anything. She hadn't picked up a belligerent drunk or a funny drunk. She had picked up an amorous drunk. Between mutterings about not having much time, he planted ardent kisses on her neck and chest.

She nearly steered the truck off the road when he slipped his hand under her skirt and between her knees. There was no way she could continue to work the clutch and accelerator with her knees clamped together. She had no choice but to allow his strong fingers to curl around the lower portion of her thigh and tease the smooth underside of her knee.

She had almost adjusted to that when his hand began to reach higher. Each touch was a jolt to her system. The floor of her stomach dropped away, and she closed her eyes for a fraction of a second when he lightly squeezed a handful of her inner thigh. The skirt of her dress inched higher. Most of it was already bunched up in her lap.

"Señor, *por favor.*" She tried to work her leg free of his questing hand.

He muttered something that sounded like "Need a woman," but Kerry wasn't sure. Knowing that they were only a few blocks from the crucial checkpoint, she pulled the truck over to the side of the road and let it idle.

"Please, señor, put this on." She reached beneath the seat where she had previously stowed the jacket and cap that she had found lying on the seat of the truck.

He didn't seem to notice her improved English or the absence of an accent, but he blinked at her stupidly. "Huh?"

She draped the military jacket over his shoulders. The jacket didn't quite accommodate their breadth, but all she needed for the guard to see was the officer's rank. The badge had been ineptly embroidered onto the sleeve, which Kerry made certain was visible. She plopped the cap down onto the mercenary's head and adjusted it, while he just as earnestly tried to lower the shoulder straps of her dress.

"Good grief," she muttered in disgust as she pulled them back up onto her shoulders, "you're an animal." Then she remembered that she was supposed to be a whore accustomed to being manhandled. She laid her hand against his whiskered cheek and smiled in a manner that she hoped was beguiling and full of lewd promise. In melodious Spanish she told him he was a lecherous pig, but made the insult sound like a lover's enticement.

Engaging the gears of the truck again, she drove the remaining blocks to the checkpoint.

There were two cars ahead of her. The driver of the first was arguing with the guard. Good. He would welcome a military truck because there would be no hassle.

"Whas goin' on?"

The mercenary raised his head and blinked, trying to see through the dirty windshield, upon which a thousand insects had given their lives. Patting his head back into place on her shoulder, Kerry told him to leave everything to her, that they were almost there. His head lolled against her shoulder as she drove the truck up to the barricade.

The guard, no older than sixteen, sauntered toward the driver's side and shone a flashlight directly into her face. She forced herself to smile. *"Buenas noches."* She lowered her voice to a sexy, husky pitch.

*"Buenas noches,"* the guard responded suspiciously. "What's wrong with the captain?"

She clicked her tongue against the roof of her mouth.

"He had too much to drink. Poor man. He's a brave soldier, but he is defeated by a bottle."

"Where are you taking him?"

"Out of the kindness of my heart, I'm driving him to my house." She winked seductively. "He asked me to nurse him through the night."

The guard grinned at her. His eyes moved over the slumping occupant of the truck. Assured that the officer was unconscious, he asked, "Why bother with him? Wouldn't you rather have a real man?" He made a crude reference to the dimensions of his manhood, which Kerry found not only unbelievable, but revolting.

Nonetheless, she simpered and lowered her lashes. "I'm sorry, but the captain has already paid me for tonight. Perhaps another time."

"Perhaps," he said cockily. "If I can afford you."

She tapped his hand flirtatiously. Making a moue of regret, she waved goodbye and put the truck into gear. The young guard commanded his partner at the checkpoint to raise the gate and she drove through it.

For several miles, Kerry tenaciously gripped the steering wheel and kept her eyes on the rearview mirror as much as she did on the winding road ahead. When it became apparent that no one was following her, she began to tremble in delayed reaction.

She had done it!

The mercenary had stayed blessedly quiet during the entire exchange with the guard. Now they were on their way and no one was even chasing them. She made a wide loop around the city and took the turnoff, which led straight into the jungle. Soon the tops of the trees interlaced over the road to form a leafy tunnel.

The road narrowed and grew bumpier with each

passing mile. The mercenary's head grew heavy where it lay against her breasts. He weighted down the entire right side of her body. She tried to shove him away several times, but she couldn't budge him. Finally she gave up, concluding that having him asleep against her was better than having to fight off his aggressive love play.

She gave considerable thought to stopping before she reached the place she had sighted earlier, but talked herself out of it. The more distance she put between the mercenary and the city tonight, the more bargaining power she would have tomorrow. So she kept driving over the corrugated road with the man's head bouncing heavily against her at every chuckhole.

She became sleepy. The monotony of the headlights being mirrored off the encroaching jungle was mesmerizing. She became so drowsy that she almost missed her turn. The moment she saw the slight break in the solid wall of trees, she reacted quickly and whipped the steering wheel to the left, then pulled the truck to a stop and cut the engine.

Jungle birds, roosting in the trees overhead, loudly protested this nighttime intrusion, then resettled. The quiet darkness enclosed the small truck like a black velvet fist.

Sighing tiredly, Kerry shoved the man off her. She arched her back, stretching out the aching muscles. She rolled her head around her shoulders. Her relief at having accomplished her mission was profound. There was nothing to do then but wait until daylight.

But the mercenary had something else in mind.

Before she could brace herself for it, he smothered her in an embrace. His nap seemed to have revived him. His kisses were more fervent than ever. While his tongue playfully flicked over her lips, his hands pulled down the oversized bodice of her dress. He plunged his hand inside and scooped up her breast.

"No!" Garnering her strength, Kerry placed her hands against his shoulders and shoved with all her might. He went toppling over backward and his head hit the dashboard. He rolled to his side and sagged forward. The only thing that prevented him from slumping all the way to the floorboard was his size. His wide shoulders pinned him between the dashboard and the seat.

He didn't move. Didn't make a sound.

Horrified, Kerry covered her mouth and waited several breathless moments. He remained motionless. "Oh, Lord, I've killed him."

She opened the door of the truck. The overhead light came on. When her eyes had adjusted to the sudden brightness, she stared down at the mercenary. Tentatively she poked at him. He groaned.

Her fearful expression turned into one of disgust. He wasn't dead, just dead drunk and passed out.

She tried to pull him up by his shirt collar, but couldn't. Levering herself up on her knees, she tugged on his shoulders until he flopped back, settling into the corner of the cab formed by the passenger door and the back of the seat.

His head was bent over. One cheek was resting against his shoulder. He'd have a crick in his neck by morning. Good. Kerry hoped he did. Anyone who drank himself into a stupor like that deserved to reap the dire consequences.

But his position made him look much less threatening. His eyelashes were long and curled, she noticed, incongruent with the masculinity of his face. With the dome light shining on him, she saw that his hair was dark brown, but streaked with reddish highlights, and that beneath his deep tan, he was freckled across his cheekbones.

He was breathing deeply through his mouth. His lips were slightly parted. With that sulky, full, lower lip, it was no wonder he could kiss— She yanked her mind away from any thought of the way he'd kissed her.

Before she started feeling any softness toward him, she thought about how he might react in the morning. He might not take kindly to being recruited for her cause. He might react violently to finding himself in the middle of nowhere before she had a chance to make her sales pitch. These mercenaries were ruthlessly short-tempered.

She looked at the machete. Acting before she could talk herself out of it, she unsnapped the scabbard and slid the long blade out of it. It seemed to weigh a hundred pounds. She maneuvered it awkwardly, barely saved her thighs from being sliced in two and tossed it onto the ground outside the open door.

Then there was the pistol.

She stared at it for several moments. Her stomach became victim to an odd flurrying. She should disarm him. That would be the smart thing to do, but, considering where the pistol was…

Now certainly wasn't the time to get squeamish! When she considered what she'd already gone through tonight, getting timid now was ludicrous.

She reached forward. Chickened out. Withdrew her hands. Closed her hands into fists, then flexed her fingers, like a safecracker about to undertake the challenge of his career.

She reached for the pistol again. This time, before she could lose her nerve, she closed her hand around the butt of it and tugged. Again. Harder. It wouldn't come free of his waistband.

She snatched her hand back and debated her alternatives. She had none. She had to get that pistol away from him, and get it without waking him up.

She stared at his web belt. Closing her eyes for a moment and wetting her dry lips, she gathered her rapidly scattering courage. Forcing down her nervousness, she touched the belt buckle. Using the tip of her index finger, she slid the small brass button forward to release the teeth clamping down into the webbing. Gradually the tension eased. She pressed harder. The teeth popped free. Metal clinked against metal softly.

The mercenary drew a deep breath. Let it out on a sigh. Kerry froze. She inched her hands forward again and, working slowly and carefully, pulled the end of the belt through the brass buckle.

There was no rejoicing. She met with another obstacle.

She touched the heavy metal button of his fatigue trousers. He made a snuffling sound and shifted his legs, drawing one knee up onto the seat. Which rearranged everything. Everything. And wedged the barrel of the gun in even tighter between his stomach and his waistband.

Kerry's hands were sweating.

She dared not think of what he would do if he should wake up and discover her fiddling with the fly of his pants. If he thought she was trying to take his gun away, he'd shoot her with it. And if he thought… The other was too horrendous to contemplate.

She reached for the button again, and this time didn't let the purring sound coming from his chest deter her. Her fingers were clumsy. It was no small task to work the button out of the reinforced hole in the stiff cloth, but at last she succeeded. She closed her fingers around the butt of the pistol again, but it still wouldn't come free.

She swore in whispers.

Gnawing on her lower lip, she pinched the tab of his zipper between her thumb and index finger. She had to yank on it three times before it moved. She had intended to lower it only an inch or two, but when it finally cooperated, it unzipped all the way. Suddenly. Shockingly. She dropped the tab as though it had bitten her, then jerked the pistol free.

He snorted, shifted again, but didn't wake up. She clutched the pistol to her chest as though it were the Holy Grail and she'd dedicated a lifetime to searching for it. Her whole body was damp with perspiration.

Finally, when she was certain that he had slept through her fumblings and that she wasn't going to have to use the vicious weapon to protect herself, she dropped it onto the ground. It clattered against the machete. She shut the door of the truck quickly, as though covering up incriminating evidence. A bird protested the noise, then silence fell again.

She sat there in the darkness, thinking.

Maybe her mercenary wasn't such a good choice after all, if he could be disarmed so easily.

Of course he was drunk, and where they were going, he wouldn't have access to alcohol. He had warned off that other soldier with one threatening look. He was physically suited to the job she had in mind for him.

She had been close enough to him tonight to know that. Those lean, hard muscles could only belong to a man of strength and stamina. She knew also that once he made up his mind to do something, he was determined. If he hadn't bumped his head against the dashboard, she would probably still be fighting him off.

She wouldn't think any more about him. Suffice it to say that she had done well; she had made a good choice.

With that in mind, Kerry settled into her own corner of the cab, rested her head in the open window and fell asleep to the steady rhythm of his gentle snores.

It seemed that she had barely closed her eyes when she was awakened by a litany of words she had only seen scrawled on the walls of public restrooms. There was movement beside her and scalding blasphemy.

The beast was coming awake.

# Two

All the jungle animals were waking up. Rustling leaves marked the progress of reptiles and rodents. Birds chattered in the branches of the trees overhead. Small monkeys screeched as they swung from vine to vine in search of breakfast.

But even their shrill racket took second place to the vivid cursing inside the cab of the truck.

Kerry cowered against the driver's door as she watched her mercenary come awake with about as much humor as a fairy-tale ogre. In fact he resembled an illustration she remembered from a childhood picture book with his hair sticking out at odd angles, his ferocious scowl, and his heavily shadowed jaw. Grunting and groaning, he leaned forward, unsteadily braced his elbows on his knees and held his head between his shaking hands.

After several moments, he moved his head around— it seemed to cause him agony—and looked at Kerry through bloodshot eyes. They had as many red streaks in them as the eastern sky. Without saying a word, he fumbled for the door handle, unlatched it and virtually rolled out of the truck.

When his feet struck the ground, lushly carpeted and spongy as it was, he let loose a string of blistering curses, products of a fertile imagination. That set off the noisy wildlife again. He clasped his head, and Kerry couldn't tell if he was trying to hold it on or tear it off.

She opened the door on the driver's side. Cautiously checking the ground for snakes first, she placed her sandaled foot in the deep undergrowth and stepped out of the truck. She considered picking up one of his weapons, either the machete or the gun, but decided that he was in no condition to do even the most defenseless animal any serious harm.

Gambling her safety on that decision, she crept around the hood of the truck and peered down the opposite side of it. He was braced against it with only his bottom touching. His feet were planted solidly in front of him, as though he had carefully put them there and didn't dare move them for fear of falling off the planet. He was bent forward at the waist, still cushioning his head between his hands.

When he heard her tread in the soft undergrowth, which must have sounded like a marching army to his supersensitive ears, he swiveled his head around.

Under the baleful gaze of golden brown eyes, Kerry halted.

"Where am I?" The words were garbled, ground out by a throat abused by tobacco and alcohol.

"Monterico," she replied fearfully.

"What day is this?"

"Tuesday."

"What about my plane?"

He seemed to have a difficult time keeping her in focus. The sunlight was growing brighter by the moment as it topped the trees. He squinted against it until his eyes were almost closed. When an extremely vocal bird squawked noisily overhead, he winced and cursed beneath his breath.

"Plane?"

"Plane. Plane. Airplane."

When she only stared back at him apprehensively, he began searching through the pockets of his shirt with a great deal of agitation and practically no coordination. Finally, from the breast pocket, he produced an airplane ticket and what appeared to be an official exit visa. The whimsical government of Monterico was stingy with visas. They weren't issued very often and were more valuable than gold. It took a king's ransom in gold to have one forged.

He shook the ticket and visa at her. "I was supposed to be on an airplane last night at ten o'clock."

Kerry swallowed. He was going to be upset. She braced herself for his wrath. But she tilted her head back fearlessly when she told him, "Sorry. You missed it."

He turned around slowly, so that his shoulder was propped against the truck. He stared at her with such undiluted animosity that she quavered on the inside.

When he spoke, his voice was whispery with menace. "Did you make me miss my plane out?"

She took a cautious step backward. "You came with me of your own free will."

He took a threatening step toward her. "You haven't got long to live, lady. But before I murder you, I'd like to know, just out of curiosity, why you shanghaied me."

She pointed an accusing finger at him. "You were drunk!"

"Which I'm living to regret."

"How was I supposed to know that you were trying to get on an airplane?"

"Didn't I mention it?"

"No."

"I must have told you," he said with an insistent shake of his head.

"You didn't."

He squinted his eyes and looked at her accusingly. "You're not only a whore, you're a lying whore."

"I'm neither," Kerry declared, blushing hotly.

Those unusual agate eyes traveled from the top of her tousled head to the tips of her toes. But this time, unlike the appreciative way they had moved over her in the cantina, they were scornful. His look made her feel exactly like what he was accusing her of being. In the daylight the cheap, ill-fitting dress showed no saving graces.

He asked sneeringly, "What's your gimmick?"

"I don't have a gimmick."

"Was business so bad in the States, you had to come down here to peddle it?"

If Kerry hadn't been so frightened of the latent violence that was causing his muscles to twitch involuntarily, she would have stepped forward and slapped him. Instead she fashioned fists out of her hands, but kept them at her sides.

Through gritted teeth she said, "I'm not a whore. I only disguised myself as one so I could go into that bar and pick you up."

"Sounds like whoring to me."

"Stop saying that!" she cried, as angered by his off-handed assessment of her as by his actual words. "I need your services."

He glanced down at his fatigue pants, which were still unfastened and riding low on his narrow hips. "I think you already had them."

Kerry went hot all over. It seemed that every drop of blood in her body rushed to her head and was pushing against her scalp. She couldn't meet his sardonic eyes any longer and glanced skittishly around the clearing.

He laughed scoffingly. "I don't remember it. How were you?"

She seethed. "You're despicable."

"That rowdy, huh?" he said, rubbing his jaw. "Wish I remembered it."

"We didn't do anything, you fool."

"No?"

"Certainly not."

"You just wanted to look but not touch?"

"No!"

"Then what are my pants doing unzipped?"

"I had to unfasten them to get your pistol out," she flared. "I didn't want you to kill me."

He digested that. "That is still a distinct possibility. And taking away my pistol and machete won't stop me. I could easily kill you with my bare hands. But I'd still like to know why you kept me from getting on that plane. Do you work for the Monterican government?"

She gaped at him, incredulous that he could think such a thing. "Are you crazy?"

He laughed without humor. "That's probably it. It would be just like El Presidente to recruit an American broad to spy for him, damned coward that he is."

"I agree with you that he's a coward. But I don't work for him."

"The rebels, then. What do you do, steal exit visas for them?"

"No. I don't work for anybody in Monterico."

"Then who? The CIA is in a world of hurt if you're the best they can do."

"I work for myself. And don't worry. I can meet your price."

"What do you mean, my price?"

"I want to hire you. Just name your fee."

"IBM doesn't have that much money, lady."

"I'll pay anything."

"You're not listening. No more jobs in Monterico. I want out of this godforsaken place." He moved toward her, sinister and steely. "You've screwed up royally, lady. That was the last plane out of here before the government shut down all international travel. Do you know what I had to do to get that visa?"

Kerry was sure she didn't want to know. His slow, threatening approach made her talk faster. "I'll make the delay worth your while. I swear it. And if you agree to help me, I can guarantee you a way out."

"How? When?"

"On Friday. I need only three days of your time. You'll go home with your pockets full of money."

She had his attention. He was studying her thoughtfully. "Why me? Beyond the fact that I was drunk and easily duped."

"I need someone with your experience."

"There are several others still hanging around. Even several in that stinking bar last night."

"But you looked more…suited to the job."

"What is this job?"

She sidestepped the direct question. First, she had to sell him on the idea of staying in the country for a few extra days. "It's a tough job. I need someone who has his own weapons available." She appealed to his vanity. "And, of course, the experience and courage to use them if it becomes necessary."

"Weapons?" He shook his head in bewilderment. "Wait a minute. You think I'm a mercenary?"

She didn't have to answer him. Her expression told him that his guess was correct.

Kerry stared at him in mystification as his face broke into a facsimile of a smile. His laugh was hoarse and deep, but eventually it rumbled up out of his chest and finally erupted as a series of dry, hacking coughs. He cursed expansively, but not so viciously as before. He rubbed his forehead and dragged both hands down his haggard face. Then he leaned against the truck, turned his face heavenward, and sighed heavily.

"What's wrong?" Kerry had to ask, though she didn't think she wanted to know. His laughter had held irony, not humor.

"You got the wrong man, lady. I'm not a mercenary."

Her jaw went slack as she stared at him. "That's not true!" How dare he try to trick her this way. "And you called El Presidente a coward. You're just trying to weasel your way out of accepting a challenging job."

"You're damn right I'm a coward," he shouted. "I cover my ass, understand? I don't claim to be a glory guy. But I'm not lying when I tell you that I'm no professional soldier."

She had recoiled at his flash of temper. "But your pistol, your machete—"

"For protection. What kind of damn fool goes into the jungle without any way to protect himself from animals? Of the four-legged variety as well as the two-legged kind." He took another step toward her. "We're in a war zone, lady, or haven't you noticed? Now I don't know what kind of game you're playing, but I'm taking myself back to town right now and throwing myself on the mercy of El Presidente. Maybe he'll still let me leave."

He glanced down at Kerry again, taking in the long, tangled hair and whorish dress. "He likes a bawdy story. I'll tell him one of the lovely ladies of his country enticed me beyond the point of no return. He'll like that."

He stepped around her and headed toward the hood of the truck.

She clutched at his sleeve desperately. "Believe me, this is no game. You can't go."

"Wanna bet?" He wrested his arm free and made for the driver's side of the truck.

"What about all that weaponry?" she asked, pointing toward the bed of the pickup.

He bent down, picked up the machete, and slid it back into its sheath. "You want to see my weaponry? All right."

He strode toward the rear of the truck and heaved one of the heavy bags over the side after removing the tarpaulin with a flourish. "Stand back," he cautioned her theatrically. "I'd hate for any of these to blow up in your face."

With a sharp tug, he unzipped one of the bags. Ready for explosive devices to spill out, Kerry stared down at the contents of the canvas bag with stupefaction.

"That's a camera."

His expression was dripping with sarcasm. "No kidding." He rezipped the bag and set it back inside the pickup. "To be precise a Nikon F3."

"You mean all those bags have cameras in them?"

"And lenses and film. I'm a photojournalist. I'd offer you my card, but a group of guerrillas and I used them to start a cook fire a week or so back and I'm fresh out."

Kerry ignored his acerbity and stared at the canvas bags. She had mistakenly thought they contained the weapons that would have assured her safe passage out of the country. It was several moments before she realized how long she'd been staring, lamenting her monumental error, contemplating her dilemma, and weighing the options left open to her.

She spun around. The man was headed into the jungle. "Where are you going?"

"To relieve myself."

"Oh. Well, I admit I made a mistake, but I'd still like to offer you a deal."

"Forget it, lady. I plan on making my own deal with El Presidente." He thumped his thighs with his fists. "Dammit! I can't believe I was stupid enough to miss that airplane. What enticed me to leave the cantina with you? Did you slip me a mickey?"

She took umbrage and didn't even honor the accusation with a denial. "You were drunk before I found you. Why, when you were so bent on making that plane, were you drinking yourself senseless?"

"I was celebrating." His teeth were angrily clenched, so Kerry knew she had struck a nerve. He was just as angry with himself as he was with her. "I couldn't wait to leave this armpit of a country. I'd been grubbing around for days trying to buy a seat on that airplane. Know what I had to do in exchange for that visa?"

"No."

"I had to take a picture of El Presidente and his mistress."

"Doing what?" she asked snidely.

Insulted, he glared at her. "A portrait that I'll probably sell to *Time*. If I ever get back to the United States. Which looks doubtful, thanks to you!"

"If you would just hear me out, I could explain why I needed a mercenary and went to such desperate lengths to get one."

"But I'm not the one."

"You look like one. Why do you think I chose you?"

"I wouldn't hazard a guess."

"I chose you over every other man in that bar because you looked the most disreputable and dangerous."

"Lucky me. Now if you'll excuse—"

"You use a camera instead of a machine gun, but you're of the same breed as these soldiers of fortune." She could still use him. If she had mistaken him for a professional soldier, it was probable that others would, too. "You sell your services to the highest bidder. I can make this worth your while, Mr...."

She stared at him in perplexity.

"O'Neal," he supplied tersely. "Linc O'Neal."

Lincoln O'Neal! She recognized his name instantly, but tried not to show that she was impressed. He was one of the most renowned and prolific photojournalists in the world. He'd made his reputation during the evacuation of Vietnam and had recorded on 35mm film every war and catastrophe since. He had two Pulitzer prizes to his credit. His work was of the highest caliber, often too realistic for the weak-stomached and too poignant for the tenderhearted.

"My name is Kerry Bishop."

"I don't give a damn what your name is, lady. Now, unless you want to see what's behind my zipper after all, I suggest you don't detain me again."

His crudity didn't put her off as it was obviously intended to. It only fueled her resolve. He turned his back on her and went stalking through the trees. Despite her flimsy shoes, Kerry plunged through the wall of green after him.

She caught his sleeve again and, this time, held on. "There are nine orphans waiting for me to escort them out of the country," she said in one breath. "I'm working with the aid of a benevolent group in the United States. I've got three days to get them to the border. On Friday a private plane will land there and pick us up. If we're not at the rendezvous place on time, the plane will leave without us. I need help in getting them through fifty miles of jungle."

"Good luck."

She uttered a cry of disbelief when he turned away again. She clutched his sleeve tighter. "Didn't you hear what I said?"

"Every single word."

"And you don't care?"

"It's got nothing to do with me."

"You're a human being! Barely, granted, but still a human being."

"Sticks and stones—"

"Oh, damn you and your jokes!" she cried. "These are children."

His face hardened. It was no wonder to her that she

had mistaken him for a mercenary. He seemed untouchable. His callousness was unbreachable.

"Lady, I've seen hundreds of kids blown to bits. Stomachs swelled up like balloons from starvation. Covered in sores and crawling with lice and flies. Screaming in terror when their parents were beheaded in front of them. Tragic, yes. Sickening, yes. Nations of them, lady. So don't expect me to fall on my knees in anguish over nine."

She released him and recoiled as though his heartlessness was a hideous, contagious disease. "You're a horrible man."

"Right. We finally agree on something. I'm not spiritually equipped to take care of nine kids, even under the best of circumstances."

She straightened her shoulders determinedly. Loathsome as he was, he was her only hope. She didn't have time to go back into the capital city and search for a replacement. "Consider this just another job. I'll pay you whatever I would pay a professional soldier."

He shook his head adamantly. "It wouldn't be as much as I'll make off the film I'm taking home."

"Three more days won't matter. Your film will be just as valuable on Friday as it is today."

"But I won't be risking my ass in the meantime. I value my hide almost as much as I do my film. I've risked it too long in this stinking jungle. I have a sixth sense that tells me when to move on." He locked gazes with her. "Now, I don't know who you are, or what the hell you're doing in a place like this, but it doesn't involve me. Got that? I hope you get the kids out, but you'll do it without me."

He turned abruptly and took no more than a few

steps before he was swallowed by the jungle. Kerry's shoulders drooped with dejection.

She slowly retraced her steps to the truck. Spotting the pistol still lying on the ground, she shuddered. He might not be a mercenary, but he was just as cold and unfeeling. He was inhumanly jaded and didn't possess an iota of compassion. To turn his back on children! How could he? How could anyone?

She stared at the pistol, wondering if she could force him at gunpoint to help her. The idea was ridiculous, of course, and she dismissed it as soon as it was formulated. She could just see herself toting little Lisa in one hand and the .357 Magnum in the other.

He would probably murder them all in their sleep anyway before they were halfway to their destination or if a better offer presented itself along the way.

Angrily, she whirled around. Her gaze accidentally fell on the bags lying in the bed of the truck. Cameras, she thought scornfully. How could she have mistaken them for weapons and ammunition? They were the tools of his trade, all right, but they were of no use to her.

How low did a man have to stoop before he could place a roll of film above the life of a parentless child? A wretch of a man. A coldhearted, selfish man, who would rather print pictures of other people than be touched by them personally. A man to whom a roll of film—

Film. Film. Film.

Kerry's heart skidded to a halt. Her eyes rounded with sudden inspiration as she stared at the canvas bags. Before allowing herself time to consider the grave consequences of what she was about to do, she bounded into the bed of the pickup and unzipped the first bag.

\* \* \*

Linc felt like hell.

Every time a macaw exercised his vocal talents, the noise went through his head like a spear. His stomach was in turmoil and with the least bit of encouragement would ignominiously empty itself. His teeth had grown fur overnight. He had a crick in his neck. God, even his hair hurt.

Wondering how that was possible, he explored it tentatively and discovered that it wasn't his hair giving him such misery, but an unaccounted for goose egg on his cranium.

But the worst of all his pains was the big one in the butt...by the name of Bishop. Something Bishop. Carol? Carolyn? Damn he couldn't remember. All he knew was that at the moment he'd like to be carving her name on a tombstone after having strangled her with his bare hands.

The little bitch had made him miss that airplane!

Every time he thought about it, he ground his teeth. And because he couldn't cope with his own stupid culpability at the moment, he directed his anger toward the woman.

Damn conniving female. What the hell was she doing in Monterico to begin with? She was nothing but a meddlesome do-gooder. Nine orphans. How the hell did she think she could secretly transport nine orphans five miles, much less fifty, then catch a plane that was supposed to rendezvous...

Hell. It sounded like a bad movie script. Unworkable. Implausible. Impossible.

And she had gambled on him risking his neck, not to mention the fortune he stood to make on the photographs he'd taken, to help her. What a laugh! He hadn't stayed alive by being Mr. Nice Guy.

Ask anyone who knew him, and they'd tell you that Linc O'Neal looked out for number one. He was liked. He was respected. He took his turn when it came to buying drinks. But don't depend on him in a pinch, because in a pinch, it was his ass he was concerned about and not the next guy's. He pledged allegiance to himself and himself alone.

He reminded himself of that as he trekked back to where he'd left the woman. He was relieved to see that she had calmed down measurably. She was leaning against the pickup, braiding her hair. The long, dark mass of hair—she had enough for about six people— was pulled over one shoulder. She was working it deftly through her fingers to form a braid as thick as his wrist.

That hair. It was one reason he'd been attracted enough to go with her last night. Hell, the last thing he had needed was a woman. He had wanted one, yes. He'd been in Monterico for six weeks. But he was too fastidious to quench his basic male desires with the tavern whores who nightly bedded soldiers from both sides of the conflict. He'd never been that horny.

Last night, of all nights, he had avoided company of any kind. He'd had only one thought in mind: catch that airplane. All he had really wanted was the numbing effect of a few drinks and to get on that airplane and put as much distance between himself and Monterico as possible.

But the liquor, potent as it was, hadn't been able to wash away the memories of the atrocities he'd witnessed in the past six weeks. So he'd kept drinking the foul stuff. And though it hadn't dulled his memory, it had severely clouded his judgment.

When the woman with that dark hair, lustrous even in the foggy light of the bar, had approached him, his common sense had surrendered to the swelling pressure in his pants. The kiss had been the deciding factor. One taste of her mouth, which had proved to be just as sweet as it had looked, had tipped the scales of his judgment.

Now, he was somewhat relieved to see that he hadn't taken complete leave of his senses last night. She was pretty. She was clean. Her figure was good, though a trifle slender, much too slender for that ridiculous dress. His instinct for women was still intact.

But how he could have mistaken her for a whore, he'd never know. He looked more like a mercenary than she did a prostitute. Her hair was dark, so it had been easy to mistake her for one of the local women. But in the dappled sunlight of the clearing, he saw that her eyes weren't brown as he had originally thought. They were dark blue. And her complexion was too fair to belong to a woman of Latin descent. It was almost too fair to belong to a brunette.

Mainly, she didn't have that hard, embittered, weary look of the women who had taken to prostitution to buy something to eat. The Monterican women who were forced to sell themselves for the price of a loaf of bread grew very old very fast.

This woman still looked fresh and wholesome, and, in the sunlight, unmistakably American. She should be living in a nice house in a Midwest suburb, organizing the Junior League's spring tea. Yet, here she was in a jungle clearing, the morning after pulling off a dangerous escapade. In spite of himself, Linc was curious about her.

"How'd you get the truck?"

She didn't seem surprised by his abrupt question and answered without hesitation. "I stole it. It was parked in front of the cantina. The keys were in the ignition. I disguised you as an officer with the jacket and cap left on the seat."

"Ingenious."

"Thank you."

"And you just drove us through the checkpoint, pretending that I was your client for the evening."

"Right."

He nodded in acknowledgment of her cleverness. "I've got a knot on my head."

"Oh, well, I'm sorry about that. You were…I was trying to—" She suddenly broke off. Linc got the distinct impression that she was keeping something from him, something she was glad he'd obviously forgotten. "Go on."

"You bumped your head on the dash."

"Hmm." He studied her for a moment, but let her lie of omission pass. There was no sense in pursuing the subject since their adventure together was drawing to a close. He was now certain that he hadn't had her last night. Drunk as he had been, he wouldn't have forgotten lying between those thighs, whose provocative shape he could see beneath her dress.

Before he got distracted by any more pleasurable thoughts, he turned his attention to what he was going to do once he reached the city. He hoped he would catch El Presidente in a good, receptive mood. "Well, I'm glad we've got the truck. It'll make getting back to the city easier. Are you riding back with me, or do we say our farewells here?"

"That won't be necessary," she said with a cheerful smile.

"What?"

"Driving back to the city."

He assumed an impatient stance. "Look, I've given you my answer. Let's not play any more games, okay? Just give me the keys to the truck and I'll be on my way."

"I don't think you'll be going anywhere, Mr. O'Neal."

"I'm going back to town. Now." He stuck out his hand, palm up. "The keys."

"The film."

"Huh?"

She inclined her head, and he followed the direction toward which she had gestured until he sighted the curls of brown film, now worthless, exposed to the fatal tropical sun.

His bloodcurdling cry began as a strangling sound. But when it left his mouth, it was a full-fledged roar of outrage. He whirled around, lunged, grabbed her, and bent her backward over the hood of the truck. His forearm acted as a bar across her throat.

"I ought to kill you."

"You might just as well," she shouted bravely. "What's one more murder? You were willing to sacrifice the lives of nine children to your own selfish pursuits."

"Selfish pursuits! That film represents what I do for a living. You just cost me thousands, lady."

"I'll pay whatever you ask."

"Forget it."

"Name your price."

"I don't want the friggin' job!"

"Because you might have to consider someone besides yourself for a change?"

"Damn right!"

"Okay, then, I'll tell you how you can turn this to your advantage. Let me up. You're hurting me."

She squirmed against him. But immediately became still. His hips were pressing against hers, and her wiggling had a profound and instantaneous effect on him. Against the softest, most vulnerable part of her body, he grew hard.

At the same time she noticed his condition, it registered with him. Instead of moving away from her, however, he pressed closer, fitting himself into the cleft between her thighs. His eyes mocked her insultingly. His breath struck her face in hot gusts.

"You invited me, remember?" he said silkily. "I might take you up on your invitation."

"You wouldn't dare."

His slow smile was anything but reassuring. "Don't count on it, lady."

"You know why I took you out of that cantina."

"All I know for sure is that I kissed you and that I woke up this morning with my pants unzipped."

"Nothing happened," she vowed in a voice tinged with anxiety.

"Not yet." He made the words sound like a promise of things to come, but gradually released her and helped her up. "However, business before pleasure. How could this possibly work to my advantage?"

Rubbing her throat and casting him venomous looks,

Kerry said, "The story. You would be involved in the rescue of nine orphans."

"And in transporting illegal aliens into the United States."

She shook her head. "We have Immigration's sanction. All the children have been slated for adoption by American parents." She saw a slight alteration in his skeptical expression and took advantage of it. "You'd be right there, Mr. O'Neal, recording it all on film. The story would have much more impact than what you already have."

"Had."

"Had," she conceded guiltily.

They contemplated each other warily.

"Where are these kids?" he asked, breaking a long silence.

"About three miles north of here. I left them in hiding there yesterday afternoon."

"What were you doing with them?"

"Teaching them. I've been here for ten months. Their parents are all dead, or considered so. Their village was burned out a month ago. We've been foraging for food and living in temporary shelters while arrangements were being made to get them out of Montorico and into the United States."

"What arrangements? With whom?"

"The Hendren Foundation, named in honor of Hal Hendren, a missionary who was killed here almost two years ago. His family founded the relief organization soon after his death."

"And you think they'll be at that rendezvous point as they said they would?"

"Absolutely."

"How'd you get your information?"

"By courier."

He barked a laugh. "Who would sell his sister for a package of Lucky Strikes. Which incidentally I need badly," he muttered, slapping his pockets until he found a pack. He discovered it was empty. "Got any?"

"No."

"Figures." He cursed. A long, disgusted breath filtered through his teeth. "Do you trust this courier?"

"His two sisters are among the orphans. He wants them taken out. His father was shot by the regular army as a spy for the rebels. His mother was...she was killed, too."

Linc propped himself against the side of the truck and gnawed on his lower lip. He looked down at his film. It was the proverbial spilled milk if he'd ever seen it. Forgiveness would be a long time in coming, but there was nothing he could do to save the film now.

He had only two choices left to him. He could return to the city and beg that despot who called himself a president for mercy. Even if it was granted, he would go home empty-handed. The other choice was equally distasteful. He still wasn't ready to become an ally of this butterfly cum Mata Hari.

"Why did you have to kidnap me?"

"Would you have come with me if I had said 'Pretty please'?" She got only a dark scowl for an answer. "I didn't think so. I didn't think any mercenary would want to bother with a group of children."

"You were right. He probably would have taken your advance money, followed you to the hideout, cut the kids' throats, raped you before killing you, and considered it a good day's work."

She turned pale and folded her arms across her middle. "I never thought of that."

"There's a lot you haven't thought of. Like food. And fresh water."

"I was counting on you...on whomever...to think about all those details."

"Not details," he said with aggravation. "Fundamental necessities."

She resented his speaking to her as though she were simpleminded. "I'm not fainthearted, Mr. O'Neal. I'll suffer any hardship I have to in order to get those children out of the country."

"They could all die before we cover that fifty miles. Are you prepared for that?"

"If they stay, they'll perish anyway."

He pondered her for a moment and decided that she might not be all fluff after all. It had taken considerable grit to do what she had done last night. "Where is the rendezvous point?"

Gladness shone in her face, but she didn't smile. Instead she turned and rushed to a hollowed-out fallen tree at the edge of the clearing. After poking a stick into it to clean out any snakes that might be harboring there from the heat, she reached in and pulled out a backpack. Unbuckling it as she crossed the clearing, she produced a map as soon as she reached the truck. She spread it out on the sun-baked hood.

"Here," she said, pointing. "And we're here."

Linc had been traveling with rebel guerrillas in recent weeks. He knew where the majority of fighting was concentrated. He looked down at the woman's expectant face, his golden eyes as hard as stones.

"That's troop-infested, solid jungle."

"I know."

"So why there?"

"Because it is so heavily patrolled. They use the least sophisticated radar equipment along that stretch of the border. The plane will have a better chance to get through without being detected."

"It's a suicide mission."

"I know that, too."

Angrily, Linc turned his back on her. Damn! She would gaze up at him with that melting look, just as she had in the tavern last night. Only this time he could see her dark blue eyes clearly. That look had made him throw caution to the wind, say, "To hell with common sense," and follow her out of the bar. She might not be a whore, but she sure as hell knew her stuff. She knew how to make a man as hard as steel, but as malleable as putty.

He'd had a helluva lot to drink last night, but he hadn't been so drunk that he didn't remember kissing her, touching her, and liking both immensely. She was a gutsy lady. He grudgingly admired her spunk. But it wasn't her spunk that he wanted to have warm and wanting beneath him. It was her body. He wanted to be wrapped in those shapely limbs and long, silky hair.

He knew, even as he made up his mind, that he was going to pay dearly for making this ill-advised decision.

"Fifty thousand dollars."

After a moment of initial shock, Kerry said, "That's your price?"

"If you can't hack it, we've got no deal."

She set her chin firmly. "Agreed."

"Not so fast. Here are the ground rules. I'm boss, see? No arguing. No bickering. When I tell you to do something, you do it without asking for an explanation." He punctuated his words by stabbing the air in front of her nose with his index finger.

"I've lived in the jungle for almost a year," she said haughtily, wanting to swat that finger away.

"In a schoolhouse with a bunch of kids. That's a little different from tramping through the jungle with them in tow. If we don't get attacked, it'll be a miracle. The only way I'll even chance it is to do everything my way."

"All right."

"All right. Let's get started. Three days isn't much time to cover the territory between here and the border."

"As soon as I change we'll pick up the children and gather supplies." She pulled a pair of khaki trousers, a blouse, socks and boots from the backpack she'd taken from the hollow tree.

"I see you thought of everything."

"Including water." She passed him a canteen. "Help yourself."

"Thanks."

She stood there awkwardly, holding the change of clothes against her chest. "Would you excuse me, please, while I change?"

He lowered the canteen from his mouth. His lips were glistening with moisture. He wiped it away with the back of his hand. His gaze never wavered from her face.

"No."

# Three

## ❧

*"No?"*

"Yes."

"Yes, you mean no?"

Lincoln O'Neal crossed his ankles, folded his arms at his waist, and tilted his head to one side. Arrogance incarnate. "No, I'm not excusing you. In fact, I'm not budging."

Kerry couldn't believe it. "You'd be rude enough to refuse me some privacy?" Sharks had kinder smiles than the one he gave her. "Then forget it," she said sharply. "I just won't change until we get to the place where I hid the children."

"I thought you said you weren't fainthearted."

Her braid almost slapped him in the face when she whipped her head around. The boor was testing her. She couldn't back down from any challenge issued by those sardonic eyes. Even now he could renege on their deal. She wouldn't be at all surprised. He obviously had no conscience. For the time being she had no choice but to play along with his asinine little games.

"Okay. I'll change."

She turned her back on him and reached behind her for the zipper of the dress.

"Allow me."

He moved up close behind her. His hands were large and manly, but sensitive enough to handle intricate cameras and lenses. Apparently he was adept at undressing women, too. The zipper didn't intimidate him or make him awkward and clumsy. It glided down her back without snagging once.

Accepting a dare was one thing, but actually carrying it out was another. She had thought that taking off her dress in front of him would be no worse than slipping out of a cover-up on the beach. But she hadn't counted on his taking an active part in her disrobing, or having him stand so close that she could feel his breath on her back. The sinking sensation in the pit of her stomach threatened to weaken her until she would have to lean against him, as she had a mad desire to do.

Inch by inch she felt her back being exposed to him. As it came open, the zipper left in its wake a ribbon of heat, caused only partially by the sun, mostly by embarrassment and the instinctive knowledge that his eyes were following the widening path of that zipper. It seemed to take forever, but it finally reached the end of its track.

"Thank you."

Kerry wished her words had carried a more authoritative ring and hadn't sounded so breathless. She moved away from him quickly. Hesitating only a few seconds, she lowered the shoulder straps down her arms. The flimsy bodice dropped to her waist. She pushed the dress over her hips and stepped out of it.

That left her standing in nothing but a pair of pant-

ies and the strappy sandals. The sun's fierce heat penetrated her naked skin. The humidity settled on it like
damp kisses. All the wildlife in the surrounding trees
fell silent, as though they were watching from above,
awed by her performance.

Her hands were shaking as she hastily stepped into
the trousers. She was barely able to button them. Next,
she shoved her arms into the short sleeves of her chambray shirt. She buttoned only two of the buttons, then
tied the shirttail at her waist. She pulled her long braid
from beneath her collar and bent down to pick up that
sleazy dress, which, under any other circumstances, she
would have been only too happy to discard.

It was when she was bent at the waist that Linc
placed his hands on either side of her waist. "Leave
me alone," she warned him in a low voice.

"No way, darl—"

The endearment died on his lips when she sprang
erect and spun around. His pistol was gripped between
both her hands and it was pointed directly at the center
of his broad chest.

"You and I have a business arrangement, Mr. O'Neal.
It's strictly business. I wouldn't give you the time of day
otherwise. If you come on to me again, I'll kill you."

"I doubt that." His features remained unperturbed.

"I mean it!" Kerry shouted. She thrust the pistol an
inch closer. "Last night I had to tolerate your disgusting gropings out of necessity, but don't ever touch me
again."

"Okay, okay."

He raised his hands in surrender. At least that's
what Kerry thought he was going to do. Instead, with
uncanny speed and humiliating ease, he knocked the

heavy pistol out of her hands. It clattered loudly onto the hood of the truck, then slid to the ground. He pinned one of her arms to her side and shoved the other one up behind her.

"Don't you ever pull a gun on me again, understand? Understand?" He pushed her arm up higher, until her hand was almost between her shoulder blades.

"You're hurting me," she gasped.

"Not as much as you'd have hurt me if that .357 had gone off," he shouted.

"I'm not even sure how it works," she shouted back.

"All the more reason why you shouldn't have tried such a damn fool thing."

"I'm sorry. Please." Tears of pain and humiliation were stinging her eyes. He relieved the pressure on her arms, but kept her clasped against him.

"I ought to wring your neck for pulling that little stunt," he said. "Instead…" He lowered his head toward hers.

"No!"

"Yes."

This kiss was just as possessive as those last night had been. His lips were hungry, passionate, hard, and yet incredibly soft. His tongue slid into her mouth. She tensed, but he brooked no resistance. He investigated her mouth thoroughly. Even though his tongue moved leisurely, Linc was the unquestioned director of the kiss. Kerry was the respondent. In spite of herself, when his tongue glanced hers, it made a corresponding movement.

He raised his head. Her eyes came open slowly, as though she'd been drugged. "Disgusting gropings, huh?" His eyes were maliciously teasing. "I don't think you found my gropings disgusting at all."

With breathtaking boldness, his hand moved to her breast and covered it. He caressed the fullness through her shirt.

"Don't." She dared not say more for fear that the moan of pleasure she felt building behind his caressing hand would work its way up.

"Why not?"

"Because I don't want you to."

"Yes, you do," he said with audacious conceit. "This could prove to be an interesting expedition after all. For both of us. We might just as well set the mood now."

"Please don't." Her voice quavered and became a full-fledged moan when the center of her breast rose up to meet the lazy caress of his thumb.

"You like it," he whispered against her neck.

"No. No I don't."

"Oh, yes." He caught her earlobe between his teeth and tugged on it gently. "Even though you put on this prickly, do-not-touch act, you're a woman who responds to a man." He smiled when a slight repositioning of his hips brought a groan to her throat. He rubbed against her suggestively. "An aroused man sets you off like a flare, doesn't he? Unless that were true, you couldn't have enticed me to go with you last night."

"You were drunk. You would have followed any female from that cantina."

"Not so. I was drunk, but I recognized your steamy nature under that cool exterior. Well, nobody stays cool in the jungle, baby. You'll thaw."

"Stop." She put all her strength into the command,

so her protest wouldn't sound as feeble as the resolve behind it.

"For now," he said, lowering his hand from her breast. "Because I'm still mad as hell at you for pointing that gun at me. When the time is right, you'll beg me for it."

His audacity had a healthy effect on her. It made her fighting mad. "Don't hold your breath."

She was successful in pushing him away only because he allowed her to. He merely laughed as he bent down and retrieved his gun. He shoved it into his waistband. Kerry watched, until she realized what she was looking at and hurriedly raised her eyes.

He was smiling at her insolently when he said, "Get in. I'll drive. You can put your boots on in the truck."

He had already assumed control, and for the moment that was fine with Kerry. Their embrace had rattled her.

Because she had been devoted to her work with the children over the last ten months, she hadn't missed the companionship of men. There was no one waiting for her to return to the United States. She hadn't been romantically involved with anyone when she came to Monterico. Because of that lack of involvement with the opposite sex, her entire being had been assaulted by Linc O'Neal's sudden intrusion into her life.

He had created a hunger inside her that hadn't been there this time yesterday. It was both thrilling and shameful. She was afraid of his virility, but fascinated by it, too. He epitomized masculinity in its rawest form. The salty taste and smell of his skin, the roughness of his beard, the huskiness of his voice, all appealed to her. His size and shape and well-honed muscles were a blood-stirring contrast to her femininity.

Unfortunately, he had a rotten character and an annoying personality. If it weren't for the orphans, Kerry would take her bruised lips and wounded pride and flee into the jungle to hide.

She had already had one user in her life. She didn't want another. Her father had been a manipulator and a fraud. At least Mr. O'Neal was straightforward. He freely admitted that he looked out for number one. When her father's corruption had been uncovered, Kerry had suffered in silence out of shame and love. She wasn't about to remain silent with Lincoln O'Neal. She owed him nothing but fifty thousand dollars. He certainly didn't warrant her devotion or respect. If he did anything that wasn't to her liking, she would tell him so with no compunction.

For all her antipathy toward him, she was grateful that O'Neal was with her. She wouldn't even admit to herself how frightened she had been at the prospect of transporting the children through the jungle alone. Their chances of surviving the trip and successfully escaping the country were slim, but at least they stood a better chance with O'Neal along.

"There's a narrow wooden bridge up ahead," she told him now. Once she had directed him to the road, they had ridden in silence. She took petty satisfaction in knowing that he was still nursing a hangover. "Almost immediately after you cross the bridge, there's a path on your left."

"Into the jungle?" he asked, looking up ahead.

"Yes. The children are hidden several hundred yards from the road."

He followed her directions, until the truck's progress

was impeded by the density of the jungle. "I'll have to stop here."

"It'll be okay. We shouldn't be here long."

He pulled the truck to a halt and Kerry alighted. "This way." She struck out through the trees, anxious to check on the children. Her long braid became ensnared in vines. Branches slapped against her face and scratched her arms. "We could use your machete."

"Hacking through the plants leaves a trail," Linc said. "Unless it becomes absolutely necessary, we're better off struggling our way through."

Kerry was instantly contrite over her testiness. "Of course. I should have thought of that."

She felt somewhat redeemed when they stumbled upon the hiding place, and it went unnoticed by Linc. She stopped, turned around to face him and was met with only a quizzical gaze before she called a name softly.

"Joe. Joe, it's all right. You can come out."

Linc started at a sound on his left. The thick foliage moved, then parted. Several pairs of coffee-colored eyes stared at him from behind fronds as wide as parasols. A tall, slender youth materialized from behind the leafy, green screen.

The boy, whose age Linc placed at around fourteen, had a brooding face that appeared years older than his gangly body. He regarded Linc with a mixture of open hostility and suspicion.

"This is Linc O'Neal," Kerry told the boy. "He's the one I picked to help us. Linc, this is Joe, the oldest of the group."

Linc glanced at her quickly, wondering if she realized that she had used his first name. She didn't appear to. He stuck out his hand toward the boy. "Hello, Joe."

Joe ignored Linc's hand and abruptly turned his back. In soft, rapid Spanish, he called the children out of hiding. In pairs and singly, they emerged from their cover. One of the oldest girls was carrying a toddler on her hip. She walked directly to Kerry and handed the child over to her.

The little girl wrapped her arms trustingly and lovingly around Kerry's neck. She kissed the child's grubby cheek and smoothed back her hair.

The other children surrounded her. It seemed that each had something vital to impart. They competed for her attention, though she spread it around as diplomatically as a candidate running for public office.

Linc knew only enough Spanish to keep himself fed and from walking into the wrong restroom. The children were chattering so excitedly that he couldn't follow what they were saying to Kerry. Only one word, repeated frequently, registered with him.

*"Hermana?"* he said.

"Sister," Kerry told him absently as she gave the child's cheek a spit bath with her fingers.

"Why do they call you—"

Linc's question was never completed. When realization struck him, his face went completely blank. If he'd been poleaxed, he couldn't have looked more stunned.

Laughing at one of the children's disjointed stories, Kerry glanced up at him and asked distractedly, "I'm sorry, what did you say?"

"I asked why they were calling you sister."

"Oh, I—"

She looked at him then, saw his sick expression and

realized the conclusion he had jumped to. He thought Sister Kerry had a religious significance. A speedy denial was on the tip of her tongue, but in a split second, she reconsidered. Why deny what he was obviously thinking? He had accidentally provided her with a way to spurn his sexual advances without jeopardizing his loyalty to their mission.

She searched her mind for a reason why she should set him right, but could find none. She also scratched the surface of her conscience, but didn't delve too deeply. She was doing this for the welfare of the orphans.

Before her conscience had time to rear up and question her motives, Kerry lowered her eyes demurely. "Why else?"

He called upon a deity, but not in prayer.

Kerry reacted with stern disapproval. "Watch your language, please." When he mumbled an apology, she knew her ruse had worked. It took all her acting ability to keep from laughing out loud. "Would you like to meet the children?"

"Are they all as friendly as Joe?" Linc asked.

"I speak English," the boy snapped with fierce pride.

Linc, unruffled by his faux pas, snapped right back, "Then your manners aren't worth a damn."

Kerry intervened quickly. "Joe, would you please stir up the fire? We'll feed the children before we go." Joe cast Linc a resentful glance before carrying out the chore Kerry had assigned him. "Children," Kerry said in Spanish and motioned for quiet, "this is Señor O'Neal."

"Make it Linc," he told her.

She told the children his first name. Eight pairs of eyes stared up at him with curiosity tempered by caution. One by one she introduced him to them. "And the youngest's name is Lisa."

He acknowledged each introduction solemnly, shaking hands with the boys and bowing stiffly at the waist for the girls, who giggled in response. He playfully tapped Lisa on the nose, being careful not to touch Kerry in the process.

He told them hello in Spanish, which just about exhausted his vocabulary. "Tell them that I'll take care of them on the journey." He spoke slowly so Kerry could simultaneously translate. "But they must obey me… at all times." He gave her a look that said, "That includes you," before he continued. "When I tell them to be quiet…they must be quiet…silent…. No moving… no wandering away from the group…ever…. If they do as I say…we'll get to the airplane…and it will take us to the United States."

The children's faces glowed radiantly when they heard the last two words.

"If they've been very good on the trip…and have done everything I've asked them to…when we arrive in the U.S.…I'll take them all to McDonald's."

"That's very thoughtful of you," Kerry said softly, "but they don't know what a McDonald's is. They couldn't even imagine it if I tried to explain."

"Oh." He glanced down at the eight faces turned up to him, and his jaded heart twisted. "Well, think of an appropriate reward," he said with feigned impatience.

After eating an unpalatable paste made of beans and rice, they began collecting their scanty provisions. When all that remained to be loaded was the children,

Linc brought one of his cameras back from the truck and began snapping pictures.

"Sister Kerry, if you would—"

"Please. Just Kerry is fine."

He nodded brusquely. He hadn't looked at her directly since learning of her vocation. "Would you please assemble everybody for a group picture?"

"Certainly."

In minutes, they were posed for him. The children were excited and smiling. Lisa had her thumb in her mouth. Joe refused to look into the lens and gazed broodingly into the surrounding trees. Kerry's smile was forced.

"Okay, let's go," Linc said as he popped his lens cap back on. Draping the camera around his neck by its strap, he shouldered a bundle of canned food that Joe had scavenged from the nearest village the night before.

"Don't you usually take action shots? Why did you want a posed group picture?" Kerry asked Linc as they tromped toward the truck.

"In case some of them don't make it."

His curt answer brought Kerry, who was carrying Lisa, to an abrupt halt on the jungle path. She turned to face Linc. "Is that a possibility?"

"Where's your head?" At that moment, he would have been hard-pressed to specify just what had made him so angry at her. "In the clouds? There are soldiers on either side who would murder these kids in a minute just for the hell of it. For an evening's entertainment."

She quailed, but refused to let him see her trepidation. "You want to back out."

Linc lowered his face close to her. "You're damn

right I do. And if you had any sense, which I'm beginning to seriously doubt, you would, too."

"I can't."

He cursed expansively and didn't apologize for it this time. "Come on, we're wasting time."

When they reached the truck his grim expression reflected his pessimism. The nine orphans were crowded into the bed of the pickup, along with his camera gear, their meager but space consuming supplies, and Kerry.

"I'm sorry you can't ride in the cab," he said, watching as she took Lisa onto her lap. "But if we're stopped, I can pass Joe off as my aid." He glanced down at her disquieting figure, which even her safari attire didn't detract from. "Without that lurid dress, you don't look much like a, uh…"

"I understand. The children will do better if I'm back here anyway. Just warn me in plenty of time if you see a patrol. I'll pull the tarp over us."

"It'll be stifling under there."

"I know."

"If we're stopped, the children must remain absolutely silent and still."

"I've explained that to them repeatedly."

"Good," he said with a terse bob of his head. "You've got water?"

"Yes. Do you have the map?"

"I know where we're going." He met her eyes soberly. "I just hope to hell we get there."

They exchanged a meaningful glance before he climbed into the cab of the truck and started the motor.

Kerry had never been more uncomfortable in her life, though she tried to put up a brave and contented front for the children. They were roughly jostled about in the bed of the truck. Its shocks were ineffectual on the washboard jungle road. At least the bouncing motion kept the gargantuan mosquitoes and other biting insects from lighting on them.

They never had to hide under the tarp, but the sun beat down on them mercilessly. And when the trees provided shade, they swapped the fiery sun for humidity so thick it could be cut with a knife.

The children complained of being thirsty, but Kerry carefully rationed their water. Fresh water might not be easy to come by. Besides, the more they drank, the more often she would have to ask Linc to stop. She wanted to avoid asking him for any favors.

He kept driving even after the sun had sunk below the tree line and had pitched the jungle into premature twilight. Darkness had completely fallen by the time they drove through a deserted village. As a safety precaution, Linc had signaled for Kerry to hide herself and the children under the tarp. He circled the village, and when he was satisfied that it was truly deserted, drove a half mile beyond it and pulled the truck into a clearing.

"We'll stop here for the night."

Kerry gratefully took his hand and let him lift her down. She planted both palms in the small of her back and arched it, stretching her cramped muscles.

Linc averted his eyes from her breasts, which were emphasized by her stretching exercise. They strained the sweat-damp fabric of her shirt. He couldn't help but remember how responsive they'd been to his touch. He cleared his throat uncomfortably. "Will you be all right if I walk back to the village and scout around?"

"Of course. Can we build a fire?"

"Yes, but keep it small. I'll take Joe with me. Here,"

he yanked the pistol from his belt and twirled it, presenting her with the butt of it.

She took it, but looked at it fearfully. "I told you this morning that I wasn't sure how to use it."

He gave her a quick lesson. "If you have to shoot it, be sure your target is as close to you as I was this morning. Then you can't miss." He grinned crookedly. She answered his smile. Then he and the boy faded into the darkness.

She put one of the older girls in charge of the younger children and sent the boys to gather firewood. By the time Linc and Joe returned, Kerry had a low fire going. Joe was carrying blankets. The bodies of two scrawny chickens were dangling from Linc's hand.

"Perfect fire," he told Kerry.

"Thank you."

"These may not go far." Apologetically he indicated the chickens. "But they were all I could find."

"I'll open a can or two of vegetables and make a stew."

He nodded and moved away from her and the children to pluck and dress the chickens. For which she was supremely grateful.

Though they had dozed while traveling, the children were almost too exhausted to eat. Kerry encouraged them, knowing that this might be their last hot meal for a few days. Eventually they had all been fed and put on pallets in the back of the pickup.

She was sitting near the dying fire sipping a precious cup of coffee when Linc joined her and refilled his cup. "See or hear anything?" she asked in a hushed voice.

"No. Everything's quiet. Which is almost unnerving. I'd rather know where they are."

"They?"

"Everybody but us." He grinned. The firelight caught his wide, white smile.

Kerry looked away from it. It was disturbingly attractive. "You surprised me."

"How?"

"By being so wonderful to the children. Thank you."

"Thank you for the aspirin. They helped improve my headache and my disposition."

"I'm serious. I appreciate your kind handling of these orphans."

"I've done some terrible things in my lifetime, but I've never abused a child," he said tightly. He sipped his coffee and stretched his long legs out in front of him.

She hadn't meant to intimate that he had, but thought it best to drop the subject.

"Tell me about them," he said after a long moment. "Mary."

"She never knew her father," Kerry said. "Before Mary was born he was executed for circulating propaganda. Her mother was sent to prison and is presumed dead."

"Mike."

Kerry had already anglicized their names so that they would start being familiar with the names they would hear in the United States. She told him about the boy. "Carmen and Cara are the courier's sisters. His name is Juan."

"And Lisa?"

Kerry smiled. "She's precious, isn't she? When her mother was only thirteen she was raped by a rebel soldier. She took her own life after Lisa was born. At least Lisa doesn't know the heartache of having had and lost."

"What about him?"

Kerry followed the direction of Linc's gaze. Joe was sitting at the edge of the clearing, staring out into the dark jungle.

"Joe," she said wistfully. "So sad."

"How old is he?"

"Fifteen." She gave him a rundown of Joe's history. "He has a remarkable mind, but he's a product of his tragic past. Hostile. Angry. Antisocial."

"In love with you."

"What?" She looked at Linc as though he'd lost his mind. "Don't be ridiculous. He's only a boy."

"Who's had to grow up fast."

"But in love with me? That's impossible."

"Hardly. By the time a boy is fifteen he's already had—" He broke off.

"I suppose so," Kerry murmured to cover the awkward pause. "Had you?" She couldn't imagine what had prompted her to ask him that. She didn't dare look at him, though from the corner of her eye, she saw the sudden movement of his head as he looked at her sharply.

"I thought taking confessions was a priest's job."

"So it is. I'm sorry. We were talking about Joe."

"Do you know what he did with that dress you wore last night?" She shook her head. "He burned it in the campfire before he banked the flames." When she gazed at him in disbelief, he nodded somberly. "I watched him throw it onto the coals and stare at it until it was consumed."

"But he's the one who stole the dress. He knew why I had to wear it."

"He also knew it helped get me here. He hates himself for contributing to your shame."

"You're imagining things."

"Nope. He's extremely protective of you."

"He's never been before. We're not in imminent danger. What is he protecting me against?"

"Me."

The firelight was reflected in his eyes, making them appear more golden than brown. He had taken off his bush shirt earlier in the day and was wearing only an army-green tank top. His skin was as smooth as polished wood. The upper part of his chest was matted with brown hair that had the same reddish cast as that on his head. It curled crisply against his tanned skin and seemed tipped in gold whenever sunlight—or firelight—struck it.

Uneasily, Kerry glanced away.

When he finally broke the strained silence, his voice was hoarse. "Why didn't you tell me?"

"There was nothing to tell," she replied honestly.

"I beg to differ, Miss Bishop." His face was taut and angry. "Why didn't you stop me from kissing you?"

"If you'll recall, I tried."

"Not very hard."

She stared at him, aghast over his righteous defense of his actions. "I chose being kissed over being killed."

"You were never under threat of dying and you know it. One word. You only had to say one word and I would have left you alone."

"This morning maybe, but what about last night?"

"That was different."

"Because you were drunk?"

"Yes." He could see that she considered inebriation a flimsy excuse. "Well, what was I supposed to think?"

he demanded defensively. "How is a man supposed to react to a whore's solicitation?"

"I'm sure I don't know," she said coldly.

"Now you do. He reacts to a whore exactly the way I did to you last night. The dress, the hair, the suggestive smile, the whole damn package was an offer no man could refuse. So don't go condemning me for taking your bait!"

"Sister Kerry, are you all right?"

They both looked up. Joe was standing just beyond the circle of the firelight. His hands were balled into fists and his eyes were trained threateningly on Linc.

"It's all right, Joe," Kerry reassured the boy. "Go to sleep. Tomorrow will be a difficult day."

He looked reluctant to relax his vigilance, but eventually he backed toward the truck and climbed into the cab, where it had been decided that he and Linc would sleep.

Kerry and Linc stared at the dying embers of the fire. The silence was as dangerous as the jungle that surrounded them.

"What made you decide to do it?" he asked.

"I needed someone's help."

"No, I don't mean recruiting me. I meant what made you decide on becoming a…you know?"

"Oh." She pulled her knees against her chest and propped her chin on them. "Things. Circumstances."

He was going to be furious if and when he ever discovered the truth. This morning's rage would be mild compared to the hell he would raise when he found out. She already dreaded the day. But until they were out of danger and in the United States, she had to continue with her lie. It served as protection against him.

And, if she were scrupulously honest, protection against herself. For all his rough edges, Kerry found him attractive to a disturbing degree. Lincoln O'Neal could have stepped out of a feminine fantasy catalog. He was ruggedly handsome, lived an extraordinary life-style, courted danger, and flaunted his disregard for established rules of behavior.

He would be an excellent lover. He had treated her roughly; his caresses had been somewhat crude; but his brazenness had held an appeal all its own. He was the kind of challenge no woman could resist. A maverick to tame. A hellion to redeem.

Kerry could deny it until she turned blue in the face, but the truth was that he had aroused her. So, to keep herself from doing something extremely foolish, she would consider herself as unavailable as he thought her to be. In a way, she was even now taking a vow of chastity.

He was impatiently jabbing a stick into the fire. Frustration was evident in his every movement and in the gritty sound of his voice. "Being what you are, how could you do what you did last night?"

"I was desperate. Surely you can see that now."

"But you were so damned convincing."

She felt flattered and ashamed at the same time. "I did what was necessary."

She could feel his gaze on her and couldn't prevent herself from meeting it. Across the fire, they stared at each other. Each was remembering his caresses, the forbidden places where he had touched her, the thorough, intimate kisses they had shared. Their thoughts ran parallel. They were on tongues, and breasts, and innuendoes that would have been better left unsaid.

Linc was the first to look away. His expression was tense. He swore beneath his breath. "Maybe you missed your rightful calling. You played your part so well," he said scornfully. "But then you had to, didn't you? You had to be certain I'd go along with you, so you lured me with a few feels. A few tastes of you—"

"Stop it!"

"Until I was crazy with lust and not thinking too clearly."

"I lied to you, yes!" she cried. She feared the seductiveness of his words and had to stop them. "I tricked and deceived you, yes. Suffered your insufferable embraces. I'd do it again if that's what it took to get these children to safety."

"Remember me in your prayers tonight, Sister Kerry," he growled. "I sure as hell need them."

He quickly tossed the dregs of his coffee into the fire. The live coals hissed like a serpent. A cloud of smoke rose up between them, symbolic of the hell he was going through to keep himself from touching her.

# *Four*

They came out of nowhere. The brush on either side of the road shifted and moved; suddenly, the truck was surrounded by guerrilla fighters who seemed to have sprouted from the trees.

Linc stamped on the brakes. They squealed as the truck skidded to a halt on the narrow gravel road. The children screamed in fright. Kerry, her screams mingling with the others, pulled little Lisa closer.

When the dust settled, everything was as motionless as a photograph. No one moved. Even the jungle birds sensed impending danger and were silent in their hideouts overhead.

The band of rebel fighters held M16s and Uzis at their hips. The automatic weapons were, without exception, aimed at the truck and its terrified occupants. The guerrillas' faces were young, but sinister. Some had yet to grow their first whiskers, but they had the implacable eyes of men who weren't afraid either to kill or be killed.

From the looks of their clothing, they had been living in the jungle for a long time. What hadn't been purposely streaked with mud for camouflage was stained with sweat and dirt and blood. Their muscles rippled. The glaring sunlight was reflected off their sweat-oiled skin. Their bodies were lean, hard, as unyielding as their menacing expressions.

Linc, having been in every war zone since Vietnam, recognized the unchanging, uncompromising expression of men who had been killing for too long. These men were inured to death. A human life, even their own, held little value for them.

He knew better than to do anything stupid in the name of heroism. He kept both hands on the steering wheel where they could easily see them. About the only thing he, Kerry and the children had going for them was that they obviously weren't part of El Presidente's army. If they had been, the truck wouldn't have been stopped, it would have been destroyed and they would be jungle fodder by now.

"Kerry," Linc called back to her, "stay where you are. I'll handle this. Keep the children as calm and quiet as possible. Tell the guerrillas that I'm going to open the door and get out."

She delivered Linc's message in Spanish. There was no response from the ring of hostile faces. Linc took that to mean that there was no argument. He slowly lowered his left hand. Several of the soldiers reacted instantly.

"No, no!" Kerry shouted. Rapidly she begged them to hold their fire and explained that Señor O'Neal only wanted to talk to them.

Bravely Linc lowered his hand again and pulled on the door handle. Warily he stepped out. With his hands raised above his head, he moved away from the truck.

Kerry gasped inaudibly when one of the guerrillas lunged forward and snatched the pistol out of his belt. He was told to unholster the machete and, even though he wasn't fluent in Spanish, he understood the threat underlying the barked order and complied without hesitation.

"We're taking the children to a town near the border," he said in a loud, clear voice, "where there's food and shelter for them. They're orphans. We're not your enemy. Let us—"

Linc's explanation was brought to a violent halt when one of the guerrillas stepped forward and backhanded him across the mouth. His head snapped around, following the impetus behind the blow. Linc, who had mastered street fighting before he had cut all his molars, came back with his fist clenched and his teeth bared. Before he could launch a counterattack, however, the soldier punched him in the stomach. Linc went down in the dusty road. The corner of his lip was dripping blood.

Kerry vaulted over the side of the pickup and ran to where Linc was lying, clutching his bruised ribs. She ignored the automatic rifles pointed at her and faced the guerrilla.

"*Por favor,* señor, let us talk to you," she said hurriedly.

"I told you to stay out of this," Linc growled, coming up on one knee. "Get back in the truck."

"And let you get beaten to death?" she hissed down at him. Swinging her long braid over her shoulder she faced the man who had hit Linc. The insignia on his beret designated him the highest ranking rebel in the group. "What Mr. O'Neal told you is true," she told him in Spanish. "We're only taking the children to a safer place."

"You're in a truck belonging to El Presidente." He spat in the road near her feet. Kerry held her ground and prayed that Linc would.

"That's right. I stole it from El Presidente's army."

One of the soldiers roughly hauled Joe out of the cab and conducted a search of it. He came back to his leader, carrying the uniform jacket and cap. The leader thrust them at Kerry accusingly.

She said, "The careless officer left them in the truck when he went inside a tavern to drink and enjoy the women." That produced a stir of resentment among the guerrillas.

"What's going on?" Linc asked. He was standing beside her now. A thin trickle of blood was oozing down his chin, and he was subconsciously rubbing his left ribs. Otherwise he seemed unharmed. Just virulently angry.

"He asked me why we were driving an army truck. I had to explain about the uniform."

Lisa began to cry. A few of the other children were whimpering in fright. The captain of the band was getting nervous. He glanced up and down the stretch of road. He rarely exposed his men to snipers for this long.

He rattled off a series of terse commands. One of his men jumped into the cab of the truck, ordering Joe into the back with the rest of the children.

"What now?" Linc asked Kerry.

"He's taking us to their camp."

Linc muttered a curse. "For how long?"

"I don't know."

"What for?"

"To decide what to do with us."

With rifles at their backs, they were nudged forward. Kerry called out to the crying children, telling them that she would see them shortly. She couldn't bear the sight of their frightened, tear-streaked faces as the truck rolled past. The commander told the soldier who was now driving the truck to take the cutoff. Apparently the camp wasn't far away.

The soldiers slipped through the jungle soundlessly. They moved through the undergrowth without disturbing a single leaf. When Linc tried to make further conversation with Kerry, he was warned to be quiet. The command was issued so threateningly that he obeyed it, though his jaw was bunched with anger.

They reached the guerrilla camp just as the truck was driven into the clearing from the opposite side. Kerry asked permission to go to the children and it was granted. They poured over the side of the pickup, scrambling toward her, seeking reassurance.

Joe was shoved against the side of the truck along with Linc. Linc's camera bags were heaved over the side and opened. Each piece of photographic equipment was examined.

"Tell them to get their goddamned hands off my cameras," he shouted to Kerry.

She shot him a glance that warned him to keep his voice low and his temper under control. She faced the leader. "Mr. O'Neal is a professional photographer. He takes pictures and sells them to news magazines." He seemed impressed, though still suspicious.

On a sudden inspiration, Kerry looked at Linc, where he was being held at gunpoint against the side of the truck. "Do you have a Polaroid?"

"Yeah. Sometimes I use it to set up shots, to check the lighting angles."

"And film?"

He nodded.

She turned to the guerrilla, whose dark eyes were moving over her in a most disconcerting way. She ignored his blatantly sexual appraisal. "Would you like Mr. O'Neal to take a picture of you and your men? A group portrait."

She could tell instantly that the idea appealed to the guerrillas. They began joking among themselves, poking each other playfully, using their automatic weapons like toys.

The leader roared for silence, and, as quickly as the joviality commenced, it ended. They all became stock-still.

"Wanna fill me in on what the hell is going on?" Linc demanded in a tightly controlled voice.

Kerry told him what she had suggested. "We might bribe our way out of this with a few photographs."

Linc glanced around at the group of hostile men. "They might get their pictures but murder us all anyway."

"Then you think of something!" she whispered tartly. "Even if we do get out alive, this is wasting precious time."

Linc looked at her with grudging respect. Most women would have dissolved into hysterics after the ambush. He knew from experience that her sharp mind could devise alternate plans as the situation called for them.

"All right. Tell the leader to line them up, call off this bozo," he said, glaring at the man who had the barrel of his M16 embedded an inch in his belly, "and let me get my camera ready."

She told the rebel what Linc had said. When she saw that he still wasn't as keen on the idea as his men were, she spread it on thick. "Señor O'Neal is famous. A prizewinner. The photographs of you and your men will appear in magazines everywhere. They will demonstrate to the world your fighting spirit and bravery."

Sullenly the guerrilla pondered what she said, then abruptly broke into a wide grin of approval. His men, who had lapsed into expectant silence, began chattering and laughing again.

"Get your camera," Kerry told Linc. "Start with a Polaroid so they can see immediate results."

Linc thoroughly enjoyed shoving aside the soldier who had been ordered to guard him. He used the heel of his hand rather more roughly than necessary and was rewarded by a scowl. He bent over his camera bag, cursing as he dusted off his expensive equipment, which had been heedlessly dropped onto the ground.

While he was loading his cameras with film, having decided that these pictures would not only be lifesaving, but profitable, too, Kerry assembled the soldiers. They stood proud and tall, showing off their Uzis like fishermen with the day's largest catch.

"They're ready," she told Linc.

"How are the kids?" he asked, as he peered through the viewfinder and motioned for the guerrillas to move closer together.

"Fine. Joe's watching them." She knew now why Linc had all those web-fine lines radiating from the corners of his eyes. He squinted into cameras a lot.

"Tell them to hold still," he said. She did. "Okay, on the count of three."

*"Uno, dos, tres,"* she counted.

The shutter clicked and the camera ejected the exposed automatic film. Kerry took it from Linc and asked, "Can you take another?"

"Yep. Give them the countdown."

After several had been taken, Kerry took the Polaroid pictures to the leader. His men inched closer, looking at the snapshots until they were fully developed. Laughter broke out. Mild insults were exchanged. They were apparently pleased with the results.

While they were passing the pictures around, Linc ripped off several frames with his power-driven Nikon. Some of these men, had they been born elsewhere, would be gloating over high school graduation pictures and toting baseball bats instead of machine guns. The contrast between their innocent delight over the snapshots and the grenade-decorated belts at their waists would make photographs that bore the famous Linc O'Neal stamp of excellence. His photographs were wordless editorials.

"Now, while they're in a good mood, let's get the hell out of here," he told Kerry beneath his breath. "You do the negotiating, since you seem to be so good at it."

Kerry didn't know whether to take that as a compliment or an insult, but she didn't dwell on it. They needed to be on their way as quickly as possible. Every hour counted. They had only two more days to make it to the border in time. Traveling with the children was slow. They hadn't covered nearly as much ground as they should have, though Linc had been driving them relentlessly.

Kerry tentatively approached the band of guerrillas. As unobtrusively as possible, she got the leader's attention. "May we leave now?"

As though a switch had turned them off, the soldiers fell silent. They all watched their leader closely, gauging his reaction and anticipating his decision.

The opinion of his men was important to him. He wanted them to hold him in the highest esteem and wouldn't dare lose face in front of them. Knowing this, Kerry pleaded her case.

"You are brave fighters. It doesn't take much courage to terrorize children. El Presidente's men are the cowards who make war on women and children, not soldiers like you." She made a gesture that encompassed the entire group.

"Would you butcher helpless children? I don't believe you would because you fight for liberty, for life. You've all left behind children of your own, or brothers and sisters. These could be your children." She nodded toward the truck where the children were huddled. "Help me. Let me move them to a safer place, away from the fighting."

The leader focused on the children. Kerry thought she discerned a flicker of compassion, or an emotion very near to it, in the man's impenetrable eyes. Then he looked at Linc and his expression became hostile again.

"Are you his woman?" he asked Kerry, hitching his chin toward Linc.

Kerry glanced at Linc over her shoulder. "I—"

"What'd he ask you?" Linc didn't like the look on the rebel's face.

She met his burning gaze across the clearing. "He asked if I was your...woman."

"Tell him no."

"No? But if he thinks—"

"He'll use you to get to me. Tell him no, dammit!"

She faced the commander again. "No. I'm not his woman."

He stared at her with cold calculation. Then, in a move that dismayed Kerry, he began to smile. The smile broke slowly across his dark, foreboding face and grew into laughter. Soon he and all his men were laughing at something only they understood and found amusing.

"Yes, you may go," he told her in Spanish.

She looked at her feet in an attitude of humble appreciation. "Gracias, señor."

"But first I want your man to take my picture again."

"He's not my man."

"You lie," he said softly.

Kerry shuddered at the triumphant gleam in his eyes. "No. He's not…he's not anything to me. I only hired Mr. O'Neal to help me get the children to safety."

"Ah," he said expansively, "then he won't mind if I have my picture taken with you."

She met his gloating sneer with an expression of astonishment and fear. "With me?"

*"Sí."*

Several of his men grunted their approval and congratulated him on his shrewdness with hearty slaps on the back.

"What the hell is going on?" Linc, standing with his hands on his hips, was demanding an answer from her as she slowly turned around.

"He wants his picture made."

"So move out of the way and I'll take one."

"With me. He wants his picture made with me." Her gaze skittered up to Linc's. His face looked as dangerous as any belonging to the men who were crowding behind her. He cast a malevolent look toward the leader.

"Tell the bastard to go to hell."

She smiled a wavering smile of gratitude. She was afraid Linc might have considered it expedient for her to have her picture taken with this animal. Proudly she turned and walked back to the leader. His eyes, directed toward Linc, were filled with malice. He reached for Kerry, encircled her wrist in a grip as hard as iron, and yanked her toward him.

"Let me go!" She wrestled out of his grip. Several machine guns were snapped into readiness, but she kept her chin up. Her expression was one of haughty contempt. "I won't have my picture made with you."

"Then your man will die," the fighter warned sibilantly.

"I don't believe so. You're not a cold-blooded murderer." She rather suspected that he was, but knew that wasn't the image he wanted to project to the free countries of the world.

Joe ordered the children, some of whom were crying, to stay where they were. He moved to Linc's side. The leader ordered two of his men to watch them. The rest of the soldiers scattered around the clearing. All of them kept their guns trained on the photographer and the adolescent boy, whose face was working with fury.

The guerrilla leader laughed nastily and wrapped his large hand around Kerry's neck. She kept her posture stiff, her body unbending. "Take your hands off me."

He only drew her closer.

"Damn him," Linc snarled from behind her. "Let her go!" he shouted to the commander.

"Why are you being so stubborn, gringa?" the rebel asked in a lulling voice. "You deprive yourself of much pleasure."

Suddenly, Joe burst into the open. He was tripped by a booted foot and went sprawling in the dirt. The soldiers laughed, none louder than the leader. The guerrilla who had tripped him, put the barrel of his automatic rifle at the base of Joe's skull and ordered him not to move.

"Oh, God," Kerry breathed. Was her stand against the whims of the rebel going to cost Joe his life? She vacillated.

"Tell him you're a nun," Linc said.

"You read the newspapers, Linc."

Right. He did. Churchmen and women were no longer spared bloody deaths. Indeed, they were sometimes the targeted victims of the cruelest executions.

The leader took hold of Kerry's long braid and began winding it around his meaty fist.

"You sonofabitch!"

Linc lunged across the clearing. A rifle butt was slammed into his middle. He went down with a grunt of pain, but came up fighting.

"Linc, no!" Kerry cried as she spun around to see what was happening.

The leader pulled a pistol from the holster at his hip. He took quick aim on Linc.

Kerry grabbed his arm. "*Por favor,* no."

"Is he your man?"

She stared into his obsidian eyes, knowing that what he had wanted most to do was frighten and humiliate them. "Yes," she declared defiantly. "Yes, yes, he is. Please don't kill him." Again and again she repeated the imploring words. Finally the guerrilla lowered the pistol to his side. He issued orders sharply and quickly.

Kerry rushed to Linc's side and assisted him to stand upright. "Hurry. He said we could go."

Wincing, holding one arm across his middle, Linc glared at the leader. He wanted to pound that arrogant face to a pulp, and if it weren't for Kerry and the children, he'd risk his life to do it. But she was tugging on his sleeve and pleading with him to get into the truck. Knowing that he was doing the wise thing, if not the thing he wanted to do, Linc turned away from the open challenge in the guerrilla's eyes.

He gathered his cameras and film rapidly as Kerry herded the children into the back of the pickup. Bravely, she pushed aside the soldier who was holding the gun on Joe and helped the boy to his feet. The glower he gave the leader was as malevolent as Linc's.

"Please, Joe, get inside the truck," Kerry said. "I'm fine and we're all alive. Let's go."

She stepped into the back of the pickup and gathered the smaller children against her. Linc came to the end of the truck. "I need my pistol and machete." She asked the leader if he would return them.

"Tell your man to get in the truck and close the door."

Kerry relayed the order to Linc. He grudgingly carried it out. The guerrilla swaggered over to the truck and laid the machete at Kerry's feet. "I am no fool. I will not return the gun."

Kerry passed along the message to Linc. He seemed inclined to argue, but changed his mind. He engaged the gears and drove the truck out of the clearing. Following the winding track through the jungle, they soon reached the road.

Before pulling onto it, he braked and stepped out of the cab. "I know it will he hotter than hell, but pull that tarp over you. We're not going to take any more chances."

He helped spread the canvas, covering over the group of huddled children and gave Kerry a piercing look.

"Did he hurt you?"

"I'm fine," she said gruffly, lowering her gaze from that incisive, golden one.

He pulled the tarp over her. Moments later she heard the door closing. The truck wheezed into motion.

"What do you think?" Kerry asked in a low voice.

"It looks deserted."

At the edge of the jungle, they had been watching the sugar plantation house for several minutes. There had been no sign of movement.

"It would be wonderful to spend the night under a roof."

Linc glanced down at Kerry. When he had finally stopped the truck—having accidentally spotted the roof of the vacated plantation house—and peeled back the tarp, she and the children had looked like a wilted bouquet. Some of the children had fallen asleep against Kerry, burdening her even more. But not a single complaint had been forthcoming. Her endurance seemed unflagging. But now he saw the traces of weariness around her eyes and mouth.

"You stay here. I'll take Joe and scout around."

They were back in ten minutes. "It doesn't look like there's been anyone here in a long time. I think it will be all right. Do you want to ride or walk?" he asked her, getting behind the steering wheel of the truck.

"I think we've all had enough of the truck for today. The children and I will walk."

She escorted the children across the sprawling yard of what must have been a lovely estate. It, however, like everything in the Central American country, had suffered the ravages of war. The white stucco walls were scarred and pockmarked with bullet holes. Vines had flourished to a fault. They had choked to death the other plants growing beneath the wide veranda, which now sagged in disrepair. Most of the windows had been broken out. The front door was missing.

But the large rooms had been shaded from the merciless sun and offered a welcome coolness that felt wonderful to Kerry and the children after having spent silent, sweltering hours beneath the tarpaulin in the back of the truck.

There was no electricity or gas in the kitchen, and Linc vetoed the idea of building a fire, so their supper consisted of cold beans straight from the can and sliced Spam. Luckily, even though the pipes were rusty, the water that came out of them was cool. Kerry bathed the children's faces and hands and put them on pallets in one of the well-ventilated rooms.

From his lookout post at one of the wide front windows, Linc watched her as she moved among the children. She patiently listened to their lengthy prayers and told them of all the glorious things that awaited them in the United States.

The moon had come up over the tops of the trees and shone onto her hair through the windows. Earlier she had unraveled her braid and combed through it with her fingers. Now her hair shimmered like a skein of black silk over her shoulders and back, catching the silver moonlight on every strand, as she moved from one pallet to another. She lifted Lisa onto her lap, kissed the top of her dark, glossy head, and rocked her gently as she softly hummed a lullaby.

Linc wished to heaven he had a cigarette, anything in fact, to distract him. Even when he wasn't looking at Kerry, he was aware of her every movement. And, curse him, he felt twinges of jealousy that it wasn't his head cushioned on her breasts.

He would surely be damned. He deserved to be. Because even now, knowing that she was chaste, he was hard and hot with the desire to be inside her. He wanted to touch her again. But not in the same way. He didn't want to subject her to his caresses. He wanted to treat her to them. He didn't want her humiliated and tearful beneath his hands. He didn't want her still and unmoving with defiance and disgust. He wanted her responsive and receptive, moaning with pleasure.

God, what was the matter with him? His thoughts were no purer than those the guerrilla fighter had no doubt been thinking. He didn't want to consider himself on that low a level, but apparently that's where he belonged. He was going to hell for what he was thinking, but he couldn't for the life of him stop thinking it.

He had been without a woman too long, that's all. But he'd been without women for long stretches of time before and had survived. He hadn't ever been consumed with the thought of having a woman as he was now. And his desires had been focused on the female sex in general, not a single member of that group.

Never before had he been unable to concentrate on anything except his feverish, thick, aching sex, which embarrassingly strained the front of his pants at inconvenient and unexpected times, like when Kerry had turned to him with a cup of water between her hands—

giving him a drink before taking one herself, bearing it like a peace offering, proffering it with a silent thank-you in her deep blue eyes.

He was angry with himself for seeing her as a desirable woman and not as what she was. His anger sought an outlet. There was no dog to kick, no missed nailhead to curse. His only scapegoat proved to be the woman who was responsible for making him act and think like a goddamned fool.

"They're all asleep," Kerry said softly as she moved toward the window.

Linc was sitting on the sill, one knee raised to ease the pressure in his groin. Kerry seemed oblivious to his black mood, oblivious to everything but the unspoiled beauty of the night. She drew a deep breath, unaware that it made her breasts lift and swell and push against her shirt until their shape was emphasized for the man who couldn't keep his eyes off them to save his soul.

"Why didn't you tell him right away that you were a nun?"

She looked at him quizzically, surprised by the harsh question. "I didn't think it would do any good."

"It might have."

"It might have also turned his attention to one of the girls."

Unspeakably vile things like that happened in time of war. Men would do things they ordinarily would find abhorrent. Linc couldn't argue the point with her. He knew she was right. But an inner demon was compelling him to hurt her, to make her suffer as he was suffering.

"I just don't get you, lady. You make out like a saint, but you seem to enjoy using that body and face of yours to drive a man crazy. I ought to know."

He slid from the windowsill and loomed over her. "Is that how you religious types get your kicks? Is that part of the convent training? Flirting, but never coming across? Promising, but never fulfilling?"

"That's disgusting, even coming from someone as low as you. I became an unwilling pawn between you and that ape in a stupid masculine contest of wills. I stood up to him, which apparently earned his respect. Then I begged him to keep you alive."

What she said had merit, making him all the madder. "Don't do me any more favors, okay? Or were you enjoying the attention so much it didn't even seem like a favor?"

"I put up with his lewd flirtation because I had to. Just as I did with you."

"And both times you sacrificed yourself for the children's sake," he sneered.

"Yes!"

"That's a hoot."

"I'm not surprised you don't understand. You've never thought of anybody but yourself. You've never loved anybody but Lincoln O'Neal."

His hands shot out, grabbed her by the shoulders, and jerked her up against him.

Joe instantly materialized out of the darkness. His liquid eyes glittered in the moonlight. They were murderously focused on Linc.

Linc cursed, released Kerry, and turned away. He was angrier at himself than at either of them. He was the one behaving like a madman. "I'm going to take a look around. Stay here." He stalked out, wielding his machete as though he would welcome something to slash into.

Kerry watched his tall shadow blend into the others on the far side of the yard. Joe worriedly whispered her name. She laid a reassuring hand on his arm and smiled halfheartedly. "I'm all right, Joe. Don't worry about Señor O'Neal. He's just edgy."

The boy didn't look convinced. Kerry wasn't convinced herself. It was a mystery to her why Linc was so angry. Why did their conversations always end in a shouting match? They swapped nasty insults like petulant children. The horrible episode with the guerrillas should have drawn them closer together, created a bond, instead it had wedged them further apart. In a very real sense they had saved each other's life today, yet to hear them, one would think they were bitter adversaries. Her feelings toward him were ambivalent. She needed time and space to think them through.

"I'm going to take a walk outside, Joe."

"But he said to stay here."

"I know what he said, but I need some air. I won't go far. Keep an eye on the children for me."

Joe wouldn't deny her request. Kerry knew she was taking unfair advantage of that as she left him standing watch over the sleeping children. She slipped through the dark rooms of the plantation house and, wanting to avoid Linc, exited through a screened porch at the back of it.

The stones of what had once been a terrace were broken and crumbling. Grass was growing up through the cracks. Kerry wondered how many parties had been held there. What had happened to the people who had enjoyed a gracious lifestyle there? They had obviously been affluent. Had they exploited the land and the laborers, as the propaganda posters proclaimed?

And Kerry Bishop wondered if she had ever met the

owners of the house. In that previous lifetime, had she been introduced to them in a gracious salon while wearing a designer dress and nibbling on canapés?

She pushed that disturbing thought aside and strolled down a weeded path. The evening was blissfully cool. She followed the path through the formal garden and beyond. The sound of running water attracted her attention. She almost stepped into the flowing stream before she saw it. It was an uncovered treasure. In the moonlight, it looked as sparkly and bubbly as champagne.

She hesitated only a moment before sitting down on its rock-strewn bank and unlacing her boots. Seconds later, she was standing in swirling, cooling water up to her knees. It felt delightful. Reluctant to leave it for even a second, she stepped back onto the rocks and unfastened her khaki pants. When she went into the water the second time, she was wearing only her shirt and panties.

She submerged herself in the natural whirlpool. The gurgling water washed her gritty, sun-baked skin, which was salty and itching with dried sweat. The swift current worked like massaging fingers to rid her muscles of their fatigue and tension. She ducked her head and let the water close over her scalp and flow through her dusty hair.

Her bath would have been divine had Linc's words not come echoing back to her. How could he possibly think that she had enjoyed the guerrilla soldier's attention? Strange, that while the guerrilla's touch had repulsed her, Linc's caresses hadn't. Originally she had been just as frightened of him, mistaking him for a man as bloodthirsty as the ones they had encountered that day. But she'd never been revolted by his touch. Disturbed, yes. Aroused, yes. But never had she found his kisses repulsive. And should he ever kiss her again—

She never got to complete the thought.

An arm closed around her midriff just beneath her breasts and hauled her out of the stream. Before she could utter a single sound, a hand was clamped over her open mouth.

# Five

Kerry fought like a wildcat.

She bit the meaty part of his hand below his wrist-bone and earned a grunt of pain for her efforts. But when she tried to work her mouth free to scream, his hand only mashed against her lips bruisingly. The sounds she tried desperately to utter were stifled.

She kicked backward against his shins, wiggled and squirmed, scratched and clawed, twisted and turned. But his strength was far superior to hers. His arms felt like a vise about to crush her ribs.

"Shut up and be still for crissake."

Kerry went limp. Her captor was Linc.

While it was infuriating that he would frighten her this way, she was thankful that it was he and not a guerrilla fighter who was dragging her deeper into the jungle and away from the house.

"Um-um-um."

"Shh! Shut up."

His words were nothing but hissing breaths close to her ear. Then new sounds registered with her, sounds she hadn't noticed before, but which were frightfully distinctive and familiar. The gruff laughter of men. The lilting, melodic tones of conversational Spanish spiced with vulgarities. The clanging of aluminum cooking pots and the clinking of armaments.

Soldiers were making camp somewhere nearby.

Gradually Linc eased his hand away from her mouth. Her lips were bloodless and numb from the pressure he had applied, but she forced them to move, forming words that were mouthed almost without sound.

"Who are they?"

"I didn't wait to ask."

"Where?"

"On the front lawn of the estate."

Her eyes widened in alarm. She turned on her heels and was about to charge through the brush. Linc's arm shot out. His hand grasped a handful of her wet shirt and, using that as leverage, hauled her back.

"Let me go!"

"Are you nuts?"

"The children."

"They're safe."

While this terse conversation was taking place, he was dragging her through the dark, dense foliage. "Get in there." He moved aside a vine as heavy and thick as a velvet drape and impatiently motioned her in.

"But the children!"

"I told you, they're safe." When it became obvious that she was going to argue, he spread his hand wide over the top of her head and shoved her down. Her knees buckled beneath her and landed jarringly on the fertile undergrowth. Before she had time to regain her balance, he gave her shoulder a push. She fell over onto her side and rolled into the leafy lair. He scrambled in after her and dropped the natural curtain behind them.

He fit his body against hers like a second skin to maximize the room in their hiding place. "Now lie still and stay quiet," he whispered directly into her ear. "Don't move. Don't make a sound."

Kerry would have protested had his arm not increased its pressure against her midriff. It was a reflexive motion Kerry understood, since she heard the sounds only seconds after Linc had. Someone was thrashing his way through the jungle, muttering to himself in vernacular Spanish as he came nearer.

His booted feet came dangerously close to where they lay, so close that the downward slash of his machete stirred the plants screening them in the darkness. Kerry sucked her breath in and held it. Linc, whose warm breath had been fanning her neck, did the same. They didn't move so much as an eyelash.

The soldier went past them, but they didn't relax. Through the jungle floor, they could still feel the vibration of his footsteps. And as they had expected, he retraced the path he had taken and came near them again, stopping only inches from where they lay behind the vine.

Kerry heard the sound of his slipping his machete into its leather scabbard, then the scratch of a match being struck. The pungent aroma of marijuana smoke filtered down to them. The soldier had decided to take a break from the arduous job of killing and looting.

Linc pressed his face into the nape of Kerry's neck, and they lay motionless and soundless. She thought of a hundred hazards that could reveal them. An untimely cough. A sneeze. A snake.

She shivered, only partially because her shirt was clinging to her wetly. The shudder was one of stark terror. What if they were discovered? And what about the children? Were they really safe, or had Linc just told her that to get her to cooperate in these self-preserving measures?

No, he wouldn't do that. But he might. He had told her once that he looked out for himself above anybody.

Thankfully, the soldier didn't smoke for long. He must have pinched out the cigarette because the sickly sweet fragrance faded away. They heard the rustling of his clothes as he repocketed the joint, then the soft, rhythmic clank of his water canteen bouncing against his hip as he moved away.

Linc waited a full five minutes from the time they last heard his shuffling tread before the pressure of his arm around Kerry relaxed and he lifted his head. For several moments neither did anything but breathe deeply, gratefully refilling their deprived lungs with air.

"What was he saying?" Linc whispered when he felt it was safe to do so.

"He was complaining that his sergeant sent him out on that scouting mission."

"Anything about us?"

"No."

"Good. I guess they don't know we're here. Are you all right?"

She was scared half to death, but she answered, "Fine. The children?"

"They're safe. I think."

She craned her head around to look at him. "What do you mean you think?"

"Shh. Relax. They were safely hidden when I came

looking for you." Over her shoulder she studied his shadowed face. "I swear it," he said, offended by her suspicion.

Kerry was ashamed of her momentary lack of trust. Linc O'Neal was a scoundrel, but he wouldn't sacrifice children to save his own hide. Even he wasn't that unscrupulous. "What happened?"

Speaking in whispers that were barely louder than a deep breath, Linc related what had happened. "I heard their trucks approaching while I was taking that last look around. I figured that if we had thought the deserted house would serve as a good camp, then soldiers would, too. I ran back, found you gone, and hustled the children into the root cellar beneath the kitchen."

"I didn't know there was one."

"I hope the soldiers don't either," he said grimly. "I put Joe in charge and threatened him with castration-by-machete if he left the cellar before I came to get them. He argued with me, of course, and wanted to go searching for you."

"I shouldn't have left."

"A little late to be thinking of that, Miss Bishop." His low volume didn't soften the stern reprimand.

She thought of several biting comebacks, but saved them. Her primary concern was for the children. "Were the children afraid?"

"Yeah, but I calmed them down, tried to make a game out of hiding. They have water. I promised them a treat if they didn't make a sound. I told them to go to sleep and said that when they woke up, you'd be there."

"Do you think they understood?"

"I hope to God they did. When he wasn't arguing, Joe was translating for me." Worriedly he added, "I'd hate to have to explain nine hidden children to this bunch of cutthroats."

The memory of the commander and his rough, insulting touch still made Kerry feel slightly sick to her stomach. "Are they the same ones we encountered today?" she asked with dread.

"I don't know. But they probably aren't any better, whatever side of the conflict they're on. I thought it best just to stay out of their way."

"I agree. What about the truck?"

"Luckily, I hid it under brush after we unloaded it."

She lay still for a moment, trying not to think about the way Linc's legs were pressed against hers. As precisely as her wet shirt was plastered to her torso, his legs were molded to every contour of hers.

"I told you to stay in the house," he said abruptly. "You agreed to do everything I told you to."

"I needed some air," she snapped.

Knowing that he was right stung her pride. It had been reckless of her to leave the house, especially at night. Now, if any harm came to the orphans, she would have to take the blame upon herself. It would be entirely her fault.

"Well, you could have gotten a lot of air...through the bullet holes in your body." He unleashed his frustration. "You almost got yourself killed, along with the rest of us. I hope you enjoyed your bath."

"I did. Brief as it was." Suddenly she drew herself up more tensely. "Linc, I left my clothes—"

"I stuffed them behind a banana tree. Let's hope they're not discovered."

"Why didn't you just bring them with you?"

"Look, lady," he said snidely, "I've only got two

hands. I couldn't collect your clothes and haul you out of your bath and keep you quiet all at the same time. So I stashed the clothes. Okay? If the soldiers had found you before I did, they would have stripped you naked anyway, and believe me, base as you may think I am, I have more respect for your modesty than they would have."

Kerry wished he hadn't made even that veiled reference to her nakedness. Now that they were out of immediate danger, she could turn her thinking to her scanty attire and her forced proximity to Linc.

How long would they have to stay hidden, lying close together, unable to move or speak above a whisper? They couldn't relax their guard for a single moment. Since they weren't hidden beneath the house as the children were, the density of the jungle at night was the only place they could hide. To go in search of another hiding place would be risky. She was just coming to realize how uncomfortable the next several hours would be.

And not only in terms of being cramped and cold. Linc's nearness was playing havoc with her senses. She gravitated toward the security his virile frame promised. Her chilled body sought the warmth of his.

"Whatever they're cooking smells good," she remarked to take her mind off him.

"Don't think about it." His own stomach rumbled hungrily. She angled her head back a fraction and glanced over her shoulder at him. "It's probably iguana…or worse," he said in an attempt to banish both their hunger pangs.

"Don't say that," she murmured, shifting her legs slightly. "I keep imagining creepy-crawly critters moving over me."

"Be still." He clenched his teeth. The slightest movements she made caused her hips to press against the curve of his lap. She was already fitted securely into that notch, and the merest shifting motion of her legs caused her bottom to rub against him.

"I'm trying," she said, "but my muscles keep cramping."

"Are you cold?"

"A little," she admitted.

The jungle was like a sauna in daylight hours, steamy and airless. But they were lying on the damp ground. Sunlight had never penetrated this dense foliage and, as a result, it was abnormally cool beneath the vine. She was so clammy that her teeth had begun to chatter.

"You'd better take off that wet shirt."

Ponderous seconds ticked by. They lay as tense and motionless as they had while the soldier was nearby. Kerry wanted to negate his idea outright. But before she could even form the words, she shivered uncontrollably. Under the circumstances, any maidenly protests would sound ridiculous.

But to lie in Linc O'Neal's arms wearing nothing but panties...?

"I'm all right," she said stiffly.

He sighed with exasperation. "I'll take my shirt off. You can wrap yourself in that."

She reconsidered, knowing that catching cold would certainly be untimely. "All right," she said reluctantly. "How...how do we do it?"

"Let me go first."

Moving as little as possible, he wedged his hand between her back and his chest and unbuttoned the few buttons on his bush shirt. With excruciating care not to move a single leaf, he eased himself into a half-sitting position and shrugged the shirt off his shoulders and down his arms. The effort made him short-winded. He was panting by the time he worked his arms free of the sleeves.

"There," he sighed. "Now you."

Kerry was grateful for the darkness which hid them. At the same time, it lent intimacy to their awkward situation. She rolled her lips inward around her teeth and squeezed her eyes shut for a moment, trying to muster her slipping courage before reaching for the buttons of her own shirt. That was the easy part. The difficulty came when she tried to peel the clinging, damp fabric away from her skin.

"Sit up as far as you can," Linc suggested.

She detected the hoarseness in his voice and passed it off as caution against discovery. She didn't dare entertain the notion that there might be another reason behind it.

Moving carefully, she raised herself until she could prop her weight on one elbow. Then, lifting and lowering her opposite shoulder repeatedly, she tried to work the wet shirt free.

"Here, let me help."

She felt the warm pressure of Linc's hand on her shoulder. It moved down her arm, taking the shirt with it, inch by slow inch. At her elbow, he had to give it an extra tug. His knuckles bumped into the side of her breast.

They froze.

"Sorry," he said at last.

Kerry said nothing. The lump of embarrassment lodged in her throat wouldn't have allowed a word to get past. He slipped the sleeve down until she pulled her hand from it. The position she had to maintain, compounded by tension, had strained all her muscles to the aching point. Tiredly she lay back down and released a grateful breath. The air cooled her back as Linc moved the wet cloth aside.

"Can you manage the rest?" he asked.

"Yes, I think so."

She rolled backward, actually bringing herself closer against him, while she pulled the other sleeve from the arm she'd been lying on. As soon as the shirt was off, she rolled forward again, hoping that in those brief few moments her breasts hadn't been as vulnerable as they had felt. It was so dark that she doubted he could actually see her. But they both knew that she was completely uncovered.

It was a disturbing thought.

So much so that, when he draped his shirt over her, she clutched at it, pulling it against her chilled skin. It was both a relief and a hazard. It provided warmth and covering, but it also smelled like him. Linc's scent filled her head and had an intoxicating effect. Holding his garment against her was like being wrapped in his arms.

"Better?"

She nodded her head. Her hair was heavy and wet. She gathered it in her fist and shifted it above her head. But that left her neck and shoulders bare. Now she could feel each breath he took. She knew without looking that he was wearing only the army-green tank top, and that above the deeply scooped neckline grew an impressive pelt of chest hair.

"You're still shivering." He laid his arm over her and drew her back against him.

Closing her eyes tightly didn't help to dispel her

memory of his arms, leanly bunched with muscles, ribboned with healthy veins. She had seen him shirtless that morning while he washed. As he sluiced water over his head and chest, she had noticed his sleek musculature.

Now she wished she hadn't paid such close attention. The muscles she had admired that morning were pressed against her back. She felt them twitch, contract and relax, as though they were as jumpy as her nerves.

That morning, the sun had streaked his hair with russet highlights and made his body hair glow a reddish-gold. She could feel its crinkly patterns now against her bare skin. And she knew that his shoulders were sprinkled with freckles, as his cheekbones were.

"Are your legs cold?" Not trusting her to give him an honest answer, Linc ran his hand down the outside of her thighs and felt the goose bumps. "I'm going to put my legs over yours. Don't be alarmed."

She could almost laugh. *Don't be alarmed.* A ludicrous statement. Like, "Don't turn around, but isn't that Prince Charles and Lady Di coming through the door?" Or like the dentist saying as he lifts his drill, "You might feel a slight tingle but don't let it bother you."

It was impossible not to be alarmed. When he laid his thigh across hers, it brought the full solidity of his maleness directly up against her bottom. The rough cloth of his fatigue pants pleasantly abraded her sensitive skin.

"Aren't you cold, too?" she asked in a high, thin voice.

"No. I've got on pants and you're wearing nothing but—"

*Right. Stop right there, O'Neal. Don't say it.* It was better left unsaid. Neither of them needed to be reminded that all she was wearing was a pair of panties, and that they were sheer and skimpy and damp. Better that they direct the conversation toward anything—books, movies, politics, the weather—than to even make mention of her attire, or lack thereof.

"I still have my canteen. Do you want some water?"

"No," she replied breathlessly. She didn't want him to move. Every time he moved, she felt him. Vividly. And her mind kept reverting to when she was trying to get the pistol out of his waistband and how his body had looked. What she had only guessed at then, she could feel pressing against her hips now.

How long would this night last? Hours. And what if the soldiers didn't break camp and pull out at daybreak, as she and Linc had tacitly assumed they would? She didn't think her pounding heart could stand the strain. Something had to be done, said, to relieve the tension.

"Tell me about yourself, Linc."

God, she didn't want to know about him. If she were smart, she didn't want to know that he sensed her with every nerve fiber in his body. They were alive and kicking, feeling her, smelling her, tasting her. She didn't want to know how his blood vessels were pumping with desire for her.

He had raced back to the house, the convoy of military trucks only minutes behind him. He had bounded into the large living room, already issuing orders for her to get the children and their pallets up and into the kitchen. He had been dumbfounded when Joe told him that Kerry wasn't there, that she'd left the house.

Cursing her even while he spoke soothing words that the children couldn't even understand, he herded them into the dark, dank cellar. It was spooky, but it provided a perfect hiding place. As he sealed the door and moved a cabinet over the floorboards, he cursed the headstrong woman who was loose in a jungle crawling with guerrilla fighters when she could be safely hidden.

Only fear for her safety had contained his fury as he had dashed through the darkness looking for her. He remembered seeing the creek when he had previously scouted around the deserted estate. The refreshing water had tempted him into taking a quick dip. Acting purely on a hunch, he had followed the vine-choked path toward it.

He had felt both murderous and profoundly relieved when he discovered Kerry splashing in the shallow water. Taking time only to hide her pile of clothing in the brush, he'd lifted her out. Snatches of erotic pictures were emblazoned on his brain.

He knew that her breasts were full, and that her nipples were so pointed and pink that a man would go through hell for a chance to touch them with his tongue. He thought about her breasts now, lying soft and unrestrained beneath his shirt and he ached to touch and reshape them in his hands. And a while ago, when she had rolled onto her back, he had known that all he had to do was lower his head and… God, it had been agony not to.

He knew that her derriere was taut and rounded, cute and saucy and sexy as hell. And now that sweet little butt was cuddling his sex. It took every ounce of self-discipline he possessed not to groan out loud with the thought.

He tried not to think of the way her hair had looked with the moonlight shining on it, or the way that silvery light had turned her eyes as deeply mysterious as sapphires. Her lips were strictly off-limits. Yet the memory of their taste lingered in his mind. He couldn't allow himself to think about the most vulnerable, most alluring part of her neck being only inches from his lips.

For someone already denied heaven, one more wicked thought didn't matter. But he would die and see the gates of hell before the night was out if he continued torturing himself this way.

They needed diversion. Anything. To get their minds off what must surely be as discomfiting for her as it was for him, though for different reasons.

"What do you want to know?" His voice was little more than a growl.

"Where did you grow up?"

"St. Louis."

"Tough neighborhood?" she asked instinctively.

He scoffed. "Lady, you can't even begin to imagine."

"Your parents?"

"Both dead now. My old man raised me. My mother died when I was just a kid."

"No brothers or sisters?"

"No, thank God."

"Why 'thank God'?"

"Because things were rough enough as it was. My dad worked all the time in the brewery. I was on my own after school until late every night. You see, he resented being stuck with me when my mom died. He was a foulmouthed, mule-headed, hard-drinking man. His ambition extended only to having enough money to pay the rent and buy whiskey. The last thing he wanted was to take care of a kid. I left home as soon as I got old enough. I only saw him twice after that before he died."

"What happened to him?"

"He was bowling one night with a bunch of his cronies and just dropped dead of a heart attack. They buried him beside my mother. I was in Asia. They sent me the details of it in a letter."

Kerry didn't know what to say. She'd never known anybody who had come from that kind of environment. "When did you get into photography?"

"High school. I was flunking something...I don't remember what now...so they stuck me in the journalism class that put together the school newspaper. They gave me a camera and appointed me photographer as a punishment." He chuckled softly. "It backfired. By the end of the year, I was hooked."

"Where did you go to college?"

"College?" He barked a scornful laugh. "Cambodia, Vietnam, Africa, the Middle East. I got my formal education on the Golan Heights, and in Beirut and Belfast, and in refugee camps in Biafra and Ethiopia."

"I see."

"I seriously doubt that," he said bitterly.

Kerry didn't know whether his resentment was directed toward her, toward his unloving father, toward his lack of formal education, or a combination of all of them. But she felt it safer not to pursue it.

It was he who finally broke the silence. "What about you? What kind of childhood did you have?"

"Charmed." Kerry smiled with remembrances of golden times. Before they were tarnished by scandal. Before the nightmare. Before the bubble burst. "Like you, both my parents are dead now, but I had them when I was growing up."

"You went to parochial school, of course."

"Yes," she answered truthfully.

"Let me guess. You wore navy blue pinafores over stiff white blouses. And pigtails so tight they made your eyes water. White stockings and black patent shoes. Your face and hands were never dirty."

She laughed softly. "You're remarkably accurate."

"And you were taught social graces along with Latin and Humanities."

She nodded, thinking back on all the formal salons she had sat in with her parents, listening to boring conversations, which to a teenager with a passion for the Rolling Stones, had had no relevance. She had never been at a loss as to which fork to use and had always politely thanked the host and hostess for the evening's entertainment. Linc had had a latchkey, and she had had personalized stationery.

"Yes," she replied, "my father's work involved considerable travel. You and I might have been in some of the same places at the same time."

He uttered another of those humorless laughs. "Honey, you don't even know about some of the places I've been in."

"I'm not that innocent."

"Compared to you, Sister Kerry, Rebecca of Sunnybrook Farm led a wild life."

Though she couldn't see his face, she could imagine the sneer on his lips. Knowing now how different his background was from hers, she could understand why he might ridicule her previously sheltered life and lack of worldly experience.

She lapsed into silence. Apparently he was of the same mind. He adjusted himself more comfortably against her. Miraculously they fell asleep.

* * *

Kerry came awake suddenly. Every muscle in her body was tense and quivering. "What is it?"

"Shh." Linc laid his fingers against her lips. "It's only rain."

The huge drops fell heavily on the plants surrounding them. They landed in hard splats. It sounded as though their shelter were being pelleted with BBs. "Oh, Lord," Kerry whimpered and ducked her head so low that her chin almost touched her chest. "I hate this."

Even though the broad leaves of the vine covering them provided some protection from the torrent, rainwater still trickled through the foliage and dripped chillingly onto her exposed skin. Her muscles were cramped. She longed to stretch her limbs in all directions in order to ease their aching and to restore circulation.

"I can't stay in here. I've got to get out."

"No," he said sharply.

"Just for a minute. To stretch."

"And get soaked in the process. Then when you crawl back in, you'll be even more uncomfortable. No, Kerry."

"We could sneak back into the house," she said in a hopeful rush.

"Uh-huh."

"No one will be watching. We could go through the kitchen and join the children in the basement. They must be terrified."

"They're probably asleep. Besides, they have Joe."

"No one would see us."

"It's too risky. The soldiers are bound to have posted a watch."

"I don't want to stay here any longer!"

"And I don't want to be shot! I don't think you want

to be gang-raped either." She sucked in her breath quickly. "Now hush about it. We're not leaving until I say so."

The racket around them was deafening. It was raining buckets. Kerry felt the jaws of claustrophobia closing around her.

"How much longer?" she asked.

"I don't know."

"Dawn?"

"I hope."

"What time is it?"

"Around four I think."

"I can't stand it any longer, Linc." She hated the tremor in her voice, but she couldn't control it. "Truly, I can't."

"You've got to."

"I can't. Please let me stand up."

"No."

"Please."

"I said no, Kerry."

"Just for a minute. I've got—"

"Turn around."

"What?"

"Turn around. Face me. Switching positions will help."

Her muscles were screaming for her to move. She turned onto her back, then did another quarter turn to bring herself face-to-face with Linc.

He laid his arm across her waist and sandwiched her thighs between his. She placed her hands on his chest and buried her face in the hollow of his shoulder. Tucking her head beneath his chin, he held her close.

She basked in the warm security he provided until the noisily splattering rain abated.

Kerry never knew how long they stayed like that. It might have been hours or merely minutes before she gradually became aware that the rainfall had ceased and that the silence was as loud as the downpour had been. She stirred and would have put space between Linc and her, had there been any space available.

"I'm sorry," she whispered.

"It's okay."

"I panicked. Claustrophobia, I guess."

"You woke up frightened. You're cold, hungry, uncomfortable. So am I. But for the time being, this is the best we can do."

His voice sounded funny. She didn't have to ask why. Her own was none too steady. The feel of his breath against her face, the way his fingers were moving comfortingly through her hair, the heat rising from the places where skin contacted skin were the reasons behind her tremulousness.

"Why did you do it, Kerry?"

"What?"

"Commit yourself to a vocation so unsuited to you."

Oh, that. She felt wretched about her lie. With the exception of their bitter quarrels, he had treated her honorably since he had mistaken her for a nun. If he had continued to be aggressive and abusive, she would have taken a blood oath that her life was committed to a religious order. But his nobility demanded the truth. At least a partial truth.

Yet, she stalled. "Why do you say it doesn't suit me?"

Linc's head was whirling with discrepancies. Kerry felt more womanly than any woman he'd ever held in his arms. He couldn't reconcile this young, beautiful, desirable woman with his concept of a nun. The sweet pressure of her breasts against his chest, the way her mouth had yielded to his those few times he had kissed her, just didn't jibe with black habits and cloistered abbeys. He was streetwise enough to know that some first impressions were sound. And he'd bet his life on this one.

In answer to her question he said, "You don't look like any nun I ever saw."

"Nuns look like everybody else."

"Do they all wear bikini panties?"

She blushed hotly. "I…I happen to like frilly underwear. That's not a sin. Feminine things appeal to me because I'm a woman."

That he didn't need to be reminded of. She was a woman, all right. He could feel her womanliness with every masculine cell in his body.

"You just don't have a holy aspect." She stiffened with the affront, but he held her tighter. "I don't mean that you're unholy, it's just that…hell…"

He paused for a moment, searching for words. "I mean, didn't you ever think about having kids? You're great with these orphans. Didn't you ever want to have kids of your own?"

"Yes," she answered honestly.

"And a, uh, you know, a man?"

"I've thought about that, yes," she said softly. She wondered if he could feel her heart pounding against his chest. Her answer was truthful. But she'd never thought about having a man as powerfully as she was thinking about it now.

She was recalling the masterful way his tongue had parted her lips and moved inside her mouth, and the manner in which his hands had been both caressing and commanding. She had felt the grinding thrust of his hips against hers. Total possession by this man must be an ultimate sexual experience for a woman.

"You've thought about making love with a man?"

She nodded, rubbing her nose in his crisp chest hair.

"You've wondered what it feels like?"

She held her lips tightly together to stopper the longing groan that pressed against them from the inside. "Of course."

He sifted his hands through her hair. "If he knows what he's doing, a man can give you pleasure. Pleasure never dreamed of."

She was liquifying, melting against him. She wondered how he could continue to hold her when surely she must be dissolving in his arms.

"Aren't you curious to know how it feels?"

"Yes."

"Well, then," he asked hoarsely, "won't you feel cheated if you don't ever experience that?"

She held her breath for what seemed like an interminable length of time before blurting out, "I haven't taken any final vows yet."

He flinched reflexively. "What?"

"I said—"

"I heard what you said. What does that mean?" His breath was hot, as hot as the widespread hand branding the skin on her back.

She was sorely tempted to tell him the truth then and there. Seconds after the words were out of her mouth, he would be making love to her. Of that she had no doubt. Swollen and hard, his manhood pressed against her belly. She was dewy and achy with desire for him. What transporting ecstasy it would be to—

But no. Her attention must be focused solely on the nine orphans. Their lives were in her hands. If they were to survive, they needed all the odds in their favor. Neither she nor Linc could be distracted for a single instant.

If they became lovers, that would not only be a distraction, but a complication. When this was all over, when they were safe in the United States, their relationship would be a heartrending dilemma to her and an albatross to him.

Kerry couldn't give herself to any man lightly, yet that's the way this man of vast experience would take her. She had no doubt that when Linc had referred to a man who knew how to give a woman pleasure he was speaking of himself. But that's all it would be to him. Pleasure. Mutual but temporary. Involvement with a man like Linc O'Neal would only open up oceans of regret for her.

She chose her answering words carefully. "It means that I'm still considering what to do with the rest of my life." It wasn't a lie. It was a solid truth. She hadn't planned her future beyond getting the nine children into the United States.

She felt his heavy sigh; it seeped out of him gradually. And with it, his tension. His compliance with her silently expressed wishes made her feel even worse about her deception.

She remained lying in his arms, but there was a tangible difference in the way he held her. Soon, grayish light began filtering through the branches of the vine. Straining their ears, they could hear sounds of morning activity coming from the soldiers' camp. The smell of coffee and food made them both delirious with hunger. Several times they heard men moving through the jungle, but none came as close as the soldier had the night before. Finally, they picked up the welcome sound of truck engines being pumped to life.

Linc waited about fifteen minutes before he lifted the vine and crawled out. "You stay here."

Kerry obeyed him. She was actually grateful for the moments of privacy. She pulled on her own shirt, which was still damp, and ran her fingers through her hair. It was a mass of tangles. She was still working her fingers through the knotted strands when the curtain of leaves was lifted.

"It's all right," Linc told her. "They're gone."

# Six

Kerry sank down onto the bank of the river. She was thoroughly dispirited. Her shoulders sagged with defeat. The toddler, Lisa, seemed to have gained fifty pounds overnight. Kerry couldn't hold her for another minute without dropping her. She set the child on the ground beside her.

"Now what?"

She got no answer. Several moments ticked by. Even the children were still, as though realizing that they faced a serious problem that might not have a solution. Shading her eyes with her hand, Kerry glanced up at the man standing beside her.

Hands on hips, one knee bent, brows lowered, eyes glowering, mouth frowning, it wasn't difficult to assess Linc's mood. Kerry watched his lips form a crude expletive that he didn't dare speak aloud in front of the children, even though they didn't understand English.

She diplomatically let a few more moments go by before she tried again. "Linc?" His head snapped around and he glared down at her. "How the hell should I know? I'm a photographer, not an engineer."

Linc immediately regretted lashing out at her. It wasn't Kerry's fault that the heavy rains the night before had caused local flooding and that the wooden bridge he had planned to use to get across the river had been washed out.

It wasn't even her fault that he was in such a foul mood. She was the reason for it, but she wasn't to blame. Ever since he had helped her crawl out of the cover where they had passed the night, he'd been ready to take somebody's head off at the slightest provocation.

"You'd better put these on." He angrily tossed her her clothes after he'd retrieved them from where he'd hidden them the night before.

She hadn't taken issue with his brusqueness, but had quickly stepped into her khaki trousers. Unable to tear his eyes away from her long, lovely, fantasy-inspiring legs, Linc had watched every supple movement. His loins had ached with the recollection of her thighs being entwined with his.

Had it really happened? Had he only dreamed that her body perfectly complemented his? Had she curled up against him, actually seeking contact, or had he just wished it so hard that it had seemed real?

Maybe so, because all morning they had fenced with each other. They hardly behaved like two people who had slept together like lovers. They hadn't even been friendly. She'd been cautious and wary of him; he'd been truculent and quarrelsome.

When they returned to the house and found the children in the kitchen instead of in the cellar, Linc had yelled at Joe. "I thought I told you to stay down there until I came to get you."

"I heard the soldiers leave," the boy shot back. "I knew it was safe."

"You don't know sh—"

"Linc!"

"When I tell you to do something I expect you—"

"Linc!" Kerry had shouted again. "Stop yelling at Joe. All the children are safe, but you're frightening them."

Linc had cursed beneath his breath as he headed for the front of the house. "Get them ready. I'll be back in five minutes."

Luckily the truck was where he had left it the evening before, concealed by jungle vines. He slashed at them viciously, working out some, but only some, of his frustration.

"The children are hungry," Kerry told him from behind the screened door when he bellowed from the front lawn for them to load up.

Stormily he had followed her back into the kitchen, where the orphans were gratefully eating stale bread and bananas. Kerry had helped them wash their faces and hands, which had become grimy in the cellar. None of them looked at Linc directly, sensing his mood, but he felt eight pairs of eyes frequently glancing in his direction. The ninth pair, belonging to Joe, openly defied him. Animosity simmered between the man and the adolescent boy, who hadn't taken kindly to the blistering lecture.

Little Lisa had squirmed free of Kerry's arms and crossed the kitchen floor bearing a dry crust of bread. Her eyes were sympathetic and imploring as she gazed up at Linc and tugged on the knee of his fatigue pants to get his attention. He looked down at her. She offered him the crust of bread wordlessly. But her eyes, as dark and rich as chocolate syrup, spoke volumes.

Linc crouched down, took the piece of bread from her, and ate it. *"Muchas gracias,"* he said and cuffed her on the chin. Lisa flashed him a dazzling smile before shyly scampering back to Kerry.

It was a while before he had cleared his throat enough to say gruffly, "Let's go."

When all the children had been placed in the truck, he drew Kerry aside. "Call off your watchdog."

"What are you talking about?"

"Joe. Make it clear to him that I didn't compromise you last night. I'm afraid to turn my back on him for fear he'll slide a knife between my ribs."

"Don't be ridiculous."

"Tell him!"

"All right!"

Those had been the last words they had exchanged until now, when, with her eyes shaded from the glaring sun, she had looked up at him and spoken his name.

Apparently her nerves were just as frayed as his. She lashed back. "That's what I'm paying you for, Mr. O'Neal. To come up with ideas. To improvise."

"Well, maybe you should have checked out my credentials more carefully before offering me the goddamn job."

Kerry had no argument for that, so she clamped her mouth shut and returned her stare to the rushing water.

Why did she always make him look like a snarling beast in front of the kids? They were watching him as though he were a cross between Jack the Ripper and Moses, afraid of him, but looking to him for leadership.

He blew out an exasperated breath. "Give me a

minute, okay?" he said, raking his fingers through his sweat-damp hair.

The bridge was clearly indicated on the map, but apparently hadn't been that substantial. The rising current, due to last night's torrential rains, had been sufficient to tear it from its moorings.

The truck had rolled to a stop where the road ended in the swirling, murky water. The children had piled out and now stood on the bank, looking to him for answers he didn't have. Joe seemed to derive a perverse satisfaction from their predicament; his lip was curled with smug derision. And quite clearly, Kerry was leaving the solution up to him. As she had pointed out, that's what she was paying him for. He would have to earn every red cent of that fifty grand.

He gnawed on his lip as he studied the river. Then he went back to the truck, picked through the supplies in the bed of it, and returned to Kerry. "I need to talk to you."

She stood, brushed off the seat of her pants, instructed the children not to get too close to the water, and followed him. When they had moved out of earshot, she asked, "What do we do now?"

"I have a suggestion, and please hear it out before you fly off the handle." He fixed his golden stare on her. "Let's load the kids up, turn around and go back the way we came. Let's throw ourselves on the mercy of the first troops we see."

He paused, expecting an explosion. When it didn't happen, he pressed on. "It won't matter which side we align ourselves with, El Presidente's or the rebels. Whichever it is, we'll appeal to their vanity, tell them what a humanitarian gesture it would be for them to help us. We'll promise to propagandize their cause to the world if they'll only help us."

He laid his hands on her shoulders and appealed to her earnestly. "Kerry, the kids are hungry and we have no more food. Our clean water is running out, and I'm not sure where we'll find more. I don't know how in hell to get across that river without risking all our lives. The truck is almost out of gas and there are no Exxon stations in the jungle.

"Even if we do make it to the rendezvous point, how do you know for certain that this Hendren fellow will be there to pick us up and whisk us away into the wild blue yonder like some Sky King?"

He saw her eyes darken and hastened to add, "Look, this was a noble idea. I admire you; I really do. But it wasn't a very practical plan, not very well thought out. Now you'll have to admit that." He smiled at her engagingly. "What do you say?"

Kerry drew a deep breath, though she never released him from her gaze. When she spoke, her voice was level and calm. "I say that unless you want my knee rammed into your crotch, you'd better take your hands off my shoulders."

His smile collapsed. His face went comically blank. His hands fell quickly to his sides.

She pivoted stiffly and marched away. But she got only a few steps away from him before he lunged, shoved his hand into the waistband of her pants and yanked her to a teeth-jarring halt. "Just a damn minute," he shouted. He spun her around. "Didn't anything I said to you register?"

She tried to wiggle free, but this time his hold on

her was inescapable. "I heard every patronizing, condescending, chicken-hearted word."

"You're determined to go on?"

"Yes! Once we cross the river, it's only a few more miles to the border."

"It might just as well be a thousand."

"I promised these children that I would get them to the families waiting for them in the United States, and that's what I'm going to do. With or without you, Mr. O'Neal." She pointed her index finger at the end of his nose. "And if you desert us now, you'll never see a penny of your precious money."

"I care more for my life than I do the money."

"Well, you've got a better chance of keeping both by getting us to that airplane instead of turning yourself over to a band of guerrillas. What happened to all your warnings about getting shot and gang-raped? Do you really think that I'd ask a favor from any of these troops?"

"Most of them, whichever side they fight for, come from Catholic backgrounds. Your profession would protect you."

"It hasn't protected me from you!"

His face turned stony. Before Kerry had time to regret her words, he yanked her high and hard against him. He snarled, "Wanna bet?"

Fleetingly she recalled the many times he could have taken advantage of her and hadn't. Unable to meet that fierce, masculine glare, which was as hard and unyielding as the lower part of his body, she moved her gaze down to his throat where she spotted his pulse beating as rapidly as her own.

"I'm sorry," she said breathlessly. "I shouldn't have said that."

"You sure as hell shouldn't have." He shoved her away, but she got the impression that it was to spare himself embarrassment and not out of any kind feelings toward her. His strong fingers were still curled around her shoulders.

"Don't be deceived," he said in a voice that throbbed with passion. "Just because I haven't touched you, doesn't mean that I haven't thought about it. A lot. You're not concealed by a habit yet. When you go flashing that dynamite body of yours around a man, you had better be willing to accept the consequences. Some might have even fewer scruples than me."

Her head came up slowly, until her eyes again met his. "Then why would you even suggest that I turn myself and these children over to the soldiers?"

He released her. Each of his ten fingers let go separately, as though being individually pried away. "I had to see how tough you really are."

She looked at him aghast. "You mean…this was all… you didn't really mean—"

"That's right. This was a test of your mettle. I had to know if you've got guts."

She backed away from him. Her hands were balled into fists as though prepared to hit him. Dark blue eyes narrowed to threatening slits. "You son of a bitch."

Linc's lips quirked. Then he threw back his head and laughed. It was a loud and wholesome laugh, so loud that it disturbed the birds and small monkeys in the branches overhead. They squawked and chattered in protest. "Damned right, Sister Kerry. I'm a son of a bitch. And I'm gonna get worse. If we make it through this alive, you're gonna hate me before we're through. Now, round up the kids while I get everything ready."

Before she could tell him just how loathsome she thought his tricky tactics were, he was stalking back toward the truck. She had no choice but to do as she was told. The orphans were hot, hungry, thirsty and exhausted, so she tolerated their querulousness. She answered their whining questions as best she could, but her attention was really on Linc. He was busy securing the end of a rope, which had been in the back of the pickup when she stole it, to the trunk of a tree. Tying the other end around his waist, he waded into the swift current.

"What are you doing?" she called, surging to her feet in alarm.

"Just keep everybody back."

The children fell silent. All stood in tense silence as Linc made unsteady progress across the muddy river. When he reached the middle where it was too deep to stand up, he began swimming. Numerous times the swift current sucked him under. And each time, Kerry clasped her hands together, holding her breath, until she saw his head break the surface again.

At last he made it to the opposite side. The water dragged at his clothes as he pulled himself up the spongy bank. Once he reached firm ground, he dropped to his knees, hung his head, and gulped air into his lungs.

When he had regained his breath, he selected a stout tree trunk and tied the rope around it. He tested it several times before wading into the river again. He pulled himself across on the rope. It wasn't as strenuous as swimming, but even so, it was exhausting work to fight the current. It took him several moments to recover once he had reached them.

"Got the idea?" He was bent at the waist, his palms resting on his knees, when he lifted his head and glanced up at Kerry. His hair was plastered to his head. Several sodden strands striped his forehead. His eyelashes were wetly clumped together. Kerry was tempted to comb the hair off his forehead and touch his bristly jaw. To keep from touching him, she actually had to squeeze her fist so tightly that her nails bit into her palm.

"Yes, I get the idea, but what about the truck?"

"It stays. We go the rest of the way on foot."

"But—" The objection died on her lips. Only minutes ago he had tested her fortitude. He had all but promised her that the going from here on would be a nightmare. She had insisted on bucking the odds. "All right," she said softly. "What do you want me to do?"

"You take Lisa. Carry her piggyback. I'll get Mary. Joe," he said hitching his chin toward the eldest boy, "you get Mike this time. You and I will have to make several trips I'm afraid."

The boy nodded his head in understanding.

"I can make more than one trip," Kerry said.

Linc shook his head no. "You'll need to stay on the other side with the children. This is no joyride, believe me. Explain the procedure to them, and for God's sake stress to them that they must hold on tight."

As she translated for the children, she tried to make crossing the river sound like a grand adventure, at the same time emphasizing how treacherous it could be and how vital it was for them to hold on to the adult carrying them.

"They're ready," she told Linc as she bent down and let Lisa climb onto her back. The child's arms folded around her neck and her ankles crisscrossed in front of Kerry's waist.

"Good girl, Lisa," Linc said, tousling the child's glossy hair.

When she beamed a smile up at him, he returned her grin and patted her back. Kerry looked up at him, marveling over his soft expression. He caught her surprised look, and they exchanged a brief stare before he turned away and leaned down so Mary could climb onto his back.

"Have you got your passport?" he asked Kerry.

They would have to travel light from now on. She had discarded everything she didn't absolutely need. "It's buttoned into my shirt pocket."

"Okay, let's go." He led the way into the churning water.

Kerry tried not to remember all the tales she had heard about the jungle river creatures. She ignored the slimy things that bumped into her feet and legs as she sought firm footing on the slippery mud of the river's bottom. She crooned comforting words to Lisa, but the reassurances were meant for herself as well as for the crying child.

The rope, not too strong to begin with, was slippery now. It was difficult to hold on to. If it hadn't meant the difference between living and drowning, she would have let go long before she reached the middle of the river. By then her palms were bleeding.

When she stepped onto nothingness and her feet were swept from beneath her, she was terrified of never breaking the surface. Finally she pulled herself up and made certain that Lisa's head had cleared, too. Gallons of water had rushed up Kerry's nose and into her eyes and mouth. She was blinded and gasping for air. But she forced herself to work her way along the rope, going hand over hand.

After what seemed like hours instead of minutes, she felt strong hands molding to her armpits and lifting her out of the water. With Lisa still on her back, she collapsed into the soft, warm, squishy mud of the riverbank and sucked in coveted air. Linc lifted Lisa off her back. Kerry's muscles quivered with exertion, but she pulled herself to her hands and knees and eventually rolled to a sitting position.

Linc was holding Lisa in his arms. Her face was buried in his throat. Her tiny hands were clutching his soaked tank top. He was stroking her back, kissing her temple, rocking her gently back and forth, and murmuring words of encouragement and praise, even though she could understand only his inflection. Kerry envied the child. She wanted to be rocked. Held. Kissed. Reassured.

"You did fine," he said.

It was hardly a lavish compliment, but Kerry had only enough energy to give him a wavering smile anyway. He pulled Lisa away and, after kissing her cheek, passed her to Kerry. Mary was sobbing quietly nearby. Kerry gathered the two girls and young Mike in her arms. They made a pitiful, soggy, sorry-looking group, but all were grateful to be alive.

"Keep this," Linc said, dropping the machete, the only weapon they had, down onto the ground near Kerry's feet. "You okay?" he asked Joe.

"Of course," the boy said haughtily.

"Let's go then."

They waded back into the water. Kerry didn't know

where they found the strength. She could barely keep her head up. Linc and Joe made three more trips each, until all the children had been safely transported across the river. On the last trip, Joe helped one of the older girls along, while Linc carried two backpacks, crammed with their meager supplies.

Tears formed in Kerry's eyes as she watched Linc sling his camera bags into the muddy waters of the rushing river. He had ripped the plastic lining out of one of the bags and wrapped his film cannisters in it, then strapped the makeshift package to his torso with his webbed belt.

Kerry had felt contrition as she watched him carry out this sobering task. She had manipulated this man unmercifully. He would be home, safe in the United States, pursuing his profession, if it weren't for her.

The only thing that eased her conscience was looking into the hopeful faces surrounding her. And she knew that, if she had it to do over again, she would take whatever measures were necessary to guarantee these orphans a brighter future.

As soon as Linc reached the bank after crossing the river for the last time, Kerry expected him to collapse and rest. Instead his movements were quick and lively.

"Hurry, Kerry, get all the children back into the trees. Have them lie down and tell them not to move."

Even as she carried out his instructions, she asked him. "What's the matter?"

"I think we're about to have company. Quick now! Joe, tell those girls to be quiet. Everybody lie down."

After having made certain that they'd left no traces behind and slashing the rope from the tree trunk, Linc dove for cover in the deep undergrowth beneath the trees. He lay on his stomach beside Kerry, staring out over the river. His breathing was rapid and heavy.

"You're exhausted," she whispered.

"Yeah."

His eyes didn't waver from the truck on the other side of the bank. Much as Kerry had despised that pickup, she missed the security of it now. "Do you think someone is following us?"

"I don't think they were deliberately following us. But someone is behind us. I heard them."

"Who?"

"It won't matter when they see the truck belonging to El Presidente's army and the rope."

"If it's El Presidente's men, they'll wonder what happened to their comrades and come checking on them," she said musingly. "And if it's part of the rebel army…"

"You got it," he said grimly. "Shh. There they are. Pass it along that no one is to move a muscle."

The whispered command was passed from child to child as a jeep chugged out of the jungle on the far side. Several others could be seen behind it.

"Rebels." Linc whispered a curse. He would have preferred the regular army since they had deserted a government truck.

Several guerrillas alighted, holding their automatic weapons at their hips ready to be fired. They approached the pickup cautiously, fearing that it might be booby-trapped. When they were satisfied that it wasn't, they examined it thoroughly.

"Recognize any of them?"

"No." Kerry listened hard, trying to catch the gist of their conversation over the roar of the water. "They're speculating on why the truck wasn't just turned around when it came to the washed-out bridge. They're wondering if the soldiers crossed the river by holding on to the rope."

"Only a fool would try crossing that river on a rope," Linc muttered.

Kerry looked at him quickly. He glanced down at her from the corner of his eye. They exchanged a brief smile.

On the far bank, one of the guerrillas produced a pair of field glasses. "Lie still," Linc hissed. The soldier studied the riverbank through the binoculars and said something.

"He saw our footprints in the mud," Kerry interrupted. "He's telling the others that there are several of us. Around a dozen."

"Pretty damn smart."

"Now he's saying—" She gasped sharply when more guerrillas moved into view.

"What is it?"

"The one on the far left—"

"Yeah, what about him?"

"That's Juan. Our courier."

By now the rebel's two sisters, Carmen and Cara, had spotted him. One gave a soft cry and made to rise. "Get down!" Linc's order, for all its lack of volume, carried with it unarguable authority. The young girl froze. "Tell her to stay put. He might be her brother, but the others aren't."

Kerry conveyed the message in whispers, but in a considerably softer tone than Linc's. Carmen whispered something back, her face working with emotion.

"What did she say?"

"That her brother wouldn't betray us," Kerry translated.

Linc wasn't convinced. His eyes remained on the far riverbank. The soldiers were conferring while they lounged and smoked and relieved themselves. Occasionally one would gesture across the river. One reeled in the rope and examined it. He gave it one swift tug between his hands. It snapped in two.

Kerry looked at Linc. He shrugged. "I told you only a fool would try it."

Some of the rebels offered opinions. Others seemed supremely unconcerned and dozed as they leaned against their jeeps. The one identified as the courier who had made arrangements for the orphans' escape kept glancing furtively toward where they lay hidden in the brush. After almost half an hour, the one obviously in charge ordered them all back into the jeeps.

"What's the consensus?" Linc asked Kerry.

"They're going to try another road and cross the river farther downstream." She was leaving something out. Her guilty expression told him so. He took her jaw in his large hand and forced her head around. His eyes demanded the truth. "Then they're going to come back this way and keep looking for us," she added reluctantly.

He swore. "That's what I was afraid of. Okay, let's start moving." He checked to make certain that all the jeeps had turned around and disappeared into the jungle before he lined the children up safari-style. He would lead, Joe would take up the rear. Kerry was to keep to the middle to encourage laggers and make sure no one wandered off the path Linc would cut with the machete.

"Tell them we'll be moving quickly. We'll take breaks, but only when absolutely necessary. Tell them not to talk." He relaxed his stern demeanor when, at Kerry's translation, the children looked up at him fearfully. "And tell them how proud I am of them for being such good soldiers."

Kerry turned warm beneath the heat of his eyes. She was included in his compliment. After she passed it along to the orphans, they smiled up at him.

They fell into line and struck out through the dense jungle, which would have been impenetrable were it not for the merciless hacking of Linc's machete. Kerry kept her eyes trained on his back. Before wading into the river, he had tied the sleeves of his bush jacket around his waist and fashioned a sweatband for his forehead out of a handkerchief. The muscles of his arms, back, and shoulders rippled with each upward swing and downward arc of the huge knife. Kerry let that supple rhythm entrance her. Otherwise, she wouldn't have had the energy to place one foot in front of the other.

Her aching body cried out for rest, her dry mouth for water, her empty stomach for food. When she was certain that she would drop on the next step, Linc halted and called a rest. Bearing Lisa, who had fallen asleep in her arms, Kerry slumped to the ground. The children all did the same, dropping in their tracks.

"Joe, pass around that canteen, but be sure to ration the water." Silently the boy moved to obey Linc's request. "How long have you been carrying Lisa?" he asked Kerry as he dropped to his knees beside her and offered her the canteen that had been hanging from his own belt. She in turn raised it to Lisa's parched lips.

"I don't know. For a while. She was too exhausted to take another step."

"I'll carry her from now on."

"You can't carry her and cut a path at the same time."

She lifted her heavy hair off her neck, knowing that she would never take a hairbrush for granted again.

"And I can't afford to have you collapse on me. You're not having your period or anything like that, are you?"

She gazed back at him in speechless astonishment. She didn't even realize that she let go of her hair and let it fall back to her shoulders. She ducked her head. "No."

"Well, that's good. Now take a drink of water." After she had recapped the canteen and handed it to him, she said, "I'm sorry about your cameras."

"Yeah, so am I. We'd been through a lot together."

She could tell by his grin that he was teasing her. "I mean it. I'm sorry you had to destroy them."

"They can be replaced."

"What about your film?"

"I hope the containers are as watertight as they're advertised to be. If they are, I'll have a helluva story to sell when I get home." He stood up. "I'll carry Lisa, and no more arguments about it. We can't go much farther before dark."

He offered his hand to her. Kerry accepted it gratefully and relied on him to pull her to her feet. He swung Lisa onto his back, hoisted her into a comfortable position, and moved to the head of the line again.

Kerry felt dangerously close to tears.

She became immune to the buzzing insects, the slithering progress of jungle reptiles close to her feet, the sweltering, steamy afternoon heat, the raucous chatter of monkeys and the keening of birds. She concentrated solely on following Linc's lead and staying on her feet even when her body threatened to fold in upon itself and never move again.

The sun had long since set and the shadows of the

jungle were dark and threatening before Linc stopped. He had stumbled upon a shallow stream beneath a slender waterfall which trickled between two vine-shrouded boulders. He eased Lisa off his back and rolled his shoulders to work the knots out.

The orphans were too tired to complain. Some of them were already asleep as Kerry circulated among them carrying canteens of cool water fresh from the stream. There was no food to distribute, and even if there had been, they were too exhausted to eat it.

Kerry longed to take her boots off and put her feet in the water. Indulging in that luxury was out of the question, however. Her feet might swell so much that she couldn't get her boots back on. Should they be attacked, she wouldn't have time. And from the way Linc was circling the perimeter of their resting place, attack seemed a very real possibility.

He moved toward her and sat down. His deep frown prompted her to ask, "Did they follow us?"

"I don't think they followed our trail, but they're on our heels just the same. I can smell the smoke from their campfires. Apparently they don't think we pose much of a threat." As he talked he was making a thick paste out of a handful of dirt and drops of water from the canteen. "Keep the children quiet. Take cover if anyone you can't identify approaches."

Terror smote her chest. "Where are you going?"

"To their camp."

"Their camp! Are you crazy?"

"Undoubtedly. Or I wouldn't be here in the first place." He gave her a wry grin. Kerry couldn't have fashioned a smile if her life depended on it. Linc motioned Joe over to them. "Will you go with me?"

*"Sí,"* the boy said.

"Smear some of this mud on your face and arms."
Linc extended his hand. Joe scooped a large dollop of
the mud from Linc's palm and began spreading it over
his exposed skin as Linc was doing.

With apprehensive eyes, Kerry watched them me-
thodically preparing to do battle. "Why are you going
into their camp?"

"To steal weapons."

"Why? We've come this far without weapons."

She struggled to keep the tears out of her voice, but
they were there. And even though it was too dark for
Linc to see her stricken features, he could hear the stark
fear in her voice.

"Kerry," he said gently, "do you really think that either side in this damn civil war is going to let an airplane from the United States land, then let us waltz on
and fly off just like that?" He snapped his fingers.

It was a rhetorical question. He didn't expect an answer and didn't get one. He went on. "If the plane is
there as you seem to believe it will be, and if we get on
it at all, it will be amidst gunfire, probably from all directions. I can't fight off two armies with one machete."

The thought of gunfire appalled her. But she realized that what Linc said was true. The fighters in this
war weren't likely to wave bye-bye from the ground as
they took off in an airplane.

Why hadn't she thought of the actual escape before? Reaching the rendezvous point had been her primary goal. Probably because of the tremendous odds
against achieving that, she hadn't thought beyond it.
What would happen to them? The children? Joe? Linc?
Her stubbornness had put them all in life-threatening
danger. She mashed her fingers against her lips to stifle
a sob. "What have I done?"

Linc took her in his arms and drew her close. "Don't chicken out on me now." He hugged her tight. Placing his mouth directly over her ear, he whispered, "You've been terrific. And it just might turn out all right after all."

Kerry wanted him to hold her longer—forever—and was disappointed when he released her. He handed her the machete. It weighted her arm down like an anchor. "Use it if you have to. We'll be back as soon as possible."

He moved away from her. She reached for him, but grasped at air. "Linc!"

His shadow solidified in front of her again. "What?"

She wanted to throw herself at him and beg him not to leave her alone. She wanted to cling to him and never let go. She wanted to be embraced, sheltered, protected from the million and one dangers lurking in the jungle at night. She wanted him to kiss her one more time.

She willed her chin to stop trembling and said shakily. "Please be careful."

It was awfully dark. He was virtually invisible with the mud smeared over his features. She might not have even known he was there if it hadn't been for his breath settling in warm gusts over her face. She sensed that he wanted to hold her as much as she wanted to be held. The tension in his body conveyed his reluctance to leave her.

But he didn't touch her again. Instead he only said, "I'll be careful."

Seconds ticked by before she realized that he and Joe had disappeared into the black shadows surrounding her. She and the eight children were alone.

# Seven

It was almost daybreak before Linc and Joe returned. Kerry, who had been dozing, was so relieved to see them unharmed that she didn't immediately comprehend their defeated expressions.

Their postures heralded the failure of their mission. Both went directly to the stream and scooped up generous handfuls of water, washing off the camouflaging mud as they drank. When Linc finally turned around, he stared at Kerry through dejected eyes.

"What happened?" she asked.

"We didn't get anything," Linc told her, keeping his voice low. "Couldn't even get close. They were on alert and didn't relax their guard for a single minute. We circled the camp all night, hoping to find a goldbricker asleep at the switch. There was no such soldier in that whole outfit."

He backed against a tree and slid down its trunk, bending his knees as he went, until his bottom touched the ground. Then he rested his head against the tree trunk and closed his eyes. "Anything happen here?"

"No. The children slept. A few of them woke up

saying they were hungry, but I managed to lull them back to sleep."

Joe, in a poignant imitation of Linc, sat leaning against another tree and closed his eyes. He was a man now, having done a man's job. He might resent Linc, but he held a grudging admiration for him, too. Kerry touched Joe's knee and, when his eyes opened, gave him a smile that said, "I'm proud of you." The boy smiled back.

She left him to rest and sat down beside Linc. "How much farther to the border?" she asked.

"About a mile."

"We won't have any trouble making it there by the deadline."

The plan was to meet the plane at noon, in hopes that if any troops were nearby they would be sleeping off their midday meal and the afternoon heat.

"I just wish to hell I knew what we were going to do once we get there."

Linc's weary sigh had a frightfully pessimistic sound to it. Kerry clutched at straws. "If we can't board the plane without risking the children's lives, we'll just slip across the border."

"And then what?" Linc asked impatiently. His red-rimmed eyes opened and focused on her. "It's just more of the same over there." He indicated their jungle surroundings with a flip of his hand.

"For miles there's nothing but jungle. God knows how far it is to the nearest outpost of civilization. And the neighboring country doesn't want Monterican refugees adding more of a strain to their struggling economy. You'll find them inhospitable if not downright hostile. If we could convince them to give the kids political asylum, what do we do in the meantime? Where are we going to get food for supper tonight? Water? Shelter?"

His negativity sparked Kerry's temper. "Well, then you think—"

"Shh!"

Joe sprang to his feet, poised to listen. He cocked his head to one side. After a moment, he shot them a warning glance and silently crept forward. Kerry made a move to detain him, but Linc's fingers encircled her wrist like a manacle and jerked her back down beside him. He shook his head vigorously when she opened her mouth to speak.

Joe disappeared into the deep green shadows of the jungle. The waiting seemed interminable. Linc eased himself up to his haunches and scanned the area with piercing eyes. Kerry felt useless. She only hoped that none of the children woke up making noises.

No more than a minute had elapsed before Joe stepped through the trees, closely followed by a guerrilla fighter. Recognizing him instantly, Kerry stood and rushed toward him, avoiding Linc's precautionary restraint.

"*Hola,* Juan," she whispered.

"*Hermana,*" he responded with a respectful inclination of his head.

Linc joined them. His guard was relaxed now that he recognized the soldier as the one Kerry had pointed out to him the day before. He looked like all the others, except that he was younger than most, sixteen maybe. His features hadn't hardened into a cold mask yet, though he already had the alert bearing of a trained guerrilla fighter. He and Kerry carried on a low, rapid conversation. When he gave Linc a suspicious once-over, she explained who he was.

"He's brought us two guns," she told Linc. "He says they're all he could smuggle out of the camp."

She shied away from the machine guns as Juan handed one to Linc and the other to Joe. Linc checked them both out. "Perfect working condition. Ammo?" The rebel handed him several clips of ammunition.

"Thanks."

*"De nada."*

"Ask him if his group knows who we are and what we're up to?" Linc told Kerry.

"No, he says," she told Linc after translating his question and hearing Juan's answer. "Since we were in the government truck, they think we're inexperienced stragglers or possible deserters looking for a band of rebels to join. They intend to follow us until they find out."

"That's what I was afraid of." Linc gnawed on his lip for a moment. "Ask him what would happen if he explained to his commander who we were. Would he let us go?"

The soldier listened, then shook his head vehemently. Kerry translated his quick response. "He says that they probably wouldn't kill us, but that they would try to take the airplane for their own use. Our only hope, he says, is to get to the plane as quickly as possible. He'll try to divert his squadron away from the designated landing place."

"Does he realize that some of his own men might get shot if they try to stop us?"

Kerry smiled ruefully at Juan's answer. "He says that some deserve to be shot."

Linc stuck out his hand and the young man shook it solemnly. "Anything you can do to help, buddy, I'll appreciate." Linc's tone didn't need any translation.

Kerry suggested that Juan wake up his sisters and tell them goodbye. He crept over to where they were sleeping. His face softened as he gazed down at them, but he motioned for Kerry to let them sleep.

He murmured something to her. His face and voice were earnest, his eyes shimmering with tears. Then, after one last glance down at the sleeping girls, he silently nodded farewell and melted into the jungle.

"What did he say?"

Kerry brushed the tears from her eyes. "He didn't want his sisters' last memory of him to be a goodbye. He knows it's doubtful that they'll ever see each other again. He wants them to start a new life in the United States. He said to tell them that he is willing to die for the freedom of his country. If they never hear from him again, they're to find comfort in the fact that he died happy, knowing that they were safe and free in America."

They fell silent, and for a long moment none of them moved. Any commentary on the young soldier's sacrifice would be superfluous. Words, no matter how poetic, wouldn't do it justice and would only sound banal.

Linc forced himself out of the reflective mood and asked Joe, "Do you know how to use that?" He nodded down toward the Uzi the boy held in his hands.

While Linc was instructing him, Kerry moved among the children, rousing them, but telling them to remain as quiet as possible. She gave them fresh water to drink and promised that there would be food for them on the airplane. Surely Jenny and Cage had thought of that.

When they had gathered what pathetically few possessions they had left, they began the final leg of their journey to the border. Kerry insisted on carrying Lisa so Linc would have more freedom of movement. Not only was he carrying the machete now, but the blunt-nosed machine gun, too.

It was almost eleven o'clock before they reached the edge of the jungle. A wide strip had been bulldozed out of it so that the border between Monterico and its neighbor could be easily distinguished. Between the two green walls of solid jungle, there was a swath of open territory about as wide as a football field.

"There, that's where he's supposed to land," Kerry said, pointing toward the open space. They remained behind the shelter of the trees, but could easily see the clearing. "See that old watchtower? He'll taxi up to that and turn around."

Linc, squinting against the brightness of the sun, studied the area. "All right, let's move as close to it as possible. Tell the kids to stay together and well behind the tree line."

"Do you see anything?"

"No, but I've got the feeling that we're not the only ones taking cover in the jungle this morning. Let's go."

They moved laterally, always keeping several yards of jungle growth between the clearing and their parallel path. When they came even with the abandoned watchtower, Linc halted them. "We'll wait here." He consulted his wristwatch. "It shouldn't be long now."

Linc told Kerry to make sure all the children understood the need to run in a crouching position should they be fired upon. "Tell them not to stop running for any reason. Any reason, Kerry. Make certain they understand that."

They prepared the children as well as they could, then Linc drew Kerry aside, out of earshot, and sat down to wait. "He's got fifteen minutes," he said, glancing at his wristwatch again.

She said confidently, "Cage will be here."

Linc's eyes, as sharp as a gold-plated razor, sliced down to her. "Who is this Cage Hendren anyway?"

"I told you. He's a Texan whose missionary brother was shot by one of El Presidente's firing squads a couple of years ago."

"I know all that. But who—or what—is he to you?"

If she didn't know better, she would think Linc was jealous. "My good friend's husband."

He stared deeply into her eyes as though looking for signs of duplicity. "What was he to you before he married your good friend?"

"Nothing! I didn't even know him. I met Jenny first, through the Hendren Foundation."

He looked away, staring straight ahead. He didn't comment on the information she had imparted, but the tension in his jaw had relaxed noticeably.

"You and I will escort the children out," he said to her, abruptly changing the subject. "Can you carry Lisa?"

"Of course."

"Even at a run?"

"I'll manage."

"Okay, I'll hold back and cover our rear. Joe will stay here until you are all on board."

"Why?" she asked, alarmed.

"To provide cover should anybody start shooting."

"Oh."

"Once you're on the plane, I'll come back for Joe."

What had been left unsaid was that Linc would be exposed to gunfire longer than anybody. His tall frame not only provided the largest target, but he would have to make the hazardous trip across the clearing twice.

"Here," he said.

She gazed down at the packages of film he had laid in her hands. "What's this for?"

"If anything happens to me, at least the film will get out." She paled drastically. "I've been in some pretty tight squeezes, but never quite this tight before. I'm just taking precautions."

"But this film hasn't even been opened," she said, puzzled.

"Yes it has. The boxes contain the film I've used. I replaced it in the cellophane wrappings so it would look like new, unexposed film. That, at least, might protect you if…if anyone caught you with it."

"I don't want to be entrusted with your film, Linc. I might—"

"Look, if target practice for one of those guerrillas pays off, just make sure the film gets processed and the pictures published."

"Don't talk like that!"

He pulled the handkerchief he'd often used as a sweatband from around his head and slipped it over hers, working it down until it hung around her neck. "Didn't knights of old give a lady they admired a token before they went into battle?"

"Don't," she said tearfully. "I can't stand this. I don't

want to talk about this. I don't even want to think about it. And you don't admire me."

He chuckled. "Yes, I do. Oh, I'll admit that I could have throttled you when I woke up and found myself shanghaied into a job I didn't want." His face lost all trace of teasing then. "But I do admire you, Kerry. You've been a trouper when you could have been a real pain in the butt. If I don't have an opportunity to tell you later—"

"Stop it! You can tell me anything you want to when we get to Texas."

"Kerry," he said gently, realizing that her distress could jeopardize her courage when she needed it the most, "I don't have any intention of dying in Monterico. I don't want my third Pulitzer to be awarded posthumously. I've never considered that there was much prestige in winning prizes if you're dead. Besides, I want to collect my fifty grand from you."

He flashed her a brief smile. He had beautiful teeth, she noticed for the first time. They looked startlingly white in contrast to his deeply tanned and bewhiskered face. She didn't know whether to slap him or kiss him.

But she didn't dare let her affection for him show. They couldn't afford to become maudlin now. So she glowered at him. "Any other last requests?" she asked sarcastically.

"If you make it and I don't, smoke a cigarette for me and have a glass or two of straight whiskey."

"Bourbon or Scotch?"

"I'm not particular."

"Anything else?"

"Yeah. Don't take those final vows."

He moved so fast her mind couldn't register it before

he had hooked his hand around the back of her head and pulled her face beneath his. Close. "I'd just as well die a sinner as a saint."

He kissed her.

His mouth came down hard on hers. Her lips parted. His tongue made one sweet, piercing stab into her mouth. The suddenness of it, the masculine claim it symbolized, made her weak. Her hands clutched the front of his tank top and her head fell back. His whiskers scraped her face, but she didn't mind. His tongue, as smooth as velvet and as nimble as a candle's flame, mated with hers and provocatively stroked the inside of her mouth.

An emptiness deep inside Kerry yawned wide, wider, yearning to be filled. Her breasts felt full, as with milk. The nipples tingled with a desperate need to be touched, kissed, sucked. Her womanhood ached deliciously. Reflexively, her hungry body arched against him. Her arms folded around his neck.

Her response drove him a little mad; he deepened the kiss. His broad hand opened wide over her back and pressed her as close to him as possible. The fervency mounted until he made a strangled cry and lifted his head. He stared down into her bewildered eyes. He gazed at her mouth, now full and red and moist from their kiss.

"God a'mighty, Kerry," he rasped.

Involuntarily, she ran her tongue over her throbbing lips.

He groaned. "Oh, God, you're sweet." He kissed her again, his tongue thrusting deeply. "And I swear to you that if we had the time—" he kissed her again "—I'd see you, all of you. And touch you. Your breasts, God, your breasts." He passed his hand over them fleetingly. It was a sizzling sensation and she moaned. "And I'd kiss you. Get inside you. Even if it meant being denied heaven."

She wanted him. Yes. But…she loved him. She loved him! And, God forbid, should anything happen to him, he would die thinking—

"Linc, there's something—"

His head popped up. "Shh!"

"But I have to tell you—"

"Not now. Be quiet." He pushed her away and stood up, craning his head to see above the trees. He motioned her to silence. Seconds later, her ears picked up the drone of an airplane's engine.

"We've got a lot to talk about, sweetheart, but now's not the time. Get the children ready." He was spurred into action, every muscle of his body tense, but executing movements with amazing calm and agility. "Joe, get into place."

"I'm ready," Joe said, taking cover behind a tree.

The airplane didn't circle the area in reconnaissance. It made one approach. The children were restless with anticipation. Their dreams were coming true. While they all kept their eyes trained on the landing airplane, Linc's were busily scanning the area for any sign of troop movement.

The pilot made a faultless landing and the airplane taxied to a stop directly in front of the old watchtower, in perfect accordance with the plan.

"Go." Linc gave Kerry a gentle push.

Tightly clasping Lisa against her chest, she took several hesitant steps into the clearing.

"Go!" This time Linc roared his command.

Kerry broke into a dead run, yelling for the children to do the same. She could hear the heavy thud of Linc's boots close behind them. They had closed almost half the distance between them and the airplane when the first shots were fired. Kerry froze; the children screamed.

"Go on, don't stop," Linc shouted.

He spun around and sprayed the air with machine-gun bullets, aiming in the general direction of their as yet unseen attackers. He saw answering gunfire. The trees seemed to spit flames no larger than those of a cigarette lighter, but he could hear bullets peppering the ground all around him. He rattled off another round and turned to chase after Kerry and the children, who had almost reached the plane. Miraculously none of them had been hit, though some of them were screaming in terror.

The door of the plane was already open. Linc turned again. The wall of the jungle now seemed to be alive with troops firing weapons. Apparently Juan hadn't been successful in diverting them. Linc only hoped that the boy hadn't been found out.

From the corner of his eye he saw Joe leave his cover and fire his machine gun. He shredded jungle plants and sent a few soldiers scampering for cover, before he jumped back behind his tree.

"Good boy," Linc muttered. He glanced over his shoulder and saw that the children were being pulled into the plane. Running backward and firing from the hip, he went to assist them on board.

It was when he glanced behind him again that he saw jeeps loaded with troops moving out of the line of trees on the other side of the border. Monterico's neighboring nation was impartial, but they were coming out to investigate. An officer in the first jeep, holding a bull-horn to his mouth, shouted an order at him. Linc didn't understand it, but he got the general meaning when the soldiers began firing warning shots.

"Shit!"

Now they had armies shooting at them from both sides.

One of the children stumbled and went down. Linc raced over to him, scooped him up, and ran at a crouch toward the door of the plane.

"Was Mike shot?" Kerry shouted over the whine of the plane's engine and the persistent gunfire.

"Just fell I think. Get in the damn airplane!"

Lisa was being lifted out of Kerry's arms and swung up into the fuselage. Linc shoved Mike toward the pair of reaching hands. The terrified little boy, tears making muddy tracks down his dusty face, was hauled inside to safety. All the children were now inside, except Joe, who was doing enough damage to frustrate the guer-rillas and keep them under cover. But his ammunition would run out soon.

"Get in the plane!" Linc repeated to Kerry.

"But you and Joe—"

"For God's sake, don't argue with me now!"

Apparently the man in the plane was of the same mind as Linc. Still protesting, Kerry was pulled inside. "If anything happens to me, get them the hell out of here," Linc shouted to the blond-headed man.

"No!" Kerry screamed.

Linc looked directly at her. The briefest but most puissant look passed between them, then Linc turned abruptly and began running back toward the line of trees, firing the machine gun as he ran.

"What's he doing?" Cage Hendren asked. "Why didn't he get in?"

"He's gone back to get one of the boys. He stayed behind to give us cover."

Cage nodded his understanding as he watched the man run in a zigzag pattern across the clearing. He didn't know who he was, but he considered him a hero. Or a fool.

"Cage, we've got to go," the pilot of the airplane shouted from the open door of the cockpit.

Kerry grabbed Cage's sleeve. "No. This plane doesn't take off without them."

Cage saw the determination on her face. "Not yet," he yelled to the pilot.

"One of these lunatics might hit us. And the other bunch is moving jeeps—"

"Thirty seconds more," Cage bargained, knowing that the veteran pilot was right. "We've got two more passengers."

Kerry screamed when she saw Linc fall to the ground. "He's all right," Cage reassured her. "He's just reducing the size of their target."

From his battle position, Linc shouted for Joe to run toward the plane while he provided cover by firing at the guerrillas. Joe emerged from the jungle with his machine gun blasting. Rotating as he ran, he fired in all directions. He had almost reached the point where Linc lay when his left leg buckled and he went down.

"No!" Kerry cried. She tried to jump from the door of the airplane, but Cage caught her shoulders from behind and gripped them hard to keep her inside.

Just then several bullets struck the exterior of the plane. They did no serious damage, but increased Cage's anxiety. The success of the mission depended on getting the children to safety. Could it be sacrificed for two who were apparently willing to give their lives?

He watched Linc belly crawl to where the boy lay sprawled facedown in the dirt. He saw them exchange words. "He's alive," Cage told Kerry.

"Oh, God, please don't let them die." Tears were streaming down her face.

"Cage, they're blocking off this makeshift runway with jeeps," the pilot yelled.

The children were all crying in terror.

"Kerry, we've got to go," Cage said.

"No. We can't leave them."

"We might all die if—"

"No, no." She struggled to get away from his restraining hands. "You can take off but leave me."

"You know I can't do that. The children need you."

She sobbed wretchedly as she saw Linc come up on one knee. He gripped Joe under the arm and slowly heaved him to his feet. Joe couldn't support himself. His left leg dangled uselessly. Linc struggled to get one of Joe's arms around his shoulders, then he began backing toward the plane with the boy in tow.

They were pelleted with gunfire. Kerry saw little puffs of dust rising from the ground where bullets struck. Smelling victory, the guerrillas left the cover of the trees and began running across the clearing, firing steadily.

"Kerry—"

"No, Cage! Don't you move this plane a single inch!"

"But—"

She cupped her hands around her mouth. "Linc! Linc! Hurry!"

Linc fired the machine gun at the pursuing enemy until it ran out of ammunition. Then, with a vicious curse, he threw it down and, in a single motion, swept Joe up into his arms like a baby and ran toward the airplane.

"They're coming!" Kerry shouted.

"Start rolling," Cage shouted over his shoulder to the pilot. He leaned as far out the door of the airplane as he could, hand extended.

Kerry saw Linc's grimace of agony a second before she saw the front of his shirt bloom red. She was too hoarse by now to make a sound, but she opened her mouth and screamed silently.

Wounded, Linc kept running, his teeth bared with exertion. He stumbled toward the door of the plane, making a Herculean effort to hand Joe up to Cage.

Cage gripped Joe's shirt collar and pulled him inside. Under his own strength and despite the pain, the boy crawled out of the way. The plane had gained momentum now and Linc was having to run to stay abreast of the door.

"Give me your hand," Cage shouted.

Linc reached as far as he could, stumbled, but miraculously stayed on his feet. Then, with one last burst of energy, he grasped Cage's hand and held on. His feet went out from under him. He was dragged a considerable distance before Cage, with Kerry's clawing assistance, managed to pull him inside. He fell in, rolled to his back and lay there gasping while Cage secured the door and shouted to the pilot, "Get the hell out of here!"

"Roger!"

They weren't out of danger yet. The airplane was fired upon from all directions before the pilot finally taxied his way clear, and the aircraft became airborne only a few feet above the jeeps trying to block their takeoff.

The children were huddled together. Most of their tears had dried, but they were wide-eyed and apprehensive over their first airplane ride. They stared at the tall, blond *norteamericano* who was speaking to them in their native language and smiling at them kindly.

Kerry's hands fluttered over Linc's chest. "Oh, Lord. Where are you hit? Are you in pain?"

He pried his eyes open. "I'm fine. Check on Joe."

She crawled over to where the boy lay. His face was ashen, his lips white with pain. Cage shouldered her aside. He swabbed Joe's arm with an alcohol-soaked cotton ball and gave him an injection.

"A painkiller," he said in answer to Kerry's unasked question.

"I didn't know you could do that."

"I didn't know I could either," he said wryly. "One of our local doctors gave me a crash course in nursing last night."

He cut away Joe's pants leg and examined the nasty bullet wound in his thigh. "I don't think it shattered his femur, but it tore up the muscle a bit."

Kerry swallowed the bile that flooded her throat. "Will he be all right?"

"I think so." Cage smiled at her and pressed her hand. "I'll do what I can to clean the wound and keep him comfortable. When we get closer, the pilot will radio Jenny. She'll see to it that an ambulance is waiting for us when we land. And by the way," he said with the smile that had made him a legend with women throughout West Texas, "I'm glad you made it."

"We wouldn't have, if it hadn't been for Linc." Now that Joe seemed to have lapsed into painless oblivion, she moved toward the man still lying prone on the floor of the fuselage.

"Who?" Cage asked.

"Linc. Lincoln O'Neal."

"You're kidding!" Cage exclaimed. "The photographer?"

"Somebody call my name?" Linc opened his eyes and struggled to sit up. The two men grinned at each other with the ease of old friends.

"Welcome aboard and pleased to meet you," Cage said, shaking hands with Linc.

"Thanks."

Linc looked at Kerry. She looked back. Cage realized immediately that something was going on there and that whatever it was, he was a fifth wheel. "I, uh, I'll see to the kids. Kerry, maybe you'd better check on Linc's wound. Medical supplies are in here," he said, sliding a first-aid kit toward her. Diplomatically he left them alone.

"What in the hell were you trying to prove back there?" Linc demanded angrily. "I told you to leave without us if anything happened. I ought to beat your butt for disobeying me."

Kerry's encroaching tears were swept away by fury. "Well, pardon me," she snapped. "I wasn't waiting for you. I was waiting for Joe. Are you in pain or not?"

"It's a Band-Aid wound," he said, negligently glancing at his bleeding shoulder.

"Cage can give you a shot to stop the pain."

"Forget it. I hate shots."

They glowered at each other. Her lips were the first

to quirk with the beginning of a smile. Then his. They surprised all the passengers in the small aircraft by suddenly bursting into laughter.

"We made it!" Linc cried exuberantly. "We actually made it. Hot damn! You're home free, Kerry."

"Home." She whispered the word like a benediction.

Then her emotions made another swift about-face. She launched herself against Linc's bloodstained chest. And while they hugged each other fiercely, she wept with relief.

# *Eight*

❧❧❧

Jenny Hendren had thoughtfully provided food. There were peanut butter sandwiches, oranges and apples, and homemade chocolate chip cookies. Cheese snacks and canned drinks had been kept in a portable cooler. As soon as their hunger had been appeased, most of the children dozed. All the seats had been temporarily removed from the Cessna executive plane, but there still wasn't an abundance of space inside the fuselage.

"How is Joe?" Kerry asked Cage.

He was bending over the injured boy, checking the inadequate bandage he had placed over his thigh wound. "Still out."

"I'm glad you had that injection ready."

"So am I. He'd be in a helluva lot of pain without it. How is the other patient?"

"Ornery, bullheaded, obstinate." Immediately after her tears had dried, she and Linc had moved apart awkwardly. No longer tender and consoling, he'd reverted to being tough and abusive. "He wants to talk to you."

Cage moved over to where Linc was propped against the wall. He looked as disreputable as when Kerry had first met him. He was unshaven. His clothes were filthy and torn and bloodstained. Without the handkerchief sweatband around his forehead, he had to constantly keep pushing his hair away from his face.

"Kerry said you wanted to talk to me." Cage eased down beside the other man.

"You said something earlier about calling ahead to your wife." Cage nodded. "Do you think she could have a camera waiting for me when we land?"

"Linc had to throw his cameras in the river when we crossed it," Kerry explained. "We barely managed to save his film."

Cage, for all his reckless living in years past, looked back at them with surprise and respect. "Sounds as if the two of you had quite an adventure."

Kerry glanced uneasily at Linc. "Yes, we did. You see, the river—"

Cage held up both hands. "I want to hear all about it, but everyone else will, too. Why don't you rest now, then tell it once for everybody?" Kerry smiled at him gratefully. "What kind of camera do you need, Linc?" he asked.

"Got a pencil?"

Cage jotted down the specifications as Linc ticked them off. "I'll see what I can do." He inched toward the cockpit.

"Nice guy," Linc remarked, his eyes still on Cage.

Kerry laughed. "Not always, from what I hear."

"Oh?"

"As I told you, I met Jenny through the Hendren Foundation. She was engaged to Hal Hendren when he was shot."

"Cage's brother?"

"Yes."

"The missionary?"

"Right."

Linc shook his head. "I must have taken a blow on the head I don't remember. Or is this as confusing as it sounds?"

"It is rather complicated. Jenny knew the brothers quite well. You see she grew up with them. The Hendrens adopted her when her parents were killed."

"So they were all one big, happy family?"

"Yes."

Linc's eyebrows shot up and he grinned lecherously. "Sounds kinky to me."

"Hardly. They were reared in a parsonage. Cage's father is a minister."

"Preacher's kid, huh? No wonder I liked him immediately. Bet he's a hell-raiser."

"Until Jenny got hold of him."

Even though Linc was bedraggled, his eyes sparkled. "I think I'm looking forward to meeting this Jenny."

Kerry laughed. "You should be, but not for the reason you think. She's a real lady. She and Cage, who was a lady killer extraordinaire, are devoted to each other. They have one child, a little boy, and she's expecting another. I'm sure that's the only reason she didn't come with Cage to pick us up."

"Well, if she had come along, I don't know where we would have put her."

Linc's comment called attention to how cramped they were. They were sitting so close that Kerry's knee was propped on his thigh. As unobtrusively as possible, she moved it away.

Both were remembering the kiss he had given her

before the airplane arrived. There were kisses. And then there were kisses. And that kiss had been the kind a man gives a woman he wants badly. It had been ravenous and undisciplined and carnal. Each time Kerry thought about it, she trembled with aftershocks. And each time Linc thought about it, his manhood threatened to embarrass him.

"Are you comfortable?" she asked huskily.

His gaze popped up to hers. At first he thought she had read his mind, or, God forbid, noticed the rigidity behind the fly of his pants. Then he realized that she was looking at his shoulder, not his lap.

"No, it's nothing," he said in a strained voice.

She shivered at the bloodstains on his tank top. He could have been killed so easily. He had risked his life. It would be impossible to repay him for the sacrifices he had made for her and the children, but she knew that some kind of thank-you, insufficient though it would be, was in order.

"Linc?"

Because he couldn't look at her without his desire running rampant, he had leaned his head against the wall of the aircraft and closed his eyes. Now, when she spoke his name with such appeal and laid her cool, dry hand on his arm, his eyes opened slowly and he turned his head to look at her.

"Hmm?"

"What you did back there..." Her voice trailed off and she lowered her eyes. "I want to thank you for everything. I...I..." The right words wouldn't come. She couldn't think of anything to say that wouldn't come close to sounding like a declaration of her love. Unwisely, she blurted out the thing that came to mind.

"I'll give you a check for the fifty thousand as soon as possible."

He sat perfectly still for several moments. It was the calm before the storm. He violently jerked his arm from beneath her hand. He wanted to tell her to keep the goddamn money. *Money! Is that all she thought this had meant to him?*

"Go to hell."

"What?"

"You heard me."

"But I don't understand."

"You've got that right, lady, you don't understand."

"Why are you snapping at me? I was only trying to thank you." By now, Kerry, too, was angry. There was just no understanding this man. He wouldn't let someone be nice to him. He was an unfeeling barbarian.

"So you've thanked me. Now drop it."

"Gladly." She started to scoot away, but noticed the fresh drops of blood oozing down his chest. "You made your shoulder bleed again."

Indifferently, he looked down at it. "It's all right."

She took a square of gauze from the first-aid kit. "Here, let me—"

He caught her wrist before her hand made contact with his injured shoulder. "I said it's all right. Just leave me alone, will you? As you've been so quick to remind me, we have a business arrangement only. That doesn't include tending my wounds." He lowered his voice. "Or kissing. Why'd you let me kiss you back there?" He moved his face closer to hers. "Why'd you kiss me back? Baby, your tongue was just as busy as mine. Don't think I didn't notice. Well, you could have spared yourself the trouble. I would have run just as hard, shot off just as many rounds of ammo, if you hadn't."

Kerry's cheeks were hot with indignation. "That's a horrible thing to say."

"Maybe. But not as horrible as making sexual promises you don't intend to keep." His lip curled with contempt. "We're even now, Sister Kerry. I hired out to do you a service. As soon as you pay me, I'm gone. Finis. I'll click off a few shots of the kids getting off the airplane for their first sight of U.S. soil, then I'll split. This whole goddamn mess will be history, and frankly, it can't happen soon enough for me."

Kerry snatched her hand out of his grip, glaring at him with patent dislike. Never in her life had she known anyone so hard and insensitive. "Goddamn mess." That summed up what he thought of the orphans, their ordeal, and her. The disillusionment was cruel, but she had suffered disillusionment before. It was painful, but not fatal. One could survive and live to tell about it.

She put as much distance as possible between herself and Mr. Lincoln O'Neal, found as comfortable a space as the crowded fuselage afforded, and settled down to sleep for the remainder of the flight.

Cage nudged her awake. "We're about fifteen minutes out, Kerry. I thought you might want to rouse the children."

"How's Joe?" The boy was moaning. His eyes were still closed, but he was fitfully rolling his head from side to side.

"Unfortunately he's coming around. But I'm not going to give him anything else. I'll let the doctor take it from here."

"Cage," she said, catching his sleeve when he moved toward the cockpit again. "I don't want to face a crowd of reporters right now. The children will be frightened enough already. We're all so dirty and tired. Can you arrange it?"

He rubbed the back of his neck. "You're big news, Kerry, because of—"

"I know," she interrupted quickly, aware that Linc could overhear everything they were saying. "But I'm sure you understand why I prefer privacy. For me and the children, not to mention the couples who are going to adopt them."

"I understand, but I'm not sure the media will. Reporters have been camped out in La Bota for days, waiting for your arrival." He saw her distress and laid a comforting hand on her shoulder. "But if you don't want to be interviewed or have the children exposed to that kind of mayhem, that's the way it'll be. I'll radio the sheriff now and tell him to cordon off the airport."

"Thank you."

The children, who were all wide-awake now, were chattering excitedly as they peered out the windows. Kerry laughed at their bewildered comments about the flat West Texas landscape, which was so different from the jungle terrain they were accustomed to.

The experienced pilot made another perfect landing. When the plane taxied to a stop, the first priority was to get Joe to the waiting ambulance, which would rush him directly to the hospital. Cage jumped to the ground and conferred briefly with the doctor.

Linc swung down and looked for a pregnant lady with a camera. She wasn't difficult to spot. Kerry was right. Jenny Hendren spelled lady from the top of her glossy brown hair to the toes of her shoes. "Mrs. Hendren?"

"Mr. O'Neal?"

They smiled at each other and she passed him the camera he had ordered. "A Nikon F3 with Tri-X film. I sent Gary to Amarillo to pick it up. We had to call around before finally locating one there."

"Sorry for putting you to so much trouble."

"I just hope it's all right," she said anxiously. "I barely know which end of a camera to point."

Linc didn't know who Gary was, but he was damned glad to have a camera in his hands again. "It's perfect, thanks. I'll settle up with you later."

He tore into a package of film and loaded it mechanically. He raised the camera to his eye just in time to snap off pictures of the paramedics lowering the stretcher bearing Joe out of the airplane. He moved toward it. The boy's eyes were open now. He spotted Linc, the only familiar face among those surrounding him. Linc said, "Hang in there, trooper." For the first time since Linc had met him, Joe smiled. Linc captured that wan smile on film.

The doctor climbed into the ambulance after the stretcher had been loaded. When he turned to close the door, he noticed Linc's wound. "You should have that attended to."

"Later." Giving his minor injury no more thought, Linc swung his camera around toward the door of the airplane.

Inside it, Kerry was speaking with soft reassurance to the children. "Everything will seem different, but don't be frightened. You are very special to the people here. They want you."

"Are you going to leave us?" young Mike asked.

"No. I won't go until I'm sure you are all happy with your new families. Are we ready?" Eight heads nodded solemnly. "Good. Then let's go."

She assisted them to the ground. Cage and Jenny Hendren escorted the pitiful parade toward a waiting van. Kerry did her best to ignore Linc as he took pictures of her. She also tried to ignore the stab of envy she felt when Cage took his wife in his arms, held her close, and kissed her.

Jenny's relief that Cage had returned safe and unharmed was apparent, as was his concern that she was overtaxing herself in her advanced stage of pregnancy. While both dismissed the other's worry, their love shone around them like an exclusive sun.

When all the children had been loaded into the van, Kerry and Jenny embraced. "It's a dream come true," Kerry said to her friend. "Thank you for everything. For making all the arrangements. You've both been wonderful."

"Hush now. You need rest and nourishment. We'll have plenty of time to talk later. Cage," she said, turning to her husband, "why don't you and Mr. O'Neal climb into the back with the children? I'll drive."

"Uh, excuse me, Mrs. Hendren," Linc said, "I'll just get a cab to the nearest hotel and—"

Simultaneously Cage and Jenny burst out laughing. "We only have one cab in town," Cage explained. "You'd be lucky to get him here the day after tomorrow if you called right now. And there's no hotel, although there are several motels."

"Besides," Jenny chimed in, "I wouldn't let you leave

without thanking you for all your help. Now get in before we collapse from this heat."

And that, it seemed, was that. Linc got in the back of the van with Cage. Little Lisa, her face a study in uncertainty, held her arms up to him. He settled her in his lap for the ride to the Hendrens' house.

"I held the reporters at bay with the promise of a press release, Kerry. You can prepare it whenever you feel like it."

"Thank you, Jenny."

"And, of course, you're staying with us," Jenny added.

"What about the children?"

"We've been loaned several mobile homes. They're at the ranch," Cage said. "We've also got nurses standing by to check them over to the immigration department's satisfaction. It'll take several days for the paperwork to be completed and the adoption papers finalized. That will all be taken care of before their families arrive to pick them up." Cage looked at the circle of young faces surrounding them. "Which ones are the sisters?"

Kerry pointed out Juan's two sisters. Cage smiled at them and told them in Spanish that their new parents were already at the house. "They're waiting for you. You'll meet them as soon as we arrive."

The little girls, who had been inconsolable when Kerry gave them their brother's parting message, clung to each other fearfully and looked to both Kerry and Linc for guidance. He gave them the thumbs-up sign and an exaggerated wink. That made them giggle.

Kerry was impressed with the Hendrens' house and surrounding acreage and commented on it as they turned off the main highway and drove through a gate.

"Thank you," Jenny said. "Cage had started refurbishing the house before we got married. We've done a lot more work on it since then. I love it."

Cage Hendren had been a wildcatter, and still laid claim to several producing oil wells. But when the price of crude began to drop, Cage could see the handwriting on the wall and began cultivating other businesses, including real estate and beef cattle ranching. He also had a stable full of quarter horses. When the economy shifted, he suffered no tremendous setbacks. They lived modestly by choice, not out of necessity.

There were three mobile homes parked end to end on the near side of the horse barn. Before the van had pulled to a complete stop, Roxy Fleming emerged from one of them at a run, her husband, Gary, close behind her.

"That's Roxy," Jenny told them.

"You wrote me about her," Kerry said.

Roxy, buxom and boisterous, would have launched herself at them, had not the easygoing, affable Gary caught her shirttail and held her back.

Cage and Jenny introduced Kerry and Linc to the Flemings. Roxy acknowledged them politely, but distractedly. She was eagerly scanning the faces of the children. "Which ones are Cara and Carmen?" Her voice was about to crack.

Kerry pointed the two girls out. Roxy extended her hands. A tense moment elapsed before the girls separated themselves from the tight little group and baby-stepped their way forward to timidly take Roxy's hands.

As discreetly as possible, Linc took pictures of the heart-wrenching scene. The most poignant photograph he got was one of Kerry Bishop, the person who had made this miracle possible. He knew it would be a good photograph. The reflected sunlight had made diamonds of the tears standing in her eyes.

Kerry descended the staircase with inexplicable nervousness. Perhaps it was because she was wearing a dress for the first time in ages. Well, that wasn't entirely true. She had worn a dress the night she had abducted Linc from the bar, but that wasn't quite the same.

Maybe her heart was pounding because this was the first time he had ever seen her with her hair clean, soft and glowing, her skin smooth and free of grime and her nails buffed to a polished shine.

For whatever reason, her knees threatened to collapse with each step she took.

It seemed that a lifetime had passed since their narrow escape from Monterico. Yet it had happened only that morning. The day had been spent getting the children settled into their temporary quarters. They had marveled over the "luxuries" they had found in the mobile homes. They had all been given clean bills of health by the nurses. Months ago, when the idea of their being adopted in the United States was first conceived, Kerry had seen to it that each child was vaccinated in accordance with U.S. regulations.

With the aid of the Flemings and Cage's parents, Bob and Sarah Hendren, all the children had been soaped and scrubbed and shampooed and outfitted in spanking new clothes donated by a La Bota merchant. Thanks to members of Bob Hendren's congregation, there was enough food in the kitchen to make the tables and countertops groan. The children had already eaten two full meals.

Roxy couldn't keep her hands off her adopted daughters and had brushed their hair so many times that Gary, almost as guilty of overindulgence as his wife, had warned her that she was going to brush them bald if she wasn't careful. Kerry only hoped that the rapport between all the children and their new families was established as easily.

At her request, Cage had driven Kerry to the hospital. The staff, carefully guarding her privacy, had let her slip in a back entrance to visit Joe. The surgery to remove the bullet from his thigh had been completed. He was groggy from the anesthetic, but he recognized her. The doctor assured her that his leg hadn't suffered any permanent damage.

When Kerry returned, Jenny had insisted that she spoil herself with a long bubble bath. Without a trace of reluctance, Kerry had stripped off the vile clothes she had lived in for almost four days.

Only when she untied the bandanna from around her neck did her fingers falter. Since Linc had given it to her, she regretted having to remove it. She laundered the handkerchief in the bathroom sink and hung it up to dry. Unless he asked for it back, she intended to keep it as a memento of her one wild, brief, unconsummated, but no less ardent, love affair.

Now, voices drifted to her from the dining room. Her stomach was queasy with a mixture of anticipation and dread. Bolstering her courage, she stepped through the arched doorway into a mellow pool of candlelight and hesitated on the threshold. Jenny was the first to spot her.

"There you are."

"Wow!" Cage whistled appreciatively. "A little soap and water can do wonders."

Linc said nothing. He was caught in the act of lifting a can of beer to his mouth. It stayed poised there in midair for several counts, before he actually drank from it. Kerry went in and took a chair across the table from him.

"This is so nice of you, Jenny." She gazed in awe at the flower centerpiece, the bright, sterling candlesticks, the china and crystal and silver.

"I thought the two of you deserved a quiet, leisurely dinner. Lunch was rather hectic. Relax and enjoy yourselves. The report from the trailers is that the children are asleep."

"I just hope I don't disgrace myself," Kerry said, running her fingers over the handle of her salad fork. "I've lived in the jungle for so long, I hardly remember how to use silverware properly."

"It will all come back to you," Jenny said with a gentle smile.

"And if it doesn't, we won't mind." Cage passed her a plate filled with food. "We're used to eating with Trent. His table manners are atrocious."

"Cute kid," Linc commented. "He made the others feel right at home."

"Yeah," Cage said. "He taught them by example how to attack a bowl of homemade ice cream."

Laughing, Kerry asked, "Where is he?"

"Blissfully asleep," his mother said wearily. "Eat quietly."

Kerry was surprised at how rich and deep Linc's laughter could be when it wasn't tinged with cynicism. It rolled over her like a wave. Apparently Cage, who was of the same broad-shouldered, slim-hipped build, had lent him a pair of jeans and a shirt. He had showered, and his hair, though it could still stand a trim, had been washed and brushed back. His face had been closely shaved. Without the stubble, his jaw looked even more unrelievedly masculine than before, which was a disquieting thought. She detected the faint outline of a white bandage beneath his shirt.

While they ate, their conversation centered mainly on the orphans. "I distributed copies of your press release to the disgruntled reporters."

"Thank you, Cage."

"We'll tell you about the applicants for adoptions, but tomorrow is soon enough for that."

"Thank you again. I'm so tired, I don't think I could assimilate anything tonight," Kerry admitted. "I'm sure you screened the couples carefully. Are all of them as wonderful as the Flemings?"

"Gary and Roxy are special friends, so we're biased. But we think the others will be super parents, too."

After a pause in the conversation, Jenny smiled at Linc and said, "I never guessed that I'd be so honored as to have a celebrity at my table."

"Where?" he asked, comically turning his head from side to side as though searching for the celebrity.

The Hendrens continued to prod him until he enlightened and entertained them with stories of his adventures as a photojournalist. He downplayed the danger he frequently encountered and embellished some of the more humorous anecdotes.

"But," he said, pushing aside his dessert plate after eating two helpings of apple pie, "this latest escapade in Monterico was about the scariest situation I've ever been in."

A major portion of the afternoon had been taken up by their recounting their tale. Cage and Jenny, the Flemings and Cage's parents had listened with disbelief as they told them all that had happened to them on their way to the border.

"I'm in no hurry to go back," Kerry said now.

"Neither were we once we got out," Cage said.

Linc looked at him in surprise. "We? You were there? When?"

"After my brother was executed."

"I'm sorry."

"No, it's all right. Jenny and I had to go down there and identify Hal's body and escort it back." He reached across the corner of the table and took her hand, squeezing it. "It was an unpleasant experience for both of us." He stared into space reflectively. "Although, if it hadn't been so spoiled by the civil war, Monterico could be a beautiful place." He gazed at his wife. "The tropical climate was rather sensuous as I recall."

Because Cage and Jenny were looking at each other with such absorption, they missed the fleeting look that passed between their guests. Both Kerry and Linc vividly remembered a night spent beneath the shelter of a vine, a heavy rainfall that surrounded them with a pounding as fierce as that of a heart on fire, and the seductive perfume of jungle flowers, naked skin and earth combined into a potent aphrodisiac.

That night seemed unreal now. It could have happened to two other people in another lifetime. They couldn't have lain together so closely and be this remotely detached from one another now. He couldn't have quieted her fears and dried her tears then and hurt her as he had this morning with his cruel words.

Kerry looked across the table at Linc; he was a stranger. They had shared cups of water and scraps of bread, passionate kisses and equally passionate arguments, and yet she knew so little about him.

"Neither of you has explained how you came to be teamed up," Jenny said. "How did you become involved with Kerry's work, Linc?"

Kerry jumped as though she'd been struck with an electric cattle prod. She met Linc's hard gaze across the table. His expression was smug. He might have cleaned up on the outside, he might look prettier, but he was still rotten to the core on the inside. He was as cunning and calculating as ever, a ruthless street fighter who never cried uncle.

"I think Kerry should be the one to tell you that," he said. *If she dares.* That remained unspoken, but Kerry clearly read the challenge in his eyes.

It was a challenge she didn't dare back down from. Setting her chin at a stubborn angle, she said, "I recruited him." He made a rude, scoffing sound. She flashed him a poisonous look. "All right, I...I..."

"Shanghaied," Linc supplied drolly.

Kerry sprang to her feet, furious with him for airing their quarrel in front of the Hendrens. "You just won't be nice about this, will you?"

He bolted from his chair. "Nice? Nice? You kidnapped me, lady. You deliberately destroyed a month's worth of hard work. You made me miss my plane out of that godforsaken hellhole. You got me captured by a bunch of cutthroats, chased, shot at, nearly drowned and you expect me to be nice about it?"

Chest heaving with agitation, he pointed at Kerry accusingly as he addressed Cage and Jenny. "She dressed up like a whore and lured me out of a tavern. That's how she 'recruited' me. I went with her, thinking I was gonna get laid and... Oh, sorry, Jenny."

"That's all right," Jenny mumbled.

"He's failed to mention that he was drunk at the time," Kerry sneered. "And I didn't lure him, I dragged him because he couldn't stand up under his own power."

"And that makes it okay?" Linc yelled across the table.

"I thought he was a mercenary," Kerry told their avid listeners. "And he is. He'll get paid for his time and trouble," she said scathingly. "Before you go pinning any medals of valor on him, maybe you should know that he didn't do anything out of largesse. I had to agree to pay him fifty thousand dollars so he wouldn't turn me and the children over to El Presidente."

"That's not why I demanded to be paid, and you damn well know it." Linc moved forward menacingly, as though he was going to climb over the table to get to her. "The money was to repay me for the film you destroyed. That's about how much revenue you cost me. But it doesn't begin to reimburse me for having to put up with you for the last four days." He tossed his napkin down beside his plate. "Cage, would it be too much of an imposition to ask you to drive me into town?"

Jenny Hendren sprang from her chair. "You're not leaving?"

"I'm afraid so, Jenny." Linc liked Cage's wife very much. They had been on a first name basis since earlier that afternoon. She was gracious and kind and straightforward, soft, womanly, and even-tempered— everything that Kerry Bishop was not. "Not that I don't appreciate your hospitality."

"But you can't leave," Jenny said imperiously. "Not now." Everyone was surprised by the intensity of her outburst and looked at her inquiringly. Embarrassed, she hastened to ask, "You took all those pictures today to go with the story of your escape, right?"

"Right," Linc answered hesitantly.

"And I'm sure that since Kerry has declined to be interviewed, she's going to grant you exclusive rights to the story. Right, Kerry?"

Kerry hesitated. "Uh, right."

"Well, the story isn't over yet," Jenny said. "Don't you want to photograph the children as they meet their new parents? And you can't leave without knowing how Joe is going to fare."

Linc considered his dilemma. Jenny was right in one respect. The story would be better if he stuck around till the end of it. He'd been on the telephone to several magazines that afternoon and was taking bids from editors who were eager to get their hands on the piece. And, by God, he was entitled to exclusive rights to it, whether Kerry had granted them freely or not.

But he didn't think he could stay under the same roof with her for another hour. He'd either make love to her or murder her, and, for entirely different reasons, he was sorely tempted to do both. The balance was precarious. A slight tip in one direction or another and wham! He was going to cook his own goose.

"I don't know," he hedged. "I guess I could get a room in town and—"

"Ouch!"

Jenny's exclamation brought all eyes around to her. She clutched her distended abdomen with both hands, cradling the precious burden it carried.

# Nine

❧❧❧

"Jenny!" Cage was out of his chair like a shot. Before Linc or Kerry could even blink, he was at Jenny's side and his hands had replaced hers on her swollen stomach. "Is it…what is it?"

She took several gasping breaths, then said, "Just one of those cramps I think."

"You're sure? It's not the baby?"

"No, I don't think so. Not yet."

"Sit down, Jenny," Kerry said, scooting Jenny's chair beneath her.

"I'm fine, really," she said, easing herself down. "I had these cramping seizures when I was pregnant with Trent."

"And they always scared the hell out of me," Cage said, running his fingers through his hair. "Should I call the doctor?"

Jenny raised his hand to her mouth and kissed it. "No. Don't make a fuss. Sorry I made such a scene." She encompassed them all in her apologetic smile.

"You did too much today and were on your feet too

long," Kerry admonished gently. "You stay right there and let us clean up the kitchen."

Over Jenny's mild protests, the three of them began carrying the soiled dishes into the kitchen. Cage hovered around his wife. Half an hour later Kerry assisted her upstairs.

No one said any more about Linc's leaving. He didn't even think about the subject himself until he stepped out onto the front porch. When Cage joined him moments later, he said, "I really should go. My being here is putting an extra burden on Jenny."

"We wouldn't hear of it. You're welcome to stay for as long as you like, if you don't mind sleeping in the single bed in Trent's room. And I warn you, he snores."

Linc grinned. "Believe me, anything will be a pleasant change compared to where I've been sleeping." Hearing his own words, his grin faded. He remembered sleeping with only the ground for a mattress and only a vine for a blanket, holding Kerry close. The memory was bittersweet and assailed him with conflicting emotions. "Is that your 'Vette?" he asked Cage. He had to say something to divert his mind, which seemed to stay on a single track lately.

"Yeah. Want to see it?"

They left the porch and strolled across the yard toward the open garage. Inside it were parked a variety of vehicles, among them the vintage '63 Corvette Stingray that had caught Linc's eye. He whistled long and low.

"It's in showroom condition. How long have you had it?"

"Several years," Cage told him. "It was in bad shape when I bought it. I hired a guy to restore it for me. We'll go for a spin in it tomorrow. It'll still bury you in the seat when you get it up to fourth gear. One of my vices is driving too fast."

Linc withdrew a package of cigarettes from the breast pocket of his borrowed shirt. He'd bummed the pack off Gary Fleming earlier in the day. "Want one?"

"I'd love one," Cage said, but held up both hands when Linc extended the pack to him. "But I've sworn off. When we got together, I promised Jenny that I'd quit."

Linc squinted at his new friend through the cigarette's smoke. "You must have had a lot of vices."

Cage laughed good-naturedly. "I did. Too many to count. I've given up most of them." He winked suggestively. "Except screwing. Jenny and I do that a lot."

The men laughed together. "God, that feels good," Linc said after a moment. "I haven't talked with a man who fluently speaks my language in over a month. Heard any good jokes lately?"

"Clean or dirty?"

"Dirty."

While Linc smoked his cigarette, the occasional silences between them were comfortable. They didn't have to work at being companionable because the groundwork for a new friendship had already been laid. It was based on mutual respect, a genuine liking, and perhaps recognition of each other's maverick nature.

That's why Linc didn't take umbrage when Cage said, "About that fifty thousand dollars…"

"I don't want the damn money."

"I didn't think so."

Cage dropped the subject then and there. He didn't probe for answers because Linc didn't seem inclined to discuss the money. Cage could respect that. And Linc liked Cage better for not probing.

"You and Jenny seem very happy together." Talking to a happily married man about his wife was a new experience for Linc, and he felt awkward about broaching the subject.

Cage, however, responded without compunction. "We are."

"You're lucky. I haven't seen too many happy marriages."

"I haven't either. I never take ours for granted though. Jenny gave up a lot to marry me."

"I know you gave up smoking and some hell-raising. What did she give up?"

Cage grinned wryly. "Her common sense." They chuckled and Cage shook his head with chagrin. "Marrying her was the only way I could have her, and, well, you know how it is. We do things for a woman that we would never do otherwise."

*You've got that right, buddy,* was Linc's self-critical thought.

"Speaking of Jenny," Cage said, "I'd better go inside and see how she's feeling. Enjoy your cigarette. See you in the morning."

"I'll buy some clothes tomorrow. Thanks for the use of these. Thanks for everything." They shook hands. Cage walked back toward the house and closed the screened front door behind him.

Linc finished smoking his cigarette meditatively. He liked the Hendrens tremendously. He also envied them their closeness to each other. He'd never been that close to another human being. Not to either of his parents. Not to a special friend. Not to anyone.

Cage's and Jenny's gentle teasing was based on affection. The love they shared for their little boy created an almost visible bond between them. By all indications, their bedsheets were kept warm with frequent and ardent activity.

Linc had intercepted numerous loving glances between them. He felt a twinge of jealousy that no one had ever looked at him with such unqualified love. In the farthest corner of his mind, he acknowledged that maybe he'd missed something.

Hell, what was he thinking about? Had a brush with death that morning turned him into a philosopher?

He had it made. He enjoyed a terrific career that involved travel and adventure. It was lucrative. It had won him acclaim. Women were easy to come by. They were drawn to him by his money, his fame, his reputation as a lover. He gave them the expensive gifts, the introductions to influential people, and the pleasure they wanted. And he was interested in only one thing from them. Once his craving for sex was satisfied, he thought no more about them.

The women in his life were bodies only. They were transitory. Women with no substance. Not like Jenny Hendren. Not like—

Uttering an impatient oath, he rubbed Kerry's name from his mind. He also tried to eradicate her image, but was less successful at accomplishing that. He couldn't forget the way she had looked when she came down to dinner. He hadn't expected her to look so…womanly. He had expected a nun's habit.

Instead, she had shown up wearing a dress that was made of some soft material that had clung temptingly to her delicate body. The skirt had whisked against her bare legs. Each time she turned, the shape of her breasts had been clearly profiled for him. Her hair had shone in the candlelight every time she moved her head. Her lips, faintly tinted with gloss, had looked as ripe and juicy as a berry ready to be plucked. And that's all he could taste.

Oh, he had done justice to the meal. His stomach had cried out for the nourishment it had been denied for the past few days. But with every bite of food, he had also swallowed a taste of Kerry.

Linc groaned with resignation as he felt himself grow hard with a desire that would surely condemn him to hell. He couldn't indulge the longing that heated his blood. He could only try his damnedest to cool it.

"How does that feel?"

"Wonderful," Jenny sighed.

Her husband had found her already in bed when he entered their master bedroom, after having checked on their sleeping son and making certain that the extra bed had been turned down for Linc. Kerry was using the guest bedroom.

Cage had undressed quickly and joined Jenny in their wide bed where he was now massaging soothing lotion onto the stretched, tight, itchy skin of her abdomen. It was a nightly ritual that both of them enjoyed immensely.

"The baby isn't moving very much tonight," he commented.

"She's resting after her performance at dinner." Ever since the doctor had confirmed that she was pregnant, Jenny had insisted that this baby was a girl. She fancied having a blond-haired, tawny-eyed daughter to round out their family.

"That was quite a show, all right."

"What do you mean by that?" Jenny asked testily.

"Only that I wasn't sure if those cramps were real or just your sneaky way of getting Linc to stay."

Jenny moved his hand aside. "I don't like your implication, Cage."

He only laughed at her pique. "That's what I thought. You're guilty as hell. Otherwise you wouldn't be protesting so much." He leaned over and stopped her flimsy denials with a kiss. When he pulled back, he asked, "Should I be jealous?"

"Over what?" She traced the hair on his chest with her fingernail. His kisses still had the power to curl her toes.

"Over your going to such great lengths to keep Linc under our roof?"

"I haven't admitted that yet, but if I did urge him—"

"Urge! I thought you were going to hog-tie the poor guy to the dining room chair when he mentioned leaving."

"Well, I do think he should stay and take photographs of the orphans when they meet their new families. And I did have a cramp."

His hands fell still and his handsome face registered concern. "A bad one?"

"No. It was one of those little contractions that don't mean anything."

"Sure?"

"Positive."

He reached for the bottle of lotion and poured some into the palms of his hands. He laid them on her breasts and began rubbing in the scented cream with lulling, circular motions.

She sighed, and her eyes slid closed. Cage gazed down at her with love. "How can you be so very pregnant and still so very beautiful?"

"You think so?" Lifting one hand, she idly brushed a dark blond strand of hair off his forehead.

"Um-huh."

"Do you think Linc thinks Kerry is beautiful?"

"I thought that's what you were up to."

She stared at him guilelessly. "What?"

"Matchmaking."

"Well, anyone can tell—"

"Jenny, stay out of it."

"That they're attracted to each other."

"They were practically biting and scratching across our dining room table."

She came up on one elbow. "Well, I've known us to bite and scratch some! And over the dining room table, too."

Cage looked stunned, then burst out laughing. "You've got me there. Helluva private party, too, as I remember it." Wrapping his arms around her, he lowered her back to the pillows and followed her down with a lengthy, mouth-to-mouth, tongue-to-tongue kiss. When he finally raised his head, her eyes were lambent, but she hadn't dropped their argument.

"I think there's friction between Kerry and Linc because they're fighting a strong attraction."

"What does Kerry say?"

"Nothing, and that's curious, don't you think? She avoids speaking his name aloud if at all possible. After what they've been through, you would think that she'd be dropping his name left and right. She tries too hard not to look at him, but I've caught her at it a thousand times today. Did Linc say anything about it when the two of you went to the garage?"

"Sorry, darling," he said, nuzzling her neck, "I couldn't break a confidence between gentlemen."

"Then he did say something about Kerry!"

"No, he didn't. But he's…restless. That's the word I'm looking for, I think. His skin is too small for him. He's angry."

"How do you know?"

"Because I recognize the symptoms. I know what it feels like to want a woman you can't have. You're mad at yourself for being hard all the time, and you can't keep yourself from getting hard every time you think about her. It's like if you don't give it to that particular woman, it's gonna fall off." He flicked his tongue over her large, rosy nipple. "And on that note…"

"We can't, Cage. The doctor said it's too late."

"I know, but—" He sighed when she placed her hand where he ached to feel it. "Ahh, Jenny." He closed his mouth around her nipple and sucked it gently.

Speaking on short gusts of air, Jenny said, "So, if you didn't talk about Kerry, what did you talk about?"

His hot mouth moved to her other breast. "You. I told Linc you were my only vice."

"Hmm, Cage." She gasped when his tongue played upon her sensitized breast. "He'll think I'm terrible."

"He'll think you're wonderful. What every man wants in a wife. A lady in the parlor—"

"And a harlot in the bedroom."

"Right," he snarled affectionately, sliding his hand between her thighs.

"We can't have—"

"There are other ways."

"But we have guests in the house." Her voice slipped another notch with every featherlight caress of his fingertips.

"That's your problem," he whispered seductively. "You're the moaner."

It was too quiet.

Kerry stood at the window of the guest bedroom, gazing out over the barren landscape, wondering what was keeping her awake when her entire body was crying out for sleep. She had finally come to the conclusion that, after almost a year of living in Monterico, she was missing the nighttime jungle sounds.

She felt exposed because, save for the mesa forming a silhouette against the sky, there was nothing to break the sameness of the landscape. No encroaching trees, no hanging vines, no dense brush. And no sound.

But then she heard a barely audible sound. A squeak. She glanced down and saw a dark shadow slipping through the gate onto the terrace that surrounded the Hendrens' lovely swimming pool.

Linc.

Her heart began its unnatural hammering, as it always seemed to do whenever he was around. This time, however, her rapid heartbeat was partially due to anger. How dare Linc blare out her indiscretion to the Hendrens! She had come to expect nothing but churlish behavior from him, but he had sunk to an all-time low that night at dinner.

His participation in the rescue must have come as a surprise to them. They might have assumed that she would need assistance at some point, but they were no doubt shocked that it had come in the form of a renowned photojournalist.

The orphans had made it impossible for her to de-emphasize the role Linc had played during their ordeal. Because, when in doubt about what to do, they all turned to him for guidance. Even though he didn't speak Spanish, he conveyed messages to them with facial expressions, gestures, and a pidgin Spanish-English that they understood and heeded.

He acted as a surrogate father to all of them, particularly to the younger ones. He might not have wanted the role, but it had been foisted upon him, and he had grudgingly accepted it. In fact, he seemed to enjoy toting Lisa in his arms and entering mock wrestling matches with the boys.

Kerry knew that Cage and Jenny had probably been burning with curiosity. Only politeness had prevented them from coming right out and asking. Linc suffered under no such restriction. Out of pure meanness, he had provided them with all the lurid details of how he had met Kerry while she stood there in mortification.

Throughout the day, she had held her breath, afraid of being exposed as a fraud. She was afraid that someone would mention a name, a name that would undoubtedly trigger a volatile response from Linc. The subject had been stamped around so many times that Kerry had become as nervous as a cat with a long tail.

By one means or another, the truth would come out. He would discover that she wasn't what she had led him to believe she was. When he did, she wanted to be as far away from him as possible. She didn't have to guess what his reaction would be. He would be livid.

That morning, after he had kissed her, she had started to tell him. Fearing that one or both of them might die, she had wanted to confess her lie. But she had been robbed of the opportunity by the arrival of the rescue plane. Then, after they had argued over the blasted money, she didn't want to tell him. It served his mercenary soul right to live under the misconception.

She had felt both relief and despair when, at dinner, he had announced that he was leaving. She wanted him to leave before he found out that she wasn't a nun. On the other hand, the thought of his leaving had crushed her. She would probably never see him again. Such a possibility was devastating. She would always be grateful to Jenny's baby for providing an adequate, but not catastrophic, diversion.

Now Kerry watched him, unseen, from her darkened second-story window as he paced the terrace, smoking. It was consoling to know that he wasn't able to sleep either. She wasn't the only one in an emotional quandary tonight.

Of course what he was feeling wasn't deep emotion. It was lust. She had seen it, blazing in his golden brown eyes, before he carefully screened them. He might be antagonistic toward her, but he wasn't indifferent. Small comfort, that. They were still irreconcilable. He was fighting a contest of wills. She loved him.

She saw him grind out his cigarette in a planter. He looked like a man bedeviled as he raised his hands to his face and rubbed the heels of them against his eyes. She thought she heard a muttered curse, but, because it was so obscene, hoped that she had imagined that.

As she watched, he leaned down and pulled off the boots Cage had loaned him. The boots he had worn out of Monterico had been so caked with mud that the Hendrens had insisted on throwing them away with the rest of their clothes.

Linc then began pulling at the buttons of his shirt until they were undone. He peeled it off quickly and tossed it onto a patio chaise. A white gauze bandage was taped to his shoulder.

He worked free the buckle of his belt but left the belt in the loops of his jeans. The metal buckle clinked softly as he unbuttoned the top button of his fly.

Kerry covered her mouth to stifle a small, yearning sound when she realized what he was going to do. It was a dark night. The moon was a slender crescent positioned low in the sky and shedding very little light. The evening was warm. The faint wind was as hot and dry as the arid ground it swept over.

It was the perfect night for a nude swim.

Especially if one's body was hot and restless.

Kerry ceased to breathe. In fact, she lifted a hand to the base of her throat as though to verify that she had a pulse, because everything inside her went perfectly still. She was mesmerized by the motions of his fingers as he worked the metal buttons from their stubborn holes. She couldn't actually see his fingers moving, but she could see the movement of his arms and elbows as he struggled with the button fly of the Western jeans.

And then he was hooking his thumbs into the waistband and pushing them down. At about his knees, he let them go. The soft, well-laundered denim pooled around his ankles. He stepped out of the jeans.

And Kerry knew one thing for certain: Jenny bought Cage's underwear. The low-slung, hip-riding briefs were the kind of undergarment a woman liked to see on a man. They were light in color and showed up in stark contrast to Linc's dark, lean body and the surrounding night.

Blood was pumping thickly through her veins.

She saw Linc raise his hands to his waist. His thumbs slid beneath the elastic band. Then...

He was splendidly, primally, majestically naked. Rawly, proudly male. And beautiful. So beautiful it hurt to look at him. The sight of his nakedness affected her like a piercing spear through her chest.

She slumped to her knees and rested her chin on the windowsill. She exercised no maidenly shyness. Her eyes boldly moved over him. His body hair grew in intriguing patterns and showed up as fuzzy shadows on his tanned flesh. It clustered darkly and thickly around his sex.

He turned. Kerry got a glimpse of a marvelously symmetrical back. Muscled shoulders tapered to a narrow waist, and the sides sloped into a straight, shallow spine. His buttocks were taut. He walked with a swagger that excited and aroused her. His thighs were lean. His calves looked as hard as apples.

Long before she had seen her fill, he dove cleanly into the water. He hardly made a splash. He swam the length of the pool underwater before he surfaced, and then remained in the shadows beneath the diving board for a long while before he began swimming laps. He cut through the water as sleekly as an eel, his arms arcing out of the water and catching the meager moonlight.

Kerry's body ached. Her skin seemed on fire. Her breasts tingled. She covered them with her hands in an attempt to contain that delicious, blooming sensation, but found that touching them brought no relief. It only made them more agitated. The merest movement of Jenny's sheer batiste nightgown against her nipples provoked shameful stirrings deep inside her.

Finally Linc swam to the edge of the pool. He opened his hands flat on the tiles and stiffened his arms, levering himself out of the water until he could get one foot up on the side. He shook the water from his head and peeled his hair back, holding it off his face with both hands behind his head for several seconds before dropping his arms. He ran his hands over his arms and legs, skimming off the water.

Kerry moaned and her body flushed hotly when he ran one hand down his chest and stomach. Before it reached that thatch of dark hair, she squeezed her eyes shut.

When she opened them again, he was stepping into the discarded briefs. He tucked everything comfortably inside before letting the elastic band snap against his waist. Kerry's mouth was dry, but she swallowed hard.

Linc bent at the waist and scooped up the rest of his clothes, then walked toward the back door of the house until he disappeared from Kerry's sight. She didn't move, but maintained her place on the floor beside the window until she heard him come upstairs and go into Trent's bedroom and gently close the door behind him.

Because her thighs had gone the consistency of warm butter, and she felt weak and feverish all over, she virtually crawled to the bed. She kicked off all the covers. She couldn't stand anything abrading her skin. Or rather, being touched anywhere, everywhere, was such a delicious sensation that she thought it best to deny it to herself.

What was this malady? A tropical fever just now manifesting itself? Or was it simply desire for the man she loved?

Linc accidently stumbled onto the intimate scene. He muttered his sincere apologies and immediately withdrew, but Cage and Jenny called him back.

They were sitting at the kitchen table. Cage's hand was splayed wide over his wife's abdomen. Both wore radiant smiles. "Come in, it's okay."

"I didn't mean to interrupt." He felt uncharacteristically gauche and callow.

"You're not interrupting," Cage said.

"Cage loves to feel the baby move."

"What would you say this is, a ballerina or a place kicker?"

Linc grinned self-consciously. "You could stuff what I know about babies into a thimble and there'd still be room."

Cage removed his hand from Jenny's tummy and poured their guest a cup of coffee. "I'm the breakfast chef. What'll you have?"

"Whatever."

"Ham and eggs?"

"Sounds great."

"Orange or grapefruit juice, Linc?" Jenny asked him.

"Orange, please."

She picked the appropriate pitcher off the table and poured him a glass. "You've never been around children?" she asked him nonchalantly.

"Not until this week."

"None of your own?"

Cage cleared his throat loudly, but Jenny didn't acknowledge the subtle reprimand. Linc appeared to be unaware of it. In fact, he was acting rather distracted, as though he were listening for something. "Uh, no, I've never been married."

"Hmm." Wearing a complacent smile that had nothing to do with the innate serenity of pregnancy, Jenny sat back in her chair and sipped her tea. She ignored Cage's reproachful glance when he returned to the table and slid a plate of food in front of Linc. "Dig in."

"This is great. Where's yours?"

"We ate earlier," Jenny told him.

"I'm sorry I slept so late. Is everyone else already up?"

"I sneaked in early and got Trent out of bed. I didn't want him to wake you," Cage said. "The Flemings and my folks have taken all the kids to the hospital to see Joe."

"Including Trent?"

"He pulled a temper tantrum. Roxy, as usual, gave in. Sarah wouldn't hear of him being left behind either," Jenny told Linc. "Between his grandmother and my best friend, I'm afraid Trent is being spoiled rotten."

Kerry hadn't been mentioned. Linc hesitated to bring up her name, but now, while she wasn't around, was a good time to ask the questions that had been eating at him.

"How did Kerry get involved with your relief organization?"

Both Jenny and Cage tried to mask their surprise. "She never told you?" Cage asked. Linc shook his head and shoveled in another bite of eggs.

"She came to us," Jenny said. "After going through the ordeal of her father's trial, she—"

Linc's fork clattered to his plate. "Whoa, whoa, what trial? What father?"

Cage and Jenny exchanged a glance. "Wooten Bishop," Cage said, as though that explained everything. And it very nearly did.

Slowly Linc pushed his plate aside and folded his arms on the table in front of him. "Wooten Bishop? The Wooten Bishop is Kerry's father?"

His hosts nodded simultaneously. Linc expelled his breath on a long gust. "Sonofagun." He shook his head in disbelief. "I never would have put their names together. I remember now that he had a daughter. I guess I never paid much attention to how old she was or what she looked like. I was in Africa when that story broke."

"He tried to shield her from the scandal as much as possible. Of course she was greatly affected by it anyway."

"Obviously," Linc muttered, staring into his coffee cup.

The Wooten Bishop family had been subjected to public scrutiny and ridicule only a couple of years earlier. After a long and illustrious career in the diplomatic corps, Bishop had been called home from Monterico when it was alleged that he had personally profited from that country's political strife. He had used information made available to him as a diplomat in moneymaking scams.

When he was found out, all his shady dealings were aired over network television. There had followed a nasty, albeit enlightening, senate hearing and a subsequent criminal trial. Only one month after his sentencing, he had died of heart failure in a federal prison.

"I asked Kerry about her childhood," Linc said hoarsely. "She said that it had been charmed."

"It was," Jenny said sadly, "before the tragedy. Kerry once told me that something inside Ambassador Bishop snapped after the death of her mother. He was never quite the same."

"Did she know about his corruption?"

Cage shook his head. "No. She suspected, but couldn't believe it. She was shattered to learn that her father had ruthlessly exploited a people who had had so little to begin with. She told Jenny and me that she went through a period of hating him. Then all she could feel for him was pity. It's little wonder that she made such a personal sacrifice to go to Monterico and try to make up for her father's wrongdoings."

"She had no business going there. She could have gotten herself killed!" Linc exclaimed, banging the table with his fist.

"You're right, Linc." Jenny laid a gentle hand over his. "She came to us, volunteering to go there and teach. We told her that there was plenty she could do here to support the cause without putting herself in danger. But she wouldn't have it any other way.

"I don't think any of us can really appreciate the sacrifices she made," Jenny went on. "Until the scandal broke, she and her family had traveled all over the world. They were highly respected, often guests of royalty and heads of state."

"She's well educated I guess," Linc remarked glumly.
"The Sorbonne."

A muscle in his cheek twitched.

Cage swirled coffee around in his cup. "It was rumored several years ago that there was a romance budding between her and a young man in Britain's royal family. But when I teased her about it, she said that's all it was. A frivolous rumor."

Jenny was reflective. "She hardly looked frivolous yesterday when she got off that airplane. I don't think she's ever been taken seriously. Maybe that's what she had to prove. She went to Monterico to announce to the world that there was more to her than what was evident on the surface."

"I still don't get it," Linc said, frowning. "It doesn't make any sense."

"What, Linc?"

"Why would a beautiful, charming, intelligent young woman like Kerry, who has everything going for her, give it all up to become a nun? I mean, isn't that going a bit overboard just to make a point? Sure her ol' man got caught with his hand in the till. There was a big scandal. But no... What's the matter?"

"A nun?"

# *Ten*

They chorused their incredulity.

Of the three of them, Cage was the first to overcome his astonishment. "Where did you get that idea?"

"She isn't a nun?" Linc croaked.

Baffled, Jenny shook her head. "No."

"Has she ever thought about becoming a nun?" Linc asked. "Taken the first steps?"

"Not to my knowledge."

Linc lunged from his chair with such force that he knocked it over backward. Still shell-shocked by his outlandish presumption, the Hendrens sat mutely and watched him storm from the kitchen and race for the stairs. He took them two at a time. If the door of the guest bedroom hadn't been made of top-grade lumber, it would have shattered beneath his hand as he shoved it open. It crashed against the inside wall. He marched in.

The bed was neatly made. The room was empty. The only movement came from the open window overlooking the patio and pool below. Airy curtains fluttered there in the soft, Southern, morning breeze.

Linc spun around and hastily retraced his footsteps

to the kitchen. Civilities were the furthest thing from his mind. "You didn't tell me she was already up," he accused his hosts.

Jenny was staring at him apprehensively and fiddling with a button on her maternity blouse. Cage was nonchalantly sipping coffee. It was he who looked up and said innocently, "You didn't ask."

"Where is she?"

"She went horseback riding," Cage told him evenly. "Got up early, even before Jenny."

Linc was holding back his explosive Irish temper with remarkable self-control. The only dead giveaways were the muscles flexing his jaw and his hands, which were held rigidly at his sides while his fingers alternately opened and closed into fists.

"We drank a cup of coffee together, then she asked if she could borrow one of the horses for a while. I helped her saddle it, and she rode off in that direction." Cage hitched his chin toward the endless horizon.

Linc looked in the direction Cage had indicated and studied the prairie through the kitchen window. "How long ago?"

Cage, secretly enjoying Linc's stewing, contemplated his answer to the simple question for an inordinate length of time. "Oh, about an hour and a half, I'd say."

"Can I borrow your pickup?" Linc had noticed a pickup in the garage the evening before. Unlike Cage's other cars, which were polished to a high sheen, the pickup had been scarred by every single mile recorded on its odometer.

"Sure," Cage replied congenially and stood up to fish the keys out of his tight jeans pocket. He tossed them to Linc.

"Thanks." He turned abruptly and left through the back door, covering the distance between the house and the garage with the long, angry stride of a man bent on getting swift and savage revenge.

Jenny got up and moved to the window. She watched Linc slam shut the door of the pickup and grind the reluctant motor to a start. He cranked the steering wheel around and drove off in a cloud of dust.

"Cage, I don't think you should have given him the keys. He looks positively furious."

"If Kerry led him to believe that she's a nun, I'm sure he is. And I can't say that I blame him."

"But—"

"Jenny," he said soothingly, moving behind her and encircling her with his arms. He linked his hands together beneath her heavy breasts. "Remember the night I chased down that Greyhound bus you were on?"

"How could I forget that? I've never been so embarrassed in my life."

Smiling at the memory, he placed his mouth close to her ear. "Well, I was just as upset then as Linc is now. Hell or high water couldn't have kept me from coming after you. We couldn't have stopped Linc either. If I hadn't lent him my truck, I think he would have struck out on foot to get to Kerry." He kissed her neck. "I just hope that his wild-goose chase meets with as much success as mine did."

Linc, pushing the old truck to perform in excess of its capabilities, had murder on his mind, not romance. He scorched the roof of the pickup with curses and disparagements aimed at Kerry's character. When he had exhausted those, he started verbally lambasting his own culpability.

What a damn fool he'd been! She must have been laughing up her sleeve at him all this time. She had duped him not once, but twice. First impersonating a whore, then a nun. Two such diverse personifications, and he'd been gullible enough to believe both of them.

What the hell was wrong with him? Had he been plagued with a jungle disease that ate at his brain? Had Kerry Bishop been slipping a mind-altering drug into his water canteen? How could he, Linc O'Neal, have been so goddamn naive?

He'd been around. He wasn't a lust-blind kid, unacquainted with the wiles of females. Why hadn't he seen past Kerry Bishop's beautiful face and into her devious mind? She wasn't a self-sacrificing churchwoman, but a cunning tease, who evidently had no scruples against manipulating a man to get what she wanted out of him.

Even when she had succeeded in achieving her goal, she had kept up the pretense. "For her own protection," he said through gritted teeth. "To save her sweet neck," he told the dashboard of the truck.

A luscious figure and a gorgeous face had cost him his common sense and quick-wittedness. He hadn't been his cold, calculating, cautious self since he'd left that damn cantina with Wooten Bishop's deceitful daughter.

The pickup truck bounced over the uneven road, which was actually no more than a pasture trail. Linc had no idea where he was going, but he was in a hurry to get there. He reasoned that Kerry wasn't well acquainted with Cage's spread either. She probably would have stayed close to the road so she'd be certain to find her way back to the house.

His instincts paid off. After twenty minutes of hard driving over rugged terrain, he spotted a stock tank as large as a small lake. Its steep banks were shaded by the feathery branches of mesquite trees. The spring grass, not yet burned brown by the summer sun, was lush and green. One of Cage's well-groomed quarter horses was tied to the lower branches of a mesquite on the rim of the bank overlooking the placid tank.

At the sound of the approaching pickup, Kerry, who was lying beneath the tree on a blanket she had taken from the tack room and tied behind her saddle, propped herself up on one elbow. She lifted the other hand to shade her eyes. She thought at first that it was Cage driving the truck, but sprang upright when she recognized the long-legged silhouette approaching her as belonging to Linc.

The incline didn't slow him down at all. Within seconds he was looming over her, his booted feet planted firmly on the ground at the edge of her blanket. Her eyes moved up his legs, up his torso, and straight into a disconcerting golden glower. She didn't have to guess at his mood. He was enraged. On the inside, she quailed, though she kept her chin up and met that intimidating stare without flinching.

"You lying bitch."

Kerry didn't even pretend to misunderstand. With a sinking heart and rapidly diminishing courage, she knew that she'd been found out. The only recourse she had was to brazen it out.

"Now, Linc," she said, quickly wetting her lips and holding her hands out in front of her as though to stave him off, "before you jump to any conclusions—"

He effectively cut her off by dropping to his knees

and roughly grabbing her by the shoulders. "Before I jump on your bones, you mean."

Her face drained of color. He hadn't made her a seductive promise but a menacing threat. "You wouldn't."

"The hell I wouldn't. But before I do, I want to know why you told me that ridiculous lie."

"I didn't!" She tried to work herself free, but to no avail. The more she struggled, the more inescapable his hold became. "I never told you that I was a nun."

"I didn't dream it up, baby."

"You heard the children call me sister and drew your own conclusions. You—"

Her teeth clicked together when he hauled her up closer to his face, which was taut with fury. "But you sure as hell let me believe it, didn't you? Why?" he roared.

"To protect myself from you."

"Don't flatter yourself."

She went hot all over at his sneering insult. "I knew what you had in mind. Don't deny it. You were thinking that our escape through the jungle was going to be a lark, during which you planned to use me for a bedmate."

"Me Tarzan, you Jane."

"It was no joking matter. You forced me to kiss you, to change clothes in front of you!"

"I didn't see anything that you hadn't advertised by wearing that cheap dress!" he shouted back. "And whether you admit it or not, lady, you loved those kisses."

"I did not!"

"Like hell."

She had to take deep, restorative breaths before she

could continue. "I was trying to think of a way to avoid your unwelcome sexual advances when the children inadvertently provided me with a way."

"Why did they call you Sister Kerry?"

"Because when I first got there, they started calling me Mother. I didn't want them to think of me that way. I was already planning to bring them to the United States for adoption. I thought that being like an older sister would be a healthier relationship. Don't blame me for your own gross mistake."

"What I blame you for is making a fool of me."

"I didn't do it maliciously," she cried.

"Didn't you?"

"No."

"Come now, Miss Kerry Bishop, daughter to one of the chief swindlers of our times, didn't you take delight in playing me like a puppet? Don't you come by those manipulative skills naturally?"

Kerry shuddered at the reference to her father and his corruption. Apparently Linc knew all about her background now. His scorn was well-founded, but it still hurt her to the core that he thought she was capable of such machinations.

"I let you think that I was a nun so that we would be concentrating only on the safety of the orphans."

"My ass. You lied to keep yourself safe from my pawing hands."

"All right, yes!"

"And my leering glances."

"Yes!"

"Not to mention all those kisses you claim to have hated."

"Yes!"

"See? By your own admission, you just went on lying."

"I tried to tell you," she cried in self-defense.

"Funny, I don't remember that occasion."

"When you kissed me that last day. Just before we heard the airplane. I wanted to…tried to tell you then."

"Not very hard you didn't."

"I didn't have a chance. Everything started happening so fast."

"It was a long airplane trip from there to here."

"We argued over the money and I was too angry to tell you."

"What about since we got back? Cage and Jenny would protect you from me, wild animal that I am. Why haven't you told me? You've had dozens of opportunities."

"Because I knew you'd react just as you are. That you'd be angry and abusive."

He lowered his voice to a sinister whisper. "Baby, anger doesn't even come close to describing the way I feel. And you don't know me very well if you think I'd be abusive."

To her humiliation, her lower lip began to quiver. "I never intended for it to go so far. Honestly. I'm sorry, Linc, truly I am."

"It's too late for apologies, Kerry."

"I know I misrepresented myself, but I had no choice. I was desperate. I needed you, but I couldn't cater to your desire. My first obligation was to the orphans."

"Do you think I'd fall for your claims to noble sentiments now?" he asked with a humorless laugh. "No way, sweetheart. I want you humbled. I want you to sink as low on the ego scale as I've been lately. Only that will satisfy me."

"What…what are you going to do?"

"What I told you that first morning I was going to do," he said silkily. "I'm gonna make you beg me for it."

"No!"

The husky exclamation died on Kerry's lips when he pushed her back onto the blanket and followed her down, covering her with his body. He trapped her hands between them. They were useless to her when he secured her jaw with one hand and lowered his mouth to hers.

She struggled, but only succeeded in exhausting her supply of strength sooner. Even her best efforts didn't budge him. Kicking didn't help because he sandwiched her thighs between his. His knees kept hers pinned together. She couldn't turn her head in any direction.

She tried to keep her lips pressed firmly together, but failed. He used his tongue like an instrument of tantalizing torture. It flicked softly over her lips, delved into the corners of them, outlined their shape until her unsteady, frightened breaths became gasps of pleasure. Finally, her lips relaxed and parted, without any force from him.

"That's it, baby. Enjoy."

His kiss was long, sensual, seeking. He firmly slanted his lips over hers, first at one angle, then another, while his tongue moved inside her mouth with sinful skill. She wanted to hate this blatant violation, but she loved it. The texture of his tongue intrigued her. She wanted to feel it not only against hers, but everywhere. She wondered if the myriad textures of his body were this fascinating and thrilling, and yearned to have her curiosity appeased.

But she steeled herself against feeling anything but contempt for him and his hateful kiss. She tried to ignore the heat spilling down her chest and into the lower part of her body, tried to disregard the desire that ribboned through her like a river of wine as golden as his eyes, tried to dismiss the swirls of sensation that licked at her thighs, her middle, her breasts. She wasn't entirely successful, but she forced herself to lie still when she wanted to writhe against him like a cat being petted.

"You might just as well participate," he rasped when he felt her body tense. His lips coasted over her cheek, pecking light kisses on her creamy complexion, now tinted pink by exposure to sun and wind during her morning horseback ride. Linc didn't allow himself to admire it too long. Feeling any tenderness for her was to be avoided at all costs if he were to regain his pride. "Because I'm not letting up until you're crazy with lust. The longer you resist, Kerry, the longer it will take."

"Go to hell."

He made a tsking sound. "Is that any way for a nun to talk?"

"Don't." When his tongue playfully batted against the lobe of her ear, she tried to sound irritable, but the protest came out as a low groan of arousal.

Linc recognized the sound for what it was. He'd never had difficulty sexually communicating with women, whether they spoke his language or not. It wasn't so much what they said as how they said it. And clearer than the single word of denial, was Kerry's breathless way of saying it.

"You like that?" he murmured, catching her ear lightly between his teeth.

"No."

He chuckled. "We both know you're a liar. I think you like it a lot."

He kissed the soft skin beneath her ear, nuzzled behind it with his nose, flirted with the rim of it with his tongue. It was hard to tell now whether her fitful movements beneath him were meant to put more space between them or to get closer.

His breath was warm as it drifted over her face. It smelled appetizingly of coffee. And that was just one of the reasons why her lips were far more obliging this time when his, with very little pressure applied, settled over hers. His open mouth moved upon hers, separating her lips for his thrusting tongue. As it speared into her mouth, she felt a correlating stab of desire in the depths of her body.

When he raised his head and peered deeply into her eyes, she thought that she might have made an involuntary sound. He asked, "Feel that?"

At first she thought that he was referring to that sweet ache deep inside herself. Then her eyes went wide with alarm when she realized that he was talking about the rigid flesh between his own thighs. She clamped her upper teeth over her lower lip and squeezed her eyes shut. His low laugh was nasty.

"I see that you do. Well, that's how it's been, baby. While you've been playing your devious little games with me, I've been hard with wanting you. All that time we were stalking through the jungle together, I was miserable not only with heat and fatigue and hunger, but with a desire that I couldn't quench. I was ashamed of it because I thought it was a violation of your holiness." He kept his voice as smooth as expensive brandy, but it had a bite as strong as cheap whiskey. "There's nothing holy about you, is there?"

He worked his hand between their bodies. When Kerry realized what he was going to do, she went rigid. "No!" It was a soundless cry.

"Why, Kerry, you surprise me. Don't you want to know the full extent of your powers?"

When he had unbuttoned his jeans, he reached for one of her hands and dragged it down. "No!" This time her protest was stifled by his kiss, a hard, possessive kiss that glued his lips to hers and sent his tongue deep into her mouth.

As he opened her hand over himself, Kerry's brain recorded a thousand fleeting impressions. One prevailed. She wanted to touch him. She wanted to discover. She wanted to catalog the smoothness, the hardness, the warmth. She wanted to sink her fingers into the hair that was coarse and springy, but soft.

She fought the temptation as long as she could, but self-discipline didn't serve her long enough. Her hand stopped resisting the relentless pressure of his. Of its own free will it molded to his shape and became inquisitive.

Making an animal sound, Linc tore his mouth from hers and roughly shoved her hand away. His breathing was unsteady and rapid. "Not that way, Kerry," he said in a voice hardly above a growl. "You won't get by with that. You never quit playing dirty, do you? I guess it runs in the family. You've always got one more trick up your sleeve. Well, your tricks won't work this time."

Perplexity filled her dark blue eyes, but he didn't

seem to notice. He was studying the buttons on her casual shirt. He negligently opened the first one. "I vaguely remember how it feels to touch you. You're small, but nice." The sexist comment brought a wave of resentment rushing through her. He saw the mutiny in her eyes and smiled arrogantly. "And as I recall, your nipples respond nicely."

Her cheeks flared with color, especially when he succeeded in opening all the buttons on her blouse and spreading it open. She and Jenny were of comparable size when Jenny wasn't pregnant. Kerry's breasts filled the cups of the lacy brassiere she had borrowed. With the sunlight pouring over them, there was little left to Linc's imagination.

His eyes turned dark and Kerry thought she saw a muscle in his cheek twitch with something akin to remorse, before his lips formed that hard, unyielding line again. "Open it."

"I won't."

"Then you can explain to Jenny how the fastener got broken," he said, reaching for the clasp.

"You're vile."

"Open it."

Setting her jaw stubbornly, she opened the clasp, but left the cups alone. After muttering a snide thank-you, he moved them aside and left her bare to his gaze. It was as scorching as the sun overhead.

Kerry's bravado deserted her. Her eyes closed in shame, so she missed seeing him swallow convulsively. She also missed the spasm of regret that twisted his stern lips as he ran his hands over her. The words he spoke fell like harmful blows on her ears.

"That's what I thought. Not much there, but what there is, is nice."

She slapped at his hands, but he secured her wrists in one manacling hold. She shrank away from his touch when he cupped the underside of her breast and pushed it up. His thumb whisked across the sensitive tip. When it responded, he laughed gloatingly. Again and again he dragged his thumb across the beaded crest, sometimes with agonizing leisure, sometimes with a quick fanning motion, sometimes raking it gently with his thumbnail, until it was quite stiff.

"Very nice," he said hoarsely. "At least to look at, play with. How do you taste?"

Her back arched off the blanket at the first deft brush of his tongue. "No, no," she groaned, rolling her head from side to side.

"I'm not convinced you mean that, Kerry." He spoke directly above her, so that even as he formed the words with his lips, they moved against the aching, throbbing flesh of her nipple.

She made a murmur of protest and had to bite her lower lip to keep from crying out, not in outrage or fear or disgust, but from pleasure. It was exquisite, the touch of his warm, wet tongue against her breast. He licked her until she was wet and glistening, then let the wind dry her while he treated the other breast to the same torturous pleasure.

"Please, no more," she begged.

"A lot more."

She gave an agonized cry when he took her nipple between his lips and held it within the satin heat of his mouth. He tugged on her gently; she made soft moaning sounds with each squeezing, milking motion of his mouth.

"Please, stop," she gasped.

He raised his head. "What do you want?" His tongue moved capriciously over the raised center of her breast.

"For you to stop."

"Why?"

"Because I hate it. Hate you."

"You might hate me. In fact, I'm sure you do. But you don't hate this." Again he touched her with the tip of his tongue. "Do you?" He repeated the question, each time nudging her with his tongue or sipping at her with his lips.

"Yes," she said, shivering with need.

"Do you?"

"Yes."

"Do you?"

"Ye…no, no, no." A sobbing sound tore through her throat.

"I didn't think so."

He lowered his head and kissed her stomach, while he struggled to open the fly of her slacks. Breathlessly, Kerry gasped for air. She was barely conscious of what his hands were doing. All her concentration was centered on his lips as they moved over her flesh, seeming to touch everywhere at once.

She actually raised her hips and aided him when he worked her slacks down. He kissed her protuberant hip bone, swung his head around and kissed the other. His lips brushed her navel, his tongue danced around it and probed it provocatively. He kissed her mound through her panties.

Kerry gave a startled cry and struggled to free her

hands. When she succeeded, she didn't fight him. Instead she mindlessly entangled her fingers in his hair. He went on kissing her, leaving her flesh fevered and damp where his mouth had been.

"I thought about this that night you slept in my arms." Linc could barely speak, and even then it was a hoarse whisper. "Your breasts beneath my mouth. Your thighs opening to me."

She didn't remember his getting her panties off, but she suddenly realized that his eyes were hungrily moving over her nakedness. She should have been terrified of his ravenous gaze, but, oddly, she wasn't. Her single thought was that she hoped he was pleased with her.

His fingers sifted through the dark cloud of hair between her thighs. Reflexively her knees came up. He parted them. Then he lowered his head and placed his mouth where she most wanted to feel him.

When his lips touched her, she cried his name. When his tongue touched her, she died a little. Holding her hips between his strong hands, Linc gave her pleasure with the same dedication with which he did everything else.

He stopped short of bringing her to climax, though he brought her to the threshold time and again. Her face was dewy with perspiration when he bent over it. "Tell me you want me."

It was a miracle that he could even form the words in his mind, much less speak them aloud. His body was pulsing with a need so great it surpassed mere desire. God, he needed to be sheathed inside her body, giving her the passion that threatened to kill him if it wasn't shared. He was filled to bursting with his need for her.

And suddenly this revenge seemed a thankless,

empty victory. He didn't want to triumph over her. He didn't want to see her cowed in defeat, but glowing with a desire to match his own. He wanted to see joy in her face, not subjugation.

But habits formed in childhood were hard to break. Nobody got the best of Lincoln O'Neal without knowing his vengeance. He'd had to scrap for every ounce of affection and respect he had ever received. He knew no other way to ask than to make it a demand.

"Tell me you want me," he ground out again, clenching his teeth in an effort to keep his body from doing what it was primed to do without playing out this senseless game. He slipped the tip of his organ between the moist petals of her sex.

"I want you," Kerry gasped.

"Inside you," he panted.

"Inside me."

Those two words snapped his control. He slipped into her body and gave a mighty push that sent him straight to her womb. He gave a cry of such anguish and regret that it seemed to echo off the endless sky. He wanted to withdraw, but his control was gone.

Knowing that he would be damned a sinner anyway, and powerless over the demands of his body, he made but three shallow thrusts before his climax claimed him. In sublime surrender, he buried his face in her neck and let the exquisite seizures wash over him. He abdicated control to the natural forces of his own body and filled the woman he had wanted for what seemed like a lifetime with the hot, potent issue of his loins.

For long moments afterward, he lay atop her, exhausted, spent, in blissful devastation. When he finally found the strength to pull himself away, he avoided looking at her. With endearing awkwardness, he draped a corner of the blanket over the lower part of her body. Lying there beside her on his back, he gazed up through the sparse branches of the mesquite tree and tried to think of a name despicable enough to call himself.

Because up until a few seconds ago, Kerry Bishop had been as chaste as the nun she had pretended to be. She had been a virgin.

"Why didn't you tell me?"

"Would you have believed me?"

"No," he sighed, knowing that that was true. He wouldn't have believed anything she had said.

He rolled to a sitting position and hung his head between his widespread knees. For several minutes, he mumbled curses and epithets aimed at himself. Then he lapsed into silence. Finally he risked looking down at Kerry. Tears had left salty tracks on her cheeks, but her eyes were clear and staring straight at him.

"Do you, uh, hurt?" She shook her head. He didn't believe her. "Do you have any water?"

"The canteen on the saddle."

He stood and hiked his jeans up his hips until he could rebutton them. He went to the saddled horse, which had been docilely grazing through it all. The canteen was hanging from the pommel by a leather strap. He uncapped it, wet the handkerchief he'd put in his pocket that morning, and carried both the canteen and the soaked handkerchief back to Kerry. He extended it down to her and tactfully turned his back while she used it.

"Thank you."

He turned back around to find her dressed and standing quietly, as though awaiting instructions. He'd not

only crushed her physically…God, when he remembered how hard he'd been when he sank into her…but
he had wounded her spirit as well. Her eyes were no
longer sparkling with lights as pure and fine as costly
sapphires. They stared at him dully.

"You'll ride back with me," he said. "I'll tie the horse
to the back of the truck."

When that was done, he came to her, took her elbow,
and led her over the rough ground with a solicitousness
that would have been comical under different circumstances. It was he who winced when she stepped up
into the truck.

It took considerably longer to cover the distance back
to the house than it had taken Linc to get to the tank.
He drove much slower, in deference to the horse that
trotted along behind them and out of regard for the discomfort Kerry must be suffering. He knew the rough
ride couldn't be comfortable for her and cursed himself
as a brute with each bumpy, bone-jarring, teeth-rattling
turn of the wheels.

When they reached the house, he pulled the pickup
into the garage and cut the engine. They sat in the deep
shadows for a moment of ponderous silence, then he
turned his head and asked, "Are you all right?"

"Yes."

"Is there anything I can do?"

Kerry glanced down at her hands, which were knotted together in her lap. *You could say that you love me.*
"No," she said, choking back tears.

Linc got out. Before he could come around and assist her, she climbed out of the cab and untied the horse.
Wordlessly they led him into the stable and turned him

over to one of the hands. Still maintaining that strained silence, they headed toward the house.

Everyone was congregated on the terrace. Jenny was bouncing a truculent Trent on her thighs. Cage was sitting in a lawn chair, staring broodily over the waters of the swimming pool, where all the children were splashing in the shallows. Roxy and Gary Fleming were sitting at one of the patio tables moodily sipping cold drinks. Sarah Hendren was clipping roses from an overloaded bush and laying them in the basket that her husband held for her.

The mood, except for that of the gleeful children, was glum.

Cage looked up and spotted Linc and Kerry coming through the gate. It was to her that he addressed his comment. "We've got troubles."

# *Eleven*

Kerry struggled up from the swamp of despair into which she had sunk and asked, "What kind of troubles?" She lowered herself into the chair Linc pulled out for her. "Not Joe?"

"No, not Joe," Roxy Fleming reassured her. "Physically he's doing all right, but the doctor told us that he's awfully depressed. Doc suggested that he be moved here this afternoon. He'll recover faster if he's not alienated from the other children."

"Here? Jenny, won't that inconvenience you?"

"Not at all," Jenny told Kerry. "We'll just move an extra bed into Trent's room."

"I'll leave," Linc said bluntly. "Then you'll have plenty of room."

Jenny glanced at him with asperity. "I thought we settled that last night. We're not going to let you leave, Linc. Besides, Joe will feel more at ease with you around."

That argument made sense, so neither he nor Kerry countered it. "Well, if you're sure," Kerry said uncertainly. "It'll only be for another day or so. Just until his adoptive family arrives to take him home."

Gary cleared his throat too loudly. Roxy shifted in her chair. Cage and Jenny glanced uncomfortably at each other.

"Did I hit a nerve?" Kerry asked intuitively. "I must have accidently stumbled onto the trouble spot you mentioned. What gives? Have Joe's adoptive parents had second thoughts since he was wounded in the escape? The doctor assured me that his leg suffered no permanent damage, if that's what's bothering them."

"Actually, Kerry," Cage said with noticeable reluctance, "Joe never was spoken for."

Stunned, Kerry could only stare at him for a moment before crying, "What? That was a condition of my bringing the orphans out, that they would have a home ready and waiting for them."

"We know." Jenny's normally serene face was filled with anxiety. "That's why we didn't tell you. Cage and I discussed it and decided that no matter what, we couldn't let you leave any of the children behind."

"Most prospective parents feel that Joe is too old for adoption," Cage said gently.

"I see."

Kerry's shoulders slumped with dejection. According to the clock, it was still well before noon. But it seemed that she had lived a thousand years since she had gotten up that morning. Her heart had already been heavy, knowing that she had fallen in love with the wrong man. That's why she had sought the solitary peacefulness of a horseback ride. Then what should have been an exultant experience had been a nightmare.

And now this. Just when she was about to accomplish the only worthwhile endeavor in her life, she was met with failure. Poor Joe. He, more than the other children, realized what coming to the United States meant to his future.

"He can't be sent back," she said fiercely.

"You can count on that," Cage said.

Jenny laid a hand on her husband's shoulder as though to hold him back. "You didn't know Cage before he settled down, Kerry," she said, "but he's a dirty fighter. He would take on the Supreme Court before he would let the boy be sent back."

Kerry smiled at Cage. "Thank you. I'll appreciate anything you can do."

"I volunteer my services," Linc said. "And I'd be willing to bet that I fight a helluva lot dirtier than Cage."

"Oh, yeah?" The other man sized him up. Then he smiled broadly. "Thanks. I'm sure I can use your help."

"Let's hope it won't go that far." Kerry stood up. "As soon as I change, we'll get to work on it. I have people in—"

"I'm afraid that's not all," Cage told her, indicating that she should sit back down.

She couldn't imagine what news could possibly be worse than what she'd already heard. She eased herself back into the chair, mentally preparing herself for a blow.

"The couple who had spoken for Lisa called this morning," Cage began.

The floor dropped out from beneath Kerry. "And?"

"And, it seems that the lady is pregnant. It was confirmed only two days ago."

Jenny filled the ensuing silence. "They've wanted a

baby for years. That's why they jumped at the chance to adopt one of the Monterican orphans."

Huge, salty tears formed in Kerry's eyes. Not Lisa. She had tried not to form a special attachment to any of the children, knowing that the final separation from them would be heartbreaking enough. But the youngest of them, Lisa, had touched Kerry's heart in a special way, probably because the child had been more dependent on her than the others had been.

"But surely, if the couple considered adoption at all, they've got enough love to give to two children," she said.

"It's not that," Jenny said. "She's had several miscarriages. They don't want to jeopardize this pregnancy. The doctor recommends that she spend the next several months in bed. It would be impossible for her to care for the child."

Beneath his breath Linc said one of the words Jenny had tried to purge from Cage's vocabulary. "Amen to that," Cage muttered.

"I see the problem," Kerry said despondently. "And I understand."

"It was a difficult decision for them. They had looked so forward to getting Lisa."

"Hell, we'd take her in an instant," Roxy said in her lovable, rough way. "But we've already got Cara and Carmen to think of. It won't be so tough now, but college and all…"

Kerry smiled at her and Gary. "You're generous to a fault. You couldn't possibly assume responsibility for another child. It wouldn't be fair to any of you. But I want you to know how much I appreciate the thought."

Kerry sought out Lisa where the little girl was splashing happily in the shallows of the pool. She squealed in delight each time the sparkling water showered her. "She's so adorable. We shouldn't have any trouble placing her in a loving home."

"That's what we thought," Cage told her.

"But tomorrow is the day they meet their families. It will be psychologically shattering if she's left behind."

"We've already put the word out through the branches of the Hendren Foundation. Of course in the meantime—"

"Cage," Jenny interjected warningly.

"In the meantime, what?" Linc asked.

Cage shrugged at his wife helplessly. "In the meantime, she'll be turned over to the immigration authorities."

"Like hell she will," Linc exclaimed.

Kerry's heart felt as hard and cold as a stone in her chest. Lisa would be frightened. She would think that all Kerry's promises had led to nothing but fear and isolation from everything familiar. "We can't let that happen."

"I'm sure it won't," Jenny said. "Two very special people will be blessed with her." She set Trent down and stood up. "Kerry, Cage has agreed to watch Trent while we go to town and do some shopping. I don't mind if you wear my clothes, but I'm sure you'd like to pick out some of your own."

"What about the children?"

"We're staying with them," Roxy said. "Gary's taken a week of vacation so we could be at your disposal."

"And we'll be here," Bob Hendren said, speaking for his wife, too.

"What about Joe?" Kerry asked. "I should be here when he arrives."

"We'll be back well before that," Jenny said, laughing.

Roxy gave Kerry an affectionate shove. "Go, enjoy, you've earned it."

However, before they left, Kerry circled around to the terrace again after showering and changing. Cage and Linc had donned swimsuits and joined the children in the water. Cage was tossing Trent high over his head, barely catching him before he landed in the water. Linc was playing with Lisa.

Kerry's eyes smarted with a fresh batch of tears as she watched him with the child. His face was split by a wide grin, and his eyes were crinkled with laughter.

Sensing her stare, he looked up at her where she stood on the deck of the pool. His gaze moved over her searchingly. Going warm with embarrassment, Kerry realized that her body was now familiar territory to him. She had no secrets from him. And she wondered, even as his eyes lowered to the spot that had known the touch of his hands and lips and sex, if he knew that she still ached there deliciously.

Lisa raised her arms toward Kerry in silent appeal. Kerry knelt down, and Linc carried the child against his naked chest to the edge of the pool. Kerry bent down to kiss the child on her slippery, wet cheek. "Goodbye, darling."

"Goodbye."

It was Linc who replied. Both surprised, their eyes clashed and held while time seemed to stand still. Then, hastily, Kerry rose and rushed toward Jenny, who was waiting at the car. But her feet didn't move as fast as her beating heart.

* * *

The two women made several stops. Kerry, using a line of credit Cage had arranged for her through his bank, bought several changes of clothes, underwear and shoes.

"I never knew a drugstore could be such a wonderland," she exclaimed. She rummaged through the contents of the sack she held in her lap on their return trip to the ranch. "I feel like I've discovered the mother lode. Skin lotion, hair conditioner, nail polish. I'm not accustomed to such luxuries."

"Maybe you should treat yourself to a week at some posh spa. Let yourself be pampered."

Kerry shook her head. "No. Not yet anyway. I've still got too much to do."

Jenny looked at her in alarm. "You're not thinking of going back to Monterico?"

"No. It's gotten too dangerous. I don't have a death wish." She carefully replaced her toiletries in the sack. "But there's still plenty to do here. Raise money for food. Medicine." Her voice trailed off and her eyes stared sightlessly at the passing landscape.

When Jenny spoke, her voice was quiet. "You can't go on making amends for your father's corruption, Kerry. Sooner or later you've got to get on with your own life."

She sighed heavily. "I know."

"Cage and I let the cat out of the bag this morning, didn't we?"

Kerry started, but she kept her face perfectly composed.

"Don't worry about it. Linc had to find out sooner or later."

"I'm sorry. We assumed that he knew who you were. Then when we realized that he thought you were—"

"Please!" Kerry held up a hand to forestall her friend from saying the word aloud. "I'm ashamed enough as it is. Don't remind me of the dirty trick I played on him."

"I know I'm being rude, but I have to ask. Why did you lead him to believe that you were a nun?"

"Jenny, you couldn't be rude if you tried. Naturally you're curious." She chose her words carefully, wanting her friend to understand her motivation. "You know how I coerced him into leaving the cantina with me."

"By pretending to be a prostitute."

"Yes. Well, I did things that I thought were, uh, you know, prostitutelike." She glanced away. "Linc is a virile man and he, uh…"

"I think I get the picture. He wasn't ready to call it quits when you explained your situation."

She nodded. "In my position, what would you have done?"

"Probably nothing so ingenious," Jenny said with a commiserating smile. "He was somewhat…upset…this morning when he found out the truth."

"To put it mildly."

"Had he calmed down by the time he found you?"

"No."

Jenny was too tactful to pursue it further. Whatever had happened out there had had an impact on them both. Linc had looked as bleak as Kerry when they returned. And, as Jenny had noticed before, they avoided touching or looking at each other, carrying the avoidance to ridiculous extremes.

"Linc accused me of being a user, just like my father," Kerry said expressionlessly. "And I suppose he's right. I manipulated him." Tears filled her eyes and slipped from her lower lids. When Jenny saw them, she reached for Kerry's hand. "You and Cage are so lucky to love each other the way you do."

"I know. But what we have didn't come easily, Kerry."

Jenny had never confided to anyone, not even to Roxy, about Cage and her. Now was the time. If her story would help Kerry, it needed to be shared.

"The night Hal left for Monterico, he came to my room," Jenny began. Kerry turned her head in an attitude of listening. "He made love to me. It was my first time." She drew a shaky little breath. "Only it wasn't Hal. It was Cage." Ignoring Kerry's gasp of surprise, she went on before she lost her nerve. "Then when I discovered I was pregnant—"

"You thought the baby was Hal's."

She nodded. "Everybody did. And only Cage knew differently. Hal had been killed. It took Cage months to find the courage to tell me."

"What happened when he did?"

"I was mortified."

"I can imagine."

"I said terrible things to him." She shuddered now with the memory. "I cruelly rejected him. It took a tragedy to bring us back together."

She squeezed Kerry's hand. "Linc reminds me of Cage. They're both volatile men. Short-tempered. There's an air of violence and danger about them. I used to tremble whenever Cage was in the parsonage. I would get as far away from him as I possibly could. Then one day I realized that the very characteristics that frightened me, also attracted me. I wasn't nearly as afraid of his virility as I was of my response to it."

She glanced at Kerry out of the corner of her eye. "Cage made me so jittery that I shied away from him. I couldn't deal with the way he made me feel, like I was stepping outside myself whenever he was around." She took her eyes off the road long enough to glance across the seat. "Are you in love with Linc?"

Kerry lowered her head and eloquent tears rolled down her cheeks. She held back sobs only by clamping her trembling lower lip between her teeth. "Yes," she said on a low moan. "Yes. But it's hopeless."

"I thought so, too, at one time. But I learned that the harder it is to come by, the more valuable the love."

The Hendrens thought that it was important for the children to be exposed to American customs as soon as possible. Kerry agreed. So that evening they cooked hot dogs on the outdoor grill. Later, Cage set up a television monitor and ran Disney movies through the VCR. It was worth all the hardships Kerry had had to suffer to see their joyous faces.

At intermission, they emptied another three freezers of homemade ice cream. Cage's parents passed out cupcakes. Even though well-meaning folks and media were still banned from the ranch, baked goods, clothing, and toys were smuggled in.

Joe, who had been enthusiastically welcomed back into the fold earlier that afternoon, hobbled over to Kerry on his crutches. "Sister Kerry, didn't you want any ice cream?"

"I'm waiting for the crowd to thin out." The children were thronged around Roxy, who was dispensing the ice cream with a long-handled spoon. "How does your leg feel?"

"A little ache. Nothing more."

"I haven't had a chance to tell you how brave you were during the rescue." The boy made a self-conscious gesture. "I was very proud of you. Without you helping him, Linc couldn't have saved us all."

Joe's soulful eyes were downcast. "He came back for me."

Kerry, reminded of the animosity the boy had harbored toward Linc, suggested quietly, "Perhaps you should thank him for that."

"He already has."

The voice came out of the darkness behind her. Her knees went weak with the gruff sound of it. When she turned her head, she caught her breath sharply. He had borrowed one of Cage's cars and gone into town on a shopping expedition of his own. He was wearing new stonewashed jeans. They clung to his hips and thighs with a soft, tight fit. He had on a Swiss Army shirt made of white cotton. The sleeves had been rolled up to his hard biceps. She smelled cologne on him for the first time and liked his selection. It reminded her of rain and wind. He'd had his hair trimmed, too, but it was still long enough to brush the collar of his shirt.

Linc moved out of the darkness and laid a hand on Joe's shoulder. "He thanked me this afternoon, but I told him it wasn't necessary. He covered my ass. In his own right, he is a freedom fighter for his country."

Joe beamed up at the older man and said proudly, "But now my country is the United States."

No one had had the heart to tell the boy that he, as yet, had no adoptive parents and that there was a very real possibility that he would be returned to Monterico. Quickly Linc changed the subject. "Did Cage tell you what an uncanny rapport Joe has with horses?"

"He's mentioned it a few hundred times," Kerry said, giving Joe a teasing smile. "You never told me you knew so much about horses."

"I never knew!" the boy exclaimed, his dark eyes shining.

That afternoon, when Joe insisted that he didn't want to lie in bed any longer, he had been taken on a tour of the ranch. Cage had returned to the house with him, marveling over the boy's natural rapport with the animals.

"He seems to speak their language," Cage said, smiling down at the adolescent.

Joe basked in Linc's compliments. In Monterico, he had seemed old beyond his years. He had shed that untimely maturity along with his hostility toward Linc.

"When you first joined us," he said to Linc solemnly, "I thought you meant to harm Sister Kerry. I know now that you wouldn't hurt her." He didn't notice the slight flinching of Linc's muscles. "I'm sorry I had bad feelings toward you. You brought us to freedom."

Before Linc could make an appropriate reply, Trent Hendren came bounding up to Joe. He halted just short of tackling him, which he would have done if he hadn't been warned earlier about hurting Joe's thigh wound. "Joe, Joe." The child had been Joe's shadow ever since he returned from the hospital. Joe didn't seem to mind. In fact, he assumed a paternal air toward Trent. The child pointed excitedly toward the television screen where another movie was just starting. Smiling shyly,

Joe hobbled toward the others with Trent tagging along beside him.

"So much a child, but so much a man," Kerry murmured as she watched him cross the patio.

"And intuitive," Linc said.

"About the horses?"

"About me." She turned her head and stared up at him. "He was right about my hurting you. Only his timing was off."

Her eyes fell away from his piercing stare. "Let's not talk about it. Please."

"I've got to talk about it." He spoke softly, even though it was unlikely anyone would hear them over the antics of Peter Pan and Captain Hook. "Are you in pain?"

"I told you earlier, no."

"Why didn't you warn me?"

"We've already established that, too. You wouldn't have believed me."

"Maybe not this morning, but—"

"When? When, Linc? Think back. At what point during our friendship would you have believed me? When would have been a good time to casually drop that into the conversation?" She expelled a long breath. "Besides, what difference does it make? It had to happen sooner or later."

"But not so—"

When he broke off without finishing, she looked at him inquiringly. "Not so what?"

"Roughly."

For a moment they stared at each other. She was the first to look away. "Oh, that, well…"

"Did I hurt you, Kerry?"

"No."

Physically her discomfort had been minimal. Emotionally, it had been fatal. He had taken her out of anger. It hadn't been an act of love, or even of sexual pleasure, but one of vengeance. Her body hadn't been bruised, but her heart had been trampled. He had dealt her emotions a crippling blow, but she would be damned before she let him know that.

She tilted her head to its haughtiest angle. "That's what you want to hear, isn't it? Hurting me would have taken some of the gilt off your trophy."

"What do you mean by that?" he asked, lowering his brows dangerously.

"Your sole purpose was to make me admit my attraction to you. You set out to make me beg, remember? Well, I did. You got what you wanted, didn't you?"

"No, goddammit."

He moved nearer. His face was dark with anger. She could feel his body heat and, madly, felt cheated for not having felt his naked flesh next to her own. She had shared with him the most intimate act between a man and woman, but she still didn't know the pleasure of her smooth skin rubbing against his hair-smattered body or the delightful friction that caused.

*And, damn him, I still want to know,* her mind cried.

"I wanted to bring you down a notch, but I would never have hurt you. I had no idea when I… I wanted to stop as soon as I…felt…" His eyes coasted down to her mouth. "But once I got inside you, I couldn't stop."

Another of those long stares followed while each remembered the feel of his body snugly embedded in hers. Linc wanted to pull her into his arms again, but knew he couldn't. So he released his frustration by lashing out at her.

"You gotta admit that you're a little old to be having your first lover."

"It was never convenient. My mother died when I was sixteen. After that, I acted as my father's hostess. Boyfriends rarely fit into the embassy's social schedule. And in the last few years…"

"You were busy keeping your old man out of jail."

"No," she flared. "I was trying to keep him from killing himself. I didn't have much spare time to cultivate relationships with men."

Linc, sincerely sorry for what he'd said, came back with, "Well, I had no way of knowing all that."

"What you don't know about me would fill an encyclopedia, Mr. O'Neal. From the very beginning, you've jumped to wrong conclusions about me, forming your own erroneous opinions—"

"And whose fault is that?" Anger was the only way to effectively douse the flames in his loins. "Why did you keep me ignorant of the facts, pretending to be what you aren't?" He took another step forward. "You've got your nerve, lady, accusing me of jumping to conclusions. And just for the record, you made a much more convincing whore than you did a nun."

She bristled in outrage. "How dare—"

"Your hands were all over me in that bar."

"I touched your thigh," she shouted defensively. "Low on your thigh."

"The hair. The juicy mouth. The come-and-get-it eyes. That crotch-teasing dress."

"I wish you would forget about that damn dress."

"Not likely, sweetheart. Were all those trappings really necessary? Why didn't you explain to me from the beginning who your old man was?"

"Because, if you'll recall, I thought you were a mercenary, a mean, low, unscrupulous—"

"Cut the insults and answer my question. Why didn't you just sober me up and introduce yourself?"

"Because I didn't know my father's friends from his enemies in Monterico. He had more of the latter than the former. So to protect both myself and the children, I thought it best not to tell you. The rebels would have murdered me on the spot if they had ever found out. My name was kept a secret."

"What the hell were you doing down there in the first place? For a Sorbonne graduate, you sure aren't very bright."

She let the slight go and addressed the question. "Someone had to go and help these orphans."

"Agreed. Someone. You didn't have to go yourself. If you've got fifty grand to pay me, you had fifty grand to pay a mercenary. You could have gotten yourself killed."

"But I didn't!"

"And I don't think you'll be satisfied until you do!"

"What do you mean?" she asked sharply.

"When will you feel like you've made restitution for your daddy's crimes? When they're shoveling dirt over your face?"

Kerry pulled herself up to a rigid posture. "What would you know about moral obligation? You, who spend your life slumming. You, who has never thought of anyone but yourself."

"At least I came by everything I have honestly."

"Oh, you're—"

"I hate to butt in."

Simultaneously, they turned toward Cage. He was wearing an amused grin. "Y'all sure are shouting a lot, and I apologize for the interruption, but something major has come up." He winked at Linc. "No pun intended."

Vivid color flooded Kerry's face. She was grateful for the darkness which hopefully concealed it. "What is it, Cage?"

"Come over here with the rest of the group. Dad has something he wants to say."

When they moved into the circle of light, Reverend Hendren stepped forward. "This will come as a surprise to all of you. Sarah and I have been talking throughout the day and have reached a decision, which we're sure will make our home a much happier one." He turned his head slightly. "Joe, how would you like to come live with us?"

It had been so unselfish and beautiful, what Bob and Sarah Hendren had done. Staring out her bedroom window an hour later, Kerry still got a lump in her throat when she thought about it.

Of course pandemonium had broken out when Bob Hendren first asked that astonishing question. At first Joe hadn't comprehended all that the question entailed. When he did, his face broke into a radiant smile. He nodded his head vigorously and reverted to his native tongue. *"Sí, sí."* When Kerry translated to the other orphans what was happening, they grouped around Joe to exuberantly celebrate his good fortune.

When they had all been put to bed in their respective temporary shelters, Kerry caught up with the older couple.

"I can't tell you how glad I am about what you've done. I only hope that I didn't pressure you into making the decision by what I said earlier today," she said with concern.

Each of them embraced her. Bob said, "We both think this will honor Hal's memory in a special way. We'll only have Joe for a few years before he goes to college. In the meantime, we can make certain that he catches up with his peers academically and socially."

"You see, Kerry," Cage's mother said, "our house emptied of all our children so quickly. Cage was gone, then Hal left. Soon after that Jenny married Cage. Bob and I can't fill those empty rooms. It will be so good having a young person there again. Trent already idolizes Joe, so he'll fit well into the family. And he'll have access to the ranch and the horses he seems to like so well. It all worked out beautifully."

That was one problem that had been resolved, Kerry thought, as she let the curtain fall back into place over the window. Maybe tomorrow would provide a solution to the problem of Lisa's future. Kerry had hugged her tightly when she tucked her into bed. She looked like a little doll in her new dotted swiss nightgown. Lisa had spontaneously returned her hug and kissed her cheek wetly and noisily.

Concern about Lisa wasn't the only burden she was taking to bed with her.

Guilt was a bedfellow. It pressed on her heavily when she recalled the scathing words she had flung at Linc. She had unfairly accused him of never thinking of anyone but himself, when actually he had risked his life countless times to save hers and the orphans'.

Why had she said that? Why did he, more than anyone she'd ever known, provoke her to do and say things that were so out of character?

Her hand paused in the act of pulling back the bedspread when she heard a heavy tread on the stairs. Jenny and Cage had retired to their bedroom as soon as his parents had left for home. The approaching footsteps could only belong to one person. Before she could change her mind, Kerry quickly moved toward the door. She opened it just as Linc was walking past. He looked at her in surprise.

"Is something wrong?"

She shook her head no, already regretting her spontaneity. His shirttail was hanging out and his shirt was unbuttoned. The dark hair on his chest was a tempting sight. She followed its tapering pattern downward. The snap on his jeans was undone. He was barefoot. His hair had been tousled, seemingly by impatient hands. He looked heart-stoppingly wonderful.

When she just stood there rooted to the spot, saying nothing, he said, "I'm sorry if I disturbed you. I went back down to smoke a cigarette and—"

"No, you didn't disturb me," she said on a rush of air. "I…I owe you an apology for what I said earlier." His eyebrow arched inquisitively. "About you thinking only of yourself," she blurted out, by way of explanation. "It was a stupid thing to say after all you did for us. You saved our lives and…and I ask your forgiveness for saying something so patently untrue about you."

When she dared to raise her eyes, she saw that his were slowly ranging down her body, which was clothed only in the nightgown she had purchased that day in town. She was backlit by the lamp on the nightstand. Her body was cast into detailed silhouette inside the sheer fabric.

"I'm glad you stopped me," Linc said huskily. "Because I owe you something, too."

She became entranced by his eyes. "You don't owe me another apology for this morning. You've already apologized."

"I owe you something besides an apology."

"What?"

He backed her into the room. "A whole lot of pleasure."

# *Twelve*

The door closed behind him with a soft click of the latch.

"Pleasure?"

"*P-L-E-A-S-U-R-E*. As in what was missing in your initiation into lovemaking. I took a lot, gave very little. I want to make that up to you."

"You mean you want to…uh…"

Nodding his head, Linc moved forward with a prowling gait. "Yeah, that's what I mean." Reaching her, he took her shoulders between his hands and drew her against him.

"But we can't." Her protest was as faint as the resistance she exerted when he adjusted his body to fit hers.

"How come?"

"Because we don't even like each other."

He shrugged. "You're all right."

"And every time we're together we fight."

"Makes life interesting and keeps me on my toes."

"You'll always hold it against me that I tricked you."

"But I admire your craftiness."

"In my mind you'll always be a mercenary even though you wield a camera instead of a gun. And—"

"And in spite of all that, we're physically attracted. Granted?"

She stared into his tanned, lean face. Her stubborn will capitulated to the urging of her body. It was awakening, as a morning glory does with the sun. Unfolding itself. Seeking the warmth. Flowering open.

Kerry tried to remember all the reasons why this was untenable and unworkable, and a downright bad idea. But her body had a memory of its own. Her senses recalled each touch, sound, and taste of his lovemaking and wanted to experience them again. Thread by thread her resistance became unwoven.

She laid her hands on his chest. "Granted."

"Then for tonight, can't we set aside all our differences and concentrate strictly on that?"

"Isn't that a rather irresponsible approach to going to bed together?"

"Don't you think we deserve to be a little irresponsible?" His gaze was moving over her face and hair. "After all we've been through?"

"I suppose so." Because his shirt was open, she could feel part of his bare chest against her palms. His skin was hot. The hair that matted it was crinkly and soft. She wanted to feel it against her face, her mouth.

"Don't think about all the reasons we shouldn't, Kerry," he said in a stirring voice. "Think about this."

Cupping her chin in one hand, he tilted her head back and pressed his lips against hers, nudging them apart, and breaching them with his tongue. Kerry's world careened. She did as he suggested and focused all her attention on the kiss, the heat and passion and hunger behind it. His lips were firm, but not forceful. His tongue was bold, but not abusive. Linc used it to make love to her mouth.

When he raised his head, she slumped against him and laid her cheek on his chest. Beneath her ear she could hear his heart pounding. Their kiss had affected him as much as it had her.

"You're good," he whispered to the crown of her head.

"You just haven't had anyone else lately."

"No. You're good."

"I am?"

"Yes, ma'am. Very good. Damn good."

Before she could prepare herself, he tilted her head back again, just in time to meet his descending mouth. He pulled her against him tightly, wedged her thighs apart and tucked the lower part of his body between them. It was a thrilling contact and one that would have made her gasp, had his mouth not held such mastery over hers. His lips ground against hers with a need close to desperation. She recognized the same kind of clamoring need within herself.

Working her hands from between their bodies, she linked them around his neck. When her breasts flattened against his chest, each of them uttered a gratified sound. She laced her fingers through his hair and stretched up on tiptoe. His moan originated in the bottom of his soul. He slid his hands down to her derriere, pressing her higher and harder against the front of his body.

They couldn't continue for long without incinerating. Gradually Linc ended the kiss. His lips, moist and soft, rubbed against hers and his hands moved to the more neutral territory of her waist. It was incredibly narrow and his hands kept gently squeezing it as though marveling over that. Kerry eased down to stand flatfooted again between his widespread feet. Her hands glided down to his shoulders, touching his ears, his jaw, along the way. She toyed with the buttons on the epaulets of his shirt.

When she lifted her shy gaze up to his, he did something she'd rarely seen him do. He smiled. She remarked on it, telling him that he had a nice smile.

He laughed softly at the innocent compliment. "I do?"

"Yes. I haven't seen you smile very often. You were usually frowning at me."

"Because I wanted to be on top of you so damn bad."

His emotion-packed words had a profound effect on Kerry's insides. They absorbed them like a blow from a velvet-wrapped fist. To put things back on an even keel, she said inanely, "Your teeth are straight. Did you wear braces?"

"Hell no."

"I did."

"I'll bet you were adorable." He pecked a light kiss on the tip of her nose. "But every day you spent in braces was worth it." He ran the tip of his tongue along her upper teeth, barely inside her lips. She shivered with the pleasure he had promised to give her. "Cold?"

"No." Then the absurdity of the question struck her and she laughed. "No," she stressed, shaking her head.

His eyes became as glowing and hypnotizing as lantern light in the middle of a nighttime forest. They were all Kerry could see. Twin stars at the center of this private universe.

"Hot?"

She nodded.

"Where?"

"Everywhere."

He pressed his open palm against her stomach. Never removing his eyes from her face, he slid his hand down, following the tapering line of her body, until his hand conformed perfectly to the delta shape. "Here?"

Kerry made a yearning sound and swayed toward him. "Yes."

"Tender?"

"A little."

"I'm sorry."

"I'm not."

"You're not?"

"No, Linc, I'm not."

They kissed, and because it was such a torrid kiss, he removed his hand, caught her, and held her close, rocking her slightly. "We're getting ahead of ourselves," he whispered raggedly. He nuzzled her neck. Kissed it. Touched it with his tongue. "You know the song that goes, 'I want to kiss you all over'?" She made an affirmative motion with her head, though she didn't move it away from the hollow of his shoulder. "Well, that's what I want to do to you. Kiss you all over. And over again."

He encircled her upper arms and eased her away. When her eyes drifted open, he said, "Desire was the only thing that kept me going while we were tramping through that damned jungle. Basically I'm a coward."

"Impossible," she said fervently.

He grinned crookedly. "You caught me on a brave week. Anyway," he said, giving a dismissive shake of his head, "the motivation that drove me was that one day, by some miraculous twist of fate, I was going to have you in bed."

"You don't fool me, Lincoln. Other people might buy that callous air you assume, but I don't. Your motivation was to get those orphans to safety."

He had the grace to look chagrined. "Well, it made the situation a helluva lot more bearable to fantasize about you along the way."

"Did you?" She assumed the posture and expression of a practiced coquette, though the gestures came to her subconsciously.

"All the time. Constantly. Continually."

His hands moved over her throat and chest. The pads of his fingers glanced over her skin, barely touching it. Even though they were sensitive to the intricate dials of a sophisticated camera, they were appealingly rough and masculine.

Lightly, he placed his hands on the sides of her breasts. He applied a slight pressure, then relaxed. Several times he did that, making her breasts move beneath the nightgown, which was made of a cotton so thin and airy that her nipples showed up as enticing shadows beneath it, even in the darkness of the room.

"Your breasts fascinated me. The way they moved every time you did. It seemed like your clothes were always getting wet. The night you bathed in the stream. The river crossing. Even perspiration made your shirt cling to you. And I'd see..."

He brushed his thumbs over her nipples. Not that they needed any encouragement. His words had already brought them to aching hardness.

"They bewitched me. All I could think of was touching, kissing."

He bent his head and kissed her breast through her nightgown. The wet, stroking caress of his tongue seeped through the sheer cloth and caused it to mold provocatively to the rosy tips. "Nice."

"You said I was small."

"You are. But I never said I didn't like small." He lowered his head to her again and kept up that particular pleasure-giving caress until her knees threatened to buckle beneath her.

"I want to see you." She surprised herself by saying that. But she didn't lower her gaze in maidenly bashfulness. She met his steadily. "Take off your shirt. Please."

Her polite afterthought amused him, but he made no comment on it as he peeled off his shirt. Holding it out to his side, he dropped it to the floor. He stood perfectly still, indulging her curiosity.

She smiled compassionately over the angry red scrape the bullet had left. She wouldn't dwell on how close he had come to being seriously wounded or killed. It made her slightly ill to think about it. She pushed the thought from her mind and, as they had agreed to do, centered her thoughts on loving.

Her touch was delicate and inquisitive when she first laid her hands on the upper, curving portion of his chest. The hair was intriguing, and she combed her fingers through it. It spread in a wide fan shape over his breasts, then funneled to a silky stripe down the center of his stomach. She bracketed his rib cage with her hands and moved them down as far as his waist, then back up, letting her fingers climb over each rib. They finally came to rest beneath the solid, curved muscles. Her thumbs came dangerously close to touching his nipples before they shied away.

She looked up at him inquiringly. "Touch me like I do you," he said tightly. His face was taut and his breath was rushing between his teeth.

Against her fingertips, the feel of his erect nipples was erotic and exciting. His trembling response to her caress gave her courage. She shed the remains of her shyness and did what she had long wanted to do, she nuzzled him with her mouth. When her lips touched his nipple, both of them sighed with pleasure. She rubbed her tongue against it with no more hurry than a languid kitten at his morning bath. It came as a mild surprise to her that she derived as much pleasure from sucking it tenderly as it obviously gave Linc. Reflexively he thrust his manhood forward, rubbing it rhythmically against her.

When he could stand no more, he pushed her away and angled her head back. "I thought tonight would get you out of my system," he ground out. "Now I'm not so sure. You're a powerful narcotic, Kerry."

He kissed her, sending his tongue into the satiny warmth of her mouth. With an impatience bordering on violence, he ended the kiss. Taking her hand, he led her across the room to a chair near the window. He sat down in it. She remained standing in front of him.

"Take off your nightgown."

Kerry swallowed a knot of trepidation. He had removed her clothing today, but they'd been in an embrace. Disrobing in front of him, strictly for his entertainment, caused her heart to flutter with anxiety.

But with something else, too. The only name she could put to this odd sensation was titillation. She had a deep-seated desire to tantalize and dazzle the worldly Lincoln O'Neal.

Her eyes took on a mysterious quality, a seductiveness, a lambency, a knowledge as old as Eve. Kerry
turned her back on him. She sensed that he was about to
make a protest but withheld it when he saw her cross her
arms over her chest and move her hands to the shoulder straps of her nightgown. They were thin. It took the
merest flick of her wrists to lower them. They slipped
to her elbows. With painstaking slowness she relaxed
her arms until they dropped to her sides. When that
happened, the nightgown slithered from her body and
fell to the floor.

She could almost feel Linc's eyes burning into her
back. She knew he was taking in her figure, the way
her waist melded into the flare of her hips. Was he
pleased? Had he noticed the dimples at the base of her
spine? Did he find them cute? Sexy? Fascinating? Was
he entranced by the shape of her bottom? Did her thighs
look heavy and lumpy?

She stepped out of the pool of fabric at her feet and
turned around slowly until she was facing him. She kept
her eyes lowered. When she gathered enough courage
to look at him, what she saw in his eyes caused her
heartbeat to soar.

"Let your hair loose."

That wasn't what she had expected him to say, but the
gritty inflection of his voice told her what she wanted
and needed to know. He liked what he saw.

She dragged the single braid over her shoulder. The
curling end of it lay against her bare breast. Her attentive audience wet his lips. She pulled the rubber band
off the end of the braid. Then, unlooping the strands
slowly, she made a ballet of unraveling it.

Linc watched every graceful movement of her fingers, as though she were executing an intricate task that required incredible talent and perfect timing. When the entire braid was undone, she tossed the heavy skein of hair over her shoulder.

"Shake your head." Kerry moved her head from side to side. Her hair undulated over her skin in a slow sweep. "Comb your fingers through it." She lifted handfuls of her hair up and away from her face, pulling it through her widespread fingers until every strand had been filtered through. It fell over her shoulders and chest, almost reaching the tips of her breasts.

Linc's chest was soughing in and out. She knew that he was about to explode, but when he made his move, she still wasn't braced for it.

His hands shot out and clasped her waist. With one motion, he moved to the edge of the chair and pulled her forward. His open mouth landed with a soft, damp impact on her naked belly and she gave a sharp cry of surprise.

He kissed her fervently, several times, stopping only long enough to move his lips from one spot to another. His arms went around her. His hands cupped her bottom, and his caresses stole her breath with the unrestricted license they took. She laid her hands on the sides of his head, curling her fingers around his ears, and watched as his dear head moved from side to side, branding her with his hot, ardent kisses. His breath stirred the triangle of downy hair before she felt his lips moving in it.

Her knees gave way and she made another whimpering sound that snapped him to his senses. He stood up and enfolded her in his embrace. He murmured endearments spiced with expletives. The words stumbled

over one another and became erotic lyrics that thrilled
and aroused Kerry even more.

When he slipped his hand between her thighs, they
parted without hesitation. It seemed right that he favored
that part of her with gentle probings that took his fingers deep inside. She softly cried his name.

"Does that hurt?" Her answer was a wordless, mindless tossing of her head. "I'll never hurt you again,
Kerry. I swear it."

As he kissed her, he unzipped his pants and shoved
them down his legs. It took some doing, but he stepped
out of them without having to release her mouth from
his tempestuous kiss.

She felt him, warm and hard and urgent against her.
In a leisurely manner that in no way matched their clam-
orous passions, he smoothed his hand down the back of
her thigh and gently lifted it up over his.

When the most intimate parts of their bodies touched,
she reacted with total abandonment, throwing her head
back until her hair almost reached her waist and arching
against him to bring his sex to the very portal of hers.

"Not yet," he whispered.

Then his hand was there again. And his fingers were
working magic, discovering secrets, finding the key
to what made her woman. When he unlocked it with
his exquisite touch, joy and pleasure and love rushed
through her. Her nails made dents in his shoulders. Her
teeth made imprints on his chest. He welcomed them.
He savored each single spasm of pleasure that gripped
her.

Kerry wasn't allowed to luxuriate in the sweet aftermath. Weakly she leaned against him, panting softly.
He cradled her in his arms and carried her to the bed,

where he tenderly deposited her on the pillows. Her eyes were almost too languorous to remain open, but the sight of Linc, naked and proud, bending over her, brought them wide open.

"You're beautiful." She could barely speak the words, but he read them on her lips.

"Who me?" He looked at her with skepticism. It twisted his smile, wrinkled his brow, and narrowed his eyes, making his expression roguish and sexy.

She smiled. "Yes you. And what you did to me. That was beautiful."

"Ah, that I agree with." He was on his knees. He straddled her thighs and ran his hands up and down them.

"I didn't make a fool of myself?"

He touched the moist cleft between her thighs. "It was beautiful to watch. To feel against my fingers."

She bit her lower lip to hold inside the yearning sounds that pushed at her throat. "It...I don't think..."

"Hmm?"

"I'm not finished," she said breathlessly.

He smiled. "Good, good."

"But I want...ahh...Linc..."

"What? Tell me what you want." He wasn't taunting; he was begging. There was no cruelty on his features. His eyes were imploring. His jaw tensed with need. His face contorted with desire kept bridled too long. His entreaty endearingly vulnerable. "Show me, Kerry. What do you want?"

She placed her hands on the tops of his thighs. When she caressed his pronounced hip bones, he hissed a vivid curse. Her fingers tangled in the dark hair, and he dropped his head forward. And when she cradled his straining manhood between her hands, he released a tremendous groan.

His penetration was swift and deep. Kerry felt again the smoldering heat in the depths of her body. Like glowing embers being fanned, it burned hot, then hotter. When he began to move, she responded, lifting her hips to welcome his thrusts.

"Not so fast. Easy. We're in no hurry this time."

Exercising amazing discipline, he relished her with the appreciation of a viticulturist for a perfect glass of rare wine. As though all of his body were covered with taste buds, he touched her everywhere, sampling her deliciousness.

His restraint couldn't last forever. And soon it was he who was rushing, increasing the tempo. Kerry spun out of control again and this time she took him with her. They whirled in a fiery dance until they either had to burn themselves out or die.

Jenny struggled to a sitting position. "Cage, did you hear something?"

"Yes," he mumbled into his pillow.

"I'd better go—"

He caught the hem of her nightgown. "Stay where you are."

"But—"

"The sound you heard was Linc going in to Kerry's room."

Jenny's mouth formed a small O. She lay back down, lying perfectly still. "Did she invite him in?"

"How the hell do I know? It's their business. Now go back to sleep?"

"Do you think he's still angry with her?"

"Jen-ny," he said warningly.

"Well, maybe—"

"Jenny!" His stage whisper shut her up. "This is what you wanted, isn't it? They're together. You've had romantic stars in your eyes for them ever since they came through the door of this house. Now be quiet so Baby and I can go back to sleep."

"Baby wasn't sleeping," Jenny grumbled. "She was kicking."

"Here, scooch back this way." Cage nudged her into the curve of his body where she snuggled, her back to his chest. He laid his hand on her swollen tummy and massaged it gently.

"You know," he commented, as his hand idly moved over her, "I sorta envy ol' Linc."

"That's a terrible thing to say to a fat, pregnant wife!"

"'Fraid I'll go tomcatting around?" She poked him in the ribs with her elbow and he yelped beneath his breath. "You didn't let me finish. I sorta envy him. I envy him the fun of the chase. But I wouldn't trade where we are now with where they are in their relationship."

"Me neither."

"Getting you in my house and in my bed was no small feat. Of course anything worth having is worth working for."

"I told Kerry practically the same thing today."

They were comfortable in their love for each other. But it still held elements of excitement, as demonstrated moments later when Cage asked, "Baby asleep?"

"Uh-huh, but Mama's wide-awake." Jenny turned to face him. "Kiss me."

"We shouldn't, Jenny. It's too dangerous now."

"Nothing else. Just a kiss. Kiss me, Cage. And make it count."

* * *

"Are you asleep?"

Kerry sighed deeply. "I think I'm dead."

Mischievously Linc blew gently on one of her breasts and, to his supreme delight and amusement, the nipple pearled. "You're not dead."

She pried her eyes open and looked at him slumberously. She was lying on her back. He was lying on his stomach beside her, propped up on his elbows and staring down at her.

"Do I look frightful?"

"Is this the woman who tramped through the jungle without so much as a lipstick or a hairbrush, worrying now about her appearance?"

"Do I?"

"Sexily mussed." He kissed her lightly. "Which is the best way a woman can look."

"Chauvinist."

"Besides, why should you care about your appearance now when you didn't in the jungle?"

"I wasn't sleeping with you then."

"Not for lack of me trying. And actually I did sleep with you. Remember the night under the vine?"

"You weren't my lover then."

"Remember the night under the vine?" he repeated, forcing her to look at him. She nodded. "Did you know that if a man could die of arousal that would have been my deathbed?" She laughed and he frowned. "It's not funny."

"I know. Because I was suffering, too."

"Yeah?"

"Yeah."

He looked at her across the pillow. "You're very pretty."

"You've never told me that before."

"I'm not usually complimentary."

She touched his hair, removing wayward strands from his forehead. "You don't get close to too many people, do you, Linc?"

"No." He saw the wounded expression in her eyes and hated himself for putting it there with his harsh, abrupt answer. He tried to soften it now by laying his hand against her cheek and rubbing his thumb over her lips. "I'm close to you tonight. I'm as close to you as I ever get to anybody. We're close to each other. Let's not spoil it by getting too analytical."

There was so much she wanted to say. Her heart was filled to capacity with love for this man. It demanded to be vocalized. But she knew that saying anything more would drive him farther away, not draw him nearer. So she held her silence.

To lighten the mood, she levered herself up and kissed his forehead. Her hair dusted his shoulder.

"That feels good."

"What?"

"Your hair against my skin."

Inspired then to demonstrate her unspoken love, Kerry began kissing his shoulders, taking careful love-bites that faintly nipped his skin. He made a grunting sound that showed his approval. She folded her legs beneath her hips and leaned across his back, dropping kisses randomly.

She sipped her way down his spine to the shallow dip just below his waist. Her hair followed the motions of her head. It draped his back, shifting and sliding over his smooth flesh as whimsically as the ever-changing surf upon the shore.

She ran her hand over his buttock, and with a gentle squeeze appreciated its firmness. He cast her a sly look over his shoulder and she giggled. "I couldn't help but notice." He grinned smugly, but the expression relaxed and softened into one of sublimity when her hair brushed across his bottom and upper thighs.

"Kerry?"

"Hmm?" She leaned back. He turned over. Her heart stopped.

He repeated her name. There was an unspoken please behind it. And a breathless anticipation he couldn't disguise.

"You don't have to if you don't want to."

Kerry smiled at him lovingly, then lowered her head.

She kissed both his knees and worked her way up his thighs, trailing her hair behind her. She took his breath where next she kissed him. He closed his eyes and sighed her name as the love play of her lips and tongue went on and on. Without inhibition. With love. Then, as a refrain, she daintily dipped her tongue into his navel. Her hair swirled around his stiff manhood. The sight was beautiful and erotic and a stunning catalyst.

He lifted her atop him. Kerry gazed down at him with wide-eyed astonishment, but, acting on instinct, impaled herself on him. He sank his fingers into the fleshy part of her hips.

"Do I—"

"Oh, God, yes," he moaned. "Just like that."

She began to roll her hips in a grinding motion. He covered her breasts with his hands, brought the nipples to ripe peaks with plucking fingers, then levered himself up to love them with his mouth.

Closing her eyes, Kerry let her own sensations instruct her on what to do. With each tug of his mouth on her breast, she felt a corresponding contraction in her womb. Inside her he was strong and unyielding, and her only thought was to draw him deeper, make him an intrinsic part of herself. Again that marvelous pressure began to build to insurmountable heights, and she was helpless to stop the avalanche of emotions that overwhelmed her.

Moments later, they lay in a tangled heap of twisted bedsheets and naked limbs. Linc was the first to regain his senses. He could have moved away. He could have left her. But he wrapped his arms around Kerry and held her tightly.

"Kerry, Kerry." There were varying elements in his voice. Yearning. Pleasure. Affection. Mostly sadness.

But Kerry, listening only to the synchronized beating of their hearts, didn't hear that.

# *Thirteen*

He needed a cigarette.

He could have lit one, but he was afraid the smell of smoke would wake her up. He could have returned to his room or moved to another part of the house to smoke, but he couldn't bring himself to leave her yet. He could have stayed away from her in the first place.

That's what he should have done.

It would have been much more prudent not to have stopped when she opened her door to him last night. He should have accepted her apology, which was unnecessary to begin with, perhaps shaken hands with her, maybe given her a friendly little good-night kiss on the cheek, and then beat it into his bedroom, locking himself in if necessary.

Had he done that, he wouldn't have to hurt her. He could have exited her life as breezily as he had entered it.

Well, not quite.

Yesterday morning was still listed in the column of his sins.

He muttered a terse obscenity. No matter how you

looked at it, it was a muddle. He was involved with Kerry Bishop. He had been since she had enticed him to leave that cantina with her. And he would be until he waved goodbye to her, saying something clever like, "Here's lookin' at you, kid," and riding off into the sunset.

It worked in the movies. Poignant, bittersweet good-byes made terrific scripts. In real life they stunk.

He placed his forehead against the cool windowsill and pressed hard, as though trying to drive his head through the wood. Saying goodbye was only half the problem. Even after he did, it would be a long time before Kerry was out of his system. He might just as well admit it. She had her claws in him, but good. He was steeped in Kerry, and she was all he could think about.

Her smile. Her voice. Her eyes. Her hair. Her body.

Again he swore and pressed down the swelling flesh beneath his jeans. His body was responding to his recollections of last night. He didn't know how he could possibly get hard again, but he was. He would have thought he'd been pumped dry last night. They had been insatiable. Their lovemaking had been earnest and playful and lusty and tender, but had always, always, left them wanting more.

Had he ever met a more responsive woman? In any country? On any continent? At any age? Their loving had gone beyond sexual gratification. Kerry had opened up something hidden deep inside him. It was that element to their lovemaking that he found so disturbing.

Having resisted the temptation as long as he could, Linc turned his head around and looked at Kerry where she lay sleeping. He couldn't hold back the smile that softened his stern mouth and relieved his face of its usual cynicism.

One shapely leg was lying outside the light sheet, which had been their only cover all night. He'd embarrassed her by raising a light bruise on the inside of her thigh with a fervent kiss.

"Who else will see it?"

Laughing, she had thrown her arms around his neck. "Jealous?"

It had surprised him to realize that he was. He had initiated her, by God. He had introduced her to the pleasure her body was capable of experiencing. He, Lincoln O'Neal, had taught her how to give pleasure. The thought of another man enjoying this wonderful, affectionate, sensual woman, whom he had discovered, had filled him with a crimson rage.

Now, he could see that slight discoloration on the tender flesh of her thigh and remembered how delightful it had been for both of them when his mouth had put it there. His gaze moved over her. There wasn't an inch of her body that didn't bring an erotic memory rushing to his mind. From the arch of her slender foot to the crescent rim of her ear, he'd caressed, kissed, licked, tasted.

Yet, for all the sensuality she had expressed last night, she looked as innocent as a child now, with her dark hair lying tangled on the pristine pillowcase, and her lips, still rouged by his kisses, slightly parted. Her lashes were dark and feathery, her cheeks creamy.

One breast was peeping from beneath the sheet. With each breath, it rose and fell beguilingly. The tip of it was rosily pink. He intimately knew its texture and taste. How many times during the night had his mouth returned to her breasts, taking and giving pleasure?

With an inaudible groan he turned his head to stare out the window again. The landscape was just being bathed with the glow of the rising sun. Where only minutes ago everything had been gray, now colors became distinguishable. The sky had been a pale noncolor; now it was vividly streaked with the reds and golds of sunrise.

The dawn was a beautiful sight, but it did nothing to lighten Linc's black mood. He had to leave today. Hanging around any longer would be just plain stupid. Any further delay would only make things messier. *Because, face it, you can't stay under the same roof with her without wanting her in bed with you.*

This thing between them, whatever the hell it was, couldn't go on. Sooner or later they both had to get on with their lives. His common sense told him that sooner was better.

Mission accomplished. End of story. Over and out. They'd done what they had set out to do. It was time to move on to other endeavors. She'd gotten all the orphans safely out of Monterico. They'd all been placed with families, except for Lisa, and that was no cause for alarm. Finding parents for her wouldn't be difficult.

Linc had decided to accept the offer an international magazine had made for his photographs documenting their escape. The price he had demanded would financially sustain him until the next military coup, or airplane crash, or volcanic eruption, or whatever it was that caused mayhem and havoc, which people wanted to see pictures of.

Odd, that he wasn't feeling his usual restlessness. He had a wanderlust that had never been quenched. At the drop of a hat he had been ready to pack his cameras and catch the next plane out. Why was he dragging his feet this time?

*That's an easy one, you bastard. Take a look behind you.*

All right, so it was Kerry. He wasn't too anxious to leave her. But what other choice did he have? What could he offer her? A cluttered, dusty apartment in Manhattan where he picked up his mail every month or so. The bathroom doubled as a darkroom. He stored his chemicals in the living room. He didn't own a car. An answering service took his telephone calls. He ate out every meal except breakfast, which he usually skipped. The only appliances in his kitchen were an unstocked refrigerator, which he used only to make ice, and a coffeepot.

But even if he had a fully equipped, lavishly furnished penthouse on Park Avenue, he couldn't ask a woman like Kerry Bishop to share her life with him. He was from the streets. A thirty-five-year-old hoodlum. He'd had no formal education. He wasn't just rough around the edges, an unpolished gem, he was seedy to the marrow.

She had lived in comparative luxury. She could probably speak more languages than he could name. She was refined, educated, and a member of the socially elite. And whether she believed it or not, no one was going to hold her old man's corruption against her. On the contrary, she was probably admired by many as a tragic heroine.

She was also the best damn thing ever to happen to Linc O'Neal, and he simply couldn't handle it.

Breathing a slow, silent sigh, he crossed the room and gazed down at her. If things were different… But they weren't, and there was no sense lamenting what couldn't possibly be. Life would sure be dismal without her. She was like a spark, constantly ready to ignite, shedding warmth and light on his cold and dreary world.

Linc braced his hand on the wall behind the bed and leaned over the headboard. He was tempted to kiss her one last time, but was afraid that would wake her up. Instead, he touched her lips lightly with his thumb. Lord, she was beautiful. She was exciting. His gut twisted painfully at the thought of never seeing her again after today.

He'd never said the words to another soul. Possibly he'd said them to his mother, but he had been so young when she died that he didn't remember. He knew he'd never said them to the dour, unfeeling man who had sired him. He whispered them to Kerry Bishop now.

"I love you."

Seconds later, her violet eyelids fluttered. He was afraid his confession had awakened her, but she came awake too slowly for that to be the case. She stretched sinuously, raising her arms above her head and pointing her toes as far as they would reach. The movement pulled the sheet away from her breasts and left them vulnerable to his gaze.

His jaw was steely with tension as he restrained himself from leaning down and taking one of those perky, pink nipples into his mouth and worrying it slowly with his tongue until she came fully awake. It cost him tremendous effort, but he kept his features remote.

When Kerry's eyes opened, she had an unrestricted view of his armpit. Impishly, she reached up and tickled it. He lowered his arm and turned away.

"It's early," he said over his shoulder. "You don't have to get up."

"I want to get up if you are. Or could I tempt you back into bed?"

He glanced at her as he pulled on his shirt. Her dark blue eyes were sultry with invitation. The sheet was draped over her lap, but she sat with back straight, breasts bare. Her hair was spilling over her shoulders. Her nipples were high and pointed. She looked like a priestess of some South Seas pagan cult.

He didn't need to be tempted. He wanted her so badly already that he could barely pull the fly of his jeans together.

"No. I need a cigarette."

"You can smoke here."

He shook his head. He heard the apprehension creeping into her voice and avoided looking at her. "I need coffee, too. Do you think Cage and Jenny would mind if I started a pot?"

"I'm sure they wouldn't."

Linc could see in the mirror over the dresser that her eyes were following every single movement he made. Anxiety crept into her expression. She had no doubt expected affection and tenderness this morning. He hadn't even given her a token "morning after" kiss. He couldn't trust himself to. If he ever held her again, he knew he wouldn't be able to let her go.

"I'll see you downstairs." Cursing himself, he headed for the door.

"Linc?" She had used the sheet to cover herself. That more than anything stabbed at his conscience. No longer a beautiful woman, unashamed before her lover, she was now self-conscious in her nakedness. Her smile lacked conviction, but she made a valiant attempt at one. "What's your hurry?"

"I've got a lot to do today. As soon as I shoot the orphans meeting their families, I'm out of here." He couldn't bear her shattered expression, so he turned away and grabbed the doorknob. "See you downstairs."

Once the door was closed behind him, he paused in the hallway. He would have been surprised by the agonized expression on his face. He clenched his teeth to hold back a cry of anguish. Then, expansively cursing life and the tricks fate played on people, he went downstairs.

Kerry let the water of the shower beat against her with punishing force.

It hadn't been a dream. Her body bore the marks to prove it. Even without physical evidence, every precious memory was branded on her mind. Linc had been her lover last night. More than that, he had loved her.

He had been exquisitely tender. Attentive to her every desire and need. Affectionate. Extremely sensual. It was as though he had read her most secret sexual fantasies and fulfilled them.

This morning, he had been a cold, remote stranger, as hostile as when he had first learned that she had shanghaied him. Only this time had been worse. Then he'd been angry. This morning he'd been indifferent. She preferred a negative emotion to none at all.

As she descended the stairs after dressing, her indomitable optimism encouraged her to believe that Linc's distant mood this morning stemmed from his need for nicotine and caffeine, and that after he had had his morning ration of both, he'd be reaching for her again and kissing her with the boundless passion he had demonstrated last night. Maybe he just wasn't a morning person.

She refused to consider the nasty alternative: that she was an "easy lay" and that once he had satisfied his curiosity and gotten his fill of her, he was ready to move on.

But the moment she entered the kitchen, she saw that the latter was true. He glanced up at her indifferently. Not a glimmer of personal feeling was to be found in those implacable golden brown eyes. He gave her a cool nod, then resumed sipping his coffee.

"Good morning, Kerry," Jenny said cheerfully as she spooned Cheerios into Trent's greedy mouth. "Cage, would you please pour Kerry some juice?"

"Just coffee please."

"What would you like to eat?" Jenny moved Trent's glass safely away from the edge of his high chair's tray and deftly wiped milk from his mouth at the same time.

"Nothing, thank you," Kerry mumbled into the cup of coffee Cage handed her. She kept her head down. What had she expected? Professions of love over the breakfast table? He had promised only to give her pleasure. He had kept that promise.

"You look smashing this morning," Jenny said.

"I was just about to comment on that myself," Cage said. "New dress?"

"Yes and thank you." She was wearing a casual, two-piece linen dress in lemon yellow. Her accessories were azalea pink and robin's egg blue. "After bush jackets, anything would look good." Kerry tried to inject some lightheartedness into her voice, but without much success. "Has anyone heard from the children this morning? Are they ready?"

"I checked in on them just a few minutes ago," Cage said. "They're in a state of controlled chaos, but they're getting packed."

"Any leads on Lisa?"

"None so far, I'm afraid," Jenny told her.

Linc scraped back his chair. He hadn't said a word since Kerry came into the kitchen. He hadn't eaten. "I promised Joe I'd carry him downstairs. I'd better go see if I can help him dress." He skulked out.

"Go wash your hands, Trent." Jenny lifted her son from his high chair, a move that earned her a stern admonishment from Cage. "Kerry, there's plenty of coffee. Cage, will you please help me in the laundry room a minute?"

As soon as they entered the utility room beyond the kitchen, Jenny turned to him and asked, "Are you sure you heard Linc go into Kerry's room?"

"Yes."

"When did he come out?"

"What are you, the dorm mother?"

"Did he spend the night?" she whispered.

"I think so, but it's none of our business."

"What's the matter with them?"

"Everybody has an off night now and then."

She shot him a look of consternation. "You never have."

Grinning complacently, he leaned down and kissed her neck. "That's true." Then her mouth got its first honest kiss of the day. "Come to think of it, neither have you."

She squirmed away from him. "You make it impossible for me to remain decent. Ladies as pregnant as I am aren't supposed to feel sexy."

"Their tough luck." Cage reached for her again.

"Cage, stop it. I know what you're doing. You're only trying to distract me from the subject of Linc and Kerry."

"Right. I am."

"We've got to do something."

"No we don't."

"But what?" she added, ignoring his response.

"Jenny." He pressed her shoulders between his hands, forcing her to pay attention. "I know I sound like a damn broken record, but I'll say it one more time. It's none of our business."

"They love each other. I know it! I can feel it!"

She was cutest when she was annoyed. He smiled down at her and bobbed his eyebrows suggestively. "You want to feel something? I'll give you something to feel."

"Oh, you're impossible!"

"That's why you love me. Now, unless you want to pay the consequences for locking yourself in the laundry room with a very bad boy, I suggest that we get down to the business at hand. This is going to be a helluva day."

It was almost dusk before the Hendrens and Kerry and Linc sat down on the outdoor furniture on the porch and drew exhausted breaths. The day had been even more hectic than Cage had predicted it would be.

A barbecue picnic had been catered by a local restaurateur to relieve the initial awkwardness of the orphans meeting their adoptive parents.

The couples who had adopted the children were all Kerry had hoped for. She tearfully waved goodbye to the children, confident that each would grow up in a home filled with love.

She had demurred from accepting any praise and shied away from the media. Reporters, who had at last been granted access to the ranch, pressed her for interviews, but she kept them at a minimum. When she did speak with them, she focused their attention on the children who had enriched her life so much over the past year and took little credit for herself.

Roxy and Gary Fleming left for home with their daughters. Reverend and Sarah Hendren had left with Joe only a few minutes earlier. His parting with Linc had been almost too painful to watch. The boy had struggled not to cry. There was a tension around Linc's mouth, too, as he and Joe solemnly shook hands, exchanging pledges to stay in touch with each other.

Now Trent and Lisa were playing together on the lawn. Lisa gave no indication that she felt rejected. In fact, she hadn't even questioned being left behind.

"There's leftover brisket in the kitchen." Jenny wearily waved her hand toward the house. "Supper is every man for himself."

"No thanks," Cage said, speaking for all of them. "I could drink a beer though. Linc?"

"I really should be getting to the airport."

He was ready to leave. The clothes he had bought in La Bota were packed in a new duffel bag and his new camera and additional lenses were stored in their protective, customized bags. They stood on the porch steps ready to be placed in the car for the drive to the airport. There was a commuter plane to Dallas leaving later that night; there he would make a connecting flight to New York.

Kerry had learned of his travel plans through Jenny. Her heart was breaking, but she refused to show it. She had assumed the same detached air that he had started the day with. Though her image was imprinted on the film in his cameras, she could have been a stranger to him. In a few weeks he probably wouldn't even remember her. She would be just another notch in his belt. Hers would be just one of many names on Lincoln O'Neal's international list of sexual conquests.

Tonight, when it was all over, tonight, when she was alone in the bed where they had shared such splendor, she would cry into the handkerchief he had given her. Until then, she would act as casual as he did. As he had pointed out to her beneath the mesquite tree, she was good at playing roles.

"Surely you've got time for a beer," Cage said.

"All right," Linc agreed. "One beer."

"I'll get it." Jenny pulled herself up by the armrests of her chair. "I've got to go inside to the bathroom anyway."

She took only a few steps toward the front door before she clutched her tummy and exclaimed sharply, "Oh, my!"

Cage shot out of his chair. "What is it? Another one of those damn cramps?"

"No."

"Indigestion? I told you to lay off that barbecue. He uses enough cayenne to—"

"No, it's not indigestion." Jenny smiled radiantly. "It's the baby."

"The baby?" Cage repeated stupidly.

"The baby. Such as in rock-a-bye baby."

"Oh, Christ. Oh, hell." Cage gripped her arm. "How do you know? Are you in pain? When—" Suddenly his chin snapped up and he peered closely into her face. He even turned her toward the porch light to see her better. His eyes narrowed suspiciously. "Are you sure?"

Jenny burst out laughing, realizing that he thought she was staging a false alarm to detain Linc. "Yes, I'm sure."

"But it's three weeks early."

"According to the calendar maybe. But Baby thinks otherwise. Now, unless you want me to drop your daughter on her head here on the porch, I think you'd better go upstairs and get my suitcase. It's in the—"

"I know where it is. Oh, hell, it's really the baby. Jenny, will you sit down please!" Cage roared when she took a step toward the door. "Do I call the hospital, the doctor? How far apart are the pains? What can I do?"

"First you can calm down. Then you can go get the suitcase like I asked you to. I'm sure Kerry will call the doctor. His number is posted on the corkboard near the phone in the kitchen," she told Kerry calmly. "Linc, would you please check on Trent? I think Lisa just fed him a June bug."

Jenny returned to her chair on the porch and watched with amazement and a great deal of amusement as they all rushed around like headless chickens, bumping clumsily into each other as they raced to do her bidding.

Cage forgot his manners and reverted to using the language he had learned in the oil fields from the roughnecks. Trent was enjoying the crunchy June bug so much that he set up a howl when Linc, who was looking a little green around the gills and moving as though his hands and feet had suddenly grown disproportionately large, fished it out of his mouth.

Of the three, Kerry maintained the most composure. It was her hand that Jenny grasped before the wheelchair rolled her toward the labor room as soon as they arrived en masse at the hospital.

"Everything will turn out fine. I know it." She smiled at Kerry meaningfully as they wheeled her away.

Since Cage was Jenny's birth partner and his participation was required in the labor room, it fell to Kerry and Linc to watch Trent and Lisa and to notify Cage's parents and the Flemings. They were told that for the time being there was nothing they could do and that they might just as well stay at home until further notice.

Cage came to the waiting room to give them periodic reports, which amounted to nothing except that the baby hadn't arrived yet.

"How's Jenny?" Kerry asked him.

"She's beautiful," he said enthusiastically. "God, she's just beautiful."

When he left, both Kerry and Linc were smiling over the man's apparent love for his wife. But when they glanced at each other, their smiles faded. Knowing that her unreciprocated love for him must be transparent, Kerry turned away to check on the two young children. The supply of picture books and Bible stories in the hospital waiting room had been exhausted. Finally Trent and Lisa had fallen asleep on the sofa. Kerry and Linc had, at different times, offered to take the children home, but Cage was insistent that they stay.

"Jenny wants Trent to be here when the baby is born," he told them. "That way he'll feel like he's a part of it."

"Funny how they can sleep through all this hospital commotion," Kerry said now as she ran her fingers through Lisa's dark hair.

"Yeah." Linc's chair was only a few inches from the corner of the sofa where she sat, but it might as well have been miles. "Any prospects on Lisa's adoption?"

Kerry shook her head. "The foundation is working on it."

"I hope Immigration doesn't start hassling you."

Kerry rubbed her hands up and down her arms as though suddenly chilled. "Surely they wouldn't send a child back there." She stared down at the sleeping Lisa, then looked up at him. "Before you leave, I want to thank you again for all you did to get us out."

He shrugged irritably.

"No, please, let me thank you. We wouldn't have made it without you. And before I forget…" She reached for her purse and took out the check she had filled in and signed earlier in the day. She extended it to him.

His eyes dropped from her face to the check. With a sudden movement that startled her, he snatched it from her hand. He read it, noticed that it was drawn on her personal account and that she had a beautiful signature, then viciously ripped it in half.

"What did you do that for?" She had been hoping that by paying her debt, she would feel a sense of finality. As long as she felt obligated to Linc, he was still a part of her life. Until he was extricated completely, she couldn't get on with the business of living without him. "It's untainted. I never touched my father's money. My mother left me an inheritance."

"I don't care where the money came from."

"Then why did you tear up the check?"

"We're even, okay?" he said harshly.

Her lips parted slightly as she sustained another painful blow to her heart. "Oh, I see. You've already been paid for your services." She drew a shuddering breath. "Tell me, Linc, was last night worth fifty thousand dollars?"

Furious, he surged to his feet.

"We've got a girl!"

Cage's sudden appearance startled them. They spun around. He was grinning from ear to ear. "Six pounds, seven ounces. She's beautiful. Perfect. Jenny's fine. No complications. You can see the baby as soon as she's weighed in, footprinted and all that." After he received their hearty congratulations, he knelt down and whispered to his son, "Hey, Trent, you've got a new baby sister."

Though Kerry protested, Cage insisted that she go in to see mother and child first. At the end of the corridor, she checked in with a nurse and was led into a postnatal ward. Jenny was the only new mother in there. Her daughter, wrapped in a fuzzy pink blanket and wearing a stocking cap, was cradled in her arms.

"I had almost forgotten how wonderful it is to hold them for the first time," she said serenely as she gazed down into the mottled, wrinkled face that she thought was beautiful.

Kerry was touched by the peaceful expression on her friend's face. Jenny's conversation was liberally sprinkled with Cage's name, and Trent's, and Aimee's, which was the name she had given her daughter.

Kerry left the room, knowing that she'd seen love epitomized. The Hendrens were filled with it. It shone from them. Kerry celebrated their happiness, but also envied it. Jenny's contentment with her husband and children only highlighted the emptiness of her own life.

She had lost her mother prematurely. Her father had died in disgrace. Kerry, hoping to rectify some of the wrongs he had committed, had taken on the responsibility of a whole nation. Oh, she had succeeded in her mission, but what did she have to show for it personally?

In a way, she had been as manipulative as her father. She hadn't resorted to corruption, but she'd been just as fraudulent. People commended her on the tremendous sacrifice she had made. But in her heart she knew that she hadn't made any such sacrifice. What she had done had been for herself, not for the orphans of Monterico.

She had used them as a cleansing agent to scrub away the stain on her family's reputation. She had endangered nine children, put their lives in peril, so she could feel absolved and guilt free. It was her way of saying, "Look at me. I might bear my father's name, but I'm not like him."

And to whom had she been trying to prove that? To a world who really didn't give a damn? Or to herself?

She returned to the waiting room. Cage was holding his sleepy son on his lap, while in Spanish, he was describing the new baby to Lisa. The little girl was sitting in the crook of Linc's arm. One of her hands was resting on his thigh in an unconscious gesture of trust and affection.

It was then that Kerry knew what she was going to do.

# *Fourteen*

⤛⟳⟳⤜

"I wasn't ready for it, were you?" Cage's question was rhetorical. The passenger riding in his classic Lincoln didn't answer him, but continued to stare out the windshield. "When Kerry announced that she wanted to adopt Lisa, I nearly dropped my teeth."

Cage looked across the seat at Linc. He'd been anything but chatty since they'd left for the airport. His rugged features were set and grim. Cage, as usual, was driving too fast, so the scenery was nothing but a blur beyond the windows. The landscape wasn't keeping Linc enthralled and silent. No, his sullenness was the product of something else. Cage had a fairly good idea what it was.

Companionably he went on, "What do you think made Kerry suddenly decide she wanted to raise a child alone?"

"How the hell should I know?" The question was explosive, angrily erupting from Linc's chest. "Why does that woman do anything? She's a wacko."

Cage chuckled. "Yeah, that crossed my mind, too." He glanced at Linc from the corner of his eye. "Sure makes for an interesting lady, though, doesn't it? That unpredictability."

Linc made a disagreeable snorting sound, crossed his arms over his chest, and slumped deeper into his seat. "*Unpredictability* is another word for irrational. I'm telling you she's crazy. Posing as a hooker. Posing as a nun. What the hell kind of rational person goes around pulling dumb stunts like that? She acts now, thinks later." He turned to Cage and pointed a warning index finger at him. "Someday her recklessness is gonna get her into a helluva lot of trouble."

Cage, hiding his smile, thought that Kerry was already in a helluva lot of trouble. Linc O'Neal was "trouble" if he'd ever seen it. Cage liked him better for it. He'd been trouble, too, and had always enjoyed his reputation of being the "bad" boy in town.

It had been a rough night. It showed on both their faces. Neither had shaved. Their eyes were slightly bloodshot. They were still wearing yesterday's clothes.

But there hadn't been time that morning for them to return to the house before the commuter plane was scheduled to take off. Linc had insisted that he make this plane and not be delayed any longer. He'd also insisted that he could hitchhike to the airport or call the town's only taxi service, so that Cage could stay at the hospital with Jenny. But Cage had been equally as adamant about driving him. Jenny and the new baby were inaccessible during doctors' rounds anyway. After he had dropped Kerry at the house with Trent and Lisa, he and Linc had left for the airport.

The goodbyes Linc and Kerry had exchanged had been brief and polite, with the two of them barely looking at each other. Cage hadn't had the heart to tell Jenny that Linc was leaving. She would be disconsolate when she found out that her matchmaking attempts had apparently failed.

Personally Cage thought that both Kerry and Linc needed a kick in the butt to bring them to their senses, but he couldn't very well lecture Jenny and then go meddling in their affairs himself. Still, it wouldn't hurt to rattle the seemingly unrattleable Mr. O'Neal just a bit.

"I would imagine that Kerry is going to have quite a bit of trouble on her hands. And soon."

Linc's feigned indifference slipped. "What do you mean?"

"First with this adoption thing. She's a single woman. The immigration people specified that the orphans could only be placed with established families so they wouldn't impose an additional burden on the American taxpayers. I'm not sure that they'll consider a single woman an 'established family.'"

"It's no longer all that uncommon for singles to adopt."

"No, but it usually takes longer. And, as you know, there's a time limit on these adoptions."

"They wouldn't send a four-year-old orphan back to Monterico," Linc said.

"Probably not." Deliberately Cage made his smile too bright and falsely optimistic. "And if they did, knowing how headstrong Kerry is, she'd probably go back with Lisa before she would give her up."

"Back to Monterico? She'd have to be crazy!"

"I wouldn't put it past her. Once that lady's mind is made up, there's just no changing it. She may look as fragile as a butterfly, but she's as stubborn as a mule. Believe me, Jenny and I found that out."

Linc lit a cigarette with shaking hands. He went through the motions mechanically, and, if his frown were any indication, he derived no pleasure from the tobacco.

"In that respect," Cage continued, "she's a lot like Jenny."

"Jenny doesn't strike me as being stubborn," Linc remarked distractedly.

Cage laughed. "Looks can be deceiving. I didn't think I was ever going to talk her into marrying me. There she was, pregnant and living by herself. I begged her to marry me. She dug her heels in and stubbornly refused."

Linc was staring at him in astonishment. "Jenny was pregnant with Trent before you got married?"

"He's mine," Cage said testily.

Linc held up both hands. "Hey, I wasn't suggesting otherwise. It just seems, I don't know, out of character for Jenny."

"It was. I take full responsibility. Someday when we've got more time, I might tell you the whole sordid story."

Linc settled back into his brooding. "Everything turned out well. That's what's important."

"Yeah, but it was touch and go there for a while." Though the speedometer registered ninety, Cage draped his left wrist over the steering wheel and laid his right arm along the top of the seat.

"I'd been tomcatting for almost twenty years before I slept with Jenny. I'd always taken extra precautions. You know what it's like. I'm sure you never go anywhere without a supply of foil packages in your pocket." Cage grinned a just-between-us-hell-raisers' smile.

Linc smiled back sickly.

"There'd never been an unfortunate accident." Cage smiled wryly. "I was damned lucky. The one time I didn't use anything, I was with the woman I'd always wanted. That first time with Jenny, contraception was the farthest thing from my mind. Who knows," he said, shrugging, "maybe I had a subconscious desire to give her my baby so she'd have to take me in the bargain."

Linc was staring through the windshield again, but he was no longer slumping. His posture was rigid, as though he anticipated being ejected from the seat at any moment. He ran his palms up and down his thighs. He was grinding his jaw.

"Turn the car around," he said abruptly.

"Huh?"

"Stop and turn around. We're going back."

"But your plane leaves in—"

"I don't give a damn about the plane!" Linc barked. "Take me back to the ranch."

Gravel sprayed everywhere when Cage whipped the large, long Lincoln off the highway and onto the shoulder. He executed a flawless U-turn and floorboarded the accelerator. He waved to the highway patrolman they passed. The officer only waved back. Catching a bat out of hell was a better bet than catching Cage Hendren when he was in a hurry.

The distance back to the ranch was covered in a third of the time it had taken to get to the turnaround point. To Linc, who was rocking back and forth in his seat while he brutalized the inside of his jaw, it seemed to take forever.

He hadn't even thought of that!

Sure, he'd planned on using something when he left the cantina with his "whore." But his supply had gotten left somewhere along the way with the rest of his gear. The morning he'd gone tearing after Kerry in Linc's pickup, he'd been so damned mad that contraception had never even occurred to him.

And, Lord, how many times had there been since then? How many times in that one night of erotic fantasy-come-true had he...? It must have been at least...! He couldn't even count the times.

Cage pulled the car right up to the end of the sidewalk. "If you don't mind, I think I'll go back to the hospital."

"Sure." Linc jerked his bags from the backseat and got out, slamming the car door shut behind him.

"I'll probably be there for the rest of the day. Make yourself at home. If you want to get rid of Trent, call my folks to come pick him up."

Linc was already halfway to the front door. He nodded absently to what Cage was saying to him. Chuckling, Cage put the Lincoln in gear and drove it back down the lane.

In the entry hall of the house, Linc dropped his bags to the floor. The sunlight had been so bright outside that it took a moment for his eyes to adjust to the dimness. Impatient and unwilling to wait, he bumped into several pieces of furniture as he scouted the rooms on the lower story of the house. When they proved to be empty, he took the stairs two at a time.

He pushed open the door to the guest bedroom, but there was no one there. By the time he reached Trent's room, he had worked himself into a froth. Where the hell was she, for crissake?

He shoved the door; it went swinging open and banged against the inside wall. Kerry had changed out of the wilted linen dress and had put on a pair of jeans and a cotton camisole. She was barefoot and her hair was hanging loosely down her back. She was sitting on the edge of the twin bed where Lisa lay sleeping. Trent was softly snoring in the other one.

For a moment, they only stared at each other.

Then Kerry bounded to her feet. "You scared me half to death!" She kept her voice down so the children wouldn't wake up, but was as angry as a spitting cat because he had caught her crying. "Why did you come barging in here like that? I thought you were a burglar!"

In three long strides, Linc was beside the bed and gripping her arm. He pulled her across the room, and out the door. When they were safely on the other side of it, he thrust his chin out belligerently and said, "No problem. If I'd been a burglar you could have impersonated a karate expert."

"Very funny. And let go of my arm." She wrested herself free of his grasp. "I just got those children to sleep. They were exhausted, but too excited to settle down. Then you come charging through the door like a rampaging bull and— Wait a minute. I thought you'd be on your way to Dallas by now. What are you doing here?"

"Proposing."

Kerry gaped at him. "Proposing? Proposing what?"

"Marriage, of course. What does a man usually propose to a woman?"

"Lots of things. Among them, marriage is usually the last resort."

His face was dark and fearsome with annoyance. "Well, that's what I'm proposing. Marriage."

"Why?"

"Because I make good on my obligations, that's why. On the way to the airport, Cage reminded me of something."

"What?"

"That we didn't use anything to keep you from getting pregnant." He bobbed his head firmly, as though he'd just dropped a bomb of startling information. "You didn't think of that, did you?"

Her hesitation was so fleeting that he didn't even notice it. For a fraction of a second, she entertained the thought of letting him go on believing that they'd been careless. But earlier that morning, she had resolved that she would never use people again for her own gain. She couldn't trick Linc that way; it would be unconscionable. By the same token, it enraged her that the only reason he had come back proposing marriage was because he felt obligated to do so.

"As a matter of fact I did."

That served to suck the wind out of his sails. Kerry took a great deal of pleasure in watching his puffed-up arrogance fall like a knifed souffle.

"I thought about it over a year ago," she told him triumphantly. "Before I went to Monterico, when there was a very real possibility that I might be raped by guerrilla soldiers, I started taking birth control pills. So, Mr. O'Neal, you've got nothing to worry about. You're relieved of your 'obligation.' Now, if you'll excuse me, I'm very tired."

She spun on her heel, but took no more than a few steps before he grabbed the seat of her britches and jerked her to a halt. "What now?" she demanded.

"You're forgetting something else," Linc said.

"Well?" Kerry folded her arms over her chest and all but tapped her foot with impatience.

Curbing an urge to strangle her, he said, "Lisa. Do you honestly think they'll let you adopt her?"

"Yes."

In spite of her ready affirmation, Linc saw the chink in Kerry's confidence and, like a mountain climber looking for footholds in the side of a sheer cliff, dug into it. "Well, I'm not so sure. And neither are Cage and Jenny. He mentioned it on the way to the airport."

"I'll exhaust every possibility."

"You still might lose."

"Then I'll take her to live someplace outside the United States, to Mexico, anywhere."

"Oh, and that would be just dandy. A terrific life for a kid, having no sense of stability, no country to claim."

"I won't give her up," Kerry cried softly. "I love her."

"So do I!"

The words echoed down the wide hallway. After the reverberation, the resulting silence was filled only with the sound of their breathing.

"You do?" Kerry asked in a soft voice.

He nodded curtly. "It was tearing my guts to shreds to leave her this morning. Did you see the way she clung to my neck, not wanting me to go?"

"She cried when you drove off, even though she had promised you she wouldn't."

Linc was visibly moved. "See? She loves me, too."

Kerry's heart had begun to race, but she wouldn't let

herself get too optimistic. She'd been disappointed too often in the past. She looked at the floor. "You could apply to adopt Lisa yourself."

"I'd have the same problems as you. Maybe even more because I'm a man. We'd have a better chance of success if we applied for her as a couple. And it would be best for Lisa. She needs both a mother and a father. I know."

Kerry's heart twisted with love. The basis of Linc's remote nature came from his never having known parental love. She wanted to throw herself against him, to cover his beard-stubbled chin with wildly happy kisses, but she restrained herself.

"That's still not a good reason to marry," she said, playing devil's advocate. "We'd be burdening Lisa with the tremendous responsibility of keeping two adults happy with each other."

"We wouldn't have to depend on her for our happiness."

"Wouldn't we?"

He turned his back to her and moved away. He slid his hands, palms out, into the seat pockets of his jeans. When he turned back to her, he looked more vulnerable than she'd ever seen him. "Lisa's not the only reason I want us to get married."

"No?"

"No. I, uh, I wasn't too hep on the idea of leaving you either. You're a pain in the ass, but I still want you."

"In bed?"

"Yeah."

"I see." Her heart sank like lead.

"And—"

"And?" She lifted her head quickly and looked at him inquiringly.

"And...I, uh..."

"What?"

He ran his hand through his hair and blew out his breath. He looked supremely irritated. "Cage said you could be damned stubborn. You want to hear me say it, don't you?" Kerry only looked back at him innocently. He swore softly. Then, flinging his arms out to his sides, he said, "I love you, okay?"

"Okay!"

Kerry launched herself against him. He caught her, closing his arms around her and holding her close. Their mouths searched for and found each other. The kiss they exchanged was torrid and left them gasping for breath.

"I thought you'd never say it."

"I didn't think I ever would either. Not while you were awake anyway."

"Awake?"

"It doesn't matter," he said, laughing. "I love you, Kerry. God knows I do."

"I love you, I love you, I love you."

"I'll probably make a terrible husband. I'm mean. Rotten. Crude."

"Wonderful. Talented. Brave."

During another hard kiss, he lifted her up to straddle his lap. She wrapped her legs around his hips and locked her ankles behind his back. He ate at her chin and neck while he fiercely whispered endearments.

When he pulled back, his eyes speared into hers. "I don't have much to offer in the way of worldly goods. I don't have a pot to—"

She pressed her fingers over his lips. "You should

have kept that fifty thousand dollars. You'd be that much richer."

"Very cute." He kissed her fingers aside. "I'm serious, Kerry. I've got money. I've been stashing it away for years, but I don't even have a suitable roof to put over our heads."

"I do. I have a lovely house in Charlotte, North Carolina."

"You never told me that."

"You never asked. It's beautiful. I know you and Lisa will like it."

"You've also got a college degree."

"But I don't have a single Pulitzer prize and you have two."

"You know how I make a living. I'll be away a lot of the time."

"No way, Lincoln," she said, shaking her head. "If you think I'm going to turn you loose on a world full of beautiful women once you're my husband, forget it."

"You can't be suggesting that you come along."

"I certainly am."

"You and Lisa?" he asked incredulously.

"Think what an asset we'll be."

"Name one."

"How many languages do you speak?"

"I've almost mastered English."

"Well, I speak four and have a working knowledge of three more. With us teaching her English, Lisa will soon be bilingual. Think of all the help we'll be to you."

"Yeah, but in a few years, it'll be time for Lisa to go to school and—"

"I'm a teacher, remember? I'll tutor her."

"But that's not quite the same. She'll need—"

"Linc, are you trying to weasel out of this already?"

"No. I just want you to know what you're letting yourself in for."

"I do." When he still looked skeptical, she said, "Look, we went through hell and came out loving each other. It can only get better from here."

He smiled and then gave a shout of genuine laughter. "You've got a point."

"Everything will work out. We'll make it work. One day at a time, okay?"

"Baby, when I can feel your heat this close, I'd agree to anything." He hitched her up higher. "If we didn't have so many clothes on, do you realize—"

"I've already thought of that."

She squirmed against him and he grimaced with supreme pleasure. Carrying her, he went into the guest bedroom. As soon as her legs slid from around him and her feet touched the floor, they began tearing off their clothes, depositing them on the floor with heedless disregard for tidiness.

They moved into the adjoining bathroom, tacitly agreeing that a shower was in order. Linc reached into the shower stall and adjusted the water taps. He stepped in and drew Kerry in with him.

Beneath the spray, their mouths met as eagerly as their bodies. Their hands were so busy they regretted having to take the time to soap them, but when they did, their pleasure was multiplied a hundred times. They moved against each other with the sleek seduction of sea animals in a mating ritual.

He turned her around, put her back against his chest, and ran his hands over her front, massaging her breasts, rolling her nipples between his soapy fingers. His hard sex probed between her water-slick thighs. That slippery friction was breathtaking. When he slipped his fingers into her, she was as wet and warm as the water that trickled down their bodies.

Their skin was still damp when he laid her on the bed and bent over her. "We'll fight."

"All the time."

"You don't mind?"

She reached for him. "Linc, don't you know by now that you have to go through a little hell…"

He gave himself to her and completed the thought. "To get to heaven."

\* \* \* \* \*

# #1 *New York Times* bestselling author

# STEPHANIE LAURENS

### unveils a dramatic new tale of desire and devotion in her beloved *Cynster* series.

Marcus Cynster is waiting for Fate to come calling. One fact seems certain: his future won't lie with Niniver Carrick, a young lady who attracts him mightily and whom he feels compelled to protect—even from himself. Fate, he's sure, would never be so kind.

Delicate and ethereal, Niniver has vowed to return her clan to prosperity, but she needs help fending off unwelcome suitors. Powerful and dangerous, Marcus is perfect for the task.

Marcus quickly discovers his fated role *is* to stand by Niniver's side and, ultimately, claim her hand.

For her to be his bride, though, they must plunge headlong into a journey full of challenges, unforeseen dangers, passion and yearning, until Niniver grasps the essential truth—that she is indeed a match for Marcus Cynster.

### Available now, wherever books are sold!

**#1 *New York Times* bestselling author**

# SHERRYL WOODS

**returns with two enthralling Calamity Janes tales—unforgettable stories of fierce friends facing challenges in life and love.**

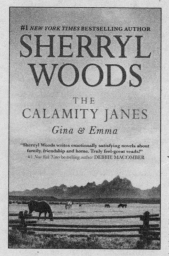

### To Catch a Thief

Gina Petrillo tried to outrun her troubles by returning home to Winding River, Wyoming. But city-slicker lawyer Rafe O'Donnell is in hot pursuit. He doesn't intend to let Gina out of his sight. And while Rafe is out to catch a thief—she just might steal his heart!

### The Calamity Janes

Struggling with single-motherhood and career pressures, Denver attorney Emma Rogers comes home for a reunion with the Calamity Janes. Can they be right that sexy journalist Ford Hamilton, the biggest thorn in her side, is actually the answer to her prayers?

## Available now, wherever books are sold!